THE SILENCE IN HEAVEN

THE SILENCE IN HEAVEN

Peter Lord-Wolff

A TOM DOHERTY ASSOCIATES BOOK
NEW YORK

THE SILENCE IN HEAVEN

Copyright © 2000 by Peter Lord-Wolff

This book is printed on acid-free paper.

A Forge Book
Published by Tom Doherty Associates, LLC
175 Fifth Avenue
New York, NY 10010

www.tor.com

Forge® is a registered trademark of Tom Doherty Associates, LLC.

Design by Lisa Pifher

Library of Congress Cataloging-in-Publication Data

Lord-Wolff, Peter.
    The silence in heaven / Peter Lord-Wolff.—1st ed.
        p.   cm.
    "A Tom Doherty Associates Book."
    ISBN 0312-86675-5 (alk. paper)
    1. Angels—Fiction. I. Title
PS3562.O729 S55 2000
813'.54—dc21   99-051783

First Edition: February 2000

Printed in the United States of America

0 9 8 7 6 5 4 3 2 1

Dedicated
to
Edith Lord-Wolff,
who tethers me to Earth
with tender love and holds
me there with the patience
of a saint . . .

Acknowledgments

To
the Spirits who arrived with
the lightness of a feather and
entrusted me with their story

To
Peter Cooper and Andy Demsky
for their greatly appreciated
role in bringing this story to
these pages

To
my agents, Eugene Winick and
Sam Pinkus, men of guiding light

To
my editor, Bob Gleason, who took
a chance and gave me creative
freedom

I thank you one and all. May my efforts match yours . . .

THE SILENCE IN HEAVEN

Innocence and Free Will

Where did it begin? Was there nothing and then something? Even the Celestials, the noblest of beings to enter the human consciousness, did not know what was in the dark before the light was turned on. These angels existed in the luminiferous ether and inherently understood they were mere embers of a great fire that had spanned universal space and innerdimensional time. They were crystalline spirits, forged from subtle matter by great heat and purged of any imperfection; bound into a communication network capable of transducing individual thought across the universal plain, their spirit is the essence of perfect pitch, made so by the vibratory constant of A-440 megahertz trapped within the crystal makeup of their very being.

These troubadours of liquid light hold heaven's song: wordless, filled with joyous meaning; soundless, and yet too loud for ears; free of music and yet full of harmony. Some angels say to hear this song truly, one must leave heaven. To know it, one must be prepared to never return. To return home, one must sing this song without knowing it is this song you are singing, for that very ignorance is the only light that will guide you on the path home.

Tashum pushed this riddle from his thoughts as he followed Paladin on yet another silly expedition of the garden Earth. Why his brother bothered, Tashum could not fathom. Why he accompanied him, Tashum knew very well.

He loved his brother better than he loved himself.

Tashum gazed up at the sun. So far away, yet apparently so important to what went on here. The round disk shimmered through the veil. He could see its radiant beams being absorbed by the tall green-leafed guardians, the lower life-forms, the very dirt itself sucking in as much light as could be held. That he had no shadow illustrated yet another difference between the universe and the universal fabric. Just what was so important about this less than lush garden, this heavy, incomplete sphere? There was no reason to argue over such a rough, harsh place.

"Over here."

Tashum turned, barely saw the arm motioning under the drooping wing. His complaint began anew as he stepped toward his brother.

"Paladin, why must we—"

A roar of pain echoed out of the glade where Paladin squatted, his hands reaching into the leafy nest. Tashum peered over his brother's shoulder.

The female lion's body contorted against some inner urging, her fierce claws shredding the foliage. Tashum started to pull Paladin away from the danger, but his brother just laughed.

"Do not be afraid, Tashum. She cannot hurt me, cannot even see us."

"What is wrong with her?"

"She is giving birth, that's all."

"Be careful." Tashum started to turn away.

Paladin's playful smile flattened. "She needs help. Shall I?"

Tashum shuddered, watched through squinty eyes as his brother's hands passed through the lion's hide, disappearing into her body. The contortions slowed, the lion's sides heaved once, and a small sac of translucent flesh dropped out from between her legs. It was covered in blood.

The lion curled, recovered her energies, and began licking at the sac.

Tashum's eyesight dizzied from the spectacle.

Paladin sat back on his haunches and sighed.

"New life, it's so amazing, isn't it?"

"Crude, brutal, ferocious. Born to kill."

"Brother," Paladin's crystal head swiveled. His radiant blue gaze fell upon Tashum. "You don't see the beauty of this, do you?" He motioned with a translucent hand. "Are you so addicted to light that this place does not affect you at all?"

"No, the effect is almost . . ." Tashum shook his head. "Paladin, don't you see the irony of life given only to be snatched away as a meal?"

"It's the way of the physical world. It's neither right nor wrong. And humans," he paused, "given time, they will become the masters of this domain."

"Masters! They're wingless," Tashum scoffed. "Why should we, the sons of fire, be involved with the sons of clay at all? They are but mere animals themselves."

"But this is wonderful sport. Think of the influence we could have upon them, brother. Look how things grow and become—"

"Are eaten and returned to rot." Tashum reached down to help his brother to his feet. "There is enough danger to this argument in heaven without your wanting to play with these creatures of the dirt."

When erect, Paladin stood an inch taller than Tashum. Paladin's long translucent wing followed his arm curling around his brother's angular shoulder. "Dear brother, you worry too much. Besides, what Sasha told you about Timean is only rumor." His expression cocked with a sly smile. "Where would he get such power?"

"Mayhem has surrendered the sword to him," replied Tashum as he stepped forward, collapsing the embrace, "Beware, brother," he said, turning to face him, "or you may wind up here as a caretaker, after all."

"Do you worry for me or yourself?" quipped Paladin.

"We are one, you and I."

"Then you see the problem as I do."

"Yes. I stand convinced that the only way to keep our place in heaven is to argue against this idea of earthly servitude." He snorted. "Celestials, subservient to the creatures of Earth—it is a travesty of creation." The blue glow in Tashum's eyes dilated even larger. "Never!"

Paladin smiled, placed his hand on Tashum's shoulder. " 'Tis true, our sport should never become an obligation. One might tire of it before the task was done. Such boredom, I believe, would be chastising."

"The humiliation of human servitude will certainly crush some of us under its weight and responsibility."

"Crush some and elate others with a sense of purpose."

"I'm not sure the Voice has really thought this out."

"How would we ever know?" Paladin's tone and smile carried irony.

"Let us not think on it." Tashum shuddered again. "Lest our debate be misconstrued as a vote in its favor."

Paladin laughed, slapped his brother on the back, and spread his elliptical-shaped wings, launching himself quickly away.

Tashum looked once more at the serene nest in the trees, before following his brother into the air. The angel caught himself smiling at the spectacle, a caring mother grooming her adorable kittens with a lick of her tongue. The demonstration of unconditional love and innocence of being was undeniably sweet. The visual harmony resonated with his vibratory spirit. He had to look away to escape its allure. At a run he took three steps and leaped into the air—wings longer than his height swept low, nearly touching the ground and in a curling-wave motion rose their length above him and he was airborn.

Tashum loved his wings and grand they were. Longer with a fuller drape than most, his wings were admired by all. When not in use he would often wrap them around his torso to keep them from being dragged behind or stepped on. He had created the first tunic apparel. By doing so he had inadvertently set the first fashion statement that lasted and with others following his example he became known.

From his bird's-eye view Tashum could see what he thought to be a male lion hunkered down in the tall grass, ears forward, tail low to the ground. The large cat was creeping up on the nest. Tashum felt an unusual sensation, an urge, concern for the new life. Then he felt as much as heard his brother's calming voice, *It's only nature, Tashum, let it be.* Tashum dropped his arms to his sides, and his massive wings pounded the air, pushing him higher, taking him away from nature.

On the heels of his brother, he passed through the layered white clouds. A mighty thrust of powerful wings took him higher into thinner atmosphere. The more distance between himself and the blue planet, the better he felt. He tried his best to put away all thoughts concerning the split in heaven over their prospective role on Earth. He believed the only reason Paladin loved visiting here was to escape the war of loud voices that rang incessantly through heaven's airy corridors. What had once been undulant cascading songs of being and wonder now careened in strident and petulant debate. Heaven itself seemed transformed by the lack of general consensus among its celestial inhabitants. The rulers of the ether were on the verge of true upheaval, and it could not be ignored; nor could it be resolved, such was their pride.

No wonder his funny and quixotic brother preferred this clump of clay rolling so regularly around in the brittle light of its sun.

The only argument Earth had was with itself.

Tashum felt the energy of heaven's sweeter light envelope his wings, pulling him home. The only earthly creatures he understood were the birds, for only they experienced the beauty and freedom of flying. But it was man whose shape mimicked his own. It would be the argument over man that opens the floodgates of heaven.

And so, the brothers joyously flew, two bright glints against a deeper blue, seemingly headed for the sun. In a blink, they were caught by a different light as the sky gave way to heaven, their true and only home.

Halfway between the spinning globe and the sweet aurora of heaven, Tashum opened his eyes wide, seeing a dark splinter that pierced this light of home. He sped forward, grabbed Paladin by the nearest wing.

"Do you see it, brother?"

Paladin did not answer, his gaze struggling to remain fixed on their target.

"Brother!"

"It cannot be what you think, Tashum. It is an illusion, surely."

"But brother—" Before Tashum could speak his awful question, both were swallowed by a storm of such darkness and hurtful wind, all thoughts of heaven and Earth fled from his mind.

Though he held tight to Paladin, his brother was pulling away.

"It has begun. Remember me! Never forget me, Tashum!" Paladin's final words echoed across the vast stellar field.

Then there was nothing but the silent roar of heaven's anger.

CHAPTER ONE

The Fall

Deep Space, 40,000 L. PALEOLITHIC.

In tiny, fluttering increments the rich backdrop of stars began to waver. As space warped, the bright chips of light moved apart, and the universal fabric of time and space went liquid. Millions of little stretch points appeared across the great sheet of black, stretching, ballooning its flatness. Concentric circles rippled out from the unseen objects trying to burst through from another dimension. Blown by solar wind, they were being pushed into this dimension of physicality.

The dimensional membrane was stretched into millions of very thin fingers, each millions of miles long and growing. The stars themselves seemed to slide down the slopes of these volcano-shaped distortions and then rearrange their relative positions in the new valleys created. The tentacles had stretched the continuum a billion miles before popping through.

A shower of ferocious whiteness exploded into cold, silent space as millions of Celestials created a crystalline sea gushing from the blackness. The winged comets gathered in an inverted cone formation, a spiraling tornado. The swirling storm of white-and-silver flame pushed across the heavens at the speed of light.

Out of the mouth of this furnace, a million beings combusted into the known universe, a fray of tumbling figures, crying out, clawing with desperation. Winged prisoners ripped from their other dimension at savage velocity, thrown into the universe of heat and cold, hard shapes and physical laws. A feverish choir of wailing voices loosed a clamor of piteous, pleading sobs, the sobs of children torn from the arms of their mothers.

At incredible speed, this celestial array shot toward an unseen target, bending light and dark matter, igniting radiation, setting gamma rays aglow, and creating a furrow as hard and black as death. The band of rebels left a ribbon of churned foam crimson particles, and cloud blue debris in their wake.

From the friction, sheets of layered lightning sprayed out before them spitting electric tendrils into the darkness of space. In a red gold arc they plummeted, throwing off spinning white hydrogen and brilliant fingers of orange pink gas sent millions of miles into emptiness.

At the front, leading the fiery host was Tashum. His translucent man-shaped figure, his enormous silver wings twisted in agony, his fingers gripped the features of his noble face, his body stretched and glowed in the particle stream of immense heat and velocity.

"Paladin!" Tashum called. "My brother!"

Paladin turned, his face distorted by the speed of their flight. "Tashum . . . why? Why!"

"Hold on," cried the first.

The two locked hands around the other's thick forearms and plummeted in tandem.

The horde of beings pulled a wide corner. They rode inertia on a carpet of lightning, shot past a dead gray moon in a continued fall from grace. And then Tashum saw it—Earth—where he and his brother had just come from.

He let out a howl of despair in the language of thunder, a cry to heaven that resonated throughout the vast stellar reaches of the universe. This wail was answered by his brother celestial, then by thousands of others. Faces cramped by terror swarmed all around him.

Brilliant sheet lightning crackled before them and spread out across the face of the planet, now partly obscured in plumes of white stratified clouds.

Heaven's own light spread through the angelic formation. The amber light shot ahead of the mass and created a glistened curved glass shell, hovering just at the ethereal cusp where Earth air meets outer space, that remote, silent place.

The eyes of the two brothers widened, then closed as they plummeted with the others toward this enormous convex sheet of gold light. Their hands instinctively raised, covering terrified expressions as their bodies crashed through—and Earth watched her sky collapse.

The tremendous sound of shattered and splintered glass filled Tashum's ears as he was engulfed in the explosion. Cascading shards of pointed, razor-sharp light peeled away his tunic and slashed at the thick roots of his wings, amputating them in deft, swift succession. They fell away, spinning and turning, joining thousands of other lifeless wings, tumbling leaves, blossoms of flame extinguished moments after they struck Earth's atmosphere.

Through the lids of his closed eyes he sensed only a fantastic whiteness, and he reeled through concussion after concussion of agony as the shards tore deeper, now at the very layers of his mind and soul. Scenes of his immortal existence spooled out of him in miles and miles of filmy memory. Faces, friends, events, cloudy palaces, and lofty pronouncements streamed out of him and vanished, leaving only an echo of his existence. He had been a vocal leader of the opposition, and now he led the way into damnation.

Emerging from the maelstrom of sparkling, spraying shards, his body went rigid with shock.

Shorn of everything except his celestial brother, he plummeted into the torrential planetary atmosphere. His translucent body—like Paladin's next to him—enriched with color as they fell. His glassy angelic form filled with blood and tissue and organs, his crystal skeleton burdened with flesh, falling . . . falling . . . falling. Faster and faster, they fell, sucked toward the surface of the planet by gravity's unfamiliar grip.

A thick rolling blackness closed in all around them. The two held tight while fierce blazing forks of lightning split the air. Throughout the cloud, Tashum heard the cries of the others as they, too, fell through this choking darkness. He felt a growing sense of isolation as their voices grew fainter, farther away—they were being split up, scattered across the face of the planet.

A blinding flash. A vein of white gigantic lightning cleft the atmosphere, turning black clouds white. A thunderous crack followed.

And now the other was gone. Suddenly Tashum's hands were both free. A split second later his vision returned, "Paladin!" he screamed. "No, my brother!" For an instant he saw the other through the veiled darkness.

Paladin clutched the place where the lightning had struck him. The terrible blackened wound in his side was smoldering. He grabbed in vain for the chip of crystal rib bone as it spun away. The crippled angel let out an agonized wail as he vanished into the cloud. He was seen no more.

"Brother!" Tashum called out after him.

At that moment, he dropped through the bottom of gray clouds and into the wide open sky he fell. It was predawn in this part of the garden, and her roundness was silhouetted against light gathering off to his right.

Tashum couldn't sort out her identifiable features. He was dazed, and the buffet of wind was maddening. It fluttered against his ears and pressed against his eyes, affording him only tiny glimpses of his destination. Above the falling angel, the round-bottomed clouds were catching a golden hue. The huge sun slipped out around the long curve of the earth, and a scream left his lips as millions of solar rays seared his new flesh a deep blood-red. He was turning and turning now, a carcass over a fire pit. The sun's brilliance raised golden blisters wherever they touched. Sputtering coals of sizzling flesh, tattooed dark, dotted his face and chest, covering his entire new body with snaked patterns.

The scent of his own burning skin swirled all around in an oily vapor and sickened his senses. The sharp acrid stench would be the first earthly smell branded into his memory.

His new weight plunged through a thin protection of billowed clouds— the moisture brought a brief relief. Back into open sky, scrabbling hands, kicking legs, panicked thoughts—he looked downward and saw the scorpion-shaped island capping a vast blue ocean. At great speed it appeared to rise up at him, enlarging in size with each beat of his heart. He could make out a rich green land mass traced in pink sand encircled by glistening waves punctuated by great leaping fish and birds riding the winds.

His would be a water landing. His figure stretched into a dive.

Clenched fists pounded the surface. His body bulleted into the water and sent up a huge plume of spray and foam that hung over the great bay, dissipating at last on the slight sea breeze.

For the longest while the surface water boiled and churned. The bay calmed her waters only to be ruffled when his head breached the surface. His new shoulder-length black hair stuck to his face and covered an eye. Tashum gasped for breath, filled his new lungs, and then felt the brand of the sun on his cheek. He dove under the surface again, deep into the blue-green depths.

He had to escape that awful sun. Each instant its terrible rays touched him, he was seared by an inferno of glowing embers. And so he swam, feeling empty of life, full of pain. He struggled in the deep water and peered forward with his new eyes. Everything looked strange. He held his hands to his face and noticed that the reflective radiant glow of his eyes upon his hands turned them amber and not his native iridescent blue.

He swam through the salt sea and broke the surface only as necessary to correct his bearing. He fought through undersea forests of kelp and veered with uncertainty amid clouds of darting fish, until he found himself following the incline of rippling pink sands. Through the distortion of shallow water, he could see the edges of the island, a skyline with curved trees and a tangle of undergrowth.

The wave force of a high tide delivered him onshore. Trying to grasp physical balance he rolled in the surf, purging his lungs, spitting up sand and seawater. His body shivered with sun shock. He stumbled and scrambled across the blinding pink beach, scattering a group of birdlike reptiles that waddled away from him on scaly hind feet. He dove through vines and underbrush and took shelter beneath the first damp outcropping of coral rock he could find.

Here in the dark ambient light, he laid back. Within seconds, he felt the pain crying out from scorched nerve endings. Every square inch of his awful flesh was inflamed. The humiliation of earthly pain torched his soul, and beneath his skin new muscles felt stretched and torn. Confined by gravity, every movement with unfamiliar arms was forced and awkward. But nothing was as harsh as the sting of singed flesh. It didn't come in waves. It was constant, and he craved the cool of darkness.

He thought of the female lion's agonizing roar when birthing the cub. Did all new life enter this forsaken place through such a wall of pain? Of course it is painful. This was not a new revelation, but the experience, the physical sensation, was new to him.

The blisters and tattoos continued to sear. In a delirium of anguish and confusion he called out for his lost brothers. The name *Paladin* passed through lips swollen and cracked.

He climbed deeper into the rock formation, where he fell into a pool of still water. He saw his reflection and wanted to scream. There was little vestige of his previous self. Indeed his eyes were those of the owl: enlarged and dilated, yellow, no longer blue. To make it go away he slapped the water with the back of his hand, but the image only fragmented. Swathed in agony, he sank into the pool and curled his body into a tight knot. The water absorbed his shuddering cries. "Paladin! What has happened to us?"

He who had once lived beyond the stars, who had commanded a legion of angels, was now banished to this wet rock crevice. This small planet, a garden to visit, a place of unique creatures viewed from the other side of the light, was now his god-awful prison.

Tashum argued this difference from the very center of himself. Such injustice—and what force could effect such unimaginable, undeniable punishment? He held his raw, burned fingers up to his face, moving them knuckle by knuckle, observing the movement of bone and tendon underneath tight strips of skin. The angel examined his fingernails—the claws of a wild beast. These were not the hands that had wielded thunderbolts, had wrestled with powers that for all he knew probably stood against him. And for what reason? He had but only spoken his mind, let his feelings be known to those whom he cherished above all others. Was he guilty of pride? How could such damnation come to pass through such innocence?

This was a strange land. He was now defenseless against even this sun, which had been such a dull thing viewed from the invisible world. All his abilities were shorn from him, ripped out of the angelic sphere by a merciless force. And why? he asked again. He was indeed intolerant of these new humans and their needs, but he had also been given free will. The *Voice* had given him free will with no mention of such consequence.

For days, he lay in this narrow cave, waiting for some semblance of strength to return, calling out for heavenly assistance, pleading with the Voice in the Light for rescue. Shouting, sobbing, beseeching, raving inarticulately in a childish fever of abandonment and complete disorientation, his ragged pleas grew weaker and less sure, trailing away at last into a whimper.

No voice answered his cries. No rescue came. There was only silence from heaven, cold, crushing emptiness was his sole shadow companion.

Over time his burns healed in the darkness, resolving themselves into deeply rooted black scars of intricate occult graffiti. He was undeniably tattooed with the mark of the fall from grace. Manual dexterity improved as he mastered gravity and learned his physical limitations. Throughout this period of adjustment his emotions remained ragged and hadn't shown any sign of improvement. He longed to go home; he was consumed by the need.

Were the others of his kind as scarred and uncertain, filled with the same longing and the same questions of their earthly existence? Would they even remember who they were to each other, to themselves after such grief?

For hours each day, Tashum would labor to remind himself of the fall, going over the details of it again and again. For he noted his celestial memories were already slipping away. To keep them alive he drew faces in the mud and inscribed angelic symbols with his finger. He was determined not to let his memories of earthly experience crowd out from his mind his celestial existence.

So much uncertainty in all of this—but he had to retain these last particles of his identity—these images he saw in pale serpentine visions, images that would float past as silvery particle fish on the surface of unreliable inner eyes.

Other developments rose up before him on the same dreamy canvas, though where they occurred in the stream of time, he could not know.

All around him on this island, he sensed an emergence of life—not just plant life or swimming lizards, but the very creature with primitive angelic aspects that had split heaven—beings with the bodies of animals and empty slated souls, tiny guttering spirit-flames that would take centuries to blossom into any kind of true essence. The dawn of modern man was being measured by a simple speech mutation and not a spiritual tone. It was too hurtful a concept but terribly real.

He sat up in the darkness. The long argument rolled through him, carefully wrought from the intricate rhetoric of heaven. This argument had resolved in his banishment, and the loss of his brother. Transduced through waves of tormented remembrance the overall injustice rang louder. He was a Celestial, an angel of the light. And as such he deserved something more.

CHAPTER TWO

Time, which had been a succulent dream for him in his pure angelic form, now became a tedious gear within this body he wore. The more the body craved its sensations, the more Tashum resolved that nothing would drive him out of the cave. If the Voice loved him and his brothers so little as to effect such a banishment, then he would resist for an eternity if necessary.

Perched on the lip of his dark isolation he sat, noting the revolving kaleidoscope of daylight and night, the growth of vegetation and its seasonal death. With each accumulating revolution of light and dark, a feeling of emptiness crawled about in his gut, a wretched demon increasing its demand for satisfaction.

He did not know how to answer the awful call that came from within. Hunched against the opening of his rock home, his glowing eyes darted about, taking in the shapes of the night-darkened island. Against the starry sky he could make out long dangling vines and slender trees, and below were collections of limestone rocks and an immense thickness of jungle growth. His powerful ears detected the creeping and near-silent movement of legged and unlegged creatures. In a moonbeam he spotted a huge glossy beetle trundling up the face of the rock. And for a moment he studied its insect legs and broad armored wings.

The pain in his stomach urged him to pick it up and turn it over. He acted before he thought. The beetle's eyelash legs worked dumbly against the air. Its underside was soft and mealy, and he was drawn to it.

An image flashed through his mind of sinking his teeth into the insect's belly. He let out a gasp, realizing that it was an instinctual image. No, he couldn't! The mere notion of being caught up and part of an earthly food chain made the humiliation of hunger all the worse.

This new demon would not be put off. Even while the groan of disgust was on his lips, the demon seemed to reach up from the stomach and into his arm and raise the insect to his waiting mouth. He threw the beetle aside— never!

For the rest of the evening he sat, taking in the life sounds of the island. He would not think of food. But he could not help but think about the nutritional needs of his own flesh. Even his intellect told him that physical flesh must be fed. In defiance, he reasoned this new pain would subside. He could wait it out, given time.

The roar of life surrounded his senses. The symphonic blend of sound was unorganized by its very nature. The bass thump of waves crashing against broad sandy beaches kept an unsteady rhythm. The onshore breeze brought with it diminished chords built from chirping birds, buzzing insects, and the screeches from other slithering life-forms. He searched for melody but found none. This was not music, no, not for Tashum.

In heaven, he had known music that flowed off the breath of angels, harmonies rich with the texture of several million voices, a sound pure and healing. Day and night it played there. Here, in the physical world, on this island, the only semblance of music came at night. Incessant, always singing the same tune, the tree frogs filled each night with their monotone messages, a lyric he could not decipher sung in the minor key of life.

He pressed his hands to his ears, squeezing his eyes shut against the great waves of this world's constant explosion of life and death.

Late in the day, the sun was sinking behind the opposing hill—in dim light he saw it—a nimble figure, upright on thick hind legs, moving through the jungle in and out of shadow and light. It leaped atop a large outcropping of coral at the edge of the clearing. It had a large hair-covered head, beefy shoulders, and long pendulous arms. It crouched over the bulbous ant pile. It held a small twig that created a bridge, one the ants couldn't resist. Lured onto the stick the ants marched into his open mouth. When it stood again, Tashum could see its relative size was smaller than his own.

Tashum stayed hidden in the shade of his cave. He watched the man beast holding a striking pose, his nose raised sniffing the air. He was searching for something hidden in the broad-leafed clearing curled around the earthen base of the knoll, where Tashum's cave crowned the rise.

A shudder of excitement collided with a feeling of disgust.

Watching it move, he instinctively knew what this was. The creature was a hideous approximation of himself. An awful angel created by an amateur god.

This was a modern human. He was sure of it.

Disgust defeated his initial excitement. An anger driven by the pain of his banishment rose in his chest, but his eyes could not be driven away.

In one hand it held a well-hewed stick, a weapon several feet in length. The creature moved stealthily, taking slow, even steps, hushing to a stop. Then two more quick steps, and he raised the stick over his shaggy head. The dance continued. The object of its intense, stupid gaze seemed to be a collection of thick grass in the center of the clearing. From a thicket of bay-grape trees, he moved closer.

The man held this position—held it, held it—and then with a thrust of the arm, plunged the stick into the hummock of grass.

A sharp scream split the air and the grass exploded with a thrashing fury. Now other man-creatures in loincloths emerged from the surrounding trees, crying out, chattering organized nonsense. From the shadows, perhaps six or seven of them dashed forward on those thick legs, throwing their pointed sticks with astonishing skill into the wildly moving grass. Their target burst out into the open—a squat four-legged beast, covered with bristled hair, tiny eyes, and a blood-wet snout guarded on each side by large, curved tusks.

The man-creatures danced aside as the boar lunged and veered at them. Bloodied sticks protruded from all parts of its wide back.

They gathered up rocks and struck the animal again and again. Still it came at them, succeeding at last in hooking one of its tusks into a leg, bringing down one of its attackers. At this returned violence, the others gave an angered shout. They descended on the boar, pounding it with more heavy stones.

Tashum winced at the crunch of bone, the tearing apart of thick hide.

Man kills animal, animal kills man, man kills man, animal kills animal in an endless display of life and death in the garden. The cycle was just as he thought. Turning away from the slaughter he sat back against the cool, moist wall and looked down at his own hands, wondering what they were capable of.

The tree frog's song brought on the darkness and safety of night. Tashum left the cave for an observer's encounter. He moved closer to the group, careful to stay out of sight. The men squatted down around their prize. They were proudly sprayed with blood; the more the better, it seemed. One of them knelt by the carcass, and, as the others watched; he produced a sharp pointed stone from a pouch and began to saw into the beast's tough hide. The man's arms bulged with the effort. In the moonlight Tashum studied the movements of the arms, how the muscles moved in concert, and then looked down at his own, turning the wrists and forearms back and forth. His own similarity with these cunning, bloodthirsty creatures was revolting. How he wished to tear off this spongy flesh in great strips and rid himself of any likeness to these hopping man-animals.

When a large enough hole was made, the leader reached inside the boar, groped about until he succeeded in tugging out several of the boar's internal organs.

A hush fell over the others as the man began a soft, singing chant, a supplication directed toward the blood-slick contents in his hand. The chant continued with an aura of reverence, and the others waited until the song was finished. At that point, the man used the stone knife to dig a small hole in the soft soil, where he placed the organs and buried them. He patted the ground and spoke a long litany of sounds over the small grave, a reverent appreciation of the boar's sacrifice to give them life.

With the ceremony over, the group again began jabbering back and forth. A number of them lifted the carcass while the rest aided their leg-wounded companion.

Language skills? This was new. Tashum sank lower behind the fern with the solid realization these were mutated men. The new masters.

Keeping a steady distance, he followed the group down a sandy trail that cut through the thick-leafed jungle, around jutting volcanic rock and through a small, rapid stream. For perhaps half a mile they moved at a trot in a slight uphill direction until they reached a large opening in the vegetation. He heard excited sounds of greeting from more of their tribe.

Tashum moved silently around the perimeter of the clearing until he found a spot where he could watch the unfolding events.

Their encampment was circled by grass huts constructed around a large fire pit. Around the fire mingled a collection of fifteen or twenty more of the humans.

Most of the humans in the group, more than half, were smaller in size than the hunters. They were shorter, though they had all the same physical features of their larger counterparts. He studied them. More active, they were, with less hirsute bodies and higher-pitched voices. And unlike the larger ones, this smaller breed wore no flaps of clothing around their waists. Some of this variety had small finger appendages hanging between their legs, whereas others did not. "Hmm, perhaps they'd been removed." He snickered quietly and looked down between his scarred legs. His own crotch was smooth and he felt relief seeing no similarity between his sexlessness and their sexed variations.

When he saw the females with their baggy breasts, he remembered how he'd watched them from the light. He quickly recognized their life-giving quality. Females kept after the smaller ones, called after them, made them quiet, and held the even smaller, fatter versions of themselves close to their own bodies. A family unit, he surmised.

The hunters now spoke in hooting, bragging voices of their adventure killing the animal. One of the men took on the role of the boar, down on all fours charging at the others while they pantomimed stabbing him with their spears and pummeling him with invisible rocks. In this theatrical version, the boar died more quickly, and the men portrayed themselves as maniacally fearless.

One of the older females took particular interest in the man whose leg had been wounded. She knelt next to him, examining the gouge, making a soft, distressed noise. They exchanged small worried murmurs.

As the angel watched, the body of the boar was disassembled by stone knives and eager hands. First, the hairy hide was peeled away, revealing layers of muscles and connective tissue. The head was cut off, as were the legs and chunks of meat hacked out and divided among them.

The females then attached the meat to the ends of sticks and placed them in the fire. The angel winced as the flesh fried and seared, dropping large globs of hot fat into the embers. Sizzling and popping. Blackening the once rich-red muscle and tissue. What kind of world was this where tender flesh was constantly subjected to flame?

The scent of the burning meat drifted across the encampment and into the leafy place where he crouched, filling his nostrils with the same stinking stench of his own flesh as it had tumbled through the sky beneath the sun's hot glare. Instinctively he began to rub at the hardened scars on his arms.

Excitement stirred in the camp as, one by one, the sticks were pulled from the fire and the small ones, the hunters and the others, fell on the cooked chunks of boar. They devoured the meat with expressions of pleasure, bright eyes and grinning mouths. Busy mouths sucked greasy remnants off their fingertips, picked at the bone for stubborn strips of remaining meat, while fingers plucked fallen pieces out of their body hair.

Tashum fell back and covered his eyes. All he heard was their grunts and smacking lips, the sucking of flesh out of their teeth. His brain reeled with oral fixation.

And worse still, a thing more terrible . . .

His own inner hunger wanted the flesh, too! This demon in his stomach had smelled the aroma of cooking meat and now demanded to be filled with it—to gorge on hot flesh and roast blood and crackling connective tissue.

He lay facedown in the soil. His outstretched fingers gripped the roots of grass and snaking ground-vines. How long had he lain in that cave, felt the demon growing strong within? The body was commanding him to nourish it. "No! I can't," he wept in silence and cried to unseen beings among the stars. "I can't eat life. I cannot be like them." He pleaded in smaller voice, "Take me back, please take me back."

He hugged the earth and thought that if he lay there long enough, the tumult in his gut might go away again. But it did not. Instead, this time it increased, spread throughout his frame, sent out spiraling, gurgling calls, clawing at his interior. The craving body would have its way. The demon would be satiated.

Beyond the commands of his mind, his body rose to knees. In a failing last effort he clutched a hanging vine, fighting what he could not control—the body staggered toward the light of the fire, the scent of seared meat. Suddenly he was standing with outstretched arms brushing aside broad leaves, raking through skeletal branches—propelled by powerful legs carrying him toward his physical need.

His angel self grew smaller and weaker yet still resisted, still clamored to return to the cave, bargaining with the demon, arguing that there must be other food in other parts of the island. But the demon saw food right here; the demon wanted food and fire and the organic companionship of these hairy angel-shaped creatures.

Those surrounding the fire grew quiet, occasionally looking up from their feast, offering a nod to a neighbor or just keeping an eye on how the boar's carcass was being parceled out. When they heard his rustling in the thicket, some stood. Mothers grabbed at their children. The hunters took up spears.

Tashum stepped out of the jungle and into the clearing.

The momentary hush was broken by a pathetic cry among the humans. They leaped away, called out at him, pointed, waved their thin arms, and chattered frantically among themselves at the sight of this sexless tattooed figure with the dilated eyes of an owl daring to stand at the edge of their firelight.

Tashum looked around the clearing in confusion. Why had they run? In the flickering light he saw only the arms and legs and soles of feet retreating away from him. Then one of the hunters pounced forward, and he felt a sting in his side. Looking down he found a spear, stained with boar's blood, buried halfway into his belly just below the ribs. As he stared at it, he heard a short whizzing noise and now another had lodged itself in the thick upper portion of his thigh. Then a third sunk into the center of his gut just above the place where he should have had a navel. He looked up at the cringing men.

"I am Tashum," he said. "A messenger of Light."

What their ears heard was loud, and it terrified them. They fled in numbers.

Tashum corrected his voice and adjusted tone and volume in accordance to the short frequency range of the human voice, but what came out was barely audible to anyone's ears. How ironic he thought, they could communicate with one another when he could not.

Out of the darkness on the far side of the clearing all he could hear was the beating of their hearts and the tiny whispered sounds of terror.

He reached down and slowly, grimacing from pain, pulled out the first spear. A luminescent golden liquid oozed out of the opening. The warm, glowing substance coagulated and slowly sealed the wound closed.

Tashum threw that spear aside and then removed the others. In all cases the glowing fluid seeped out and adhered the wounds together.

"I will not harm you," he said in tonal sounds borrowed from nature that emoted his harmless intention. He repeated his plea while taking another step forward.

A shriek went up among them as they flung themselves deeper into the jungle, but for a few brave men who stayed behind.

"I only want to do as you do!" he called after them, advancing toward the fire. He felt the draft of a near miss; the second stone struck his left ear. He glanced to his left in time to see the stone thrower wind up and throw again. Tashum easily caught his pitch and returned it just as quickly.

The thrower ducked away behind a broad leaf.

Much to the amazement of the other hunters, Tashum's thrown stone was boldly embedded in the trunk of a bay-grape tree.

After a few panicked words shouted back and forth the bravest of men joined their fellow tribesmen in a full rout.

The jungle was now filled with the panic and shrill wails of the villagers as they fled from the sight of this monster.

They scattered through the trees and undergrowth, scampered wildly over rocks and fallen logs. Beyond the social rejection and attempted murder, Tashum was amused at their flight. Soon a laugh fluttered up out of his throat, and he found that he was chuckling at their feeble attempt to flee.

They broke through foliage, sent up clouds of birds, slipped in wet mud, and scampered away, sometimes on all fours.

Tashum knew that his majestic body could catch them, could taunt them, break them, and he determined that if indeed this were their domain, he would not be dominated.

The fire had burned low, and he threw their spears into the embers, watching as the flickering light returned to a hot glare. He picked through the remains of their meal until he found a fist-sized lump of boar meat attached to a handle of bone. By the fire's light, he examined its burned black appearance and felt its greasy texture. He brought it to his nose, sniffing. And finally, complete resignation . . .

The demon gurgled with delight. The flesh tasted salty but just sat there warm on his tongue. He swallowed the lump of meat, surprised to feel its descent into his interior. He took another bite, a larger one, and chewed slowly. He looked around, up into the treetops. Beyond their leafy heads he could see the stars.

"Life eating life," he said to the sky that hid the Voice, the Light. "Flesh devouring flesh. Is this part of the noble lesson I'm to learn?"

He felt the puny pinpricks of light watching him. He lifted the food to his mouth again and the demon, the body, growled with delight.

"Is this what you want?" he asked the dark canopy. "Is this your great purpose?"

He tore ravenously into the meat, steadily eating his way down to the bone until it was slick and white.

CHAPTER THREE

With the passage of time, the humans' fear of Tashum subsided, and the primitives returned to their normal activities: the survival game. He could hear them muttering and skulking, masterfully moving through the vegetation, seeking him out. Though more often than not, he spied on them.

He studied the nature of their various transactions, males trading foodstuffs and meat for sharpened sticks and small works of art, carvings of wood and stones that served no apparent purpose but were imbued with some power or value beyond the angel's comprehension.

Tashum witnessed the birth of one of their offspring, fearing at first the woman had lost one of her internal organs until a vague memory of a lion giving birth informed him better.

Watching them for any length of time was petty sport. They simply were not his kind. Once noted, their patterns bored him, though he did grudgingly incorporate some of the lessons he learned by watching them. This voyeurism led to the discovery of his first earthly delight.

At the mouth of his cave stood a large tree laden with an exotic fruit. Under these heavy boughs, Tashum would sit and occasionally eat the soft-skinned reddish orbs as he had seen the humans do. He eschewed meat unless a long season without fruit sent him crashing after a boar, which he cooked over a fire as did the humans. Though he felt shame at this mimicry, he decided their only advantage over him was their evolving experience at survival.

He learned to control his hunger by feeding it just before the scream in his stomach became too fierce, and since his dietary needs were not great, he found he needed to eat only once a month. His body efficiently absorbed nearly all the nutrients he ingested, and once a month, he would regurgitate a small hard black object, nearly obsidian in color and texture. That object was his waste—which decidedly proved he was more advanced than the humans, who seemed forever searching out some bush or tree to leave a token of a previous meal they had eaten earlier in the same day.

Most evenings under the fruit tree he could feel the humans watching him. Tashum pretended not to notice their incursions, choosing to ignore the growing audience of eyes staring up at him.

Still, they kept their distance, which Tashum didn't mind. He had studied them sufficient to his interest and found the repetition of their lives dull—until the evening one of the smaller ones became lost in the jungle just before dark. The female responsible for the child shrieked when she discovered it was missing, and the others fanned out through the jungle with purpose, looking worriedly at the last colors of dusk, as if the impending darkness itself might devour the child.

Their panic assaulted his ears, his inner feelings rose up sharply in his chest, and he found that he could not still it with his former disinterest. So he rose and moved through the trees, keeping thirty yards or so between him and their search.

The elders repeatedly called out a single word, and Tashum realized that it was a name. The child's name. He smiled, as if his understanding of this new advancement had somehow contributed to their naming each other.

The smile faded quickly when he heard a soft growl and a low whimper. Off to his left he spied a hunkered boar, moving slowly toward a thicket. Without thinking, Tashum sped toward the thicket just as the boar began its charge. They arrived at the same moment, and the angel grabbed the creature by its tusks, heaving it mightily against a tree. The boar squealed as its bones cracked against the hard wood, then it died with a sigh.

Kneeling down in waist-deep grass, Tashum pushed aside long blades and spied the missing child. Its cheeks were tear covered and dirty. Tashum reached down and lifted the child into his arms, at first being careful not to let it touch his body.

The child was warm in his hands, though it shook with fear. He pulled it against his chest, instinctively, to soothe it. Through his skin he could feel the rapid pace of a tiny heart. In his embrace the flow of tears stopped. Tense little arms relaxed, and a wet face nestled against Tashum's neck.

He stood and carried the child toward the clearing.

The others, having heard the boar's scream, had started to return, then stopped at the edge of the clearing when Tashum emerged carrying the child. Their eyes were large with fear. The hunters held their weapons in check. One of the women started forward, then hesitated.

Tashum held the child out to her. She rushed forward and snatched it from his arms, then rushed back into the hushed crowd.

Not knowing what to do next, Tashum turned and headed back toward to his roost. He made three steps before a single spear flew over his shoulder and stabbed the tree in front of him. He glanced back and witnessed the chastisement of the spear chucker by his fellow hunters. They beat him with sticks while making reference to the child.

For days, he pondered this event, attempting without success to decipher the rampaging conflict of emotion. Finally, he understood that similar feelings had resided within him since his arrival here. He needed his brother, Paladin, just as much as they needed that child.

Following this incident, as it was now obvious that he had little interest in hurting them, the humans began to present themselves in twos and threes. Each group came accompanied by the hunting leader, that nimble, wiry leader Tashum had first seen in the moonlight long ago.

Visitation occurred only when dusk still lent some hint of color to the sky and when Tashum could be seen sitting under his tree gazing out across the vast blue to a curved horizon. Alone the hunting leader would emerge from the trees bowing and chattering, a solemn, favor-asking expression on his broad, earnest face. He would leave his weapons at the base of the knoll and climb to the awaiting angel. He would stand in front of Tashum, blocking his view of the sea, and in long, apologetic phrases and with many shrugs and much wringing of hands he would ask Tashum's permission to bring out two or three of his tribesmen.

The first time this happened, when Tashum got the gist of what the human was requesting, he simply nodded and grunted.

At this, the four-foot-tall human frowned and bowed, bobbing his hairy head many times in alarm and launched into another long compilation of remarks of praise and favor asking until he paused at last and looked up for a response.

Tashum realized it was his turn.

Emulating the man, Tashum moved his arms about, gesturing and pantomiming. At first all he spoke was meaningless grunts and syllables but this seemed to puzzle the hunter. Joy of music? The ecstasy of light? In his tongue it was all nonsense.

The hunter took charcoal from the fire pit and drew on his arms lines that approximated Tashum's tattooed scars. Then he pointed at the difference between his almond-shaped eyes and the angel's glowing owl eyes.

Tashum's gaze followed his pointed finger to the sky.

A silence followed.

Tashum stood, holding his fist in the air and in his own celestial language he spoke to heaven. "You told us that this new age was to be an ascent into greater beauty, more wondrous joy. But the reality has been a stripping away of all our former happiness."

Tashum folded his arms across his chest and fell silent, awaiting a heavenly reply, and not to his surprise none came.

The small man searched Tashum's face, urging him to continue the dialogue. Tashum realized that his tone bridged the language barrier and softened his voice, letting the sadness he felt roll out.

"An unanswerable riddle turned into an unthinkable argument that arose suddenly and fiercely in heaven. One day I was horrified to discover that I had become a leader of the opposition. An accidental rebel against the Voice."

Tashum pantomimed, as he had seen them do regarding the killing of the boar. "For my audacity, I was thrown out of heaven, sent smashing through the angelic barrier that separates one universe from another, our world from yours."

The smaller man hung onto his words as he gazed at the stars.

When Tashum had finished this speech, the hunting leader stood silent with his eyes closed as if deeply grateful, still taking in the shower of words and sounds, as though cloaked in their drama and wisdom and mystery. Then he brightened and opened his eyes and motioned toward the trees. After much cajoling, he succeeded in persuading two of the hunters out of hiding.

The two men crossed the clearing and scurried up the hill to join them. Near the top they dropped to their hands and knees and with heads lowered they crawled toward the angel.

Once near the fire pit both men nodded with rapidity and offered small wooden bowls in exaggerated gestures supplicant in nature.

Tashum gave an exaggerated nod of his head and watched as they filled one of the bowls with blackened embers from his fire pit. From their glances and the way they chose the embers they seemed to be interested in his tattooed scars. The leader stayed standing and directed the harvesting of ash. He indicated they had taken too much and ordered three of the embers put back. Then he turned his smile to Tashum and gave to him the second wooden bowl. Without ceremony all three men went back down the hill.

The hunting leader—whom Tashum came to call Shrug—brought more gifts as a sign of gratitude for the angel's willingness to go on display. Over time he collected a waist covering of animal skins, dried fish, and, occasionally, small wooden figurines carved with stone knives. He appreciated their craft abilities much more that he was willing to admit and the art of trade and value was interesting, because it was unique to only humans.

It did not pass Tashum's notice that Shrug, in turn, received gifts, or payments, from those he escorted across the stretch of beach to view him.

It amused the angel to think that Shrug sold visits with Tashum as others of their tribe sold sharpened sticks and effigies to eager buyers. It was less amussing that Shrug and his band were using the ash from his fire pit in a tattooing paste. Once mixed with plant extracts the ash was applied to their limbs and torsos loosly imitating the patterns and designs that crisscross Tashum's body, marks of the fall.

Then a gift arrived that took Tashum by surprise.

After a litany of simple words accompanied shrinking shoulders and up-lifted palms and much supplication—followed by Tashum's formal acceptance—Shrug brought out a withered figure.

Tashum watched as this human limped across the open sand, colored in the lingering deep orange of the sunset. His dragging twisted foot left a unique track in the sand: a single footprint alongside a long unevenly plowed trail.

Tashum recognized the cripple as the hunter who had been injured so long ago by the boar's tusk. Having never seen a human injured in this way, Tashum was curious. He leaned forward—as Shrug calmed the man—and closely examined the place where the pointed tusk had wounded the leg. A wide, glossy scar began at about the ankle and extended upward a hand's length.

He looked up at Shrug, questioning his intent. Shrug pointed to Tashum's side, where the first spear had penetrated. He made a signal for smooth, then pointed to the man's leg.

It took Tashum several moments, but finally he understood. Shrug wanted the angel to heal the crippled man as he had done for himself.

The tusk had damaged the man's organic machinery. The skin, muscles, and connective tissue had rearranged. And as a result he could no longer run about like the others. He was less useful to the group, slower and therefore more liable to boar injury than ever before.

All of this ran quickly through Tashum's mind as he touched the scar, turning the leg gently from side to side.

In his observations of village life he had seen instances where injury and minor illness had healed without long-term damage. But when he looked at this misshapen figure, he sensed that some wounds were not subject to healing.

Shrug made a sign between his heart and that of the other man. Then he circled his face, and, again, the other man's. Tashum's intent stare into the man's eyes brought forth something completely unexpected; he entered the man's thoughts. How they were transduced without sight or sound was no more mysterious to Tashum than his ability to do so; he now knew the two hunters were brothers.

His tattooed fingers touched the scar and felt the lumps of twisted, useless flesh beneath. He thought of the child he had carried, how the resonance of warm flesh sang a song of health throughout her frame. The flesh of this leg would never again sing such a song. He was compelled to let the energy of his being flow into and correct this detuned body. Tashum's eyes glowed brighter as the charge built up in his fingertips. Under his touch, the cripple's body hair stood on end. The tiniest of sparks leaped from finger to scar.

Shrug stumbled backward as he, too, felt the tickle of static emanating from doctor and patient. Tashum's internal focus could see the damage done by an angry boar and the resulting strangled muscle and scar tissue. He sighed heavily and realized that the disharmony would not be corrected by his simple celestial tuning fork. He shook his head with disappointment and sat back.

Shrug grunted in kind acknowledgment, then reached over and patted the angel's head gently. Suddenly the two men started pointing and laughing at one another. Comically, their long tangled hair and beards were still standing erect. Shrug did a little dance that even curled Tashum's lips into a smile. These men had found humor in the failure of cure. How interesting, observed the angel. Their great joy in laughter was irresistible. Tashum's chuckle eventually grew to a full-size belly laugh. A first for him.

A bit later, as the three sat around the fire, Shrug nudged his brother. From a pouch tied around his waist the cripple produced a gift: three round stones. He balanced the smooth stones in the palm of his hands, letting Tashum examine them for a moment.

To Tashum they were only worn stones, dull and lifeless.

With a shy smile and a look of significance, the crippled man expertly tossed one of the stones into a perfect arc, then a second stone from the other hand in the opposite direction, also in an arc, then a third, juggling the stones about in the air. In almost magical fashion, the little human kept two of the stones busy in the air, while a third was hitting a palm and being launched again, creating a small fountain of stones.

Tashum watched the performance feeling a sensation of spinning in his head. These stones—this ability to keep them moving in opposite directions, their hypnotic movement—they seemed weightless, a whirling, flying magic.

Suddenly Tashum laughed and plunged his hand out, trying to catch one of the flying stones. Instantly the man dropped them and leaped away, landing on his back and crab crawling in fear. The withered man watched from his awkward position in the sand. Shrug broke out in a chatter of denunciation directed at the angel, pointing first at him, then pointing at the stones.

"Enough," Tashum said to the angry hunter leader. Then addressing the other he apologized and made the kinds of supplicating gestures with his hands that he'd seen Shrug use time and time again.

The man crawled back and plucked the round stones from the sand and held them out for Tashum to take.

"For me?" he asked, pointing to his chest.

The two humans indicated they were indeed a gift. Tashum accepted the stones. The wounded man made a bouncing motion with his hands, encouraging Tashum to give it a try.

The angel looked down at the stones in his hands. A tiny throbbing sense of importance seemed to beckon from his deepest memories—the parts of his mind that were virtually blank now and featureless. But what? Three smooth stones, washed up no doubt on the beach. What was the significance in that?

As the two humans watched him with growing expectancy, Tashum tossed one of the stones, then another. The first of them fell into the sand, another settled into a bowl among the roots of the large fruit tree.

But this was, after all, only a first attempt. The two humans bent closer, giving small sounds of encouragement and the juggler himself offered a number of pantomimed hints for success.

Tashum tried again. And again. And again. The juggler took the stones back many times and demonstrated the ease with which such a thing can be done. And just as many times, the angel took the stones back only to see them fumbled to the earth.

Long after the evening light had died, when the moon slice in the night sky cast only a feeble glow, Tashum was still struggling with the stones. Finally, in self-disgust, he threw the stones to the ground. Shrug took this as the signal to leave, and he and the limping man withdrew back down the slope into the jungle, trading quiet grunts that Tashum had no wish to translate.

That night, Tashum walked the island with his thoughts scouring the blankness—the empty vaults where his memories were once stored—looking for some crumb of remaining recollection. He held the stones in his hands, feeling their water-smoothed surfaces, sensing their weight in his fingers. It was not a far leap to assign these stones some association with divine numbers. The Voice often sounded as three. The trio of celestial visions that encircled the Voice's rare, if ever, seen image. These fragments swirled in front of his eyes, then fell away, as surely as the stones had fallen to the ground earlier. But what could he make of his attraction to the sight of the stones whirling through the air? And what of his inability to master this simple sleight of hand even though it was a feat performed by the least capable of these animal-men?

As the moon arced across the sky he crept through the jungle growth.

Perched high in a tree, he looked down at the sleeping collection of twenty humans, scattered in twos and threes around their fire pit.

By comparison, his body was completely different from theirs. More capable in most ways—he could swim farther and faster, he had more powerful vision and hearing—and yet, strangely, he seemed incapable of certain minor tasks.

For weeks afterward, he refused all Shrug's requests, and eventually the little man stopped coming.

At dusk Tashum sat alone under his tree, staring at the stones, lying where they dropped after another failed attempt to make them fly. His inability to master the art of juggling was very troubling. He could not bear the thought of being less divine than they.

One afternoon, while the sun sat high in the heavens, Tashum's thoughts were forced back into the world of the humans. He awoke from his sleep to the sound of excitement and disarray coming from the villagers, some way up the sandy path. He crept to the mouth of his cave, turning his head slightly, trying to tune in on their distress. It had the sound of alarm. Alarm from what, he did not know. The hunter's voices were sharp and harsh, women and children simply cried. He wondered if they were under attack. But as he listened, he could not make out the sounds of an attacker—the shrill noise of boars, or any other dangerous creature, for that matter.

The intensity of the ambient sunlight meant dusk was still many hours away. Trapped by the sun, there was little he could do but wait. He fought off his want of sleep, yawned, and listened as best he could. Within minutes, the voices grew fainter—not quieter, just more diminished as though receding into the distance. For the remaining hours until dusk, the island became devoid of any human noise—the sounds he'd become so accustomed to: children running, children's laughter, women speaking to each other softly as they tended the children and gathered berries and fruit, and the louder, broader voices of the men chattering, breaking small branches with their feet as they traversed the island looking for prey. Even the sounds of their snoring at the midday nap—a noise he had first mistaken for rutting pigs—was absent.

The island now seemed a strange place, where he could make out only the calls and moving-about sounds of animals and insects.

When the sun finally disappeared behind the sea, Tashum raced from his cave down the sandy path to the clearing where the humans had lived. The small lean-tos were demolished, sticks and clusters of palm branches scattered in the dirt, the fire pit was cold and white gray, the stones kicked out of their circle. Their spears, their cast-off animal skins, their dried fish—everything was gone.

He stopped and closed his eyes, searching out now not only with his ears, but with a beam of thought, searching for some remaining sign of the humans. He crossed the village grounds and followed the path heading toward the ocean. It led him to a cove where Shrug's people kept a small fleet of fishing dug-out canoes. The signal became stronger: a dull, wordless agony somewhere near the beach. Breaking out of the jungle, his eyes swept the area. All the boats were gone.

He searched the dark horizon, hoping to pick out their tiny silhouettes. For some time he ran the length of the beach searching desperately for some visual clue to the direction of their retreat but found none. Long ago a great storm brought them here, washing their small broken boats up on these shores, but tonight the air was still, there was no storm to take them away. Why would they leave? Where would they go?

Then he heard it again—that slow agonized harmonic of human suffering. His body seemed an antenna for the static sound wave.

Again, Tashum began to focus on the sound—not an audible sound, but a crying out of thought energy that some part of his ancient ability could still capture. He brought a stillness to his thoughts. There it was! He picked up the vibration and followed it, turning one way, then correcting his direction until it grew stronger and filled his mind. Finally he found it. . . .

Shrug lay in the grass near the sandy path.

The small human's knees and hands were lacerated and bleeding, his wounds filled with grit. He had apparently crawled from the village the few miles to this stretch of sand, no doubt trying to join those fleeing the island. Why?

Tashum bent over, placed his hand on the human's shivering body. The night was warm and balmy, and Shrug should have been stalking through the forest or sitting by the fire. He should have been gesticulating and calling out orders.

The hunter's eyes were dim now and watery. His face felt hot to the touch. A foamy spittle leaked from one corner of his gasping mouth. Tashum took some of this on his finger and smelled it.

The scent was wrong, more acrid than organic.

And why was he shivering as though the night were frigid?

Cold.

Tashum searched Shrug's eyes. Had he spoken?

So cold, came the words again. But they were not words. They were spasms of thought.

Tashum sent back a reply: *I can make a fire*. But Shrug turned away, and the angel couldn't tell if the human could read thoughts or not. Tashum ran three of his fingers across the length of a gash on Shrugs forehead, and the lesion slowly closed.

My family, came another thought message.

"Your family?" Tashum asked out loud.

Come back my family. . . . So cold.

At this Tashum straightened and noticed another male figure lay lifeless in the tall grass. There were no signs of battle or an enemy. No weapons, no blood trails.

He moved away from Shrug. He stood over the other man. But the man was silent. He found no warmth in his touch, no thoughts, just a body stiff with death.

He returned to Shrug and lifted the man into his arms, hoping to share with him some of his own body's heat. He held him close and rubbed the backside of the failing body.

Shrug's head lay on the angel's broad shoulder, his gazed fixed on Tashum's raised wing nubs.

Tashum . . . A shudder ran up through his body and froze his curious expression.

Shrug? Tashum waved a hand across Shrug's visual plane to no response. The angel lifted the small man onto a shoulder and took off running down the path.

Back at the village site, Tashum rebuilt the fire in the pit as he had seen Shrug and others do on countless evenings. He propped Shrug against one of the blackened fire stones and quickly gathered a large bundle of dry sticks and leaves from the demolished lean-tos.

Soon the fire roared and sent a shower of sparks into the night sky. Raw heat radiated powerfully from the flame, and still Shrug seemed to get colder and colder and sleepier. He fell away from the stone and laid on the ground.

Tashum knelt beside the little man and rubbed the man's hands between his own. He could smell that other scent. He could taste its foulness being absorbed through his touch. It rose from the man's body increasingly more pungently. It was disease killing him, not injury.

The body that had been rigid with cold relaxed, and Tashum heard a long, satisfied breath pass out of Shrug. The angel witnessed a brilliant flash of pure light streak across the man's eyes. But it was more than a breath and an illusion. Shrug was notably lighter than before. Tashum's hands slid down Shrug's length. The harmonic resonance was dissipating.

For a moment he felt Shrug's presence still in the village. Shrug's spirit was hovering over the body, and Tashum was confused by such a migration.

He studied the corpse for some time, placing his ear to the still chest, pressing fingers to the pulse spots: the neck, the wrists. Then he took a breath and, opening Shrug's mouth, blew air into his lungs. He did this many times, but Shrug's presence was gone and refused to return. Tashum could not see the spirit, but he felt it being carried away with the gentle island breeze.

He took the body in his hands and shook it. Shook it again, trying to reawaken Shrug from this deep, enchanted sleep that had come over him. Tashum shook him violently until he heard bones in the neck breaking, and arm bones and ribs cracking under the pressure of his fingers.

Then he placed the body on the ground and knelt over the man, closed his eyes and sent probing thought beams into the hunter's brain. Tashum's energy probe moved around in the deepest recesses, searching for some sign of life presence. But he may as well have been listening to a stone, for there was nothing waiting to be discovered.

When daylight crept over the horizon, Tashum drew himself up and left the clearing.

Each night he returned to the clearing, only to find the body still there. Pigs and insects had violated the corpse. Fingers were missing, as were toes. A line of ants had formed, toiling in and out of the unmoving lips. Shrug was truly inert, as helpless as sand.

He carried Shrug's remains back to his cave for safekeeping. Since the body had not been completely consumed, Tashum reasoned it might be possible for Shrug to return. Perhaps these humans had another ability he did not—that of leaving and later returning to their bodies. As the days passed, the smell of the corpse became hideous and unbearable, and within a fortnight in that tropical climate it became clear that should Shrug return, there would be very little left to return to.

At the end of week three, Tashum carried the rotting corpse to the beach and fashioned a bed of sticks and leaves to carry it out to sea. He sat on his haunches and watched the remains float for awhile in the moonlight.

Eventually, the mat of sticks and leaves lost buoyancy. Slowly the raft settled and sank under the waves. Shrug was gone. . . .

When their bodies stopped functioning, the life force could leave. He could not be certain where the spirit would go. Was it a place or a state? Was there another planet that Shrug had been consigned to, in the way Tashum had been remaindered here? There were obvious clues, but he wasn't ready to admit to himself a reality where the human spirit migrated to the very Light he had been ejected from.

What had been Shrug's final thoughts? *So warm* . . . followed by that sensation of light. Light that tasted of fruit, the freedom of birds. Light that bathed and caressed. Light that enwrapped one in joy and flights of wonder.

The Light of home.

He was, thus, not alive in the same sense as these humans. Tashum understood he could be wounded, and like the lizard that could lose a tail or leg and have it grow back, in time he could be healed, made whole again. But even the lizard eventually dies and does not replace itself, except through its offspring.

Why couldn't his life be similar to theirs, in the way their souls cycle through nature, the way rainwater falls into the ocean, then is pulled back up into the clouds, only to fall again?

Where their arrivals and departures were as natural as the weather that cleaned and greened this planet, his weather was naturally quiescent.

He wiped at his eyes, pondering these thoughts, staring up into the maze of stars beyond the sky and beyond his reach. The light of his celestial birth-place—a place where insects did not sting, where hunger did not torment, where friends did not die and deliquesce into nothing.

Why must he be here? Why, when every day he dreamed of that world of careless delight from which he'd been rejected?

Grief filled his mind, "Take me back," he whispered. Why was he here? What was his purpose? Why was he kept so alone?

The only thing he knew with certainty was his organic machinery could not be permanently wounded. Even in the flesh, he didn't share the fragile mortality of Earth's children. For the ensuing centuries, he would wonder who was really better off. . . .

CHAPTER fOUR

1509 A.D.

The moon crept over the dark horizon, unfurling its jagged carpet of silver across the undulating surface of a black sea.

Tashum followed a rutted path, taking him through thickets of bay-grape trees and dense jungle shrub to a broad open beach. He was dressed in animal skins, walking as he had for many a millennia on the still-warm pink sands. He gazed out across vast, heaving waters and sent out his silent call.

Come, my brothers . . .

For whatever reason, Shrug's people never returned. Nothing remained of their habitation. And for some forty thousand years, Tashum contented himself with their memory—a memory now bleached into a faint mythic tale—hunters who had taught him the ways of this tiny, tiny world; hunters that tattooed themselves with ash and blood to mimic his likeness.

For centuries, he studied the properties of plants and animals, observed the slow movement of the stars as they circled heaven's dome. He swam in the cool, dark sea discovering the other world under her waves. He could drown himself if he wished, which he did several times, only to awaken washed up on the beach, mouth full of water and sand.

Tonight he sat under his fruit tree, one of many successors to the original. He picked up the three smooth stones given to him so many eons ago by a wounded hunter. He felt their familiar weight in his palms, took a breath, and tossed one into the air, then the second. They passed each other in mid-arc, and he gave the third a quick launch. For a moment the stones hung in the air in a perfect triangle, weightless. His hands continued to move, and the stones spun and looped upward in a dance. Not only had he mastered many of nature's mysteries, he had come to master this simple juggling trick. It pleased him to know he could not be bested by bestial man. Given time and practice he reasoned he could master any earthly sport. In a swift playful movement, he tossed all the stones into the air at once and let them fall among the roots of the tree.

He eyed them. With the full weight of his gaze on the stones, in tiny increments, they began to move. One stone shifted slightly to the left, another moved forward, a third budged backward until they sat in a straight line. After more intense concentration, he caused them to form a triangle— his mind reaching out with an invisible hand. Here was a trick he knew man was incapable of mimicking. A thing the creator had not given. . . .

He heard a foreign noise.

A great moan of tearing timber. His heart quickened and he calmed himself, drawing back into the silent place where he could detect the tiniest snapping twig or thread of thought.

There it was again. It wasn't a tree falling. The birds were now screeching the announcement of new arrival. The breeze brought to him a new scent and human sounds in the din.

He took off at a run down the beach, his eyes scanning the ocean's thin black horizon. So many centuries after disappearing in their dug-out boats, maybe Shrug's people had returned without a great storm.

Tashum reached a curve in the shoreline and his gaze went to the outer reef, the partially hidden crown of coral that encircled the island.

And he saw it—two hundred yards across the water the broken hull of a massive sailing vessel lay moaning, its belly torn open by the outer reef. The ship's bow was crushed and holed, exposing her innards; large white sails lofted over the sides and dipped into the water, pressing against her damaged hull. He watched her settle, listening to her wooden cries for help.

He turned and looked farther down the beach, sharpening his radiant gaze. The sand was littered with broken crates, scattered debris, wooden casks rolled in the surf. On the surface of the moonlit water bobbed corked bottles and splintered planks, drowned chickens and rats. At his feet, the waves delivered a single boot.

He picked up the boot and examined its soaked leather sides, its pliable sole. He tossed it aside and moved toward the shoreline. The body of a man dressed in rough cloth pants and a large, loose-fitting shirt drifted toward him. The man's hands were leather-lashed together behind his back.

Tashum bent and studied these unfamiliar body coverings and the face. The face.

Human certainly, but so unlike the human appearance of Shrug's people. The forehead was flat and broad, not low and protruding as he had remembered. The nose was sharp and narrow; the staring eyes were oval and set wide apart. And the face had hair, but not the animal hairiness he recalled from so long ago. This clipped hair went over the lips and around the bottom of the chin in an oval, not so much as natural, unkempt growth but more an adornment. The figure was so tall—or would be had the drowned man been upright. He might have shared Tashum's height.

The ear on the near side of the head was large and also hairless, and at the fleshy lower tip, Tashum found a circle of gold pierced into the skin. Another glimmering adornment.

These were not man-animals, but a new breed of being. A shedding of the outer beast had taken place. Albeit wingless, these humans were almost divine, almost celestial in shape and appearance. How had such a change occurred? Where did they acquire such fine things?

His heart quickened—could this be? Had they come at last?

Then he caught sight of the blood.

Tashum moved aside the wet slop of hair and discovered a long, cruel slash opening the man's throat, creating a second mouth. This was no death by water, certainly no fever. This was a death—the slaughtering of a boar for hunger. His eyes examined the thin cleaved wound, made by some kind of sharp instrument, perhaps a bladed implement traced across the flesh.

In death the humans had left him and now in death they returned. Returned from a salty sea, the conduit of abandonment and reclamation in Tashum's world.

His eyes scanned the waves. Others floated toward the beach. But were they all dead?

He went from one arriving corpse to the next—all wore similar garb, made not from animal skins but from some kind of material that appeared to be fibers meshed and woven together. Thin strips of bark, perhaps, or tough grasses but softer to the touch than what comes from nature. Thread.

Most had hands tied behind their backs. Most were slashed at the throat, though a few seemed to have died from drowning, their faces blue and distended.

"No," he murmured to himself, panicking. "No, no, no."

He darted from one washed-up body to another, kneeling over them, probing their brains for even the faintest sign of life presence.

He found nothing.

He stood, looked up to heaven. "Why? Haven't I been in the dark long enough?"

The only light he'd known had come with Shrug and his little band of humans. This was too cruel, to show him more, to taunt him with more death. These new men, they had real beauty; that was apparent even in their death state. He reached his hands up, a silent supplication, the ache in his chest unbearable. Where was the Voice, the Light, the mercy—

"H-help us . . . p-please."

Tashum looked around. He'd heard it—a tattered human voice. His head jerked, eyes scanned the debris.

"Where are you?" he cried out in a vocal tone that mimicked the other man's voice. The sudden ease with which he spoke a language unknown to him seemed magical, and he was curious if he had used the right sounds.

"P-please . . ." sounded from the water. "Here, out here I am."

Tashum noted he not only heard the jagged cry but the man's words were also being transduced into mental images of understanding. At last organized language had reached his ears.

In the darkness, Tashum focused on a flotilla of debris rising and falling just a few yards off the shore. Stumbling toward the edge of the water, he spied a long and narrow wooden box. Clinging to one side was a human hand with dark, broken fingernails and snake-white skin. In a moment another hand appeared and then, emerging up out of the water, a face, that of a modern human. A round, almost dull face with short, dark hair and skin as white as an unearthed grub.

And glowing owllike eyes.

Tashum nearly fell facedown into the water, his leg joints broken loose from their moorings. He stumbled again, catching himself. The eyes! On earth the only other glowing eyes he had ever seen had been his own reflected in a pool of moonlit water. He was at a loss to recognize this creature's face or physique to be one of his fallen brothers.

"Please help us, you must," the man spoke in a weak, uncertain voice. Clearly in ill health, he raised an arm and pointed to another body-length wooden box swirling in the surf. "Bring her ashore," he pleaded as a wave carried him ashore. "Do you hear me, don't just stand there, we need your help!"

Tashum stared at this pitiful weakling balanced on all fours, struggling against the pull of the surf. He crawled to dry sand before collapsing. The angel measured the time the man lay there by counting the cycle of waves splashing against the shore. It took six sets of seven waves before the man's breathing relaxed to normal rhythms.

When the man lifted his face from the sand Tashum was standing over him. He appeared too weak to find Tashum's eyeline and spoke to the angel's knees. "Please. Bring her ashore!" he urged with pointed finger. "She's in that box. Bring her to me and I shall reward you. Be quick!"

Tashum was immediately put off by the man's commanding tone. Had it not been for the stranger's desperation and his own curiosity he would have waited until ready before wading out into the surf and pulling the odd-shaped box up onto the beach.

When he pried off the lid, at first all he could make out was the orange moon dazzling on the surface of the water inside. Then he saw a serene face framed by a swirl of dark hair. He lifted the sleeping beauty up into the open air. Seawater drained from her clothes, sucking her blouse tight against her rounded breasts.

At first it seemed unreal, this creature in his arms. He stared down at her with disbelief. Never had he seen or dreamed of this—a face of such perfect innocence, sacred beauty—awakening in him some new revelation.

Centuries ago he had experienced pain for the first time, and now he felt pain's opposite—an exaltation so rich, so tumultuous, it was itself almost painful. The sheer, sharp agony of beholding a thing so beautiful, so exotic and unreal rising up out of the murk. How a creature such as this could exist in a world such as this—astonishment rose up and out of him as a sob.

He lifted her fully from the box and knelt to place her onto the bed of sand. Her clothing, heavy with water, was intricate, with threads of gold on a scarlet cloth, more fanciful than clothing worn by the other bodies on the beach. His hands gently moved across the soft, whispering surface finding small beads and broad threaded designs skillfully woven into the fabric. Then he touched her face, surprised to leave a white stain. He stopped, his frown deepening. He touched her again, leaving another stark white stain. He looked at his fingertips and found smudges of the flesh color. His fingers scrubbed her face, washing away all of the darker coloring, revealing a salt white complexion underneath. She was more worshipful than before.

He bent closer.

"She's not dead—she can't be dead," the other said, springing forward, taking her by the shoulders. "Please say she's not dead!"

Tashum pressed her eyes open and found dim, unfocused owl-colored eyes. As he watched, the light flickered, brightened for an instant and then extinguished, becoming glassy, insensate orbs.

"Fanny," the man cried, then turned to Tashum. "If the light leaves her eyes, she's dead. I've seen it before. Fanny! Wake up, come back!"

The plain-looking man swung one arm down in a snapping motion and a small dagger slipped from his shirt sleeve into the palm of his hand. He let her go and slit open a wrist and stuffed the bleeding wound into her slack, gaping mouth.

Slowly the man's gaze lifted from her face to find Tashum's eyes.

"Bloody hell!" he said, his mouth quivering. "You—you're one of them! She needs your blood, not mine! Don't you see?"

Tashum didn't know how to respond to such a request. He pushed the man aside and took her head in his hands, her wet hair slipping between his strong fingers. He closed his eyes tightly and projected a fierce thrust of energy into her mind.

"She needs your blood!" the man insisted. "Please! You must bring her back."

"Silence," Tashum murmured. The man's language rolled off Tashum's tongue with relative ease. It shocked him, how he knew these words he could not fathom. He rocked back on his haunches, worried to speak it again.

"Don't just sit there!" The man commanded in the King's English. "You must do something!"

Tashum gripped her head, pulling it to his chest, pressing waves of heat into her. Her mind was a blackness, a solid, opaque wall. "Come back," he whispered. "Return."

His fingers found the contours of her skull, the flashing energy pulsing out of him, swarming through the chambers of her brain. Silently he searched for life presence, for a dim, single nub of thought, for the sensation of warmth he had felt so often in dying creatures. Diving inward, thrashing about—a swimmer trapped in the rocks of the outer reef searching for signs of starlight above the dark sea. But he found nothing. None of the living illumination that should envelop a receding soul.

"Come back," he repeated, smoothing back her hair, filling the chill darkness in her skull with a warmth of his own. A desperate strength forced dreams of life into her closed shelter. "There." His hands relaxed their grip. "She is here."

Her eyes unsealed and gradually opened. The bold yellow light fluttered, then gained brave, delicate strength in the core of her dilated pupils. Her tongue moved across her lips, taking in the pools and smears of the man's blood.

For a moment Tashum was caught in her sad gaze, glowing low-burning candles, transfixed by their otherworldly stare.

Slowly and without a word her arm rose and her thumb rotated the ring on her third finger. Light glimmered off the small blade that snapped out of the ring just before it sank into Tashum's neck and slid down to his broad chest leaving a thin trail.

A trail of golden amber fluid.

Her eyes widened with disbelief. Yet without hesitating, her open mouth moved toward the wound. Her full lips pushed forward—a calf wanting milk.

He pushed her away, rubbed at the wound at his neck. He thought of Shrug, not needing or wanting his blood. And he died. Then he looked at her. Could his blood that so healed his own wounds heal hers as well?

"Just once more," she moaned softly, "I'm so hungry, my darling Pal-a-din."

Tashum reeled back, pushing her down, pressing her into the sand with his hands. For a moment she lay pinned under the weight of him. "Paladin." His lips traced the sound of his brother's name. After these countless empty centuries, a name he had given up ever hearing from another's lips.

"Paladin, my love, feed me, please, please."

"It's not Paladin, Fanny," her companion said. "But he is one of them. I'm sure of it."

He loomed over her, staring down into those hungry eyes—lovely, demon eyes. He knew what it was to feel hunger—to be driven to madness by an unstoppable wanting, by unthinkable desire. Yet, this felt wrong. Absolutely wrong—wanting his *blood*. He was no wild pig to be eaten from. No.

"I'm so terribly hungry," she gasped. "I need you, my darling."

"Fanny, can you not see, this is not Paladin," her companion said a second time.

Tashum turned and looked at the other. The man crawled closer toward him. He was more alert than she, but his eyes ached in the same manner. The man's drawn face burned to quench some furious hunger.

The angel's eyes raced back and forth from one to the other. Suddenly, a thrill of terror passed through him. He released her and fled. He stumbled toward the black gate of vegetation rising up before him. His hands rose to his face but he could not leave the beach—them.

Life feeding on life, he thought. Another permutation of the ancient law of this world. They wanted his celestial blood. She wanted it—she needed it, obviously wavering in death's delirious grasp. He had the ability to give it, give it freely but for the instinctive clash of one rogue wave smashing against the flow of his inner tide.

Some ancient voice cried, *Sin*. And yet a sensation of wanton love filled him suddenly. He wanted to give it to them, *wanted* to do it. Some new gentle demon had risen to life inside him and now urged that he give of himself.

He panted and fell to the sand, weak, overcome with emotion. These strangers were angelic and yet demonic. Human and inhuman. Paladin's lifeblood? Is that really what she moaned for? To drink the blood of an angel—was such a thing possible?

Upon his backside he felt the strange tingle of a million pinpricks. He pulled himself up off the sand and turned to face them. In his line of vision appeared an object, haunting and unfamiliar, a glistening round ball—a fantastic radiant thing—a sun in miniature. It hovered in the night air, dancing gently there before his eyes.

A glowing orb. A living light—a heavenly sign.

His hand opened at his side, his eyes hypnotized by the shimmer playing across the orb's glossy surface. Dare he touch it? In stops and starts he reached out for it.

The image hung before him, a celestial thing, a lantern filled with the Light of home. It was the light he had searched for, had hungered for, had hoped to see inside the dying woman's soul. Slowly he reached out, his fingertips nearing its surface. He wanted to take it, to taste it, to drink in the fantastic energy.

Yet when he lunged for it, he felt no physical sensation. His hand passed through the orb as if it were a fume. No! He snatched at it. Grabbing now with both hands, taking swipes at this insanely luminous image.

It had appeared. Finally, a silent messenger from his distant celestial world. After four hundred centuries a message had finally come.

"A sign," he whispered. "A messenger."

A cold breeze passed through the trees—no. No, wait. Not a breeze, but a voice. Again it spoke in the language of the universe, murmuring its soft, cold wind through his very being.

"A sign of what?" asked the chilled whisper in the English language of his visitors.

Now Tashum could make out a vague shape standing between him and the black jungle beyond. A translucent presence, thin smoke from a dying fire. It rose, leaped, and perched itself high on the coral outcrop.

"Who are you?" Tashum asked, his vision groping the shadows. A ghostly voice passed through his memory. "Do I know you?"

"You only need to know that I am where you want to be."

"What is this vision? This orb of fire?"

"Guiding tools. Follow your logic."

"Who are these humans with the eyes of the Fallen?" Tashum asked, his mouth dry, "I know them not," a choking sound in his voice. The figure flickered, as though it might vanish. "Don't leave me, spirit!" he cried out. "Please, I have need of your help."

"Your brother calls to you," the spirit whispered. "Through her you find Paladin. Someday you will need her as she needs you now."

Tashum raised a shaking hand to his mouth. "Paladin." A breath caught in his throat, and he felt dizzy and ill.

"Your brother calls to you," the voice spoke again.

"Where is he? What does he want? How can I find him?"

The voice rose in pitch, blending now with a true breeze on the island. "Paladin—your gentle brother—your forsaken brother!"

"Where is he?" Tashum shouted. "Forsaken how?"

"Time is fluid, but their needs are static. Do not forsake Paladin by wasting precious moments."

"I would deliver rescue for my brother, show me the way."

"Do what you must."

The spirit rose from its perch, and Tashum followed its flight, hearing the soft snapping of wings. For a moment, the spirit was illuminated by the moon. A wavering, glasslike angelic shape, a being with fully spread wings. The image appeared fluid on the wind. In one hand he held a sword, but his right hand was missing at the wrist.

"Mayhem!" Tashum called. "Is it you?" he screamed. "Mayhem!"

Memories of heaven blazed as fiery images. The thousands of Fallen Ones blazing from their world of everlasting delight, faces contorted with anguish and terrible grief. Among them, the face of Mayhem.

"He sends for you. Tashum, he begs of you—find him," the spirit said finally, and then he vanished.

"Find him," Tashum murmured, his eyes darted about in the empty air. "Find him, but where?" he shouted, running up the beach, desperate for a final glimpse, a last word. But the spirit Mayhem had disappeared. Still Tashum's eyes searched the sky, hopeful of further contact. The crash of distant thunder brought his thoughts back to earth.

He turned, seeing the two creatures gazing at him with insatiable appetites. The message had come with them, just as he had dreamed. Somehow these new humans would help him if he helped them. But who were these two who had arrived on a death ship? Sent from Paladin along with the magic orb? Sent along with Mayhem, appearing as a mere fleck in his eye? Most shockingly, Mayhem was missing a hand, but how? Why?

With great effort, the woman rose up from the sand as he approached them.

"We're bleeders," she said in a soft, pale voice, as if she knew the questions raging inside him. "If you have a brother named Paladin, then you are of our family."

Paladin. At last, the gates of his prison creaked on the verge of opening. And what was the meaning of the visionary orb? What was this mysterious riddle?

He bent closer, examining her eyes. He listened to her language, created by the complex movement of the mouth. English seemed natural to him, but he relied upon the stacked images in her thoughts for truth.

"Feed us," she begged. "Give us your gift. Your blood. As Paladin did."

"He saved us," the man said, "as we need you to save us now."

The two sat at his feet—starving chicks looking up at him with eyes the same as his own. What had they said? He was of the same family?

"Paladin gave to you his blood?" Again, his words came out in their language and left strange feelings in his mouth.

"He took us in his arms," said the woman. "He fed us his divinity in a flood, allowed us to drink the glowing wine of his body."

"The blood of angels," the man said.

Tashum stared down at their drawn white faces, the only survivors among the wreckage. "Do you live in the sun?"

"No, in direct sunlight we burn. Like you, presumably. Bright light hurts our eyes." He finished with a quiver, "Please help us, father."

"Father?" Tashum leaned away.

Join him . . . your gentle brother, came a message on the breeze.

The decision arrived without further thought.

Without a word, Tashum moved to a dead seaman nearby, and from his waistband the angel took a long curved knife. He stood in the sand between them. Holding the knife by the bone handle, he pressed the blade across one wrist, his eyes clenched at the pain. A spurt of glowing blood oozed out at the knife point. Fanny struck the wound with her open mouth, sucking at the golden sap, her cold, urgent lips pressed to his arm, her hands reaching up to caress his body.

The man whimpered wordlessly, hovering around her, nervously, eagerly awaiting his turn.

Tashum handed the knife to the man and held out his other exposed wrist.

"Drink of me," Tashum said.

Tashum failed to notice the glow fading out of the visionary orb as the woman drank from him.

The man's eyes widened, and he plunged the knife deep into the arm. Tashum let out a sharp gasp. The man pulled the blade roughly toward the wrist, tearing the skin. He let the knife fall away and grabbed the arm with both hands, pushed his face into the gash, frantically nursing the wound.

Tashum felt their voracious mouths on his ruptured veins, heard their small murmurs of wonder and ecstasy, felt their caresses of amorous appreciation.

Tashum first knelt and then a moment later laid down in the sand between them, feeling his thick, golden blood draining out of him, gazing up at the thinly outlined and quickly dissipating orb, which gave way to a large moon hidden behind it.

The two humans curled up next to him, their mouths pressed to his wrists, their bodies tight against his. Adoring him, drinking from him. His supernatural life force flowed into them, twisting through their veins, filling their skin and organs and bones with harsh, pungent force.

Tashum breathed in deeply, his eyes still on the moon hung against the black cosmos—another orb he could not reach. As he focused, he noted a wide, round corona of silver white, giving the impression of a huge staring eye.

Was heaven watching? Did heaven approve? It must have, he thought.

The two humans moaned softly now in a sated half-sleep, burying themselves in his sides with small, rocking motions. And he could feel his knife wounds closing, the pain was dissolving. This act of regeneration had been so simple, once performed.

He gazed up at that god-size eye and wondered if this was another bend in the long road that had brought him here or, finally, his first true step on the path to redemption.

He closed his eyes and he shared their sleep.

CHAPTER FIVE

Tashum's solitude had been lifted, the sounds of his island now included the regular music of other heartbeats, pictures of a world Tashum had only been able to imagine in abstract, ghostly visions that had no meaning, anchored in no reality.

Fanny and Dickey—their chosen English names—had intellect, he decided. Intelligence and passion that went beyond the simple survival needs of Shrug and his band. He embroidered their tales and descriptions of the life on other continents into a tapestry that now decorated his mind in glorious color and sensation. Ruling kings and queens carried the same modern visage. When they spoke of armies, he imagined a thousand soldiers with Dickey's face advancing against a thousand Fannies. The paintings all had the same subject. Even their mention of saints, of Christ, Mary, and the Magdalene, carried the same two faces within his mind.

Whereas Shrug had been an amusing if beloved puppet, Dickey was thoughtless, carefree, moody, unpredictable. And Fanny, she embodied a mystery of reaction and attitude that left him constantly off balance, at once clumsy and unable to please, and a moment later, the very sun that sustained her.

These two new-style humans, which he knew to be different than the others they spoke of, others who had bobbed null as corks onto his beach.

They were his only reference to a world that had moved forward, grown, evolved, become civilized and social—more barbaric and criminal—with all the majesty and mystery of a great undertaking. The world had grown without Tashum's participation, and these stories of the new masters only heightened his sense of isolation on this womb of coral and dirt.

Marooned as they were, Tashum never tired of asking them questions, though they occasionally tired of answering. They were bored easily and at times desperate to return to their world they called the living. He drank from them, from their memories, as readily as they drank from his arms, particularly when the subject was Paladin, or questions of other Fallen Angels.

"How many others have you seen like me?" Tashum looked to Fanny for a response as she ran her fingers over his face and neck. The scars, once hard and black, had over the centuries smoothed and faded into deep bronze, appearing now as swirls of soft, glossy texture, indecipherable letters of a lost alphabet embossed across his pale body.

"Besides Paladin, you're the only one," she said.

As they lay together in the cave, waiting for the death of the twilight, Tashum wondered what Paladin had told his children. They seemed aware of his angelic origin, but to his satisfaction they did not grasp what that meant.

Dickey sat on his haunches closer to the cavern's mouth, tossing small stones into a pool of water that ran along one wall. "They say there's a monastery in northern Africa. With monks." He struggled for the words. "Like us."

"Did Paladin tell you of them?" Tashum asked, glancing up.

"No. But the last I heard of him, that's where he was going—with Fanny."

Fanny withdrew her fingers from Tashum's face.

Dickey was now staring at Fanny with teased expression: "He wanted to see them for himself. Like you, he often spoke of brothers and sisters."

"Did he find them?"

Fanny's eyes narrowed and glanced at Dickey.

Dickey shrugged, not understanding Fanny's expression and said, "Don't know, ask her."

Fanny kept her dark expression away from Tashum. "I'll never know. We went our separate ways," she said, her face softening as she leaned over to kiss Tashum's scars.

Tashum sensed that she was withholding something, but he let it go. "Where is this Africa?" he asked. "I mean, is it far?"

"The world's a big place," Dickey replied. He tossed his last stone and sat back, lounged against the rock wall. "Bigger than anyone ever imagined."

Fanny finished the thought for him, "This speck of an island—it's part of what they're calling the New World."

"The New World," Tashum repeated with a laugh. "It's very old for me. How does it all fit together? You know, Africa, the New World?"

Fanny tossed her head, "Well, Africa is a long way from here." She leaned across him. Her finger touched the dirt and drew a circle, "England is here." Then her index finger randomly pointed to the far wall, "Africa is over there somewhere."

"No, it's not, it's over here!" complained Dickey.

"Oh, shut up! How would you know?"

"I just know if that's England," he pointed to her drawn circle, "then Africa wouldn't be there where you put it. Would it?"

"You really are rotten," she said with a scowl, and laid back into Tashum's arms. In the quiet they both stared up, watching a small green, lizard clinging to the domed coral ceiling above them.

"How did you happen to come here?" asked Tashum.

"We sailed from England four months ago. By the grace of God we survived terrible storms, followed by days when there was no wind at all. The ship simply sat in the middle of a flat wasteland of water. No signs of life, no sight of land. It was horrible."

Tashum was familiar with the story but stumped by the actual geography they described. They had recounted many times for him the tale of their passage to the island, the changing details keeping it fresh. Through their stories, Tashum had relived their other travels, escaping plagues and famine and cannibalism in a high mountain village in Eastern Europe. Always hoping and dreaming of a cure for their disease, always hearing stories of physicians in the west who could effect a miracle. Before meeting Paladin, they had been bleeders. When cut, they simply bled and kept on bleeding, the flow from the smallest wound would cascade unchecked, unstoppable, until such weakness overcame them, they would lie as dead for days.

In northern Italy, they had fallen in with pilgrims who told tales of the appearance of St. Osmond's disembodied face on the wall of a blessed chapel in the Alps. Those who touched the face were supposedly cured of all disease. Old men were made young again. Virginity was restored to harlots. The mute were made to speak. Those afflicted with demons were freed from possession. It was an endless list of mythic calamity and cure.

When their ragtag procession reached the church after days of hunger and sleeping in snow, eating moss and the leather of their own belts, they found the place deserted, the tombstones broken, the door to the chapel smashed. And on entering the building, they were attacked by a band of robbers, who beat and stabbed them, violated women and men alike, took their shoes and what coinage they had and left them all to die.

Fanny and Dickey crawled as far as the doorway, their wounds bleeding profusely. They wept and held tight to each other, calling out for miracles. And as they lay on the cold stone entryway, warmed only by their pooled blood, a tall robed figure appeared above them. Thinking he was a priest, they begged him to say the last rites.

Instead of whispering the magic words of the church, he took a knife, opened slits upon his chest and let them drink of his blood—not the scarlet blood of man, but the glowing life fluid of a god. In this way he saved them, made them his children and created for them a life in death.

The father, this giver of new life, called himself Paladin. This, if nothing else, made them family enough to one another who had known no other.

Tashum would have drifted off into slumber, but for the restlessness of his companions.

"I'm hungry," Dickey muttered. He unfolded his short, thin body and laid down in the cool, sandy earth of the cave floor.

"So am I," Fanny said, speaking into Tashum's ribs.

Tashum stroked her hair. So temperamental, these strange children.

"Remember how we feasted in Budapest?" Dickey said, his hand lying across his face.

She gave several small shakes of quiet laughter.

Tashum recognized her gestures. The sideways glances they shared were a reaction to a private, almost secret, joke they would not share.

"Tonight I'll show you how we feast on the island."

"Not that again." Fanny groaned.

Tashum bent down and kissed the top of her head. He felt love for her, and her sibling, Dickey. But his instincts warned him against coddling them too much. He thought of the ancient Shrug: the father teaching the children of that long ago tribe.

"Yes, that again." His chest puffed proud, imitating his memory of Shrug. "There are things you must learn."

Fanny rolled her eyes. Dickey yawned, smacking his dry lips.

"Come on, the both of you," Tashum said. "If nothing else, at least you should be amused, and probably delighted."

"Must we really?" Fanny moaned. . . .

A warm, coastal breeze slipped through forking branches, rustling the leaves masking their approach. In unison the three dark figures stopped and silently split up.

The sow boar sniffed the air, lifted her tusked snout, and detected a dangerous scent. She snorted, snuffed, and shook her bristled head, then trotted on short legs through waist-deep grass when . . .

The jungle exploded with movement, vines flung aside, young saplings snapped from their roots. A movement so swift it left an image lag; a succession of ghosts attached to a figure flashed through space, faster than thought, unearthly eliminating any chance for reaction. The grass parted and in seconds the sow lay dying, her neck broken by a single deft stroke.

Fanny stood over the animal. The image lags joined her physical form, as her chest rose and fell. Her open mouth sucked in air.

"At last! That's how it's done," Tashum said, emerging from a curtain of bay-grape trees. "You've done it," said the proud teacher to his student. "You've mastered movement."

Following Tashum, Dickey broke into applause. "Brava," he called out, "I didn't think you could do it, but you did!"

Fanny sat next to the boar and caught her breath. Moonlight brought her white cheekbones into sharp relief.

"It's easy," she said, trying to hide her own amazement at what she had just accomplished.

"Easy, once you've learned the technique," Tashum answered, and knelt next to her. "Paladin never taught you this, did he?"

"No," she huffed, and leaned against his leg for support.

"Paladin taught us almost nothing," Dickey said. "You should have seen yourself, Fanny, you were just a blur. Ain't that right, Tashum? Just a blur, she was."

"She's learned to move as fast as a solid object can fall," answered Tashum.

"How did I do that?" she asked with pure innocence.

"Well," the angel said, settling next to Fanny, "it's a matter of realizing that the air is not empty. It's filled with particles, much like water, but it can be split open."

"Like lightning," Fanny said.

"Precisely."

"But my thoughts weren't of lightning."

"They don't need to be." The angel smiled.

"It's cheating." Dickey's yellow eyes glowed. "And we love cheating, we do." He slid his hands into the front pockets of his trousers and kicked up his heels. Humming a sea shanty, he began dancing, whirling all around them, creating a dizzy, circular wall of his own image lags, showing off his own newly learned ability. Then he fell to the ground hooting and howling with glee.

"Can others do this?" she asked the angel.

"Others of my kind? I don't know. . . . I would hope so."

"How about other humans?"

"It would be hard for me to say, but I believe not. No, I wouldn't think so," Tashum replied. "You have celestial blood in your veins. It makes you different. It opens new avenues."

"And it closes others," Fanny said with sharp irony. "Like the sun. I miss the sun terribly."

Tashum searched her face for a moment, almost speaking, then turned his attention to the animal. "Let me show you how to carve up the carcass."

"Allow me," Fanny said, rotating the ring on her finger. The blade rose from the ring and slid across the beast's throat. Blood bubbled up. She pressed her hungry mouth to the wound.

Dickey's Mad Hatter display ended with the first suckling sounds. He rolled up on all fours. "Fanny, please," Dickey whimpered, "I really need that."

Her eyes looked up at him, amber and radiant. A moment later she pulled away from the animal, wiping the blood from her lips with a moan of delectation. "I haven't forgotten you," she assured him.

Dickey dropped to the slit, he sucked hard at the open artery.

Tashum lurched away from the spectacle of these blood drinkers attached to the pig. It made him dizzy to watch. His thoughts colliding with a sense of coldness that emanated from them. Their absolute hunger, their absolute lack of sanctity over a life taken was overwhelming. Even ancient Shrug knew to bless that which fed him. A shrill alarm stitched up his back. If they had no feeling of gratitude for the pig, how long before they lost their ardor for him?

Dickey looked up from the animal, thick blood drooling from his lips. "Tashum, would you care for a taste?"

"No. I never—"

Fanny's head turned to see the expression of horror and disgust on the angel's face. So long was his time spent alone, he had no practice at hiding his feelings.

"I should have let you drink first," she said.

"No." He shook his head, glanced away, then turned back, forcing himself to look at the scene. "No, I eat fruit, flesh if nothing else, but I never drink blood." His voice carried a tad of arrogance. "I could never drink blood."

Her eyes narrowed, "I wasn't always like this." She paused, her eyes reshaped, and her voice softened, "Since Paladin gave us his sacred blood, we must find nourishment this way."

"Do you not eat flesh at all?"

"Blood is better than flesh," she answered. "Blood carries life. And it's better to drink from the living."

Tashum licked at dry lips. "I see."

"I'm not sure you do, my darling." Fanny came to him, caressed his face with her hands. "When Paladin gave us life, this life, it took away some part of us that was human. My body doesn't," she searched for the right words, "it doesn't work as it did."

She pressed him with urgent kisses. Her lips found his, her cool tongue brought blood-salt taste into his mouth. Her hands brushed through his long hair.

"Please . . . ," she whispered into his mouth. "Take away the clouds in your eyes. My Tashum, my beloved. Are you not glad we're alive? Are you not glad that I'm here?"

"Yes," he answered, but not fast enough to suit her.

Tears spilled down her cheeks and onto his lips, his mouth.

"Don't despise us so," she wept. "I couldn't live with that."

He wrapped his powerful arms around her shuddering body.

Dickey moved closer, whispered into his ear, "You're our father now. Our teacher. Our savior."

Tashum added Dickey into his embrace. "Why should I despise you? Here life feeds life," he said in a broken voice. "I can't hate you for your need to survive."

She gently pushed away and looked up into his face. "Don't pity us, please promise me that."

"How could I ever pity Paladin's creation?" He pulled her close.

They pressed their cold vampire bodies against his, these undead children, born of angelic pity, nourished on hot living blood. He felt such longing for them, such inexpressible love. For once, he did not look to heaven for approval. He accepted his own heart.

Days later, the argument between love and disgust still followed Tashum as he strolled across the pink beach. A quick downpour had earlier imprinted the coral sand with rain punctures and upon drying left a brittle, pebbled surface. He made it a game, counting how many steps he could take before breaking through the mantle. He stopped and his gaze lifted upward, where rotund clouds were sweeping across the night sky, leaving thin carpets of vapor, reminiscent of cosmic dust.

He sat on the edge of a tidal pool. He stared up at the twinkle of stars. From memory he identified the relative position of the Sisters, the Bear, and the Hunter. Dickey and Fanny had taught him about constellations and myth. These star clusters and attendant stories were informative for Tashum. He was learning about the human world that had developed beyond his island. Betrayal, treachery, heroics, masculinity, femininity, parents, and children—the night sky was for him now a pageant of human dreams and aspirations, rising up and falling down. These stars were pegs on which they hung their history. How he longed to be out among these humans. Understanding them might be the key to understanding himself. As he gazed at his reflection on the water's surface he wondered where Paladin was tonight. He tried to envision his brother gazing at the same stars, lost in the same milky spectacle.

A soft footfall and the snap of twigs ended his reverie.

Fanny approached him from around a tumbled collection of coral stone. Her hands were held behind her back.

"What are you hiding?" Tashum asked.

She smiled. "I have something for you."

He nodded. "If you want to give me a true gift, tell me more about Paladin."

Her eyebrows rose and fell. "Such as?"

"To begin with, where was he the last time you saw him?" Tashum stooped and picked up a tiny white crab off the sand with one finger, watching it scamper across his palm.

She knelt beside him, still keeping her hands out of sight. "Another time, perhaps. I've told you so many of the stories." She sighed. "Not now."

"Very well, then, tell of the Black Knight that haunted you."

She frowned. "The Black Knight again? Must I?"

He leaned back on his elbows. "If you are too tired to speak of it, open your mind so I can see it for myself."

"I'd rather tell you than having you mucking about in my brain." She gave him a spoiled-child frown and sat heavily across from him. "Paladin stole three round things, orbs, he called them. And the Black Knight wanted them back. There—that's what happened."

"But you never tell me the details of what happened," he said, his voice rising with insistence. "Or why Paladin was even interested in the orbs. There had to be a reason."

"Yes, I know there must have been a reason. But please, old stories, events bygone . . . I have so little interest in them anymore. Why should you?"

"I think you know my interest."

"What difference does it make? He's gone and we're here." She moved forward and brushed his face with her lips. "You are here. Flesh and blood now, same as me."

He watched as the delicious grin returned to her face, and she brought her hands around, opening her fingers. Tashum's head turned slightly to one side as he examined a small pile of glassy stones that filled her palms.

"What are these?"

"Tashum, my beloved, I can't take you back to your stars, but I can bring these stars to you."

The glow of the moon threw myriad sparkles off the stones. "What do you call them?"

"Diamonds," she answered, her voice low and full of a reverence he had never seen in her. "They're from the ship."

He plucked a large one from her hand and held it up to the light of the moon. He turned it and studied the flashes of color held in its facets.

"You look so sad, I thought they'd bring you cheer," she said. "I swam out to the ship and retrieved them for you. It seemed a shame to let such beautiful stars sink into the ocean."

"They are beautiful." Tashum lowered the stone. "But they're not stars, Fanny."

"But of course they are, they have the same appearance, they're even the same size. Go ahead, hold one up to the sky." When he didn't, she did, held between thumb and index finger, "See, Tashum, they're the same size."

"Fanny, the stars are very large. They only seem small because of their great distance from Earth."

"Oh, well, to a lot of people they are stars, and that's why they're so valuable."

Tashum returned the gem to her hand and looked back up into the sky. "Fanny, if . . . if you could only see the Light of the universe. Light so pure. I was once part of that Light, that brightness, existing in a dimension that your language cannot contain. Just as you hunger for blood, I hunger for that Light. Not the formless, senseless illumination of your sun, but light that is the tissue of the universe—music and thunderbolts and communal thought." He struggled for a moment to find a phrase, a descriptor that she might understand. "When you were on the beach that first night, when the light had gone from your eyes, did you not enter into a shining, glorious world, a place of color and . . . ?"

She poured the gems from one hand into another, clattering them back and forth, pondering the question for a moment. She looked up at him, a pout on her lips. "I beheld nothing, felt nothing. It was more—floating down a river. A river of black ink is what I remember."

"No light?" he began and then stopped, glancing away from her. "Black ink?"

"Not literally. An underworld. The lands of Morpheus," she said, then added impatiently, "I don't know—it was darkness. A kind of dark, dreamless sleep. There was nothing, I was nothing. Thank God you brought me back."

He shook his head. "Compared to the Light of the universe . . ." He sighed. "These diamonds are no more than the droppings of a pig."

The yellow glow in her eyes flared. "What good is light? You can't touch or hold it. Besides, you're here with me now. And nothing is more precious to me, except . . ." Her expression grew still and uncertain. She dumped the stones into his open hand.

He accepted them, rolling them around in his palm. "Except what, Fanny?"

"You know, it is a common and decent practice to return a good deed with a good deed."

"What are you suggesting?"

"A taste of your light," rubbing his wrist with her thumb. "I won't take much—just a sip. Please, a mere taste."

He held the stones out for her, waiting for her to take them back.

She seemed startled by his disinterest in her gift.

He held her gaze long enough to see faint images of countless faces— her human victims in their final expression of death. He was tapped into her subconscious and suddenly realized why the blood of animals failed to satiate her taste. He withdrew his probe in fear of further hideous discovery. After a long moment he let the diamonds tumble from his hand. She fell to the ground feverishly picking them out of the sand and shooing away tiny white crabs.

"You . . . ," she said. "You monster! I know you've been stealing my memories." Her voice leveled, "They're mine and they have worth. I give you so much and you return so little."

"I am sorry, Fanny." He stood and brushed sand from his legs. "I understand that these stones are the prettiest things in this world. I also understand the nature of the transaction you offer. Those days are over."

"It's far from over, Tashum." Tears that had been forming leaked from her eyes as she watched him go. Leaving the moonbeams, his large frame went black against the blackness of the jungle.

"Someday, I'll have something you want. Something you can't live without," she said with a quiet breath, "and we'll see how you act then."

"You know what I want," Tashum called back to her.

He slipped through the trees, wishing his hearing wasn't so powerful, his understanding of his stepchildren so complete. He had been so thoroughly seduced by their arrival, he had neglected his own sense of purpose. They were so loud in his mind, his inner quiet was drowning.

There was only one way to teach them the next lesson, much as he himself had been taught so long before. He would give them a number of revolutions of the sun alone. Let them hunt boar without him, drink pig blood instead of his. Perhaps then they would learn reverence, learn respect for the island, for him.

How could they not understand the food of life was a gift? Not to be bought with artifacts of light, such as diamonds, but with the true currency of the soul, gratitude straight from the heart.

He would teach them by staying away himself. If he was their stepfather, he would set the example, as Shrug had done eons before. He would show them his frown and let them earn his smile.

CHAPTER SIX

For the first few days away from them, Tashum could not block out the torment that emitted from their hearts. And for the first time the angel realized his crystalline skeleton served as an antenna for such emotional transmissions. He felt the twinge of their anguish, the devastation of unanswered entreaties for forgiveness—the psychic anger, spit as lightning from a storm cloud.

He shadowed them, remaining hidden, until they sensed his nearness and mocked him: children playing a game they called hide-and-seek with a watchful parent. So he moved to the far end of the island. Their confusion came to him in murmurs of thought. Their slow ideas of how to get along reached across the fifteen or so miles he put between them and himself. What he couldn't see he felt.

After ten days, he sensed they had found a kind of equilibrium within themselves, each other. He fought his deep urge to see them, to spy on them at least. Even though the rules of banishment were his own he needed to complete the experiment, for his own equilibrium, his own true self.

He was proud of himself, of his experiment, and felt he had done them all a favor by exacting this small punishment.

The experiment ended quickly when Tashum sensed the distant presence of other humans. For days, the trade winds carried their scent. Their thought energy traveled in bright bursts but was not clear enough to decipher. The air in general was full of change, and from somewhere across the water, they were coming.

The night the ship arrived, he slipped back through the trees to their favorite beach on the north shore. Fanny and Dickey were feeding a bonfire ten yards from the water. And he knew that they sensed the humans as well.

Higher and higher Fanny and Dickey fueled the flames, illuminating the rocky coral cove with a brilliant red orange glare, creating a halo that could be seen all over the island and for miles, certainly, out across the waters.

They spoke to each other in short, whispered words, exchanging subtle sidelong glances and murmured confirmations, codes they had no doubt developed over some ninety years of nocturnal companionship.

Such a curious relationship. Neither wedded to each other nor related by blood, other than the blood of animals they so greedily shared, they were indeed bonded by their disease.

Tashum regretted hiding from them the moment he saw them again. But their thoughts were not of him, and this produced a minor ache. His self-imposed exile seemed almost a silly exercise relative to their excitement over the pending arrival. Had he taught them too well not to need him? That was a painful notion but nonetheless he decided to stay put. Hidden and unseen, he would simply observe their interactions with the new arrivals.

The ship appeared over the horizon's razor summit. He watched as it drew closer and closer to the torrential fire and he realized that on this world, flesh loves flame. Even though life can be scorched by it, tormented by it, they can't refuse its allure. Another curious relationship—to love the thing that inevitably consumes you.

The vessel grew larger and more distinct, tacking with surprising speed given the lackadaisical wind pushing her large square sails. She sat heavy in the water, and the outer reef lay hidden beneath a high tide. Tashum saw the danger and wondered if the fire was indeed a warning to stay away. They fed the flames and she kept coming, until the ship gave a sudden, violent shudder some two hundred yards out. Having run hard against the reef, a towering mast toppled forward, and he saw a jagged gash open up across the bow. In minutes, the vessel listed to one side and began lowering into the water. The ship's demise was accompanied by the shouts and answers of the men onboard.

Soon a small boat carrying nine men was being oared toward the shore, coming closer to the raging bonfire. Four men jumped out and dragged the boat to a resting position on the sand.

Their leader, dressed in a long, flamboyant coat with white ruffles around his neck, stepped off into ankle-deep water. His gaze searched the beach area.

When he first spied Fanny at a distance wearing her tattered European garb, he halfheartedly smiled. His ambivalent expression faded when she leaped down from her perch atop a coral mound. He hushed his oarsmen's banter after they witnessed the superhuman feat. With squinted eyes they watched her cross the sand to where she stood above them on the sloping shore, with her dead-white skin and glowing eyes. Dangling from her right hand was a large wooden club, an instrument deeply stained with the blood of boars and birds.

The disembarking sailors, dressed in rough textiles, gathered behind their leader and brandished their ball-and-powder weapons. The leader's new face, a drawn-down mask of aggression, called his men to the ready. He in turn unsheathed an impressive curved, shining cutlass.

"Madam, your signal fire fooled us and brought us hard aground on that bloody reef," he said, full of reproach.

"Yes," Fanny answered, "we expected it to do so."

"Then you are pirates!" His body shook with fury.

Dickey appeared at the top of an outcropping of tinted orange coral. He grimaced down at them while twirling through his fingers a club fashioned from the leg bone of a boar.

Fanny took a few steps closer, enjoying the moment.

"Not pirates, sir," she said. "We're only hungry."

The men were startled at Dickey's sudden scream of laughter. Unnerved at this display, and Fanny's steady, threatening approach, they cocked and aimed their weapons.

Without warning, Dickey leaped in a broad sweep. His feet had barely touched the sand when he swung his club in a ballet motion that felled three oarsmen in a single stroke. Knocked free, their weapons left their hands and discharged into the night sky. He pounced on them, before they could gain their senses, and, rearing back his thick arm, pounded and howled. His club opened first one skull just above the ear with a sickening crunch. A second stroke smashed another's face to raw meat. The continued swing clubbed a third head clean off its shoulders. All of this carnage in just seconds. His arm left image lags of his actions lingering in the air to the bewilderment of those left standing.

He turned to face a knot of three sailors. Two of the men panicked, dropped their weapons, and ran. They wailed and crossed themselves as they sought the cover of the jungle's dense undergrowth. The remaining man, a huge Spaniard with a head of thick, shaggy hair, let out a roar as he lunged at Dickey with a long, fine blade. The vampire leaped into the air as the cutlass whizzed under his feet. He landed on the Spaniard's shoulders, his powerful legs wrapping around the man's throat. In a quick, sharp movement, Dickey snapped the man's neck and rode the sailor down as they toppled to the sand.

"Shoot that woman! Fire!" the leader shouted, as Fanny continued her menacing approach.

At point-blank range, the trumpet-shaped blunderbusses belched fire and smoke. But she was gone and the musket balls pierced twin holes through her ghostlike image and embedded themselves in the coral wall behind.

"Where'd she go?" the leader gasped, looking for the woman who had . . .

Fanny dropped from the air and was behind them.

The leader just caught sight of her, as her club made solid contact with the side of his head. The blow broke open an eye socket and dislodged a spray of blood and brains. With a despairing shriek, he fell to the sand, his body jerking and shivering.

Fanny had just turned to the remaining men, when her eyes bulged. A wheeze caught in her throat.

She looked down to see a blade of steel emerging tip first from under her left breast. As she stared down in horror, more of the blade emerged. Its taper widened and passed through her. The steel grated against the bottom of her rib cage until she felt the thud of the sword's hilt punch her backside.

From his vantage point, Tashum cried out and lunged forward.

Fanny buckled to her knees, gagging and choking, her eyes large and staring. The swordsman withdrew the blade, swathed in blood and raised it for a quick slash to her neck when a sudden light flashed in Fanny's eyes, and, without even a sideways glance, she snapped the club back and found the sailor's ankle.

The man bellowed in agony as the club shattered bone. He fell to the sand and clutched at his useless leg. Fanny turned, and, with grim determination, bludgeoned him—each blow evoking a fresh wail. Finally she ran him through with the saber, still gleaming with her own blood.

As she made this final thrust, another sailor leaped from behind with a cocked pistol to her head. In a lightning move, Tashum latched onto his shoulder and spun the man around.

The gun fired into the angel's stomach, blew a hole of fire and metal into him, and hurled him backward onto the ground. The burning pain roared through him and he gazed in numb fear at the opening in his shirt. A scorched hole, ringed in black, oozed liquid amber. The sailor didn't notice, or didn't care, and rushed him with a drawn dagger. In an instant, Tashum reached for the weapon, snapped it around on the attacker, and drove the knife deep into the sailor's own ripe mortal frame.

The sailor dropped to his knees, his wide eyes staring into Tashum's expression. For a moment time seemed to halt. The angel clasped the hand of the sailor, while his gut drooled red over their joined fingers.

And in that moment Tashum saw that this was no rogue, no murderer— he was a young man, no more than seventeen years old. And as his thought energy flickered and sputtered, an ember growing cold, images crackled through his dying brain: a young, raven-haired woman—sunny days in a green countryside, warm fire—boyhood friends—songs and limericks and mugs of ale—he and the young woman intertwined in an embrace of heart-breaking tenderness—saying good-bye to her just weeks ago—promising to remain faithful—saying good-bye to the child growing inside her.

As life faded from the young man's eyes, Tashum heard the name *Rosalind* weep out of him, and a choking, shocked cry bubbled in the back of his throat. The eyes went corpse white. His life was gone, and his body toppled to the wet sand.

Tashum stared down at the dead youth. A sense of appalling evil, stronger than a pistol shot, raged through him.

"What have I done?" He closed his eyes with a moan.

Over the sounds of groaning, dying victims, and the continued butchery carried on between Fanny and Dickey, he shrieked again, "What have I done!"

His eyes open now, he stared up into the sky, rich with stars, and rounded hills of silver dust. His tears formed a lens that weighed heavy against his pupils and made his world of Light appear so much farther away.

Fanny and Dickey ignored him, fully intent on their banquet, bent over dying men, and drew blood out of their gashes with bestiality. They leaped from body to body with expressions of delight and complete disregard for the sanctity of life. These unsuspecting voyagers whose only visible crime had been to seek safe harbor now lay butchered.

Tashum understood now. That first evening when the beach had been littered with the bodies of sailors, hands tied behind their backs—now he knew it had been their work. Their appetites. Their fetid need for human blood. These lonely children he had taken charge of now showed him their true nature.

Hovering over a flowing slash of crimson, Fanny stared back at the angel. And over the crackling fire and the giddy, slurping noises from Dickey, a slow, beatific smile opened on her face, exposing pinkened teeth, and her lips glistened with blood. Fanny's body was poised in a feline slink. She was putting forth an invitation, in the form of a long, grateful sensuous exchange.

Tashum broke his intoxicating gaze. He leaped to his feet, kicking sand at the scene as he had seen Shrug do in times of distress. Fanny watched, perplexed, as Tashum ran off into the jungle, screaming madly, "We are killers!" Over and over, he screamed the same words.

He who was their father, their savior—he had made all this possible. His celestial blood, which he had given in pity and gentleness, his life force which had pulled them back from the brink of sickness and death, had made this slaughter possible.

With a torrent of fury, he fled, leaving the carnage behind. He ran through the jungle with little thought of direction. The vivid scenes taken from the young man's mind played and replayed in his head. No change of consciousness could drive the images away. And he ran, faster and farther. At last he came to the place where, thousands of years ago, he had come to know that band of primitives; he cast himself down where their fire pit had been. Here in this private, sacred place he broke down into choking tears of despair.

If his original sin had been pride, surely he was guilty of murder now. He was the stepfather of some new form of hideous evil. He and his brother, Paladin, once locked in childlike fright as they were cast out of the heavenly kingdom, were now locked together in the creation and fostering of this different kind of fall. Through ignorance they had perverted the new children of this world. They had filled their flesh with a celestial flame only to see that divine spark used to trick and maim and destroy not just subspecies, but their own brethren. Knowing his own role in this tragedy, it was unfair to place blame squarely upon Fanny and Dickey without shouldering the weight of the crime. Surely, it was this capacity for evil that had caused he and his brother to be banished from the Light.

Several hours later the scene that had earlier exploded with screams and gunshots was now suffused with a ghostly peace. Tashum stood concealed by thick foliage and bay-grape trees bordering the beach. His eyes were trained forward, his gaze set.

In waist-deep water, Fanny washed the traces of blood from her soiled nude body. It washed as white and perfect as a statue come to life in this silver moonlight. She pretended not to notice Tashum's advance from the jungle backdrop. Slowly, he made his way out onto the moon-glistened beach.

He stopped within a stone's throw of her. They gazed at one another. Neither knew what to say. After an awkward moment Fanny's lips shaped a smile. Then his thoughts as well as his head turned to the crack of a gunshot.

A bit dazed, Dickey sat in the sand with a broken rifle laid across his lap. The blunderbuss had misfired, blown-up, knocked him down and sprayed him with burned black powder without injuring him further. He threw aside the musket's remnants, rose to his feet, staggered away from the massacre.

Beyond the stumbling drunk, Tashum could see the dying fire and the bodies of seven sailors heaped in the sand.

Dickey tripped over a piece of driftwood, tumbled, and splashed up sand. "I'll never get used to walking in this stuff." He cursed the fine gains that clung to his face, hair and blood- and powder-stained clothing. "Look at me, I'm a bloody mess."

Tashum would have laughed at such comedic moves yesterday. But things were different now. Innocence had given way to conspiracy, survival had switched to murder. These thoughts ran through Tashum's mind, keeping the smile from his face, and his gaze fell back onto Fanny.

Dickey followed Tashum's line of sight to his sister. "Lovely, isn't she?"

Tashum's head rose and fell in a nod, "She's more than that." He felt entangled by the complex web of hot and cold emotions, the doubts she brought out in him.

"What about the sailors who ran?" he asked finally.

Acknowledging his role in the food chain, Dickey smiled. "Now that you've taught us to hunt, there's no place on this island they can hide, is there?" He raised a finger and pointed to the gutted and dying ship hung up on the reef. "And their mates out there, they'll soon be in and we'll have them, too. . . . When we're ready."

Dickey's proud expression faded to wonder, as if he could feel the jabbing pain his words had afflicted upon Tashum.

The angel's rigid frame sunk a wee bit. "Did Paladin drink blood?"

Dickey smiled, slowly stretching out his reply to play with him. "Let's see . . . hmmm . . . I know he watched us."

Tashum's jaw tightened. His eyes looked to the heavens.

Dickey laid his hand on the angel's shoulder. "Tashum, don't take what we do too personally. I'm certain the guilt would ruin you."

"I ask you again. Did my brother drink blood?"

"No," he admitted in earnest. "Paladin didn't drink blood. And like you he needed nothing to get him through the day except darkness." And with a smile, "Join us for a swim?" he asked, peeling off his filthy clothes.

Tashum stood silent and weighed Dickey's words. He watched the vampire's backside wade into the water, then he looked to Fanny.

She glanced back over her shoulder and stared back with eyes transmitting her message, the same invitation, a simple longing to be with him. The song of the Siren was supported by sensual images of her physical beauty: the slicked-back hair clinging to her sculpted alabaster back, flowing down to curvaceous hips. She turned, exposing her breasts—wide and heavy, rising and falling with the gentle surf. As she stepped forward, the receding water revealed a patch of hair at the top of long, thin-stemmed legs. She extended her hand, and the elegant index finger curved in invitation. And she sent a thought, *What more can I offer?*

Tashum felt an urge rising within himself he thought was purely reserved for humans. Killed by intellect, the urge quickly faded from his mind and was replaced by a new fear, a realization of how far he had actually been corrupted by the flesh. He knew he was standing at the crossroads. Time could not be undone, nor could these murderous events be changed. He remembered how violent Shrug's people had been when it came time to feed, how they, too, killed to survive.

Tashum's thoughts were interrupted by Dickey splashing water at Fanny. The angel noticed then that their wounds were closing with an accelerated healing. He looked at his own gunshot wound. His fingers raced around the new flesh that had covered the bullet hole, erasing all signs of his sin against man. Tashum smiled as he watched them frolic in the surf, so childlike. From what he had observed and what he had been told, all species in the realm have their predators, a system of checks and balances devised and enforced by nature. Before Paladin's little experiment, mankind's only true predator had been other men. If the Fallen Angels are the forefathers of this new breed, these vampires, was it then not his role to teach and raise these children of less responsible gods? And finally he recalled the pride of lions he and Paladin had observed. The memory had a sharp sting to it, for in the end the lioness's kittens were killed and eaten by their stepfather. Was it not the design of life to feed life and to live by that example? Tashum felt the surrender to this unsuspected commitment engulf him, drawing and pulling him toward Fanny and their ways. His clothes began dropping to the sand, discarded there with the sense of right and wrong. He knew he was crossing the line of impossible return. Tashum's feet carried him down the sloping sand, across the white lace of sea foam and into water kept warm by the gulf stream. At their shouts and invitations he dove beneath the waves. Tashum followed the sea floor to Fanny's feet. He slid up her body, emerging in the night air just inches from her face. Tashum let the heat of her passion burn away his sense of foreboding over this new union. Dickey joined the huddle, and together they showered Tashum with drunken laughter and salty kisses. The moon cast down a fountain of splendor on these strange lovers. The trio of silhouettes, dark except for the glow in their eyes, had come together in a carefree embrace of lively mouths. This image swirled around in the water for hours beneath the changing hues of the night sky.

The following night, Tashum sat beneath heavy bows of his favorite tree perched atop the highest point on the island. He was contemplating the events from the night before. All day while Fanny and Dickey slept the angel fought his internal battle over his own actions.

From behind, he heard a crackling of underbrush. He glanced over a shoulder and saw Fanny. She stopped to wipe away clotted blood, the remnant of her late night snack, disappeared from her mouth with a swipe of her hand. She caught Tashum's uncomfortable expression. "I swam out to the ship. Don't be alarmed."

"But I am alarmed," he said, the sob still heavy in his throat. "And I am distraught with the knowledge of what we have created."

"And what is that?" she asked, approaching slowly, walking in a semicircle, bringing herself into his frontal view.

"The damned." He said looking away. "You taught me that word and showed me your ways."

He stood with his back turned to her.

Still she approached, forcing him to look at her.

"Paladin gave us his blood in innocence. Just as you have," she said. "And there was a price."

"When he found out," Tashum paused, bowed his head, "he must have been devastated."

"No, Paladin saw us for what we are—and still he loved us. We are physical beings, Tashum. He saw that. He didn't understand it, not utterly, because he was like you. His body was on Earth, but his head was somewhere else. Up in heaven or wherever it is you come from."

"Beyond the darkness is light, your heaven possi—"

"I don't care!" she interrupted, "We are entirely here, we live here," she persisted. "Body, mind, soul—here on Earth. We have bodies, we have desires."

"Desires beyond bloodlust?" he asked.

She watched him with unwavering, unapologetic eyes. "If you want to know . . . ," she said, "touch me. Please touch me. The way you did on that first night when you brought me back from the darkness."

He stood unmoving, as if locked in place. He watched her hand to see if she now sought his blood. But she was drunk from feasting on some poor shipwrecked sailor. There was a different hunger in those catty eyes.

"Touch me," she said, drawing closer. "Come on Tashum, touch me."

In short increments, his hand reached out and his fingers found her throat and lingered gently. "Did Paladin touch you?"

Her head fell back, her hair falling across his hand. "Yes," she murmured.

His other hand found her face and his fingertips traced the strong line of her nose, the softness of her lips. He pulled her body close to his.

A luminous heat passed out of his celestial hands and into her face, her throat. He tugged at her clothing, which spilled down to her hips, and then slid down her slim, strong legs.

The gash in her chest was all but healed. He bit at his finger until amber blood oozed out. He traced her closed wound, watching the sparks of healing popping in the dark. She took his hand, held it until the blood stanched.

"No. I don't want to be healed."

"But—"

She shook her head, took his other hand. "I want you to touch me in a better way."

She pulled him down until they were both kneeling, facing each other as if in prayer. She drew his hands to her breasts, forcing his hands, moving in circular motions from her nipples, hard as pebbles, to the soft dome. And she released him. He sensed their weight in his palms, their ponderous undersurface.

Now down to her belly, where his hands sensed a spark inside her, something burning deep inside her body.

Touch me, came her thoughts.

His fingers spread and ran slowly down her legs.

A soft moan passed through her teeth. *Please* . . .

She wanted his palms on her, and something else of his inside of her; he had no penis standing erect to satiate her needs, no, the very molecules of her body ached for the unseen fire in his hands that moved in circles with the lightness of smoke above her stomach. And the glow of some insistent, spitting ember inside of her grew with the incandescence of his fingers.

She sank to the ground, stretching out, pulling him with her. Not missing a beat of the tummy rub, he stayed balanced on his haunches looming over her prone hungry body. His fingers were drawn to the heat port between her legs, Finding their way through a mound of hair, radiant fingertips pried open the vent, not going deep, but just hovering there. His immortal energy fed into her human flesh as heaven and earth crashed together, the innocent and the carnal colliding. He directed the beams of light particles flowing from his fingertips into a single beam. With gentle back and forth movement, he pushed and pulled the light in and out of her elongated opening. A shock wave convulsed through her. She laid on the ground looking up at him, and he down at her.

Her legs opened wider, enlarging the invitation.

She wanted to hide the beauty of her eyes, her mouth, so he could see her real beauty, her primal labyrinth of pleasure. The images in her mind were a swirl of things he did not understand. She wanted to be fouled and debased, but at the same time she needed to be loved and held in an endless gentle embrace. She longed for a place of safety. She wanted to be exposed, she wanted to be unclothed and unprotected; opening wider still, she wanted the moon to go there, his eyes to go there. She wanted her pleasure to come from giving him pleasure. Pictures spun through her brain of priests and schoolboys, thieves in a ruined church. She wanted to risk shame, enslavement, humiliation, and enchantment. And she was asking him to do the same, be truly naked with her.

His need to have more understanding of her met her need of debasement straight on. The incandescence in his hands became a hot arc. She stiffened, absorbed this bolt of lightning from his touch, opening more fully as a cat scream spilled out of her, splitting the silent glade. Through this orifice, he had sent a bolt of energy into the core of her being. Microdots of light rose like bubbles from the pores of her skin, popping and dissipating in the night air.

But it was too great a charge being released into her. He felt lightheaded, dizzied by his strange act. His eyes dimmed. With a jerk he pulled away from her and fell onto his back.

She rolled over and her arms stretched up over her head as if bound. Offering herself without condition. A deeper, more gasping groan escaped her lips, passing into the earth.

His inner anger spent itself, replaced by a sensual spell of amazement. He couldn't stop, she wouldn't let him, he kissed her legs, her hips, evoking new moans, her face pressing into the dirt.

His hands moved in circles on her back, finding the tops of her vertebrae, feeling the tautness of muscle in her sides, in her armpits, reaching forward to her shoulders.

Her buttocks rose in circular movements while flames rose higher and hotter within, her muscles cramping and releasing in an endless loop.

Now there was fear in her mind, a desperate, clawing terror that the fire was growing too hot. These sensations flared uncontrolled, and her fear burned greater. Her fingers dug into the soil, her hips rocked forward and back, her mouth open and panting. The heat was too much, the scorching, roiling, churning—don't let it stop!

And then, with a startling shudder, her life presence seemed to uproot and pass out of her body and loft into the air. Her perfect, creature-body continued to writhe and stretch in his grasp, but she was somewhere over herself, over him.

The female life presence that was Fanny whirled all about him, and then it hovered at the far end of her body. And when the white hotness inside reached a fevered peak, beyond her capacity to withstand it—her legs set to trembling, her head bucked up and down—the life force plunged back into her, entered through that deep, wet enfoldment held up to the air, and fired back into the body. She let out a cry of pain. Her body went hard and rigid, lying there at his knees, feeling a sharp, hot, ripping agony, but soon the pain unfolded, petal by petal, and within the pain was a delicious, warm, trickling fountain of pleasure. And then the pleasure unfolded further, blossoming, and within the pleasure was eternity.

He took her in his arms and pressed her face against his chest. She was the irresitable child again seeking warmth. The little remnants of electricity still tickling through her were released through small spasms.

"What did you do?" whispered her mouth dry. "I was outside of myself. I saw my body, I saw your hands on me. How?"

"I don't know," he said, speaking into her sea-wet hair.

"You laid your hands on me," she said, answering her own question. "I can still feel you, your handprints glowing on my skin. The shroud of your essence covering me."

Her head rustled against him, as if to draw closer.

"Now you know, Tashum. You've seen me, you've melted me. And now you know me."

He looked down at her, this undead woman in the cradle of his arms. This killer, driven by thirst, this being of inexpressible wonder, this child.

Of her he knew his touch could evoke an explosion of physical sensation capable of forcing surrender. That she wanted his otherworldly touch, his companionship and love, as much as his blood. She had all of that, in a way he could not fathom. He felt such tenderness for her. But what, if anything, did he understand of being bound to Earth, body, mind, and soul?

He leaned down and kissed her head, and Fanny wrapped her cold arms around him. Her thoughts now were of tranquillity. The fire subsided.

Fire.

There it was once more. Fire and flesh, the ever-present, entwining enigma of this world. In her mind she had visualized a kind of fire within her body. She felt the blaze that stung, erupted, and consumed, that forced her consciousness from her physical body.

He looked up through the treetops. Perhaps that was the bond—that sensation of fire burning flesh, the moment when she knew life, when unimaginable physical pain plunged her senses into immeasurable pleasure.

The avoidance of flame was the avoidance of life. And thus, exposing the most tender part of her, the drapes of flesh that could feel the most pleasure and the most pain. The raw, boneless unmuscled flesh, the vulnerable enfoldment that opened into the deepest part of her body—that's what she had raised up to him, raised up to the universe.

She wanted him to look at it, take it, tear it open, put something into her. To fill her unfathomable emptiness.

Life. Blood. Humiliation. Exposure. Pain. Pleasure. Eternity.

All this was wrapped up inside her—a complete lack of fear, a brazen demand to know life, to *feel* it. And now having passed through the fire, such peace, as she nestled against him, her face turning up to him now, a pool of perfect serenity.

He had seen it, felt it, but he was not certain he could ever truly know what it meant—this lying down that was really a rising up. This vulnerability that was really a kind of awesome power.

"You will always be my beloved," she whispered. "My angel."

"Fanny, doesn't 'always' mean forever?" he said gently into her hair. His eyes snapped closed, his cheek pressed against her brow.

Her eyes sprang open above the questioning frown developing on her lips. "Always means . . . Say that you love me." Her voice was desperate and words hurried. "I must know that's how you feel. Please say it."

"Did Paladin say it?"

She shuffled restlessly against him, turning so he saw her face in profile. "He said he loved all things," she said in a small voice.

"And so do I."

"Yes, but how do you feel about me? You've been alone on this island for how many centuries? Surely now that there is a woman here who loves you, who adores you, surely I rank above birds and the sea and whatever else."

He was silent for a moment. "I feel many things for you. One of them is a kind of love."

"I know even if you don't," she murmured. "You will love me. God created me the first time, and left me forsaken, diseased. Then Paladin created me anew and then he, too, left me. It was you who pulled me out of that river of blackness, that hollow black death. And where I come from, when a man's wife is left alone, husbandless, his brother takes her as his own. We're meant to be together always. In this world and the world to come."

Tashum's eyes remained on the dark horizon behind her, "Where is Paladin, Fanny? You must tell me."

He touched her face and attempted to probe her mind for Paladin's image, but nothing came. All chambers were blockaded. Were all women like this? Could they all close their mind hard and impenetrable as stone?

"Don't keep it from me!" he demanded.

She reared up, her eyes bright and fierce. "Can't you stay here with me?"

"This is not my world, Fanny." His gaze raised skyward.

"Why must you always blunder into the past, into the stars? Why can't you live in this hour?" She took his hands into hers. "Be with me. Enjoy my flesh, my caresses. I know this world must seem to you flat and spiritless, but it is my world and it can be yours through me. There is beauty here as well as terror. There is ecstasy, companionship. Could it be you are here on this world to learn something? To see something that all of heaven is blinded to?" There was a hint in the tone of her voice, but that was all she would give.

To see something that all of heaven is blinded to. Was it a riddle?

"Fanny, please." He sighed, and looked away from her.

"Look into my eyes." She reached up and caressed his cheek. "Whenever you touch me, you will find the heavens by bits and pieces. Love me and then you will know your redemption." Her words sounded a prophetic ring.

He gazed down at his hands cradled inside hers. Why must she always challenge him with such sweet harshness? He took in a long breath and let it out. Finally he kissed her fingers and withdrew his hands from her clutch.

"I love you, but . . . ," he paused, "but I fear your joy in killing. You speak of a god and yet you blaspheme him with your every breath. I cannot hate and yet . . . I cannot be consumed with adoration for . . . for you."

"So you don't love me." Slowly she stood, rising above him. Her fingers traced gently across his face. "You will, Tashum," she said, stepping back. "That's why you're here with me. That's why I'm here with you. I hold your destiny. . . ."

Tashum flinched but had no words to counter her gentle threat.

She took a step back, then turned and walked away.

He felt dirty over his pleasure, confusion in his deeds, and could not shake the feeling that Fanny harbored deep secrets about Paladin, something she could not dare to divulge, at least not now. His eyes closed into a second darkness.

The island was again filled with human sounds—hunting and eating, with one major difference. The hunters were rustling through thickets and dashing through water hunting man. Tashum would have none of it, preferring to walk on the bottom of the sea from dusk till dawn. Angry words whispered at midnight, laughter at sunset, calling out for each other through the flowering vines and trunks of trees, Fanny and Dickey were having the time of their lives tracking down the last of the sailors. Armed with Tashum's lessons they had no equals. The blood orgy lasted barely a fortnight.

When they reunited with their angel, Tashum knew that recent events had forever changed his relationship with Fanny and for that matter Dickey too. He preferred to think of them as they were before the massacre but they seemed proud of the event and grateful for the tricks he had given them to make it happen. As a result the art of murder was a popular topic of conversation around their fire pit. For a distraction Tashum taught them to avoid the dangerous tides near the reef, and they gave him the names of fish and undersea things he described to them. He instructed them in ways to predict the phases of the moon, and they told him about the points of a compass. And so it went, his knowledge for theirs. There was indeed a new openness to their relationship and the honesty of acceptance was mutual but all innocence was gone. They were beasts of the night.

Dickey and Fanny soon started to build signal fires nightly. Within a month, they had lured another ship up onto the reef, this one Portuguese. Tashum kept a distance to their activities, which were never discussed in his presence. Even without words the vampires thought energy was intrusive, and their wanting ever present. When a third ship arrived, bringing a crew of Dutch and Spanish sailors to their deaths, Tashum expressed total dismay.

Attempting to placate their angel, they hid the bodies in the sand, knowing all too well that in the tropics, flesh would soon disappear. What they couldn't hide was very evident; the blood of man had sparked a deep-seated insanity within the two. Tashum avoided their company for days afterward. He wandered the solitary beaches and cursed himself at the sight of toe bones and grinning skulls revealed by blown sands and receding waves.

Loot from these wayward vessels sat in cluttered heaps in their cave. The two vampires luxuriated in their life of piracy and avoided Tashum's wordless, remorseful gaze. They bragged of spending their amassed fortunes and plotted their escape from the island with little effect on the angel. Tashum simply had no interest in their fantasies.

Swirling fire. A fountain of jetting flames. Orange leaping into silver. Red spiraling into white. The vampires danced about the flames, kicking a jig, their mouths stained with blood. Slowly a thin outline of a figure appeared in the flames—stood in the center of fire, his feet buried in embers, his winged body filled with tongues of flame, his hand reaching out, beckoning.

"*Join him,*" came a voice cracking of hot coals. "*Join your forsaken brother.*"

Tashum's left eye opened. There was no fire or dancing vampires. His neck muscles rigid, chest out of breath, trembling. Fanny, asleep next to him felt his arrhythmic motion. His hand unconsciously gripped the leg of her linen sailor pants. Her head rose off the water-stained red velvet pillow as her gaze fell on him.

"Tashum?" she whispered.

His head rolled toward her. "I'm fine," he said.

"More wicked dreams?" she asked.

He nodded and closed his eyes.

The afternoon sun whitened the far wall of the cave. In summer's heat, the natural cool moistness of his cave had turned uncomfortably hot and steamy. They wore pants but their tops were bare.

She rose to an elbow, unfolded a small Oriental fan and began churning the air above his face. He thanked her with a smile.

For more than a year he had been visited by sleep visions of swirling fire and death and dancing vampires. He recollected the spirit as Paladin, but his face and features were never clear or identifiable, and his brother was always dressed in a variety of indecipherable costumes, always calling to him through pursed lips.

He sat upright and searched for something to clear his mind. There at his feet he found the three time-smoothed stones. He picked them up, ran his fingers over their surfaces. He tossed one into the air, then the second, and a third, idly juggling them. Then he snatched them out of the air and lay down again.

"Let me see those," she said.

He flagged one hand at a buzzing fly and handed the stones to her.

"These are the stones ancients gave to you?" she asked.

"Yes. They were a gift."

She flicked at the ring on her third finger, snapping out the small, curved blade.

"What are you doing?" he asked.

"Patience, you," she said, as the knife blade scratched a thin *T* on the stone's soft surface. She quickly carved an *F* and a *D* on the remaining two stones. The blade slipped back into the ring, and she pushed the stones at him, punched into his side. "Here, now they're monogrammed proper."

"What is the symbol?"

"*T* for 'Tashum,' " she said with a sleepy smile.

In the dirt she spelled out his name with a fingernail. And for a moment he studied the lines and shapes of the letters.

"The other two—this is a *D* for 'Dickey.' And the *F*, that's the beginning of my name."

With a finger, he traced the jagged etchings on the stones.

"Will they fly better?"

She sighed and closed her eyes. "Where I come from, jugglers are fools. Entertainment for children and drunkards."

"How fitting," he said, and rose to his feet. Lightly he spun the stones in the air, watching them leap and whirl.

"They don't fly any better."

"You place greater value on those damn rocks than on my diamonds," Fanny said. "More than anything we've given to you." Her hand gestured to the rear of the cave, to the heaps of clothing, silver and gold eating utensils stacked upon tea crates. Everything precious the vampires found aboard their victims' ships lay stacked in unorganized piles of rope and rifles, sails and swords, boots and lanterns, punctuated by a variety of wooden casks.

"None of this means anything to you, does it?"

Dickey's head rose off his strung hammock at the sound of their unhappy voices. He tugged a confluence of linen from the crotch of his pants. "I'm hungry," he said, voicing his almost hourly complaint.

Tashum closed his eyes, letting his hands rise and fall, manipulating the stones, keeping them airborne.

"Tashum, are you not going to answer me?" she said. "Well?"

Tashum ignored them, fascinated by the flight of the stones.

"I'm tired of boars and birds," Dickey said, and sat up, pulling on a three-cornered white-plumed hat taken from the Portuguese quartermaster.

"Yes, and so am I," Fanny groaned, rolling on her back. "And I tire of this cave and this island. I'm ill with the sight of you, Dickey, and I'm equally sick of Tashum, and I'm terribly tired of myself."

"Why not drink each other's blood?" Tashum suggested.

"You don't need to be so cruel, Tashum."

"How about a dram or two of yours?" Dickey said with a cocked grin.

Tashum smiled quietly. "I'll not be juggled with."

Fanny glared and turned away from him. She played with the gold-threaded pillow fringe. "Tell us about this dream of yours."

He caught the stones and glanced down at the new lettering. "I rather like these decorations." he said. "I want to learn to read and write."

"Me, too," said Dickey as he slipped out of the hammock. "She ain't much of a teacher."

"Dickey, you have trouble lacing your boots," she said.

Dickey mumbled something in Italian that neither Tashum nor Fanny heard. He waved them off, moved to the wardrobe pile, and picked up a wide-brimmed felt hat.

"What is this dream that keeps awakening you?" Fanny asked in a softer, more manipulative voice. "You know it is better to share your needs with those you love, in order to get what you want."

"Put that way, how can I refuse?" He played along, holding her gaze. "I dream of the Light. I dream of Paladin, and one day you must tell me where he is, Fanny."

For a split second she was trapped in his gaze. His mind thrust forward and through Fanny's wide-open eyes he snatched her unguarded thoughts.

If I tell him, he'll have no more need of me. . . .

Sensing his intrusion she turned her head quickly.

"How dare you trespass my mind!" she snapped. "How dare you!"

"How dare you lie to me by omission," he answered in a steady voice. "How dare you take my blood, take my comfort and protection all this time and offer me nothing in return but blood feasts and complaints."

Dickey faced them, alarm flashing from under the brim of his hat. He started to speak but held his tongue when he saw Fanny's expression.

"Offer you nothing?" Fanny demanded. "Nothing!" She shrieked and leaped on him, beating his arms and chest, then backed away.

"What about love?" she shouted, tears filled her angry face. "What about my body, my diamonds—everything I have! Is that not enough for you?"

Dickey stood frozen and watched them struggle.

Tashum lifted her off him and flicked her across the cave. Dickey ducked out of the way of Fanny's flight. She landed among mildewed boots and rusty lanterns.

, She rose to a crouch, breathing hard, staring at Tashum with ruthless eyes. She swayed, then pounced and grabbed up his juggling stones.

"Fanny," Tashum cautioned. "Please—"

"F," she said, holding up the first stone, "is for 'fallen,' 'foul,' 'fiend.' " She threw the stone against a far wall, where it hit a patch of sunlight, and ricocheted out of the cave. "D for 'damned,' " she snarled, throwing the second stone at Dickey. "And T, is for 'thieving,' 'trickery' and 'trespass. . . .' " With a howl, she threw the last stone at Tashum. "I hate you! God, how I hate you!"

Tashum ducked away from the whizzing stone.

Silence filled the cramped, dank cave.

She pulled her knees up to her chest, looking out toward the entrance of the cave. "I want to leave this place."

Tashum looked from her to Dickey.

Dickey avoided his gaze at first, and after a moment of hesitation he pulled off the hat, toyed with its felt brim, and gave the angel a furtive, sidelong glance. "So do I wish to leave." He glanced at Fanny. "That stone hurt, you know? I think you broke one of my ribs."

Tashum rose and moved toward the mouth of the cave, his fingers lagging along one wall. He stood looking out toward the sunlight. He moved his hand forward along the wall, stretching until his fingertips almost touched the fringe of sunlight. His hand remained steady until, the physical searing heat forced him to withdraw—until, it was less painful to be with them.

Slowly he turned to the vampires. "There is a ship just beyond the horizon."
He spoke with quiet restraint. "If you don't butcher the crew we will leave
with them."

"I favor that idea," Dickey said.

"You can't feed off the crew." His eyes narrowed. "Not this time."

"No feeding," she said. "That's an easy command for you to froth off.
He who is sober."

"When she's right, she's right," Dickey added with a grin. "Can't go
without it, you know?"

The angel nodded, "I know."

She pulled her pillow to her stomach. "I command you to stop your
stargazing."

His mouth twisted to one side, "What you ask of me is the impossible.
What I ask of you is only reasonable."

Tashum went to the piles of loot, pulled back a wool blanket and moving
aside strands of pearls and clinking silver goblets, found at last a small dagger,
which he unsheathed.

"Upon your vow to feed only from me, I, and I alone will give you the
strength for the voyage," he said.

Fanny and Dickey stared at him, unable to speak. Both wondered about
Tashum's ultimate power. How could he have conjured up such a vessel
only when it suited him? Whatever the truth, it seemed trivial to the notion
they would soon be off the island. And of more immediate importance was
the thought of his essence coursing through their veins.

He placed the knife in Fanny's hand and held out his upturned wrists.

Fanny hesitated, looking from the dagger up into his face, testing his
intent. A swallow slid down her white throat as she watched him.

"Fanny," Tashum said, almost inaudibly, "By these actions you agree to
my conditions."

Her slender white fingers wrapped themselves around his upturned forearm. She brought the point of the knife to the surface of his etched skin and
pressed it down into the flesh until the blade punctured through.

Dickey scooted across the floor and settled next to Fanny. The two vampires watched with expressions of bedazzlement as a bulb of glowing, golden
fluid flooded out of Tashum's arm. Fanny moved forward and dipped her
tongue into the succulent honey-colored blood. A moan began deep inside
her body and came out in a long, rolling guttural breath.

After they had taken their nutriments, Fanny and Dickey lay back, their eyes glazed, their bodies slack and opiated.

Tashum wiped the blade of the dagger on his shirt returned it to the metal scabbard.

"We welcome the ship and we leave with them," he said, and in a firmer parental tone he added, "I will let you feed from me—and you have made a vow not to drink from the ship's crew."

He bent over Fanny, waiting for a response.

Her heavy-lidded eyes looked back at him. "Yes," she mumbled thickly. "Yes, my angel." Her mouth curled into a Cheshire smile, "Not even if they offered it to me would I drink from them."

He turned to Dickey.

Dickey managed to wiggle his fingers. "By this hand," he said slowly, "I swear I will only drink of you." He licked his lips and grinned. "My angel." His chest lurched and a tinkling of laughter came out of him.

Fanny smirked and giggled, and the two vampires lay on the cave floor, tittering new-fledged drunkards.

Tashum strode to the edge of sunlight, nearly risked another scalding, just to escape his hateful love for them. Then his thoughts drifted into the arena of practical and social intercourse with normal humans. Tashum knew it would be difficult to blend in and go unnoticed. After all, he himself was unnerved the first time he saw his own demonic eyes and tattooed skin reflected in a tide pool. There was a new word in his vocabulary—disguise. Fanny's unearthly skin tone had been disguised by colored paste, and both vampires had arrived on the island possessing colored spectacles, which, oddly, they had never used again. They had no need of disguise here, for they were the hunters, and he was their king. Fear, not disbelief, had always been the emotion and reaction from the terrified sailors once lured ashore. He sensed it was not fear of death these men had displayed. No, their fear came from the physical differences between us and them. Fear of the demonic transcends fear of death. He knew leaving the island would bring certain dangers—his appearance would be judged before his actions. He would need disguises for the journey into this new world where he would no longer be a king. . . .

CHAPTER SEVEN

W_{eeks} later Tashum stood on an aft balcony of the merchant explorer ship, *Merciful*. He listened to the calm sound of water rippling in the ship's broad wake. He watched his island recede under the feathery light of a half-moon. His earthly domain was a mere ink spot on the captain's sea chart. It was identified as an atoll made of coral and limestone, and the mariners had named it the Somers Islands. It lay to the west of a vast coastline called the unexplored New World, and to the east across a vast sea was Britannia.

He watched his little paradise sink into the sea and into his memory. Soon, all he would be able to see was the small spark of Fanny and Dickey's final signal fire.

"How does it feel to leave?" a voice asked.

Tashum glanced at Dickey. He started to smile, then fingered the dark eyeglasses in his hand. "I thought we agreed that you and Fanny would stay down below."

"It smells awful down there."

"That should come as no surprise," he said, looking back to the island.

Dickey shrugged his shoulders and followed his gaze. "I know what it's like to take leave of the only place you've ever called home," he said, and leaned fully against the rail.

Tashum ran a finger under one eye and then the other. Still no answer to Dickey's words.

"So many emotions," Dickey said. "Eventually, they will fade away."

Tashum nodded, sufficient encouragement to Dickey to continue.

"I left my village in Romania when I was only seventeen years of age," he said. "Leaving behind my younger brother, Vladimir, was the hardest thing I've ever done. We had no father, no mother—and I had been to him both. My brother was all I had. I loved him but I had needs."

"If you cared so much, why did you leave him?" Tashum gripped the railing.

"Only to seek a cure," he said, with the shake of his index finger that made his words appear truer. "He was a helpless child, but I was dying. If I did not find a cure, he would have been alone anyway."

Tashum cocked his head, silently questioning why Dickey didn't take his brother with him. Heaven alone had the power to separate him from his brother, Paladin. Dickey, vampire or not, was even more selfish than he imagined. "Obviously, you found your cure."

Dickey raised a brow to the chill in Tashum's voice.

"How old were you when you met Paladin?"

Dickey fumbled with the mental math, unable or not willing to figure it out. "Don't know really. I didn't keep track of time back then."

"You look about forty now, and as your age was frozen in time by Paladin's essence. From what you have said, I would guess you were away from your brother for some time."

"Hmm, years I would guess."

"Did you ever return for him?"

"Yes," Dickey said. Then he remembered Tashum's sense of family. "Understand, the only reason I went at all was to save myself so I could care for him. That was my only thought, to care for my brother, truly, Tashum."

There is a funny smell to a lie, made no less noxious by the innocence of the unaware liar. Tashum resented these connections to himself, he resented Dickey's half-truth sincerity tainting the aroma of this lie.

Dickey and Fanny were the first modern humans he had known, and they owned a place within him that he could not deny. He withheld his disapprobation and simply refused to look at him.

"My cure was his undoing." Dickey continued his embroidery. "My brother had a wildness within him, a defying spirit. Vlad had a predilection for breaking into houses, but no talent for it. He was forever being discovered by angry neighbors who had found him with their food in one hand or making off with their heirlooms tucked under an arm."

"Did Vlad steal for pleasure?"

"Yes, I rather think he did." Dickey sighed, and followed Tashum's gaze across the water. "Two years after Paladin saved Fanny and me, I journeyed back to my village to give him my blood, to bring him into our nocturnal family."

"What!" Tashum's head jerked, his mind filled with images of hundreds maybe thousands of these vampire creatures.

Dickey couldn't help but recognize Tashum's distress, his sense of responsibility, a weak link. "Vlad would have known what to do with these vampire powers, much more than myself," he continued. "Vlad loved the adventure of life."

"Did you feed him?"

"He had quite the appetite."

"Did you give him immortality?"

Dickey stretched the moment with a long pause, "When I saw him next," his voice lowered, along with his mood, "he had been blinded and crippled. Living in the forest when I found him. An outcast, he'd become."

"What had he done?"

"His crime, he stole a loaf of bread and a ladle of milk." Dickey's chest puffed up with anger. "And for that, the village priest had his eyes gouged out and his hands cut off at the wrist." Dickey's voice wavered. "After they crippled him, they put him on display in the village square."

Tashum had profound understanding of brotherly love and felt Dickey's sense of loss, but he had to know. "Did you feed him?"

Dickey's eyes flared hot, and off his acerbic tongue rolled fiery words. "No! He fed me!" Dickey shook with defiance.

Tashum leaned back knowing this wasn't a lie. Dickey's words burned with the passion of truth.

"That's right, Tashum, I drank the blood of my own brother. I sucked the life out of him. This poor crippled, whimpering man was more terrified of me than he was of death. I didn't have the heart to identify myself. He never knew . . ."

A silence settled between them. A thorn of fear pricked Tashum's heart, a remembrance of Mayhem's message. How would he react should he find Paladin broken and blind? Tashum faced Dickey.

"What did you do?"

"What did I do?"

"With your brother, did you make arrangements for him?"

"Yes," a half smile appeared, "I buried him with the eyes of the priest and the hands of the village axman."

Tashum glared at Dickey. Some shallow truths have the same smell as the worst lies. This was no lie. Dickey not only avenged his brother by killing the priest and the axman, he also drank their families bone dry and left their bodies hanging off sticks for all to see. In the final act of his vengeance, he burned the village, razed it to the ground. Dickey said he left fair warning; that he would drink the blood of anyone fool enough to follow after him.

For the first time, Tashum realized Dickey was capable of standing on his own.

Before the vampire could speak again, heavy footsteps sounded behind them. Tashum quickly put on his dark spectacles, once the property of a Portuguese monk. The deep blue lenses covered the soft yellow glow of his eyes.

"Time for you to go below," he whispered to Dickey, adjusting the lenses on his nose.

"We've paid enough to be left alone."

"Avert your eyes, at the least."

The captain of the *Merciful* appeared up a short flight of steps, a tall, narrow-faced man with massive muttonchop whiskers and a wide mouth with uneven, protruding teeth. The captain lifted a thick mug of ale to his bearded face. He eyed Dickey, who turned away, pretending a hacking, consumptive cough.

"How're ye wards, doctor," the captain asked. His gaze seemed stuck on the glow of Dickey's dead white skin.

"There's been little change in their condition," Tashum answered.

"They won't be bringing their disease among me men, now, will they?" he said, looking for assurances.

"If you're requesting more gold pieces—"

"Keep your gold, keep your gold, ye've give me plenty." He emptied his mug and took a breath. He looked at Tashum with a steady, open gaze. "I ask only for your assurance, sir."

"You have my promise."

"Aye, I've no reason to doubt you."

"I thought a quantity of night air might assist his cure. Of which he has had plenty." Tashum turned to Dickey. "You should go down below, now."

Dickey gave another cough, then mumbled a farewell, keeping his own yellow eyes from the view of the other man. When Dickey was gone, the captain gripped the rail, taking a long inhalation of the salt air.

"Ye've made me a rich man," he said to Tashum. "And I've tickled the palms of the crew, to be sure. Not a man among them will be scouting about in yer affairs. But if that dread sickness appears elseplace among the men, I'll not be able to hold them back. There's enough talk, even with their purses full, if you follow my meaning."

"I believe I understand you, Captain."

"Yer tale is as leaky as a sponge." He chuckled softly. "Though you don't seem the criminal sort."

"We were shipwrecked, marooned," Tashum explained. "The natives gave me these scars. The island was festering with a pox that with certainty robbed us of our ability to withstand the sun—"

The captain held up a hand. "You need not lead me down that path again, sir. Your gold speaks the truth of Jehovah. Save yer speeches for the harbour master and English bailiffs."

"Bailiffs?"

"Aye, there will those interested in your peculiarities." The captain reached out and clamped Tashum on the shoulder. His touch sent myriad images through the angel's mind: the rain-drenched man fighting a ship's wheel through hurricane squalls, comforting frightened men, singing to a young daughter sitting on his knees. This was a good man and Tashum knew he had no further need of explanation. It was a preposterous tale he and Fanny had concocted, but it was enough. To belabor it was to weaken it.

The captain patted his arm roughly. "If yer of a mind to win back some of that coinage ye chucked at us, come by any eve for a game of Queen's Rummy."

Tashum nodded, "Queen's Rummy? Yes, I thank you," he answered.

"Are you a gambling sort?"

Tashum's forehead wrinkled briefly. Gambling was not a word that had been entered into his new vocabulary, though it sounded like a good-natured enterprise from the man's tone.

"I gamble when . . . it's proper to do so," he answered flatly.

"Aye, a cautious one, then. That's fine. That's fine with me." The captain smiled and gave him a small salute before descending the steps and returning to his duties.

Life on the ship took on a routine of its own. The squawk and groan of the masts in their moorings, the slow, massive purl of wind filling sails, the ocean's waves breaking against the wooden hull, the shouts of sailor voices—all became as commonplace as any noise on his island. The scent of rotten meat and unwashed bodies soon became unremarkable. Tashum and his patients stayed below in their cabin during daylight and listened to the curious whispers of the crew outside their door. From these *sotto voce* remarks they knew of the rumors spread about them—the suspicion of murder and devilment. But as the captain had promised, no challenge was ever advanced.

To Tashum's surprise, some of the sailors blocked out his mind probes, not intentionally, but naturally, he was sure. He concluded, that the unity of consciousness in these modern men was as individualistic as were their sizes and shapes. This was a unique concept for a being that had been connected with his brothers and sisters in the light by thought shared through a communication network that spanned the heavens.

Though Dickey and Fanny complained that their treatment was worse than that of African slaves, they kept to their cramped quarters. Both vampires recognized the wisdom of playing their roles as the bedridden, and remained invisible to the crew. Tashum, alone, ventured above deck, always wearing his eyeglasses even in the darkness, and he generally kept to himself.

In his solitary way he watched the crewmen scamper with practiced agility through the rigging, adjusting and repairing sails. He was impressed and amazed by the fearlessness of men who went hand over hand up into the leaning crow's nest, far above the deck, to watch for other ships, oncoming weather conditions and sea monsters.

One night Tashum's curiosity, and want of a better view led him aloft into the standing rigging of the ship's main mast. He enjoyed the feel of man-made rope in his hand, and the ascent up the webbed ladder known to him as ratlines seemed an easy maneuver. His island's tallest tree had never taken him this high, or swayed as boldly. Standing high aloft in the thimble shaped crows-nest, he soon discovered his own fear of heights. An awful, paralytic fear of falling overtook him when he looked down to the churning motion of the sea. The continual pitch and roll created by the ship's forward and lateral movement and sea swell made the nausea all the worse. The physical sensations were sudden reminders of his fall from grace. The light-headedness and dizzied eyesight collapsed him to the floor of the crow's nest. His cheek was flat against the floor plank when he opened his eyes to find the ship's cat poised near the trapdoor. He watched the sleek hunter calmly cleaning some invisible debris from its claws. Then he noticed the dead rat at the feline's feet. The tabby held the angel's gaze with confidence until Tashum slid the dark glasses down the bridge of his nose revealing those eyes. The cat's tail flicked three times before it picked up the limp rat and slinked closer. Within arm's reach of the angel the cat dropped and nudged the carcass with its nose. Tashum realized it was a gift and in turn allowed the cat to rub its body against his face. The cat only wanted a single pass and leaped away. He glanced back, meowed once and stepped off into what looked like thin air. Tashum crawled to the opening of the trapdoor and watched the masterful climber descend the well-traveled lines. For hours Tashum remained a lofty prisoner. Near dawn, his fear of the sun beat his vertigo and forced him back down the ratlines. His less than gracious descent was observed and laughed at by those sailors who routinely set the ship's sails. His pride despised being the brunt of other's jokes, but he did love laughter.

The angel learned new words and the curious rituals of human inter-action: handshakes, friendly insults, and the art of the well-timed spit.

He listened intently to the songs they sang of ale and the devil, easy women and brown-eyed girls. His brows furrowed at their slang, phrases used during moments of surprise or pain: "God's wounds" or "God's blood," and he puzzled over these words being interchangeable with "shit" and "piss" and "fuck." He did not see a connection, but there it was.

He saw his face in a mirror for the first time, and he studied drunkenness after sucking down several pints of cider brew. A sailor pointed out to him the man in the moon. And he listened through the floorboards to Sunday prayers. This talk concerning a great collection of words bound together in a book that had come from the mouth of their god, delivered by winged angels piqued his curiosity and wonder. All of this interplay, these facets of human life, he absorbed with the eager agility of a child and the instinctive caution of an adult.

The third week out a storm hit, and they all stayed below while the vessel heaved and fell into the deep troughs between giant waves and yawed side to side blown by gale-force winds. The storm was followed by days of windless doldrums, a feature that, to Tashum's surprise, engendered more angry restlessness in the crew than did the dangers of foul weather.

With little wind the ship's sails luffed and sank. She drifted slowly, pushed along by mysterious ocean currents that kept her heading in the right direction, according to the stars.

Tashum was laid out across the large double berth of their aft cabin. Half conscious, he listened to this buffeting sound as he waited for the setting of the sun. Half asleep, he dreamed of the Light.

He bolted upright—holding a brief fragment of his time near the Light, he held the dream memory; two angelic choirs positioned opposite each other, their wordless music rushing toward the space between them. They were creating something of importance, but its message hovered just beyond Tashum's ability to retain the dissipating meaning. And then it was gone. He glanced at the vampires.

"I . . . ," Dickey said in a bored voice. His gaze drifted off Tashum and down to a chessboard covered with gold and silver playing pieces.

". . . am hungry," Fanny finished his thought. She stared at her finger resting on the golden queen. "Tashum, it's time you took care of us," she said without taking her eyes off the game.

Under a dim lantern swinging side to side with the rhythm of a slow heart, Fanny and Dickey were draped over wooden chairs at a small table near the cabin door.

His vision of heaven interrupted, Tashum let his head fall back against the wall. "I just fed you three days ago. Besides, England is so close," he said.

"Not without wind," chimed Dickey. "Some days we've gone nowhere. We could wander the seas for months, couldn't we?"

"Years," Fanny added.

"You can conquer your hungers if you try," Tashum said in a firm fatherly voice. "You need to be weaned off me. There is the ship's livestock. I could buy for you a pig."

"You said," Fanny spoke evenly, "you would give us the strength, with no mention of pigs. If you go back on your vow, we have no choice but to go back on ours."

"Must the world, must the very universe, revolve around your constant hungers?"

"Of course it does." She glanced at the playing board. "Dickey would you please move!"

"I'm beginning to worry about you two," Tashum said as he stretched and shook off his sleep. "You need to learn more self-control and fight these urges."

"You bound yourself to a vow," Dickey said quietly as he finished moving a silver pawn. "And we have upheld our portion of the bargain, have we not?"

"Have we been gluttons?" Fanny asked in the same reasonable tone. "Dickey, that's an illegal move," she said, pointing to his pawn.

"No, it's not. You made the same move last game."

"You should have said something then. Move it back."

"Only if you let me win."

"Dickey, I was letting you win."

Tashum crossed to the door and fumbled with the latch. At first it held against his gentle efforts. With a jerk he pulled the door open and stepped partway into the stairway outside.

"Before you leave, tell us of your decision," Fanny said.

Tashum looked back at their hungry faces. "Can you wait until midnight?" he asked, reluctantly.

"If that's the hour you wish to impose, so be it," Fanny answered.

Dickey began to speak, just as Tashum banged the door behind him.

Tashum breathed deeply as he stepped on deck. His hands were busy fidgeting with the bent arm of his dark glasses. He made his way toward the ship's bow, moving past crates of cargo and livestock pens—goats nattering and kicking—caged chickens settling in for the night with small, comforting clucks. He excused his way through a small knot of men who let him pass without a word.

For an hour he watched as the stars began to appear in the sky's darkening dome. No, they had not been gluttons, he admitted to himself. In fact, under the cramped circumstances, Dickey and Fanny had been undemanding. A draft of his blood apparently replenished them for weeks, fueled them at the very deepest level. It had only been since the storm their hunger had resurfaced in shorter intervals. Life below decks was miserable, and the angel understood their boredom. So why couldn't he bring himself to give more? Why, indeed? For a moment, he pictured the white-lipped gashes, their victims' faces drained and contorted, and, lastly, he recalled the ghastly skeletal bones bleaching in the sand. His angelic blood powered Fanny and Dickey, saved them. Made it all possible. Made him the accomplice to every murder that had taken place and every murder they would commit for the rest of their nocturnal lives. It was a sobering thought. He wanted to continue walking, but he was already standing on the narrow bow sprit and had walked as far forward as the ship's design would allow. Cantilevered out over unbroken waves he leaned into the breeze with nothing before him but empty ocean.

The wind picked up, billowing *Merciful's* sails and to great effect lifted the mood on deck. Tashum walked aft down the port side of the ship. He stopped at the sound of laughter and banter. The door of the captain's cabin stood open on crude hinges. He saw three men seated around a round table.

"Doctor," the captain called out. "Join us, sir."

The men held playing cards in their hands. They slid their chairs and stools closer together and made room for him at the table, inviting him to enter into their game with little fanfare. Dickey had explained to Tashum some days earlier the idea of the card game and the angel sat down, taking up a position. The boatswain, a bluff red-headed Scott named MacGregor, asked if he was familiar with Queen's Rummy. Tashum nodded, explaining, however, that it had been some years since his last game. Briefly, the quartermaster, a hook-nosed, broken-toothed Englishman named Riggett, took him through the rules and explained the relative value of the face cards.

MacGregor shuffled the cards and dealt each man a count of seven. Tashum took them in his hand and studied the crude illustration of a king in profile holding a sword before him. He flipped through the others, examining a jack and two aces, two spades and two diamonds. He sensed immediately that the cards represented stories about humankind just as the constellations did. He looked from his cards to the other men and he smiled and laughed.

"This king—," he began.

"Hush, man," the captain said, "ye keep them to yerself, ye know."

"I be interested in what ye've got there," said Riggett holding his yellow grin.

"Yes, yes," Tashum chuckled, and rearranged his hand as the others did. At last he was among humans, living the dreams of so many centuries, hearing their stories, stumbling into their world, playing their games.

The game began and the men anted up their coins, Tashum peered into the mind of each one, reading the cards in their hands. He made sense of the simple rules, played with secret knowledge, and won the pot.

"Ye've got new-man's luck," Riggett grumbled, slapping down his hand.

"Aye, better luck than you, Riggett," said the captain.

"Perhaps those spectacles are magic and allow him witness to our cards," Riggett said.

"Ye know better, Riggett," scoffed the captain. "Ye were right the first time. New luck is what's his."

"Well, thank you for an enlightening evening," Tashum said, and began to stand.

"Stay yerself there," the captain said, gesturing for the angel to reseat himself. "Ye must give us a chance to win back a bit of what we've relinquished."

"I do?"

"Shit, man," MacGregor said. "Ye've got to be a gentleman about this."

"Oh, of course," Tashum answered, glancing to each anxious face. "Yes, a thousand pardons. I fear I exhibit the manners of one who has spent too long alone on an island."

"Ye weren't quite alone now, were ye?" MacGregor piped.

As the new hand was dealt and coinage anted up, Tashum's mind went back to the island, that night with Fanny when he had seen the knife's edge of fear and desire. Ah, that was what this gambling was all about.

Chance.

A dance of flesh and flame.

These men put forward their valuable bits of gold, balancing themselves on the pinnacle of chance where much was to be gained and much to be lost. Just as the faces on the cards represented royalty and the stars represented history, this game represented the risk of life. This was no mere entertainment. It was a pale reflection of life itself.

Tashum played the next few games without using his mental ability and found to his delight that he was beaten badly. He folded out after an hour of play but continued watching Riggett and the captain bluff their way toward a conclusion. Riggett would lose a number of small hands, then win a large pot. In the games he won, Riggett showed an uncanny ability to recall which cards had been used and to calculate which cards were in the hands of the men around him. For this he was called a blighter and a rapscallion. They would seem to forget the epithets when they lost to the captain. After another hour of play, only the captain and Riggett remained in the game.

Once again, Riggett followed his previous pattern, losing hand after hand when the pot was small. But at the final hand, when the pot was large, Riggett's luck would change.

Riggett's wicked smile spread across his face when he pulled the coins toward himself at the final lay of the cards.

When Riggett and MacGregor had gone, the captain invited Tashum to drink a mug of ale with him.

"Ye don't seem to mourn the loss of yer coin," the captain said. "Can ye be that rich that bad fortune makes ye smile?"

Tashum tasted the effervescent liquid. "I found the evening illuminating."

"Ha! Illuminating, ye say?" He laughed bitterly. "Did yer illumination cast enough light to let ye see what I saw?"

Tashum shrugged his shoulders. "What did you see?"

"The way Riggett played. The devil seemed on his side."

"He did seem to play with extreme skill."

The captain grunted into his mug. "Aye, good fortune never loved any man so well." His eyebrows drew together. "Nor the devil."

"The devil and fortune?" Tashum shook his head. "Perhaps I was on that island too long."

The captain laughed. "They're just sayings, my good man."

Tashum winced at the idea of being called a man, despite his disguise.

The captain faltered and put his hand on Tashum's arm. "If I have offended thee, 'twas not my intent." He patted Tashum's arm. "I know there are men who wear their religion inside their vest, close to their heart, for only God and himself to share. To some men, the mere mention of the devil is blasphemy. Aye, but with you I feel it's different. I believe you to be as honest as ye need be. . . . Aye, sometimes I talk too much. Forgive me."

Tashum looked deep into the captain's eyes, realized he had met his first truly good man. Here was a man born into ordinary innocence, a man who had held on to his honor through the storms of life. And yet he was capable of expressing true regret over a paltry, and imagined, misuse of a stray word.

Tashum, stood, extended his hand. "You have not offended me in the least, Captain. I thank you for such good sport, and a splendid evening of chance."

The captain didn't take his hand but did wish him a good night.

Buoyed by his discovery, Tashum went down the steps and into his cabin, where Fanny and Dickey waited for him. His good cheer faded a bit at the sight of their hungry eyes, but he steeled himself to the task.

He withdrew a small knife from a travel chest and opened his veins. Fanny offered a grateful smile and bent her head toward one of the wounds, while Dickey simply landed on the other without any form of acknowledgment or gratitude.

Tashum stood between them and turned his head at a soft sound.

The latch on the cabin door had come undone, and Riggett stood outside with one wide eye on the thin opening.

Tashum pulled away from the vampires, leaving them openmouthed, drooling.

Tashum reached for the door, but Riggett was gone. He tugged on the stubborn door, pulling it closed.

"Tashum, please," Dickey said, "I need more—"

"Quiet! We've been seen."

"What?" barked Fanny.

"The quartermaster," Tashum said, and began pacing about in the small cabin. "This is very bad."

"Throw him overboard. Go!" Fanny cried. "Do it now, Tashum."

"She's right. He'll tell the others. Kill him Tashum."

His eyes flicked from Fanny to Dickey, taking in their worried expressions. Then he rushed through the door and bolted up the stairs.

Moments later, on deck, he spied the man near the ship's beam.

Riggett twitched as though he were waiting, expecting to meet someone. He settled against the rail and awaited Tashum's approach.

"Doctor," the man said, grinning. "Luvely evenin', ain't it?"

"Yes, Riggett," Tashum answered, "it is."

A breeze ruffled through the man's beard and he glanced up at the sky.

The mizzen mast sail snapped and filled. "A new wind is a-blow'n."

"Perhaps we'll make England soon," Tashum said.

"Aye, most of us will." Riggett's eyes narrowed, an animal studying his prey. "Just what sort of medical arts will ye be practicing there, doctor?"

"My wards are infected with a strange illness," Tashum answered. "I pray that it passes."

"What sort of devil needs sup on blood for restoration?" the man said. His grin flashed again, then fell away, his mouth went small and tight.

"It was you at the door?"

His breath light and panting. "I've heard tales, sir, of demons who lurk in the night and drink the blood of men. Tales of the vampire and his black arts."

"Riggett, I—"

"Ye've bought the captain's silence, doctor. Ye've closed many mouths and eyes to who ye are and what yer wards are. But if tales were to be told of vampires walking our boards, no amount of filthy lucre could keep you from tasting salt water."

Tashum reached into a pouch and withdrew a large diamond. He held it up to the light of the moon.

"Perhaps this can medicate your fears, sir," Tashum said, dropping the stone into the quartermaster's hand.

The man walked over to a storm lantern, tilted his palm back and forth, watching blues and whites refracting off the gem's surface. "What is it, ye give me?"

"It's a diamond."

"So, that's what the bloody things look like," Riggett said, his smirking mouth revealing broken yellow teeth. He bit the stone softly, and checked it for scratches. "Where there's one there's always more," he teased. "Would that be fair to say?"

Tashum nodded. He reached into the pouch and produced another stone. "That's as much wealth as I have to share," he said.

The quartermaster rubbed the diamonds in circles in his hand. "Hmm, this should stop up me lungs."

"Very well, keep them," Tashum said, and held out his hand as he had seen others do.

The quartermaster paused, then took his hand and gave it a strong grip. In the rear of the man's mind, Tashum saw a series of ready calculations,

several having to do with Tashum and his wards, others involving a complicated formula for losing just enough to win a great deal during each evening
of card playing, centered around little notches and irregularities in the cards
that informed Riggett what value lay in each man's card hand.

Back in the cabin, Fanny and Dickey quizzed Tashum on the transaction.
Fanny grew silent. She exchanged a long, sullen look with Dickey. Tashum
moved to the bank of small paneled windows at the end of the cabin. He
could see the moon-glistened water churning in the ship's wake. He stood
there until she spoke.

"We shan't be able to purchase his silence for long, you know that, don't
you?" Fanny asked.

"Why? I gave him two of the finest stones," Tashum said.

"They weren't yours to give away," Fanny said. "But that's not the issue."

He adjusted the flame on their lantern and held a diamond up to the
flame. "I've still got this one."

Fanny pulled his hand down into her line of sight. "You don't understand
men like him," she said as though she were teaching him something. "The
size of the ransom doesn't matter. It's never enough for men like that." She
pulled him closer. "You think that Dickey and I are wicked because we are
bleeders. What you don't see is that we simply live out the darkness that lies
within all men."

"But he took hands with me," Tashum jerked loose from her grip.

"He took hands!" she scoffed, and turned to Dickey. "Oh, well, he took
hands. Everything's squared then. I seriously doubt it! Riggett." She faced
Tashum, "He's the bloke who wins at cards all the time, correct?"

"Yes." Tashum smiled. "He alters the cards so he knows which cards are
being dealt to whom."

"You fool, if you knew he was playing with marked cards," Dickey said,
"why did you play along?"

"Shut up, Dickey! Tashum, the point is, men like Riggett brag to their
mates about such deals with the devil."

Dickey laughed. "Guess what? You're the devil, Tashum."

Tashum snarled at him. "Devil," he said, and wondered exactly what
that word meant. He looked down at his hands. "If the goal in gambling is
to test your skill against the others, why would he need to mark cards?"

Dickey laughed. "To cheat—to win, for God's sake, didn't you notice
there was money to be had?" He gestured to his sister. "Fanny, tell him about

robbery and gentlemen's games." Dickey seemed to have measured his luck against the edges of the angel's pride and stopped just short of angering him.

Tashum just stood there gazing at his hands.

Fanny said nothing and drifted away from him to a darker corner of the cabin.

Dickey took his chair at the table, picked up his silver bishop from the playing board, and twirled it through his fingers.

Fanny's voice came out of the shadows. "For centuries you've dreamed of humanity—now you're getting your chance to finally see them, Tashum. Perhaps now you'll realize that we're not the evil you believe."

"We're not devils but we are top of the food chain, and I'm still hungry," Dickey said, clubbing Fanny's golden queen with his silver bishop. "Now can we finish what we started? Our dinner, please."

Tashum was trapped between logic and emotion. He stumbled backward and sat on the double berth. With closed eyes, he forced out Dickey's whine and listened to only the sounds of a new breeze outside the porthole, fluttering across *Merciful*'s decks, filling her sails and pushing her along. Concentrating on the serene image of a ship at sea, he was mentally able to block out their physical advance. Fanny gently opened his wrist.

"You've had enough for now," Tashum said, after ten minutes of listening to his wards' soft moans. He despised their need; it was the act as much as the source that seemed inherently and morally perverse. He wondered how it might end. His thoughts went back in time to a male lion cannibalizing his brother's offspring; infanticide, a murder for preservation of the killer's genes. Instinctively the male lion was securing a safer place for his yet to be conceived children to grow up in. The moment it entered his mind, Tashum rejected any correlation between the lion and himself as inconceivable, he loved them beyond their needs.

In the days that followed the wind gained strength. Now the sails were full and taut. The captain and crew had high spirits as the trade winds pushed them toward England.

For Tashum, the biggest change came with the new palate of scents on the wind. As they approached the British Isles, the feral, familiar smells of his island evaporated. He sampled the air and discovered small traces of animals and vegetation he had never known. The overwhelming scent of humanity took him by complete surprise—he had no idea there could be so many men, women, and children inhabiting this planet.

Tashum used every spare moment to prepare himself for his impending contact with this new world. He allowed Fanny to cut his hair. In the next card game, he played particularly hard and won an impressive waistcoat, matching pants, and silver-buckled shoes from MacGregor, as they were about the same size. He made sure to lose a reasonable sum to the Scot later in compensation.

He labored over the English language and with the eagerness of a bright child taught himself to read the few books onboard. He studied the captain's maps and sea charts, and in the process he learned about celestial navigation. His interests mushroomed away from the needs of Fanny and Dickey. He saw less of them with each passing day.

In a tiny room at the ship's stern he created a small library for himself, complete with candles and shelves. He fashioned a small desk made from crates, and a stool. Near his desk was a small round window that allowed in fresh air to combat the odors of bilge water, mold, and rat droppings.

One night, under dim candlelight, Tashum was hunched over the small table carefully turning the pages of a yellowed manuscript. The book's title identified it as *Palace of Honour written by Gawain Douglas in 1501.*

He glanced toward the window for a moment. A faint murmur. Then something splashed into the sea. There were no shouts, no call of alarm, so he returned to his pages and resumed reading. A stream of wax sped down the side of a candle and across the table toward his papers. He lifted them and waited as the stream stopped and hardened from clear to yellow.

His brows furrowed after hearing a quick succession of splashes. He jumped up, crossed to the small porthole, and flung it open.

Tashum froze. He watched as the bodies of several men drifted silently past the ships bulbous hull. Another splash into the sea. This new body floated past, bobbing and listless. A face emerged up out of the water—MacGregor! With a thick, bloodied slash across his throat, exposing his windpipe.

Tashum grabbed his dark glasses off the table, darted out of the makeshift library, then down the corridor, and flew up the steps into the night air. On the main deck, the sails ruffled in a light breeze. He crossed to the other side and glanced around, listening to the eerie silence enveloping the ship. He looked around her decks piled high with cargo. Not a man in sight.

Then another splash came from the bow. He stepped lightly forward and saw a pair of lifeless booted legs sticking out from behind a crate. The legs shifted slightly, then began to disappear, dragged out of sight. Tashum craned around the edge of the cargo. A flash of heat passed through him.

Dickey's mouth was smeared with blood. He struggled, pulled the dead seaman next to the port rail. Fanny stepped out of the shadows. She comforted the ship's cat held in her arms. Her hands and face were dark and gleaming with red gore.

"It wouldn't hurt you to help me," Dickey grunted. "This bloke must weigh twelve stone. Come on, Fanny."

"Can't you see, I'm busy," she said, and continued to stroke the feline.

"You're always busy when it comes to the hard bits, Fanny."

Dickey lifted and rolled the dead sailor up onto the side rail.

"I don't like physical work, you know that." She glanced out over the water.

"As if I do." Dickey grunted with his labors. Another splash . . .

Tashum slipped through the dark and latched onto Dickey, throwing him hard into the forward mast. The vampire fell heavily against the base of the mast and crumbled, onto the deck. He quickly recovered and started to reach for a cutlass lying a few feet away.

"Who's faster, you or me?" Tashum said, looming over him. "And what are you willing to wager?"

Caught in Tashum's stare, Dickey cowered away from the cutlass. "It was all Fanny's doing," he eagerly volunteered. "It was her I say."

"Dickey, you're such a little worm," she said, and dropped the cat.

"Well it was your idea, Fanny."

"You both stink of blood! You . . . ," Tashum said through his teeth. He pointed an accusing finger at Fanny. "You swore to me that you would leave the crew alone! I let you *drink* of me!"

"Drink? We were starving and you let us *sip* of you occasionally," Fanny snarled. "You acted the miser, parceling pennies. We're accustomed to riches."

"Fanny, at the very least, you could have bled the livestock onboard!"

"Goat blood? You'd have us drink from chickens, I suppose?"

He turned away in disgust.

Her voice hardened. "Besides, we need the money they took from us. Tashum, we're about to embark on a voyage into the true world—one you know nothing about. And in that world, you must have money."

"Money? What in hell's name is wrong with you? Will money sail this ship?"

"We don't need it to," she answered, pointing toward the port side. "Tashum, look, England!"

He followed her gaze and saw a coastline that filled the horizon with solid shadow.

"The tide will take us as close as we need. Then we'll row ashore with our loot in the launch." Fanny rubbed up next to him, trying to pull his arms around her.

"It's ours for the taking. You'll see, Tashum." Her eyes were big and round. "I'll make you a good queen, my king." She flashed a prideful smile still dirty with clotted blood.

Her appearance sickened Tashum. He pushed away her attentions and turned his back to her. Out of sheer frustration, he rubbed his face and hair. He would try and keep emotion out of it. "It appears you've figured out everything—but me," he said, calmly.

She grabbed for him. "Don't be cross now, not at this moment when our future—"

He pushed her back, wiping at fresh blood she had smeared on his neck. "Our future? Our future, you say? You broke your word to me. The two of you slaughtered the entire crew. These were decent men!"

"But darling, we don't need them anymore."

"You'll always need them! That's the problem!" His jaws clamped shut and he turned again to take in the English coast. He kept his back to her. "I'm finished with you, the pair of you." He flicked her hand off of his shoulder. "I'm leaving you. Now. Tonight."

Dickey let out a growl. "Tashum, they were plotting to throw us all overboard," he clenched a fist. "Riggett and the others, for weeks they've been waiting for the right moment. Once we were gone, there was nothing to stop them—they would simply divide our booty among themselves."

"I had given Riggett more than enough—"

"He wanted more!" Fanny said, trying to get into his line of sight, trying to reason with him. "His kind always want more."

"Tashum, you killed that boy on the island, to protect Fanny." Dickey rubbed his back where he hit against the mast. "And we killed the crew to protect you."

"Through our actions . . ." Fanny picked up the cat again, stroking its fur. "We were protecting all of us."

Tashum shook his head. If just being near this many people so confused him, how would he ever walk the streets among them. Shame crept into his cheeks. He hadn't known the sailors that shipwrecked on the island. But these men . . .

"What about the captain?" Tashum said, a stone in his throat, tears glistening in his eyes. "What—what about MacGregor? These were good men, Fanny, not simply goblets to drink from!"

"Tashum, I admit we went back on our vow." Fanny's voice was smooth and calculated. "But you're angry with us for the wrong reasons. These good men were ready to murder us, you included."

"We're monsters to all men. The sooner you realize that, the safer we'll all be." Dickey said. "They hate us, Tashum."

"They will kill you, Tashum," she said with finality.

"Can you really blame them?" He scanned their messy faces. "They hate us and we hate them. Kill or be killed? Is that what I've traveled here to see? To be a part of?"

There was a brief silence.

"Perhaps you should take some time on your own. We'll meet up later. In the warmth of the Mediterranean," she said in her most seductive voice. "We have an eternity for togetherness you and—"

"No, Fanny we don't. My road is quite different than yours. We part company here."

She read right through his stern expression. "Do you really think that you'll find Paladin or the secret of the orbs on your own?"

The sheer mention of his brother's name on the lips of such a dark siren added coals to the flame burning deep inside his soul. He lunged at her. Held firmly in his grip, she defiantly opened her eyes to him. Ghostly faded images, thinly projected on the back wall of her mind. Where was this place of cascading waterfalls and high mountain peaks, of night sky holding different star formations? Joyous tears grew in the corners of Tashum's flickering eyes as he absorbed the essence of Paladin and Fanny, he could see them as well as feel the heat of their entwined embrace. He could taste the fragrance of pine trees, and above all, he could taste Fanny. She blinked, and the images and sensations disappeared. Tashum found himself staring into Fanny's eyes, but the pictures were gone. She was fully aware and content with her power to give and take away the very things Tashum believed he needed most.

"You need me for that if for nothing else, Tashum," Fanny said.

"Fanny! Where is Paladin?"

"I'm sure it will come back to me," she paused, "in time."

His frame shook with rage. She watched his right hand form into a tight fist.

"Tashum, don't hit me . . . unless it's the only way I can keep you."

"Fanny, if you want someone to beat you up, ask your friend." His glare shifted to her companion. "If I am on this world another forty thousand years, I will not waste another hour on either of you. Dickey, put a boat in the water!"

Dickey nodded numbly and rose to his feet. "I'll need help, they're bloody heavy you know."

Fanny's hurt enflamed to anger and her eyes swelled with tears. "You need me, Tashum! No one else will take in a demonic thing like you!" The cat leaped from her tight clutched arms.

"I'm well practiced at being alone, I'll survive."

"You can't leave me!" Her demeanor broke apart in sobs, and she pounded her fists against his chest. "No! No! No! You can't leave me, I forbid it!"

He lost himself in her grief and started to caress her forehead, then stopped with a sudden jerk, thinking on the flow of widows' tears that will result from this slaughter.

"Good-bye, Fanny." He allowed her to sink to his feet, weeping and crying out. Tashum turned and glared at Dickey. "Get my boat ready!"

He disengaged from Fanny's clutch and walked away. He followed Dickey aft.

Together they put upright the smaller of two rowing skiffs. Tashum watched Dickey untie a line from the side rail. The rope's other end was strung through a pulley attached to a yardarm high above the deck. As Dickey rigged the skiff to be lowered over the side, Tashum found himself leaning on the ship's port rail, gazing at England.

At last he was at the start gate of his journey. The realm of man awaited, and he was prepared to cast himself into their world in order to get back to his own.

Far down the coastline, he could make out the shapes of moored ships and the stacked rooftops of a village. He stood mesmerized by the web of torchlights and signal fires beckoning to him.

Tashum startled at the creak of running rope and the splash of his boat dropping into the water. He ran down to the cabin and threw gems, money, and belongings into a wooden chest, and a short time later he stood on the port side of the ship. He kicked a rope ladder over the side.

He listened for a moment to Fanny's staggered breathing and lamenting sobs. He placed the chest on the edge of the deck and went to her, finding her crumpled at the bow of the ship. She looked up at him, her yellow eyes awash in tears.

"Tashum, you can't. Please," she said in a broken, child's voice. "Please, don't take leave of us."

He gently pulled her to his chest and for a moment he felt her cold, convulsing body next to his.

"I am sure we shall see each other. From time to time."

Slowly she pulled back and took his face in her hands. "I know you love me, I've got knowledge you will need!"

"Yes you do, Fanny," he said as he forced her hands back down to her sides. "But you'll never share it with me, and I don't know why. If you loved Paladin as much as you've displayed, then why won't you tell where he is?"

On the verge of speaking, Fanny's mouth just froze. A quiver followed, but her tears revealed more than her mouth ever had. He kissed her forehead and then let her go. She supported herself on trembling legs and watched him walk the ship's length to where Dickey was standing.

"Take care of her," Tashum said. "I'll be in touch with you from time to time—I'll pay you a handsome reward for any information regarding Paladin, the orbs, or others of my kind."

"You've done wrong by us," Dickey whispered.

"I've done wrong to myself," Tashum added in a soft tone. "Take me up on my offer."

He gave them a final glance. He pitched two soft bags of belongings into the skiff and gathered up his chest of gems under one arm. As Tashum lowered himself down the ladder he noticed Dickey raising a boot.

"Dickey, don't do anything foolish."

"Actually, I was planning to do a little jig."

"No you weren't. But I accept these little betrayals as part and parcel of our relationship."

Dickey lowered his boot, crossed his arms, and leaned back in a pout. The vampire watched Tashum clamber down the ladder.

The small boat rocked under his unsteady foot. He sat and took up the oars. He was clumsy with the long oars and spun himself around in circles several times before grasping the nature of oars as a steering mechanism. With no wind the water was smooth. He navigated his small boat through a cluster of partially submerged bodies. Tashum's friend the captain was face-down. The drowned man bumped and rubbed against the skiff's hull. Tashum grabbed for him, snagged him by the belt, and tried to pull him into the skiff. The boat started to capsize; water rushed in over the oarlocks. He had no choice but to relinquish the captain's body back to the sea. The release of dead weight tumbled him backward, and the skiff rocked to upright. Tashum lay sprawled across its width. He waited until she settled before moving.

"Tashum! You'll sink that boat if you're not careful." Dickey laughed. "Good God man, you can't save the drowned."

"He was a Christian. He deserves burial," Tashum called back.

"Sailor's are buried at sea. Let him go."

Tashum rose to his knees and watched silently as the captain drifted away into total darkness.

Dickey watched Tashum take the oars and begin rowing. He couldn't think of anything to say, so he whistled a sea shanty and walked along the deck, keeping up with Tashum's progress.

When the skiff cleared the ship's bow, Tashum was serenaded by Fanny's despair. Her shrill wail hurt his ears and pierced the night. He rowed with vigor and little concern of his skiff's true bearing. He figured that as long as the stern of his boat continued to move in any direction away from the bow of the ship, he couldn't help but make landfall simply because the coastline was so large—he was just bound to hit it. He felt the shedding of emotional chains with each stroke of the oars. It felt good to leave them behind.

Eager to begin his quest, he pulled the oars deeper through the water, the tiny increase in speed across a smooth sea was instantaneous and worth the effort. Heaven was his final destination, and the journey home would begin on the shores of England.

CHAPTER EIGHT

Tashum gazed across the grass-covered dunes rising gently from the wind-swept beach. He could see a narrow dirt road leading to the outskirts of a small village comprising several dark silhouetted buildings. He counted eight figures milling around a large fire. He thought of Fanny and Dickey, but there was no murderous reef.

Tashum knew more about the contents of his pockets than he did about England. Henry VIII was king, and Fanny called his kingdom nothing more than a damp rock surrounded by water. With barely a glimpse of Henry's realm, Tashum could see that it was much more than that.

He turned and scrambled back down the sandy incline to where his boat lay beached above the receding tide. He studied his bags, mentally going over their contents and finally decided to take all three. This was his first contact with native civilization, and despite his slight prejudice against hu-manity he did want to make a good impression. He had a sudden moment of concern, then patted a breast pocket for his dark spectacles. He felt their shape, safely there, and relaxed.

Later, he stood on the road a mere stone's throw away from the small group-ing of fishing shanties. The buildings appeared to be only a generation beyond

Shrug's huts—without beauty, thrown together with sticks and stones and topped with roughly thatched roofs. He felt a tinge of disappointment, which puzzled him because he had no preconceived notion of what to expect.

The aroma of fish being smoked over an open fire took him back to his island and memories of Shrug's people doing the same. He wondered if this is where the descendants of Shrug's tribe had ended up.

The moment Tashum stepped into the firelight, he sensed he might have miscalculated his attire, a fashion fiasco that dropped the jaws silent of those dirty-faced peasants dressed in rags. They gathered in closer with squinted eyes to see the apparition glimmering in faint light at the edge of their circle. The only sound other than the fire's crackle came from the jingle-jangle in Tashum's step. From the top of his feathered floppy blue velvet hat crowned by a diamond-crusted tiara, he was dripping in a treasure chest of gold and silver jewelry. Inca necklaces clanked against the Spanish conquistador's breastplate armor, covering a woman's deep red velveteen frock. Over the knee baggy green leather boots carried the clown closer into the circle of unbelieving eyes.

Tashum quickly sorted out who was in charge. It was easy. He was the toothless man sitting on the only stick-built chair. Rocks and barrels suited the others of his tribe.

"My name is Tashum. Where is it I have come to?"

Where's me weapon? resounded the man's mental reply, and he stood flexing his leather-covered chest. "Ye've come to Corfe," the codger cackled. "Ye've come alone have ye, blind man?"

Tashum noticed the other men fanning out flanking him both left and right. The hunter's pheromones filled Tashum's nose.

"I'm not blind, just sensitive to bright light."

"Dressed like that here, you should be." This brought laughter from his tribe.

Tashum mustered up a laugh. But his laugh quieted theirs.

"Ye've still come to Corfe," he continued. "The castle and village are down the road." His eyes narrowed. "Come alone have ye?"

Tashum felt the bristle of the hair on his neck. He surveyed the hungry faces inching in from the darkness to the fires glow, adding to the ranks of the dozen or so men already encircling him. An odd patchwork of men and boys brandished knives and clubs. He'd seen these patterns before. How disappointing.

At lightning speed, Tashum leaped over the burning pyre and fish racks. Through the smoke he flew. His feet landed lightly. His hand wrapped firmly around the conspiring leader's throat. The man's eyes bugged. His cider breath was cut off. Tashum pulled him out of the sheepskin-covered chair and on to his feet and then off the ground an arm's length for all to see. With desired effect the hunters stood down.

"I'm here to see Henry VIII," he growled at the bewildered crowd. "I don't wish to harm any of you." Tashum dropped his wheezing trophy back into his rickety throne. Two haggard women rushed to the limp man's assistance.

"I have gifts," he said. He removed the jeweled hat and tossed it beyond the fire. No attempt was made to pluck it from the air. It landed in the dirt. To his amazement they continued to just stare at him like stunned mullets.

Standing with his back to the seated man, he only heard the click of a hammer locking, then saw a bright muzzle flash as he turned to face the shooter.

Tashum's head snapped back, and his blind-man's glasses flew from the bridge of his nose. At its hinged points his body crumpled, folding down upon itself.

He landed facedown.

They didn't wait to see a puddle of blood, or even movement. Conformation wasn't needed for a head shot, not at point-blank range. His clothes and jewels were torn from his body by greedy hands. The bits and pieces were then fought over once safely away from the victim. He was naked before the small boy dipped his finger into the amber liquid puddled beneath the sleeping stranger.

Tashum's eyes blinked four times before he realized he was staring into dirt. The musket ball had entered through pursed lips and ate away his cheek when it exited. His tongue swept the inside of his mouth and fell into the dirt through the ball's gaping exit hole. He turned his head slightly, seeing the boy's reflection in the puddle of his own essence. The mere thought of the boy tasting this poison prompted Tashum to spring up off the ground, grab the boy's finger. He rubbed it furiously in the dirt. Tashum's monstrous return from the dead with burning yellow eyes, fluorescent blood, and sexless body would become an instant legend. The boy would carry this story with him into manhood and old age.

Tashum was furious. He had come here bearing gifts, but they had stolen the moment and were pillaging his belongings in the premature celebration of his death.

He was catching his breath and planing his next move, as clubs were raised, and gun barrels stuffed with powder and ball. They were a mad crowd bent on ridding this world of this monstrous aberration, and they gathered courage from their shared hysteria.

Tashum threw up his arms and tried to shout, "I wish you no harm!" But all that came was an inaudible gargle from a pair of split lips hanging off a mangled face. Peeled back flesh exposed the glowing white crystal of his jaw and cheekbones heightened the villager's fear. He backed away from them, toward the less threatening rumble of the surf over his shoulder.

They skulked around, moving in and out of the fire's glow, taking up hunter's positions. Then they formed ranks and moved in unison as a group, counter-checking his lateral moves, backing him toward the sea. He repeated his slurred plea for nonviolence.

Their intent was set, and no amount of words would appease them.

Hopelessly surrounded, the angel crouched in a last-stand defense.

Suddenly their advance was stopped and their ranks split. They shielded their eyes from a ball of flame and then a series of explosions erupting at a distance in the blackness behind their prey.

Tashum was just as surprised as he turned to witness the night sky lit up and flames burning on the slow-cresting waves.

"Aye, 'tis more devil's work!" cried a voice in the crowd.

In the corner of his eye Tashum noticed the archer raise his crossbow. He heard the whistle, then felt a thud. The sting of the feathered bolt sticking out of his upper thigh brought a shudder. A series of misfired gunshots chased him out of the grassy dunes, dragging a leg across the wide beach and into the water.

He glanced back once to see them lining the dune, screaming insults, weapons waving and still pointed in his direction. He threw himself into the waves and furiously pumped his arms, fueling his escape. In his anger and disappointment it was easier to understand the vampire's disrespect for mankind. If this was the centuries-old cultivation of their civilization, he'd just as soon swim back to Somers Island.

*   *   *

Tashum swam for hours, hugging the coastline, riding the in-going tide, and was finally delivered into the wetlands of a broad estuary. He'd never been in fresh water and couldn't help but taste its sweetness through his wounds.

Near the tree-lined shore, under a rich blue and pink canopy of the new day forming, Tashum dove beneath a large floating mound of woven branches and twigs. His head broke the surface, and he glanced around the hollow mound's interior. Whatever furry beasts had created the shelter were long gone and had left for him a dry dark place to heal. He slithered out of the pool, up onto the log worn flat and smooth by generations of small otter's feet. He was relieved to be alone and simply lay there staring up at tufts of auburn-colored fur woven into the thatched ceiling. Were there animals here that could build such shelter? What an amazing concept. It was a momentary thought quickly fading as he considered the feathered shaft embedded in his thigh.

It had to go. He pried loose a hefty branch from the weave, raised it, then brought it down hard against his thigh. The archer's dart popped out the backside of the thigh muscle and plopped into the pool of water. He lay back down, knowing time would heal all his physical wounds but wondering if wounds of the heart were ever truly mended.

Before slipping into a deep sleep, he recounted his reception with the natives. Of all the possible explanations, the explosions had to be the work of Fanny and Dickey covering their treachery by blowing up the ship using the deck gun's black powder. If his lips weren't so ragged, he would have chuckled at their inadvertent intervention.

Perhaps he should have stayed with them. With their cunning and killing skills it might have been a fair fight. Or no fight at all. Slowly, his mind emptied of exhaustive what-if scenarios until he was weightless. Darkness was replaced by the dreams of brilliant white Light that medicated his recuperative sleep.

How many days, even months, had passed, he wasn't sure. He awoke consumed by shivering cold. He barely recalled his wounds that had long since healed. His movements were stiff and labored. Must be the cold, he thought and rubbed his hands together. It was darker in his cocoon than he had remembered. Then he noticed the pool he had emerged from was no longer fluid; he could see moving water beneath, but the surface was hard, like stone. Everything he touched was painfully cold and covered with hardened water. Vaguely, lodged in the back of his mind, he remembered Dickey complaining about something called ice that came during a season named winter. Whatever its name, he needed warmth more than he'd ever needed food or anything physical. His legs swung out off the log, and his feet landed with a crack against the ice. His feet pounded the ice until they broke through and made a hole. He pushed his torso off the log and slipped into the frigid black water.

Submerged, he kicked free of the hut and swam freely. He panicked when he looked up, expecting to see blurred night sky beyond the surface and saw only the blackness of no light. He let buoyancy be his guide. He floated up, and touched the hard surface, his hands pushed against this heavy, solid ceiling. He searched for a soft or weak spot and found nothing but an impenetrable wall. He felt trapped in blackness. He dove to the bottom, crouched down, and sprang up with all of his might. Rocketing behind leading fists, he crashed into the frozen barrier. It cracked and split with a moan.

Tashum's nude body breached up out of the small hole. His feet cleared the frozen surface before he lost inertia and tumbled down onto the snow-covered surface. Now a barren, flat landscape surrounded by leafless trees and rolling hills, the estuary was deep into winter's slumber. The dark, moody sky was leaking small delicate white flakes that fell uniformly, keeping everything white.

"What world is this? . . ." he cried aloud as he stood. "Where am I? . . ."

"Well, it's not France!" was hollered out in the laughing mocking tone of male gentry English, with a foreign accent like Dickey's. "It's not Scotland, yet," the voice continued. "Or Cornwall!"

Tashum turned in circles, his glowing eyes narrowed and scanned the ridge. He found a candlelit window placed high in a wall of a structure obscured by thickets of tree limbs. He ducked low and began running toward the frozen incline. He crossed a hundred yards of ice in seconds.

"It's not Wales. Are you still with me?"

Tashum climbed the heavily wooded embankment. The exercise warmed away the chill and the snowflakes melted as they landed on his skin. Only his feet were numbed by the ankle deep snow.

From a higher vantage, he could see, in sharp profile, the silhouetted shapes of the building's steep-pitched roof and adjoining spired tower. Fanny had called such dwellings manor houses when she had drawn them in the sand.

Tashum passed through an arched gate set in a thick wall of neatly stacked stones. He recognized the acrid smell and knew the meaning of mounds marking newly dug graves that lined the inner wall. His powerful hearing picked up the gurgling sounds of lungs purging themselves of sickly fluids. His eyes followed his ears to the exterior window on the manor's second floor. He crossed the small courtyard to the manor's side entry. The heavy door sat unhinged and crooked in its frame. A large red letter *P* had been painted across its carved wooden planks. Tashum slipped inside through the diagonal opening.

Even with his vision, he couldn't see the details, only the shapes of man-made things lining the walls of the long hallway. The man's hacking and delirious rantings grew louder with each step.

"It's bloody England, isn't it!" the man's voiced echoed through the otherwise dead corridor.

Tashum moved into a large open room. He was drawn to a formal staircase dusted by diagonal moonbeams filtered in from long narrow windows set midway up the wall. He froze when he looked to his left. Two metal-skinned figures flanked the main entry door. They didn't move and, not sensing life within them, he crossed the room, reached for the banister, and sprinted up the broad staircase.

That nostril-burning smell again. Tashum's eyes focused on the far end of the hallway; light flickered across a body heaped prone in the doorway. Tashum's step creaked the floorboard; he stopped.

"William, is it you?" the voice cried out from the adjoining room.

Before stepping over the corpse, Tashum glanced down at the young well-dressed but putrefied man, still clutching a paper document in his outstretched gloved hand. His frilly shirt and coat were stained with dried blood surrounding a gunshot wound to the chest. Gunned down where he stood, so it appeared. Tashum heard something hit against the wall. He ducked back. With care, he peeked around the doorjamb.

What he had thought to be candlelight from afar was actually the dying glow of embers burning in a large wall opening—fireplace. The dull thud he had heard was a bed-ridden man's feeble attempt to pitch a book across the room and into the fire pit, as witnessed by his next attempt, high and wide, a miss.

The four-poster bed was strewn with his weapons: half a dozen pistols, several daggers, and a broad sword. The gray-haired old man laid back against a stack of feather pillows stained brown from body sweats. Dull black eyes on a gaunt face stared blankly upward.

Even from the doorway, Tashum sensed a difference in this man. For a long while he stood there, silent, ready to dart if needed. He wondered if he was invisible to this man whose eyes were constantly moving and had passed over him several times. Each time Tashum caught his gaze he was shut out, left unable to connect. But it was the nonresponse to his presence that baffled the angel. His chill was returning, and the embers were dying. He moved in silence to the fireplace. The ember's heat was weak, but even that felt good. From the last book to have been thrown, he quietly tore pages and wadded them as he had seen Dickey do, so many times. He stopped on the title page; *Coverdale's complete English Bible printed by James Nicholson, London 1535* A.D. This was a book he knew he must read, and he put it aside. A log was added to the pile of paper already smoldering on the embers. A steady stream of his breath brought the flame back to life. Tashum forgot everything in the luxury of the radiant heat against his naked skin, and not until he turned to warm his backside did he think of the immediate situation.

The man's head was cocked. His ears seemed to be searching for telltale signs of what his eyes were staring at. Tashum cautiously moved toward him.

The man reached for his pistol, fumbling to locate and handle the weapon. Tashum was removing the weapon from his hands before the hammer was cocked.

"You have no need to fear me," Tashum said in a gentle and honest voice.

The man's dead eyes widened as if it might make a difference. He blindly patted the dark wool fabric, searching with his left hand, pitted with open sores.

"You're not William?" he moaned.

"No, my name is Tashum. Do you not see me?"

"Sir, I see nothing but blackness," was his a bitter response. "I'm blind."

Tashum fought to control his own fear over the phrase, the most horrifying and restrictive form of confinement. The blindness he had seen in animals always brought a lingering death. To see the same condition in a man was more gut-wrenching. He realized that his own eyes, as powerful as they were, could not penetrate dead eyes. He leaned across the helpless man and placed a pistol in his hand. He stood straight, an easy target, even for a blind man.

"Pull back the hammer, if it makes you feel better."

He did, then waved the gun wildly. Tashum stood passively watching the muzzle swing left then right, searching.

Blind, but no fool, he rested the gun in his lap with a sigh. "If you are here to steal from me, take what you wish. Possessions mean little to me now."

"Did the man lying in the doorway try to steal from you?"

"Good," his tone reclaiming his manhood. "I thought I got him. Hmm," wiggling his long thin nose, sniffing the air, "explains that awful stench."

"Yes." Tashum held his position.

"William always was rotten, avarice by nature. I suppose that doesn't speak very well of me or my own cupidity. William was my only surviving heir," he said choking on sputum.

"You need food, sustenance."

"No, my water's turned black. I'm diseased. Steal from me what you will. And leave."

Tashum sat on the edge of the bed.

"Did you hear me? Go!" The man shooed him with his hands. "Take your leave, or die rotting away here!"

Tashum noticed the lesions hidden in the man's scalp beneath an unkempt tangle of shoulder-length hair. He could see Shrug so clearly in his mind; the same sores, the same death. He reached over, took the man's hand and sandwiched it between his.

"What is it that kills you?"

"Plague, you fool!" he said, jerking his hand away from Tashum's clasp.

Tashum noticed a lesser degree of infection around open sores on the hand as he released it. The angel wasn't sure how harmonic touch worked, but he knew his healing power had limitations.

"Take your leave, sir!"

"I have nowhere to take leave to."

"If you stay here you will surely die."

"I have nowhere else to go."

"I will share my house, but I will not share my disease with another soul. Please leave me to die—"

"No doubt you are dying, however, I am immune to such disease. I need your accommodation, and you need fresh clothes and bedding in your final hours. Perhaps we can help one another. Tit for tat."

"You never did answer my question. Did you come here to steal from me?"

"No, friend. I came because you answered my call," he said with a smile.

"I'd never heard a Christian man screech like that before. Where the devil did you think you were?"

"I didn't know. I simply fell asleep in a land of lush green, and awoke in a sea of white."

"Mmm—a poet. Winter kills everything . . . ," he said as bloody sputum formed in the corners of his quivering mouth, "but this damned disease."

Tashum glanced at the snow swirling just outside the window. "Hmm, yes . . . winter."

Seasons were not a new concept for Tashum. His seasons, the seasons of his island, were punctuated by great storms, violent wind and rain, but never was the landscape virtually suffocated beneath a cold white blanket.

By morning Tashum was wearing the sensible clothing of his new best friend—his Dutch benefactor. And three nights later the angel committed the neatly wrapped body of Van Spinoza Huidekooper into the grave already occupied by his wife. The man had truly loved his wife. Let them spend eternity together he thought as he smoothed the mix of dirt and snow with the soles of his fine leather boot. He stood back gazing at the headstones of two generations planted within the walls of this courtyard. Huidekooper in his final hours had told Tashum how much he loved his wife and children and regretted bitterly bringing them to this godforsaken land only ten months before the plague arrived at their doorstep. For a brief moment, Tashum considered digging up the rest of the Huidekooper family and planting them all together. Perhaps another night. The early morning chirp of barn swallows drove him from the predawn back into the manor house.

Tashum remained in the manor house, a prisoner of cold and snow, until one day everywhere he looked, green was replacing white. The landscape had been washed clean by spring rains.

He had settled in, in of doors, a first for him. The home and trappings of the country squire suited him very well. Some days he would duck through the fingers of painful sunlight flooding the great hall, to stand in a special place where he could see the beautifully painted portraits of over-dressed people striking poetic poses. He learned about fashion and color scheme from these images. He envisioned his own face superimposed over that of his benefactor. Frozen in oil as they were, he sought to emulate the strength through arrogance he recognized in these immortal's facial expressions and delicate body language. Never had loneliness of station been indicated by so many revealing artifacts.

Daylight was reserved for reading the thoughts of these men whose ideas had been machine printed and handwritten on the pages of books that lived in the Huidekooper library. Added up, they numbered more than five hundred.

The Bible was very troublesome for an angel who had missed most of the events described between its covers. Even aided by *Sir Thomas Elyot's English Dictionary* the wordage seemed ambiguous. The text written in the form of stories outlined very dire consequences for believers and nonbelievers alike if the book's instructions were not followed to the letter. He searched the text for similarities and reasoned that it wasn't out of the question that his Voice and their God could be one and the same; mysterious existence created the most common bond. The stories describing the violent deeds of angels seemed unlikely, but he couldn't deny the acute similarities in the individual description; Michael could be Timean with a change of name. Likewise, Lilith was probably Sofia, and Uriel was no doubt Trybar. Satan and the idea of hell troubled him greatly. Mainly because it appeared that heaven couldn't exist without hell, and he knew of no such place. Initially he reasoned that good and evil were intangible, merely descriptive words of one's actions. Later, he would discover evil to be a very real concept, and upon further reflection, he wondered if he weren't already in hell. Tashum was elated and disappointed not to find himself or Paladin on the roster of God's messengers and outraged to read the most important statement he had ever made was attributed to someone unknown to him. Tashum's infamous declaration that "The sons of fire should not stand subservient to the sons of clay" had been more than words lifted from his mouth. It was a belief that reshaped him, that split heaven and led to his fall from grace. The great book described the legions of angels of Light and their hierarchy in an invisible world. He had no memory of such order and importance of station. When he read about the Fallen Angels he realized the book had not been written from their point of view. He wondered if his fallen brothers and sisters shared his sense of abandonment. Were they hidden from mankind in fortresses of their own? Were they truly joined in a force of evil? And if so, why was he not included in the band of rebels? Tashum read the Bible three more times before he put it away. Each reading created more questions than were answered. He elected to search for his own truths.

Eventually, it was curiosity as much as loneliness that drove him outside and soon he developed a routine of exploring his surrounding countryside by cover of night. His new home sat on a twenty-acre plot of recently purchased woodlands that overlooked the Stour River. The small thatched village of Christ Church was the nearest town. Christ Church lay to the south, the bustling port city of Poole to the west, and to the north was the Salisbury plain and the Druid's monument of Stonehenge. He became a phantom of the dales and fells, crossing the moors like invisible wind. A master of shadow and the silent ways, Tashum would eavesdrop on his neighbors with regularity. He encountered caped figures lurking in the shadows, some were thieving highwaymen, but most were drunkards just trying to make their way home unnoticed. Along the Cornish shore he watched smugglers row their contraband ashore, where it was loaded onto carts pulled by horses. Seeing horses enslaved to labor made Paladin's predictions ring true. But to his constant disappointment, he never crossed paths with a being like himself.

Four months had passed quickly. Already the autumn was leeching the green from the leaves and the surrounding landscape.

Inside the Huidekooper house, off the kitchen in the hallway, Tashum had discovered a small trapdoor covered over by a crude wool woven rug. A ladder hung down into a small sanctuary, an elongated secret room. He envisioned the Heidekooper family hiding there in times of danger. This place became his favorite morning study, due to its only feature: an oval-shaped stained-glass window placed high on the wall. During daylight hours, sunlight was diffused amber through painted panes of glass, casting a golden glow that was enhanced by the white sand particles used in the white plastered walls.

He would spend the morning hours staring at the depiction. The brilliant painted image of the winged angel descending through a pyramid of golden light. The effect was best at sunrise because the level sun drove its radiance square against the window. He found that stirring up dust to be caught and refracted in the light was an interesting addition to the show. By noon, the magic was over, and he would fill the remainder of the day in the library, or napping.

This day seemed no exception. Tashum climbed down the hand-hewn ladder into his little sanctuary. It was early and it was quite dark, which for him posed little problem. He sat on the stone ledge that stood out from the building's foundation, waiting for the light to come shinning through the window.

"From animal skins to silk. That's quite the evolutionary leap, Tashum."

Tashum's head jerked, his eyes focused down to small beams searching the gloom for the familiar voice.

"Don't strain your eyes. You're as blind to me as your benefactor, Herr Huidekooper, was to you."

"Mayhem?" he questioned softly, his head slowly turning, searching. "It is you, isn't it?"

"Listen to you. Your voice is so English, and your dress so gentrified. You even move like them." Mayhem's translucent image rippled through the dark. He came from the far wall, floated over the stone floor, and landed next to Tashum. He bent at the waist to be face to face with his brother. "This place suites you, Tashum."

"I feel your presence, but I cannot see you."

"The Bible speaks of visible and invisible worlds, does it not?"

"Yes! Come to me in the visible world, show thouself, lest thou be misconstrued as something less grand," replied Tashum in a daring tone.

"But, Tashum, you already know me. You know my former glory."

"Former glory? You're in the invisible world. How could you be anything less?"

"You need to see for yourself."

"Show me a way home, Mayhem, so I can experience your glory for thyself."

"In time, you'll know my full glory." Mayhem's transparency stood erect. He glanced up and stared at the illuminated window. First rays were diffusing through the stained glass, and the amber light was slowly creeping its way down the wall.

Mayhem's glassy shape levitated twelve feet up the wall to be at eye level with the glowing window.

"What do you see being portrayed in the window?" he said after a brief pause. "What exactly is the Celestial doing?" asked the spirit as he cocked his head, "and how is it happening?"

Tashum looked up, studying the painted angel suspended in the pyramid of light. He had no reference to the face that had been painted by man. Then he noticed three prominently painted orbs securing the three corners of the pyramid. He expanded his concentration to the border of red Latin script— EGO SUM LUMEN PURUS SUM EGO—stretched in an oval around the circumference of the stained glass.

"Well?" teased Mayhem. "Do you not see it?"

Tashum was more interested in Mayhem. His hand reached into the clay ash bin and threw a handful of ashen dust into the air. Gleaming dust particles filled the room and poured down from the ceiling. Suspended by their lightness, they formed and created an outline of Mayhem's angelic shape. Mayhem spread his wings, sending the dust particles swirling away in large circular flight patterns. Tashum was quick to notice the outlined sword held in his left hand and a stump. Mayhem's right hand was missing at the wrist.

"Your hand?" Tashum choked, "What happened to your hand, brother?" Tashum's mind was reeling—there was no imperfection in heaven. "Lost your hand but got your sword back?" He was dumbfounded. "How?"

"Brilliant observation. And you're not a clever lad, Tashum."

Tashum could almost taste the indignation in his tone. "I'm . . . I'm sorry, I didn't mean—"

"Don't humble yourself. Redemption isn't easy, but there are ways."

"If not through redemption, how did you get back into the Light?"

"That would be too easy, I have already given you clues that were denied me," Mayhem said as he leaned closer to the lit window, positioning himself so Tashum would have a flash-quick glimpse of his face.

Tashum's eyes widened at what he saw. Mayhem was scarred and owl-eyed, like himself.

"We all ended up looking like this," Mayhem said with disdain. "It's the mark of the Fall."

Tashum spoke without thinking, "You didn't redeem yourself—"

"Watch your tongue! How I got here is my secret."

"Where are all my brothers and sisters?"

"They're around," he said in a sly way that raised Tashum's short hairs.

Tashum felt a wave of anxiety roll through his mind. A new fear sprung from nowhere. "How exactly did you get the sword of banishment back from Timean?"

Mayhem's expression turned wicked and threatening but he held his tongue and simply turned his head in profile, gazing at the winged angel painted to such glowing perfection: clear skin, radiant blue eyes.

"Mayhem's, please, please help me." His eyes big and round, pleading with the spirit. "I don't understand this world, its stories and legends, please help me. I need your light. Reveal your true self to me, as you would come to a man."

"I don't do such things."

Mayhem's outlined image melted away as gravity settled the dust particles out of the diagonal swath of colored light. He hung there completely invisible to his brother.

"Mayhem, if you will not help me, then deliver a message to Paladin."

"I'm not a messenger."

Tashum saw a slight waver in the stained glass. He jumped to his feet. "You can't leave me here like this! Please!"

After a few minutes, Tashum knew he was alone. He sank back down onto the stone slab, weak with self-pity and the torment of envy. Tashum stared at the stained glass, studying it for meaning. Within two hours the sun's luminous rays had crossed over the roof line, and the room returned to dark ambiance. He had sussed out that the window was a vortex depiction, and the orbs were key to the magic. That he had never read or heard about such an inner-dimensional window only assured him all the more that it was the secret way home. This reaffirmed what Fanny had told him—Paladin knew something of the vortex. Furthermore, Mayhem's dark hints convinced him, the where and how would come to him in time. He found relief in the frustration but hardly satisfaction.

At midday, Tashum rested his eyes. He was stretched prone on the bed he now thought of as his. He heard a sound relatively new to him: a clippity-clop riding on the light breeze. The polyrhythms and soft sound of hoof tapping against cobblestone sent him deeper into his state of relaxation. He rarely drooled when he slept, but today the corners of his mouth were wet. Muted voices stopped his eyelid flutter.

"I thought he was dead. See the *P* painted on the door?"

"'E's grave's been dug but it ain't been filled, is it?"

Tashum's eyes popped open. In a flash he was off the bed, flat against the wall, sliding toward the window.

Through the crack in the shutter, he could see three men standing in the courtyard examining the graves. Two of them wore shiny chest armor and the helmets of the king's army. The third was simply well fed and well dressed.

"I hope he ain't dead in there," quipped the tall guard pointing at the manor.

"Why should you be concerned? We're not grave diggers. We're just here to collect the land," the portly man with an air of power said, looking up from the paper scroll he had taken from his attaché bag.

Tashum's heart sank as he thought of losing this place, his temple of refuge, the window. He seized the moment by pushing open the shutter, and in a commanding voice he shouted from the shadows, "What are you men doing down there?"

All three jumped. One of the soldiers pointed to an open window on the second floor.

"Good God! You scared the wind from us!" said the fat man in a turbulent voice.

"Desecration of the grave deserves a good scare," came Tashum's firm voice from the shuttered window.

"We are not desecrating anything." The man turned to the guards and quietly asked, "Do either of you see anyone up there?" They shook their heads.

Tashum placed another bet, hedged as it were. "Would you like to come in? But for me, the plague's killed all it will here."

The mere mention of plague shook the three mortals.

"I don't think that's at all necessary, but I ask of thee to identify thyself."

Tashum was living in his house, wearing his clothes, and now taking his name. The angel did not want to lie, or tell the truth, so he asked a question in answer to theirs. "Who's missing from the grave that you stand over?"

All three glanced at the awaiting open grave. The fat man's lips read the name carved in the headstone. Looking up he squinted into the sun rising over the ridged roof line. "I'm terribly sorry, Herr Huidekooper, I should have come to your door. We . . . I, mistakenly thought you had died with the other members of your family. We'll take leave of you and your sorrow, sir."

"You don't wish to come in?"

"No, no. I don't think that will be necessary, but for the record, sir, are these your family—"

"You can read! Who do you think they are!" Tashum barked.

"Yes, sorry to bother you, sir." He raised his hand. With a wave of his fingers, the guards followed him out of the courtyard.

Through the small slit in the shutter, Tashum strained to watch their departure. When they disappeared through the courtyard gate, he turned and bolted out of the room.

From an narrow archer's slit in the towered staircase Tashum watched the three men mount their horses. He still thought it incredible that men had domesticated creatures three times their size to be such loyal servants. And what beautiful creatures they were, Fanny's descriptions were mere stick drawings measured against the real thing.

When the horsemen clippity-clopped back over the rise and disappeared from sight, Tashum realized they had taken his voice without face value and considered him a man. Those men had been fooled because they expected him to be a man and could not fathom anything beyond that. Perhaps that was why there was no mention of vampires in the Bible. Tashum wondered how much mythology and reality moved back and forth before the eyes of these self-centered humans. He hadn't planned the deception, he merely played along with those incapable of understanding anything other than reflections of themselves. So be it.

Tashum hurried into the small chamber that served as the master's office. He scoured the documents and discovered a new word: *slavery*. The Huidekooper family business centered on the importation of African slaves to the new world. He poured over bills of lading, letters of intent and introduction, ship charters, and ship design. He now had sailing vessels, ships that would carry him to Paladin's world. For him *slavery* was just a new word, but Africa was a place, indeed, the very last place where Paladin had been seen.

With his morale lifted he filled the house with candles and lit her seven fireplaces. He powdered his face and dressed himself in the finest clothes of his wardrobe. From room to room he danced, kicking up his feet to the whistled tune of a sea shanty. In the great hall, a suit of armor stood in for a dance partner. To give the tin man life he put a candle inside the chestplate. Round and round he skipped. Metal arms and legs flailed, clanked, and moaned, crashing into everything they came in contact with until they tumbled over, drunk with joy. The armor landed facedown, torso crossing Tashum's legs.

Tashum, up on elbows, lay there watching the hot liquid paraffin seep out through metal seams in short streams that quickly froze to the metallic skin of his lifeless dancing partner. Gazing at the bulky exoskeleton, his thoughts drifted back, remembering beetles, crab, and lobster, Somers Island . . .

One year later, the family business ran hard aground on Tashum's maiden voyage to Africa's Ivory coast. From the outset the ship's design didn't make sense. He complained about the claustrophobic living conditions aboard ship for the slaves and argued against the need for leg iron restraints. The captain of the converted German frigate *Tulpe* assured him that once they had picked up their live cargo, it would all make sense, even to a blind man. Tashum hated being patronized, but it was the price he knew he must pay to play this role of human.

The first night in the Niger River delta, he went ashore and saw them— hundreds of them, huddled and chained together, not the monkey-men he'd been promised. No, to his horror, these were man, woman, and child torn from God's paradise. Their fear and grief hung heavy in the air. It engulfed and overwhelmed him, dropped him to his knees, and filled his eyes full of tears. For a dizzied moment, he was falling through the sky again with his brothers. He and his brothers had themselves stood proud not to become slaves to mankind.

As reality chimed its song of utter misery, he leaped to his feet. Quoting words from their own great book, Tashum demanded the immediate release of God's children. His demands echoed in the lobes of deaf ears. He was firmly reminded he had only contracted to purchase 175 of the 1,200 black skins imprisoned within the compound. Furthermore, if released, they would just be captured again and sold to the next ship. The blind man was urged to complete his end of the bargain. Tashum snapped when asked if he wished to be part of the selection process.

His actions spoke brighter than his words. Under cover of darkness, Tashum swam from ship to ship, setting each ablaze before the human cargo could be loaded the next morning. He returned to shore and kept out of sight as the captain and crew stumbled out of the brothel to witness flames licking up into the ship's standing rigging. The fire quickly spread through the *Tulpe*'s wooden hull. The moans and cries of stranded sailors rose above the fire's roar.

By daybreak, Tashum and his 175 black-skinned river people from the Gwari, Nupe, Igala, and Ibo tribes had followed the Niger River, marching twenty miles north of the slave encampment. At an opportune time, Tashum slipped away from the arguing chiefs to find safety in the hollowed trunk of a mangrove tree.

That night, he was on his own again. A simple thank-you gift was dangling from the branch outside the entrance to his hiding place. He took the beaded necklace and looked closely at the small charm attached to it. The inch-long figurine was very clearly an effigy of a tattooed man. Then he noticed the flesh tone makeup had washed off his hands during the exodus, revealing his own tattooed skin. He couldn't help but wonder if he was related to the original tattooed man. He placed the necklace around his neck. Not sure where to go he climbed a neighboring mangrove thick with foliage. Atop the lush canopy, he stretched out in a bed of broad leaves. Overhead, the was a sky filled from horizon to horizon with twinkling stars set against the blackness of infinity. The sailor's lamentations echoed in his ears, but their grief was shallow compared to the sorrow of the enslaved. Slavery— what a hideous concept. Surely the blinded eyes of his benefactor never witnessed the misery of his wicked business. And just as surely, Spinoza Huidekooper must have known where his wealth came from. Did that make him an evil man? Tashum wasn't sure. He lay there content, believing he had done the right thing, and could only hope that during the process he had somehow lifted a curse from his benefactor's name, a man he had uniquely admired, until now.

CHAPTER NINE

Lost Years

When next Tashum stood at the gates of the Huidekooper manor it marked the end of his two-hundred-year walkabout. He felt as run down and tired as the house he had left unattended. He had gambled his way around the circumference of the Mediterranean basin. On his side trips, he journeyed to the far northern reaches of Russia and the southern tip of India. From the mountain ranges of the Himalayas and eastward to the strait of Gibraltar. Upon his return to Britain, the duke of Wellington was the most popular man in England, and Bonaparte had been reduced to a jester on the run. Tashum had crossed the bloody battlefields that dotted Europe. He saw the broken bodies and knew that the glory of war left a ghastly odor upon fields that once smelled of sweet clover. This disappointment in man's warring habits and their thirst for destruction was only the dessert course to a meal that had left a bad taste.

Africa had provided little in his search for Paladin. At a distance, he saw the fortress situated on the rocky Moroccan coast. Its shape and color fit Fanny's description of the place where she had spent time with Paladin. But he could never be sure, as there were many such fortresses situated along the coastline. And at the time of his visit, the fort was being fought over by warring Berber tribes. It was battle weary, under siege, and he was denied access.

He journeyed eastward, crossing great barren deserts and grass-covered plateaus to the lands of biblical description. For Tashum, life in Jerusalem was no more enlightened than what he found in Mecca or would later find at the Vatican. In these spiritual centers, he saw men who put themselves on pedestals above their brethren. These men were given special treatment because they claimed to have access to God's ear and could speak for God, but none of them had a God-given ability to create miracles or even produce an angel. Tashum wanted miracles. He wanted man to put him in touch with angels.

Stories regarding Angels of the Light and the Fallen were plentiful, but they were always told in the past tense. He questioned countless dozens of men who claimed to have met or seen angels. With few exception he found lies in the eyes of the storytellers. There was, however, one story that held his intrigue—the story was more than a hundred years old when it was told to Tashum and impossible to verify.

For years he had heard rumors claiming Joan of Arc had not been burned at the stake but had been whisked out of France and neatly tucked away at a monastery, hidden somewhere in the Alps. It was reported she eventually died of consumption at the ripe old age of fifty in the alpine retreat. Tashum never believed the fantastic rumor. He preferred the widely published and printed in Latin account *Thomas de Courcelle's, The Trial and Execution of Joan of Arc*. The trial and execution were very well documented and left little doubt in his mind Joan of Arc, at the age of nineteen, died at Old Market Square in Rouen, France. Her death was caused from being burned at the stake. For him the most fascinating bit about the popular rumor was the names of three new characters: the Black Knight, a Dominican Monk named Paladino, and a convicted heretic. The heretic claimed he was an angel named Timean. Timean swore he guided Joan of Arc through her battles and had come to Earth to save her. At Joan's trial during a closed session, it was reported that Timean testified on her behalf. He demanded her immediate release and was imprisoned himself. In the story he simply disappeared and presumably went back to heaven. Meanwhile, with the help of the French dauphin Charles, the other two characters, Paladino and the Black Knight, smuggled Joan out of the dungeon and delivered her to the monastery in the Alps. They were paid handsomely by supporters of the future king of France, Charles VII. They vanished into legend after that.

After hearing the tale, Tashum, often weighed the odds of chance and coincidence. He knew a fallen angel, Paladin. He also knew an angel of the Light, named Timean. Was it possible the Black Knight was one and the same from Fanny's stories?

Tashum concluded that it must be a unique coincidence that these names had been chosen at random; credence given to anything beyond that was wishful thinking.

Occasionally, he encountered rumors of vampires and always listened for a description of Fanny or Dickey. The stories were widespread and sometimes simultaneous in occurrence. He was convinced there were many such aberrations of nature. Vampires had never been authenticated and were seemingly invented by authors for nightmarish entertainment. Mostly useless tales, they rarely attempted to chronicle documented accounts or disengage from the fantastic. In 1897, regarding the novel *Dracula*, a critic for *Punch* wrote

> It is a pity that Mr. Bram Stoker was not content to employ such supernatural anti-vampire receipts as his wildest imagination might have invented without rashly venturing on a domain where angels fear to tread.

Occasionally, small hints could be discerned by reading between the lines, but the stories and novels never answered with any real satisfaction whether vampirism was a physiological condition or something measured in purely metaphysical proportions. Science was spilt on the issue of their very existence until the latter half of the nineteenth century, when it was generally accepted that vampires, with rare exception, did not exist. The subject of vampires was constantly reopened with each new discovery in the blood sciences.

By the early 1800s, English obstetrician James Blundell had with great success revived the practice of blood transfusion from healthy human to anemic patients. This idea wasn't new, but experimentation was ghastly and lent support to those in the scientific community interested in vampirism, which in turn led to debate.

Earlier in 1665, through correspondence, Tashum had discouraged physician Richard Lord from transfusing lamb's blood into the veins of a man institutionalized for insanity. Lord's proposal was widely posted, and he refused Tashum's objection, but he did accept Tashum's idea of using silver tubes as opposed to his traditional quill for the puncture process. That the man remained quite mad was a mild disappointment for Dr. Lord. For Tashum, that the patient even survived the cross cut of animal blood was a bewildering success. Tashum sensed instinctively that each species held its own set of keys and locks for the continuation of its own kind. Of course, evolution pointed out nature's exceptions. Fanny and Dickey could conceivably live off the blood of most mammals and birds, but they were aberrations of nature, something far beyond the realm of cross-breeding. Fanny had once been human. She might carry over the species' propensity to proliferate, which would account for the far-flung rumors and supposed evidence of vampiric activity beyond the ability and appetite of his two stepchildren.

Over time measured in the unremitting course of two centuries, these thoughts, these worries, would torment Tashum, buried, perhaps, under layers of his own needs and desires, but there nonetheless. Lurking in the back of his mind, a single image would continue to haunt and beguile him above all others: Fanny's treacherous and lovely face.

CHAPTER TEN

Information Age

Reacting to your hunger is not enough, Victor," Dickey said as he scanned the near empty London street. "When you've been alive as long as Fanny and I, you'll understand that just feeding becomes boring after awhile. A little ritual or playacting adds a bit of spice to the game. It's hard to keep interested otherwise."

"I'm sick of rules, dude." Victor's gloved fingers slicked back his hair. His thin black-leather-clad figure absorbed more light than it reflected. He struck a pose, arms crossed, leaning up against the red telephone kiosk that served as their temporary observation post. "Why didn't you make someone else immortal, if you wanted 'em to play stupid games?"

"Immoral and immortal. That's my godforsaken Victor." Dickey's eyes grew warm. "My American cowboy." He stroked the younger man's sleek jaw.

Victor stepped away. "I never punched no cows." Strikingly handsome, almost effeminately beautiful, the young vampire had a model's face: high, defined cheekbones, a wide mouth protecting the perfect smile, and very unique feature, the eyes of an owl. Tonight his eyes were thinly disguised by wraparound sunglasses. He accented his troubled teen aura with a black leather jacket jangling with chrome over tight black leather pants stuffed into biker's boots. Beauty and terror, an irresistible combination for Dickey. The elder sighed. "Besides, you remind me of someone from a long, long time ago."

"Who, not that bloody angel you're always goin' on about?"

Dickey lifted his shoulders and gently smiled.

Victor spit into the street. "If you wanted an angel, why didn't you shag someone from a bleedin' monastery—make 'em immortal?"

"I wanted you, Victor." He teased, "Didn't I?"

"The day you show me a fuckin' angel is the day I believe your little fairy tale."

Dickey chuckled. "Angels are a bit like honest men, very difficult to spot, and even then you don't believe it half the time."

"Yeah, well, if I don't feed soon, I'm gonna shag some bobby and suck him dry right in the street."

"Patience, lad." Dickey patted his arm. "That's one rule I don't want you ever to forget. The last thing we need is to have the coppers looking for us. We'll . . ." He stopped, smiled, and pointed as he spied a prostitute across the way. "We'll finish this later." He nodded to Victor.

Victor returned the nod and was absorbed into the blackness of the night. Dickey moved up the street, walking slowly toward her, keeping the hunger out of his manner.

"Beautiful, aren't they?" he said when he reached her side.

The woman turned her silent gaze from the spangled night sky to the thinset, rather ordinary fellow who had approached from out of nowhere.

"The stars, I mean," he added.

"Where'd yee come from?" She said in a thick Edinburgh accent.

He smiled and gestured, "I saw you from across the way." He continued, as he lit a cigarette: "The Greeks say that the stars were created when a goddess sprayed her breast milk across the heavens."

With a clink, his lighter lid shut, killing the flame. He glanced at her through a smoky cloud, his gaze moving down the lines of her gaunt cheeks to the smooth surface of her neck and came to linger on the rise and fall of her small, high breasts giving shape to a cheap silver-colored blouse.

"Breast milk, ye say?" she said.

"No, not me dear. It's what the Greeks say."

She blinked slowly, unimpressed with his overly ordinary appearance, his Bogart-lipped cigarette and his wrinkled cream-colored suit coat over a tatty shirt and stained tie.

"I fancy the diamond theory myself," she quipped.

A bulky London taxi rumbled past them. Its headlamps washed across Victor standing in the shadows behind her.

"Are you working, love?" Dickey asked.

Her stomach growled loudly, and she leaned lightly against a parked car. "Truth to tell, I'm a wee bit hungry."

Dickey's eyebrows rose with interest. "Ah, what a coincidence," he finished with a wide grin.

He took the woman by the arm before her instincts warned against it. He led her up the street. Dickey's nod was imperceptible as they passed Victor, now slumped against a brick facade. A moment later, Victor flipped his cigarette stub into the street and followed the pair at a distance.

"Shit," he muttered. "Another fuckin' hooker."

Dim blue light drifted through hundreds of unwashed windows in the abandoned factory. The eerie light brought a wan shape to overturned work tables and hulking World War II–era machinery, partly dismantled, covered in dust and grease. Marble-sized ball bearings lay scattered across the littered floor.

From somewhere deep in the cavernous building erupted a series of huffing, seething moans. Two shadowed figures were entwined among broken crates and litter.

Dickey's muscular body kneaded and pressed into the slight woman who worked mechanically at first against his pounding grunts, ignoring his theatrical shouts of building orgasmic pleasure that rose and sang among the high rafters of the factory.

The woman's eyes suddenly grew wide, lips trembled, so surprised that such powerful currents surged out of her Milquetoast client.

Dickey thrust her roughly against a wall, knocking a gasp from her mouth as his stout hips raised her up and up. One scuffed white heel fell from her foot to the floor. Then at the brink of ecstasy he reared back, now a medieval monster, his neck thick, his chest expanding and his mouth sank to her throat.

His raging growl of fantastic pleasure grew louder and more ferocious as he tore at her flesh, eating through the skin and tendons until he found the thick, rich artery that exploded with blood. The woman writhed and screamed in his iron clutch, feet kicking, fingers tightening in his hair, fighting his animalistic onslaught.

He reared back again, his mouth painted in wide swaths of runny red fluid and bits of tissue, her naked breasts awash in dark liquid. With a final howling cry he lunged at her again, drinking in her hot, lavish blood. He tasted its desperate, frightened life, her deep, thudding heart. He pressed his face into the fist-sized wound and sucked, stopping only to breathe. It ended with a broken sigh. Her body sagged in his arms, and he let her fall to the floor.

A figure leaped out of the shadows. "Gimme some a that," Victor cried, shoving Dickey aside.

"Victor," Dickey said, sprawling on the floor. "Mind your manners."

"Fuck manners," Victor mumbled. The younger vampire stooped over the dying woman, picked her limp body up into his arms, raised her above his head and buried his face into the gapping wound.

Dickey sat back against a large crate. From his trouser pocket he produced a small plastic-wrapped sponge. He was already remarkably clean in the aftermath of such a gruesome act. He ran the damp sponge over his face and hands with feline persistence until he was squeaky clean.

"You didn't leave me much," Victor said, and dropped her body. She landed at his feet, all bent up, in a pile.

Dickey watched Victor, hungrily licking at the backs of his hands, slurping, cleaning away with his wide tongue the remaining pools. He sat beside the corpse and sucked on each of his fingertips one by one, grinning, saturated, fat-gutted, and sighing.

"Tasty, little bitch," he murmured. "Tastes like vodka."

"And you didn't think you'd like your meal," Dickey said.

"Meal, my ass! I didn't get enough outa her to fill my pecker."

"The night is young, my boy," he said with a smile. "Come lie with me."

"I'm way too wired to take a nap. Yuh got another one of them sponges?"

Dickey tossed his sponge to his partner. "Victor, you need to learn how to concentrate."

"What the fuck's that got to with nappin'?" He put the sponge to the red slick on the lapel of his jacket. "That bitch was drinkin' vodka. That's the only reason yer sleepy."

"If you can't quiet yourself and find your inner stillness, you will never comprehend the tricks I can teach you. . . . You do want to learn, don't you?"

"Aw, fuck—man. Yuh know I hate that meditation shit." Victor ran his fingers through his swept-back hair and let it fall across his face. "I just don't get it, dude."

"Well it's your choice. The only thing I insist—" Dickey was cut off in midsentence.

A hard flash. A blaze of crystal white light.

Spears of solid, pure illumination shot through cracks in boxes and machinery. The two vampires threw hands to their face, eyes wincing in the shock and pain caused by the brilliance.

The epicenter of this sudden solar radiance came from another part of the factory, just beyond a mountain of metal garbage and splintered crates. When Dickey realized he wasn't going to be melted into eternity, he glanced at Victor and began to pick his way through the debris, keeping a hand to his face, blinking, readjusting his blue contact lenses until, after feeling his way around, he came to a place where he could take in the scene.

Victor peered from behind him. Tapped him on the shoulder. "What the fuck is that?"

"That, my boy, is the fairy tale I was telling you about."

"Fuck-oh-dear! You shitin' me—"

Dickey shushed him. They stared with awe at the scene unfolding in the main room of the factory, where a pyramid of living amber light now hovered just off the floor. Each of the three corner points were anchored to the floor by a small red-orange orb. Through the apex of this pyramid came the form of a translucent man-figure descending, as if riding an invisible elevator.

The winged man landed softly on the bottom layer of the pyramid's translucent surface, a being with large transparent wings and a magnificent, equally transparent body. In a whispering unisex voice it stated, "I am pure light am I."

The being then thrust forward with arduous effort, breaking through the walls of the pyramid. The canted walls shattered like sheets of glass. The amber pyramid collapsed in on itself, raining jagged shards, tinkling and breaking, dissipating into thin air before hitting the floor.

The angel's wings shuttered and spasmed as they were sliced into by a blade of sheet light. Wings amputated at the shoulder fell away and melted without a trace before touching the floor. Then a wave of light washed over the luminous being, softly erasing all traces of the celestial costume, leaving in its wake a body filled with skin and flesh.

A naked human, more male than female in physical appearance except for one shocking detail—he had no penis or sex of any kind. He stood before them on quivering newborn legs, unaware that his entrance had been observed.

"Where's his dick?" asked Victor in a whisper.

"They don't need them," he replied while clamping Victor's lips together with his fingers.

The man crouched on the floor, unsteady, seeming to catch his breath and bearings. After a moment, he rose and moved swiftly to a bank of dented metal lockers. He opened the third door from the end and quickly dressed in modern street clothes—a pair of jeans, a shirt, and a waist-length dark leather jacket.

"Dickey, you said the night was young. I want some a that!" Victor whispered, trembling with excitement.

"You'll have your taste, lad. That you will." He pointed in the direction of the angel's trail. "But for now, you just follow him, and don't let him out of your sight."

"Where you goin'?"

"I've got to get a message off."

"Message? To who?"

"To whom, boy. To whom."

"Never mind, I know who you're talkin' 'bout."

The older vampire patted Victor's arm. "Patience, lad."

"That's somethin' I ain't got much of."

He tightened his grip. "If we play our cards right, and if that's what I think it is, we've just hit the lottery *and* the blood bank, all in one fell swoop."

"How you gonna find the sons-a-bitch?"

"He has a special phone number. It doesn't matter where he is."

CHAPTER ELEVEN

Tashum stepped out of an air-conditioned neon-orange taxi and into the glare of the Atlantic City casino. He cut an elegant figure in his white dinner jacket draped over black trousers. A thin black attaché case dangled at his side. His manicured fingers tugged against the jacket lapels straightening his custom padded shoulders. He glanced at his reflection in the casino glass facade.

The hotel loomed above him into the night sky, its vainglorious main entrance belching out tourists and red-jacketed bell boys.

Tashum chuckled thinking how the Puritan settlers of this coast would curse the heavens to see what had become of their brave, moral adventure.

He smirked, taking in the noise of accelerating limousines, the chatter of honeymooners tabulating their losses and intoxicated grandmothers clutching heavy coin purses, making their unsteady way toward tour busses. How Tashum had despised the superstitious and murderous nature of early Puritans. This heartbreak hotel constructed on the former site of their church seemed just reward for the purgative cruelty they inflicted upon their own.

"Gregory?" Tashum said clearing his thoughts. "Are you coming?"

Behind him, a British voice spoke from inside the cab, "Sir, do you have any cash for the fare?" Wynn Gregory smiled apologetically from the back-seat. "I've got nothing smaller than a hundred. Sorry."

"I pay you too much," Tashum said, patting his coat.

"Gentlemen, this ain't a parking lot!" bitched the cab driver, his foot gunning the engine.

"Gregory you have my wallet. Pay the man."

"I nearly forgot." Gregory reached inside his charcoal jacket, his eyes darting about. "It's here somewhere."

"Forgot?" Tashum teased, "You never forget anything."

Tashum's finger tapped against the roof of the cab, counting off the seconds until the cab driver would erupt. Then he glanced back at Gregory, so young when he signed on, but now a man in the middle of his fifties and graying at his temples. Had they been at Oxford instead of the Jersey shore, his butler and aide-de-camp could easily have been taken for a scholar in medieval texts. He more than amused Tashum.

"Got it," he said with a sigh of relief. He pulled out a long black wallet. He pried it open and flipped through the cash inside.

"Come on, guys! Come on, come on!" the driver ranted throwing up his hands, "I'm missing fares left and right!"

Gregory's beseeching glance shot up to his employer. "You only have hundreds as well."

"How much do we owe you?"

"Same as it was the first time, thirty-three eighty five! Thirty-three eighty-five!" He twisted around, eyeballing the displayed bills. "And I ain't got that kind of change, mister!"

Tashum caught the cabby's eyeline and tried to probe his mind but was shut out of the crude oil even before the driver's eye moved. Tashum had grown accustomed to opening up and strolling through people's minds at will. It was an unconscious game. Over the years, he had come across many from this tribe of slightly different humans. However, from their actions he guessed they must think alike. He knew from experience they made great gamblers and poor losers.

"Surely you have proper change," Gregory asked, holding out the bill.

"Fuck you, pal! Gimme my fare!" The flustered driver swung around and snatched the bill from the Englishman's hand. "Get outa my cab!"

Tashum beckoned Gregory out of the car, handing him the case. Then he leaned in and in a flash of movement had the driver's pouch in his hand and began counting out change.

"Hey! Hey!" The driver's chubby face jiggled. He twisted his rotund bulk around and launched himself over the backseat. With one hand, Tashum gripped the man's face, squishing his lips together.

"Muvver vugger! Gooddamn euuu!" the driver bellowed through his pinched lips, squirming wildly as Tashum wrestled him down and stuffed him in the foot well. All the while, Gregory calmly counted out the rest of the change.

"Shall I give him a tip sir?"

"Ten percent," Tashum replied.

When Gregory had finished, Tashum tossed the bag into the front and released the man, letting him flounder about in the backseat.

Tashum shut the door and led Gregory to the entrance of the hotel. "Gregory, in the future, do carry portage fare. Hmm, on second thought, from now on limousines only. And what's with this sudden interest in tipping cabbies? You're English."

"Right sir. It just seems so American."

"Well, it is, and you're not."

A gust of hot summer wind caught the black attaché case in Gregory's hand, turning it first one direction and then another. "That was uncomfortably warm air, wasn't it?"

"Puritans called it devil's breath," Tashum remarked.

"I suppose anything that stirs this humidity is a blessing. It's so oppressive."

"I hadn't noticed."

Gregory tucked the case under one arm as they entered the dazzle of the casino's cavernous main lobby, past the clatter of quarters spilling out of slots, the ding of dollar machines, and the tat-tat-tat of roulette wheels, toward the gold-mirrored door of a private elevator.

The tall, thin attendant in the short jacket eyed them as they approached.

"We're on the list, Marcus," Gregory said in his unruffled London accent. "Mr. Diamond, as you know. And myself."

The young attendant nodded and smiled as he scanned a list of names on a computer screen. He highlighted a code on the screen and turned a key on his console, allowing the elevator doors to slide silently open.

"Good evening, sirs," offered the attendant as they stepped through the portal.

"This should cover our stay," said Gregory, slipping a hundred-dollar bill into the young man's hand.

"You're good for a century. Thanks."

The elevator doors were barely shut before Tashum spoke, "Was that my money or yours?"

"That depends on how well you do," Gregory said playfully.

"In that case, I'd better see the profile of tonight's opponent."

Gregory flipped the latches on the case, which opened to reveal a collection of file folders. He thumbed through them and withdrew one. "Here you are. Wade, Billy-Joe Wade."

Tashum opened the folder and glanced at the large black-and-white photograph of the man, balding, with dark hair cut close to his head. A potato nose. A man-of-the-people grin. Tashum flipped the photo sheet to a page of comprehensive statistics. "You got all this bio-information off the Internet?"

"Frightening, isn't it?" Gregory said with a flat smile.

Tashum's brow raised. "Frankly, yes."

"What sort of strategy will you employ for the CEO of Westin Hawker Petroleum?"

"I use technique, not strategy," Tashum quipped as he flipped through more pages, allowing himself a slight smile. "Strategy is random, changing with condition; technique is constant, regardless of condition."

"Isn't the game really about luck, though?"

"Winning. It's about winning Gregory."

"But you lose all the time . . ."

"You're awfully frisky. Have I sacked you lately?"

Gregory smiled. "Not for," looking at his calendar watch, "four months and six days." He glanced up. "Is it time for another evaluation?"

Tashum shook his head. "If your wit were wine, Gregory, I don't believe it would flow out of the bottle."

"Is the cork in?"

"Point made."

"I take it that's a compliment as well."

The elevator's ascent began to slow.

"You would, Gregory, you would."

Gregory reached up and rubbed briskly at a lump in Tashum's cosmetic cover. "Just a sec, your Avenger mask is in need of a little repair."

"Avenger. That's a bit much." Tashum snapped the file closed and straightened the folds in the red silk pocket square popping out of the breast pocket of his Armani jacket.

Gregory jerked his hand away as the doors whispered open. A moment later they stepped into a dark gaming room high above the streets of Atlantic City. Gregory whispered a few words to the room manager, and they were led past a bank of huge windows that looked out over the flicker of city lights. They stopped at a large round table under a soft white light in the center of the quiet room.

"Mr. Wade will join you in a few moments," the manager said.

"Very well," Tashum said, seating himself and running his palms over the green felt of the tabletop. "This is new. It was blue last year."

"Will there be anything else?" Gregory asked.

"No. Try not to lose too much downstairs," he added with a grin. "Check in from time to time, and a few treats wouldn't hurt. Oh, do keep your cell phone on."

Gregory jotted down a few lines in his daily reminder book. "Treats?" he said, thinking out loud. "Anything in particular, sir?"

"You know my taste," Tashum said with a smile. "But surprise me."

Gregory nodded. "With pleasure." Then he bid his employer good luck.

Tashum took a cigar from inside his jacket and went through the ritual of lighting it. He let the smoke roll around in his mouth before blowing out a long, slow plume.

In the 489 years since he took leave of his island, now called Bermuda, one thing alone had remained constant in Tashum's life on earth. There was nothing quite as satisfying as the taste of well-turned tobacco, backed by the exclusivity of impunity to the harmful effect of tobacco, which made the ritual that much better.

His potato-nosed opponent entered the room, and Tashum smiled through a low cloud of blue smoke.

Forty-six hours later, the two men were still at the table, obscured in shadows and separated by a tower of poker chips crowning the green felt. All of it on Tashum's side.

On seeing Wynn Gregory enter and stand at the edge of the circle of light, Tashum leaned forward, letting the overhead light wash across his face, a half-smoked cigar and his rumpled suit. "I believe this may be a good time for a short recess."

With a nod from his boss, the Englishman stepped closer.

Billy-Joe Wade possessed a thick-necked pudgy-face and sour frown. With a damp handkerchief, he wiped at sweat around his eyes. "Damn it, Diamond!" he snapped in a west Texas drawl, pointing his fat little finger decorated with a squat diamond ring. "What is this, amateur night? You can't just stop the game now! Not when there's a pant load of my money—"

"Your money!" Another nimbus cloud uncoiled across the table. "You mean your company's money, don't you?" Tashum grinned. "I'll forgive the outburst—you have a right to be nervous. It's a lot for you to lose."

Billy-Joe sat back, flushed and uncertain, looking first to Gregory and then around at the shadows as if searching the darkness for some reply. With shaky hands he lit a cigarette. "You want a break, take it."

Tashum took a long, contented draw on the Havana stub, and his eyes turned toward Gregory.

"Did you bring me a treat?"

"Not exactly." The Englishman pulled a stiff white envelope from the interior of his jacket. "This telex just came in over the ship-to-shore, marked urgent."

"From whom?"

"It's just postmarked London."

"Hmm, Potter."

Tashum settled back in his comfortable oxblood leather chair. Only the glowing coal of his cigar remained in the circle of overhead light. "My eyes are tired. If it's not too personal, read it to me. I'm sure my generous friend won't mind."

"Whatever it takes to get this game goin'," moaned the Texan.

Tashum's perfect smile appeared in the shadow.

Gregory tugged a finger across the seal of the envelope, unfolded the sheet inside and read, *"I've seen a winged man and have certain round objects I'm sure you're interested in obtaining. Look forward to seeing you soon. Love and kisses, Dickey."* Gregory looked up. "The word *soon* is underlined."

Tashum felt an odd sensation, a cool breath brushed across his neck.

You wanted help, this is your chance. Take it!

The white of his smile vanished, followed by a sudden exhalation of cigar smoke. It was Mayhem's voice, Tashum was sure of it. He looked left and right for any trace of the spirit.

No need to look alarmed. You know it's me.

Am I supposed to be thrilled? replied Tashum's inner dialog.

Gregory cleared his throat and asked quietly, "I don't understand the urgency. It sounds rather silly."

"No, it's not silly. We leave immediately for London." Tashum rose from the table.

At this the Texan awoke angrily from his astonishment. "Wh-what are you doing?"

Tashum thought he saw a slight distortion above the game table.

"Hey, come on now, you gotta give me a chance, for Chrissakes!"

Mayhem's translucent image was sitting on the edge of the table. He bent down looking at the Texan's cards held in a quivering hand. The spirit then whispered into the Texan's ear, "You haven't got a chance in hell. Let him go." The Texan gazed at Tashum, wondering where the voice came from.

Tashum caught the Texan's gaze. He thrust a pod of energy into the man's brain and heard a thunderclap of fear. *If I walk out of here a loser, I'm dead. If I win, I swear I won't ever step inside a casino again, please God.*

Tashum glanced at the gambler's sparkling diamond. "Would you rather play your last card, or simply trade the pot for that ring on your pinkie?"

Billy-Joe wheezed. "My goddamn ring for the pot? What is this, a joke?" He chuckled. "It's a nice ring, but Jesus—look how much money is out there."

"They're only poker chips. A two carat *D* flawless Russian cut stone interests me much more."

"You got a deal, mister." Without further discussion, the Texan wrestled the ring over two red knuckles and tossed it to him.

Tashum slipped the ring into his pocket without a glance. He gestured at the pile of poker chips. "Take them, they're yours."

"That's it? We play for nearly two days straight, and it ends like this?" the Texan said, raking the chips to his side of the table. "Anytime."

Tashum leaned across the table. "One other thing, when you beg heaven for a second chance, it might be wise to honor the wager."

The man's face emptied of color. He nodded weakly.

Tashum reached into his jacket, pulled out a small case, and handed a metallic business card to the Texan. "But when you decide to game again, leave a message at this number."

"Diamond, you're one strange feller," he said, accepting Tashum's card.

Tashum took his extended hand, gently turned it over, and examined the lifeline cut deep in the blotchy pink skin, stretched across a fatty palm. "Stress kills," he said, releasing the man's hand.

"That's what Doc Benson told me, but he's a doctor, I ain't sure about you."

"No, probably not," Tashum spun and grabbed Gregory by the arm, spewing out commands as they headed for the elevator.

"Now, you have a lot to do," he said to Gregory. "I want my crew assembled and *Lofty Vision* made ready. Call ahead and have the Kensington house opened, aired out, and filled with flowers. Make them all orange—and glorious. Oh, yes, Hamley Potter must be notified of our passage."

When the elevator reached the lobby floor, Tashum was still thinking of chores for his manservant. He grabbed his arm gently and guided him toward the casino's main entrance.

If Dickey was up to no good, at least his lures were showing improvement, thought Tashum. And Mayhem, silent for so long, for whatever reason, seemed now willing to point the way home. That, too, was improvement.

Mayhem, struck a stoic pose on the casino's rooftop. His arms were crossed, held in cocoon of long, pliable wings that wrapped tightly around his shape. From his perch, he watched Tashum and Gregory hail a taxicab. His lips curled into smile as massive wings unfurled and lifted him into flight.

The good ship *Lofty Vision* was a long, sleek vessel of Italian design equipped for voyages that might last days or months, depending on the destination Tashum dictated to his crew. Registered in Bermuda, she sailed under a Union Jack against a red field, but she hadn't been to the island in donkey's years.

Her sharp prow sliced effortlessly through the dark Atlantic, leaving the New Jersey shore in her wake. She would make passage across four thousand miles of open sea before her next landfall at Poole Harbour, on the south coast of England.

Tashum loved standing on the ship's bridge, the cool sea breeze pressed against his face. He took a final deep breath, then crossed the threshold and entered the bridge through a side door. The interior of her operations room was outfitted with the latest in electronic communications gear, radar, sonar sounding equipment, satellite weather tracking systems, cellular phone tracking devices, an array of auto pilot technology, and more.

The officers in crisp military type uniforms snapped to attention when he appeared.

"Good evening, gentlemen," Tashum said with an air of command.

He moved swiftly toward the helmsman. Tashum gazed at the only ancient navigation tool onboard: a compass. Then his intense gaze went to the broad skylight, getting a fix on the position of the stars and moon.

After glancing quickly at a simple wristwatch he said, "In four minutes, change our course . . . ," he paused, looking at the compass needle, swift calculations running in his mind, "ten degrees north by northeast. Maintain that heading for three hours at our present speed and we'll pick up valuable time."

"Aye, aye, sir," answered the helmsmen in an accent from the north of England.

Tashum turned to the communications officer, an American with closely cropped blond hair.

"I'd like to see today's closing figures on the Japanese gem market."

"Yes, sir," the American replied, "I'll put them up on the monitor in your cabin right away."

"No rush." Tashum nodded, searching their faces, then moved toward the door. "All right then, that's all for now. Good night, and thank you, gentlemen."

When he had gone, the communications officer removed his cap and ran the back of his hand across his hairline.

"Tell me it's just not me, he is strange, right?" He looked at his mates for confirmation.

The sonar man looked up, green light reflecting on his face from the scope.

"Strange? That's putting it mildly," he said in a low voice. "I mean he's got more electronics onboard this rig than most war ships I've been on. Not to mention this crew and our training—and still he takes his bearing from the stars. Go figure."

The helmsmen eyed the other two, his face sharp and unmoved.

"He's also got keen hearing, and more money than God, so put a cork in it."

"I was just curious, that's all," said the sonar man, putting his cap back on. "But have any of you guys ever seen him on deck during the day?"

"I told you to drop it!"

Ironically, Tashum was just as mystified by his inability to probe the sonar man's thoughts. He hired him for that reason only, to study. But after five years Tashum was no closer to understanding this slight genetic difference than he was the first time he had encountered Riggett onboard the good ship *Merciful*, his first voyage.

Outside, Tashum stood at the rail, once again enjoying the cool, breeze on his face. From a pocket, he withdrew the note from Dickey. *Seen a winged man*—after all these years . . .

He considered the possibility of an elaborate hoax. But he had to know, and he was willingly bound to respond to such tips. He was encouraged by Mayhem's presence and smiled with the possibility it could be real. He withdrew a cigar from an inner pocket, then took his time igniting the tip. In a moment smoke twisted and unfurled from his mouth, dispersing quickly in the wind as did his thoughts.

Fanny, Dickey. Stranded as they were on that lush green spit of sand, it hadn't been all bad. Along with the terror came family. Fanny and Dickey also brought the world to him, and in part had taken him to the world of wondrous invention.

Over the intervening centuries, while the vampires cavorted with their victims on this continent and that, Tashum's quest alternated between searching for signs of Paladin and discovering a tangible understanding of how his blood could have physiologically changed Fanny and Dickey. Their needful bodies seemed to have lost the ability to generate their own new blood cells. The secrets of his blood had given them a fragile immortality and afflicted them with the same condition that kept him a prisoner of darkness. Tashum recognized one last draw. It struck him that his time on Earth may be as short as the cigar stub, that the final effort to unlock these blood secrets lay with one Shelly Green, M.D.

For the next three days, Tashum studied the young hematologist's résumé. She seemed perfect for what he needed. A detective named Malvern had put together Shelly's bio just before his strange disappearance. Tashum was contemplating his first meeting with Shelly when *Lofty Vision* crossed the fiftieth parallel. This invisible mark put them two hundred miles south west of the Emerald Isle and making good time under clear skies and a smooth sea.

Five hundred miles away in a posh Mayfair office in the heart of London's financial district, Hamley Potter had just finished his brown bag lunch. His wrinkled sixty-year-old hands shook slightly, pushing the half-eaten cucumber sandwich into the bag. With neatnick precision, he dusted breadcrumbs off the highly polished rosewood desk top into an etched brass waste bin. Martha sat in the client's chair across from him, sharing the desk as she had done every noontime for the past thirty-seven years.

Neither cheap nor even frugal, Potter coveted the exclusivity of his private club memberships such as the Hurlingham Club and the affiliations with noteworthy men and women that come attached. His dining table at the Connaught Grill was permanently reserved, as were seasonal box seats for the Royal London Ballet. He rarely lavished his friends or clients with gifts, but when he did, the gifts from Aspreys were charged to his personal account and no doubt valued somewhere between a diamond bauble and a small car. Potter was comfortable with the belief he had earned the spoils of success, which he recognized as being the price of admittance to his position in life.

"Martha, after we've finished lunch, I want you to ring Robert McDonnell. Ask him where we stand in regards to the Chasen billing."

"Ham, I did that this morning. I'm waiting to hear back. Robert said we'll probably be taking this one in the knickers, unless we sue, or unless you're very nice to him and exchange dates for the Brighton condo."

"Hmm, the old stodge said that, did he?"

She nodded. "He needs the condo the weekend of the fifteenth. He wants to trade that weekend for the following, I believe it's the twenty-second."

"Give him the days if it will save us some money. I can't go to Brighton anyway, Tashum is coming back to England."

Martha noticed a blinking light on the sleek desk phone.

"Here, let me get that," she said as she picked up the phone and spoke into it. "Hello? No, this isn't Potter but yes, this is his private line. One moment please." She looked to Potter. "Speak of the devil, it's Tashum."

"Put him on the speakerphone."

She tapped a button on the phone's base and sat back to listen. Potter leaned closer to the phone's mic.

"Potter here."

"Good morning, Potter. Thought I'd give you something to do."

"It's hardly morning and I'm already quite busy."

"Presumably with a cucumber and butter sandwich."

Potter raised a brow looking at his lunch bag. "You couldn't be more wrong. Doctor has me off butter, and I'm bloody well overworked."

"And overpaid. Mostly by me, I might add."

A short pause, as Hamley winked at Martha. "If you didn't get your money's worth, I wouldn't be able to sleep at night."

"If it weren't for the gin, I'm not sure that you would sleep at all."

"Doctor has me off drink as well."

"I can see that's not helped your disposition much."

"Tashum, I really am busy, what can I do for you?"

"I'm quite curious about Malvern. If you haven't heard anything from him by tomorrow, I want you to go see him in person."

Potter's expression drooped. "Tashum, I'm afraid I've got some rather bad news for you." He rubbed his brow. "Malvern is dead."

The speaker box was silent but for static.

"Tashum, are you there?"

"Yes, I heard you." The deep fullness of his voice rattled the speaker box.

"I should tell you it was suicide."

Martha cringed hearing that word.

"I suppose it's big news when a retired Scotland Yard inspector kills himself?" asked Tashum with concern.

"Page seven, *Daily Telegraph*. Did you know him very well?"

"You read that rag, do you?"

"Sometimes," he said softly. "Did you know Malvern well?"

"Apparently not."

"Hmmm." Then his voice firmed up. "I have his report titled *Paladin* here. Perhaps I should just fax it to you."

"Have you looked at it?"

"No, it's addressed to you and it's quite thick."

Martha spoke up, "Ham, the note attached—"

"Oh, that's right," he said, cutting her off, "Martha just reminded me that Malvern included a note stating there was more. What 'more' is, he didn't say. It was all scribbled, practically unintelligible."

"I'd like to see the note with the document. How many pages is it, anyway?"

Martha reached for the packet on a side table.

"Martha's checking now." Potter's eyelids were heavy. His focus drifted to the far wall and lingered on the model of a nineteenth-century sailing ship encased in glass. "It's amazing, isn't it?"

"What?" questioned the angel after a pause. "What's amazing?"

"Nothing really. Just that you're somewhere out there on your yacht and I, from my office here in London, can send a document over the airwaves, that's all."

"You need a holiday, Potter. You'll take one after my visit, I hope."

"That'll be the day."

Martha jotted down a number onto a pad and pushed it across the slick desktop.

"The document is four hundred and seventy-three pages in length."

"Fax the report to me and expect to see me on the fifth."

"Looking forward to it."

"Give my best to Martha. Good-bye, Potter."

Potter broke the line by tapping a button on his desk phone. When his eyes lifted and crossed the rosewood desk, they met Martha's middle-aged, and still hopeful, gaze. "Good Lord, that man wears me out."

"Shall I cancel all of your appointments after the fifth?"

He didn't have to answer, she knew the routine. No telling what she thought of Tashum. Potter wasn't even sure what he thought of his number one client. Even after fifty years Tashum remained an enigma in his life. He never aged—Potter was more than curious, but he was also a gentleman cut from the same bolt of cloth that had produced Gregory, men who *never complained and never explained*. Tashum's physical condition wasn't discussed, and it wasn't a problem. However, Potter would admit that his curiosity burned when Tashum pressed him about training a successor. After all, Potter had faithfully managed Tashum's amassed fortune for half a century. Tashum controlled accounts still collecting interest on investments made during the Industrial Revolution. He had investments in Shakespeare's Globe Theatre, Scottish wool exports, and glassworks in Amsterdam. His bank accounts swelled with wealth from locomotive and weapon-based transactions apparently dating back to the American Revolution and textiles from the age of steam. He had original stock certificates connected to the invention and early development of the automobile. Always in the shadow of great men, Henry Ford was but one of many innovators Tashum supported. Wealth was only a byproduct of the angel's interests. . . .

Yes, Tashum probably did have more money than God. And yes, Potter was content to work a bit harder for this unique client.

Gregory was hunched over the fax machine watching the incoming printed messages drop into the collection basket. He rarely read what came through the machine, but seeing the name *Paladin* referenced so many times piqued his curiosity. He collected the twenty-odd pages in a single swoop and added them to the thick stack off to his left.

Gregory exited the small telecommunications room, entering the unusually wide, dimly lit hallway. He passed several shut doors. For obvious reasons, but unique to luxury yacht design, the owner's stateroom and dayrooms were all windowless and situated deep within the ship's hull. Gregory stopped at a set of double ornately carved wooden doors. After three raps, knuckle against wood, he entered uninvited.

Tashum's stateroom, a suite of three rooms, included a library, where he was seated reading from one of the many books that surrounded him in this lush wooded retreat.

He looked up from the pages of yet another hematological reference tome and eyed the report in Gregory's hand. "Potter was quite right," Tashum muttered, "it is amazing."

"Sorry, was that meant for my ears?" Gregory asked, and handed him the freshly printed stack of faxed pages.

"No, not really. I was thinking out loud."

"Would you like some tea, sir?"

"No, no thank you."

Tashum's eyes hit the report. He was instantly absorbed and didn't notice Gregory's activities, the fluffing up of the two flower arrangements and straightening seams of the floor-to-ceiling drapes that hid an imaginary window. In the brief tour, he dusted the bright work, the highlighted tops and edges of the two overstuffed chairs and the fruitwood coffee table that separated them. Gregory surveyed the room for further problems in perfection. Satisfied, he left quietly.

Tashum's thoughts weren't as content. He hadn't expected miracles from private investigator John Malvern and was incredibly surprised by what he read.

The information was culled from the unpublished diary of a fifteenth-century English clergyman named James Sunderland. Malvern had discovered reference to a monk named Paladino and a heretic named Timean.

Malvern paraphrased the diary and wrote:

In late January of 1431, Henry VI sent an envoy of English theologians to Rouen, France. James Sunderland was among the clergymen. His mission in Rouen, was to interview Joan of Arc and stay witness to her trial. Sunderland describes a clandestine meeting taking place in the castle of Philip Augustus. At this meeting Philip introduced Sunderland to a blind Dominican monk named Paladino. The monk shared his sparkling wine with them and brought forth someone who wanted to give official testimony on behalf of Joan of Arc. He claimed he was the angel who had guided Joan of Arc. He insisted he'd come to Earth as a man and wished an audience with the powers that be. Sunderland described Timean as uniquely different. His eyes were extraordinarily large, with a blue tint, unlike any human eyes Sunderland had ever seen. He displayed a pair of nubs raised on the backs of wide shoulders and claimed his wings attach there. When accused of deception Timean reportedly stabbed himself with a dagger to fully demonstrate his immortality. He, along with Paladino, was quietly jailed on charges of heresy and crimes against the church. Sunderland advised the tribunal on Timean's wizardry, and the consensus was to banish Timean into permanent exile, as they did not know how to dispatch such a demon. Timean was secretly taken to the French coast and placed aboard a Royal caravel. The ship set sail for the Azores never to be seen again. Paladino managed through unknown means to escape from the castle's dungeon and disappeared. I thought it suspicious that such an amazing event should produce no notice in the transcript of Joan of Arc's trial when all the other details were so thoroughly documented. I've been to the library of the Chambre des De'putés and read the original transcript. There is no mention of Timean.

Tashum took Malvern's point perfectly. Timean was Joan of Arc's star witness.

Chirp-chirp, the electronic chirp of a phone broke his concentration. He glanced at his cellular phone sitting on the side table. His gaze drifted back to the report, and he set it aside.

"Hello?" He said into the small device. "Yes. I'm busy. Can't you handle it? Tell the official we'll clear customs in Poole. On second thought, I'll join you in the communications room in a minute."

The rest of Malvern's report, the culmination of four years of steady research, would have to wait. As Tashum walked to the door, he tried to imagine a probable connection between Malvern's suicide and his research on Paladin. No, it must have been something else in Malvern's personal life that had caused him to snap so completely, Tashum concluded. A woman or perhaps money.

Once on the line with British Customs and Emigration, Tashum, quickly smoothed over the problem one of his crew members was having with an expired Brazilian passport. His chef was very upset to learn he couldn't leave the ship until a new passport was issued. He complained he had tickets for the Brazil versus England football match and had to be there. Tashum allowed him to throw a hissy and calmly assured his chef that he would indeed miss the game and be arrested if he left the ship. At Tashum's request, Gregory spent the rest of the day trying to locate a very large screen television that could be delivered to the yacht on the day of the football match.

*   *   *

Gregory joined Tashum on the port side of *Lofty Vision*'s exterior bridge. Tashum lowered the high-tech binoculars.

Gregory could see the twinkle of lights set into the dark outline of a low-lying landscape. "The Swanage Peninsula," he said with pride. "Fantastic."

"Fantastic, might be too strong a word," moaned Tashum, handing the binoculars to Gregory. "Did you find a suitable television screen for Ramon?"

"Yes. Well I think so."

"If you enjoy his talents, I hope you mean yes."

"Hmm, I've ordered the largest screen made," Gregory chuckled. "I used to come down here from London when I was a child. Ever been?"

"Oh, yes, I've been."

"Castle Corfe." Gregory waxed on, immersed in the memory, "I had so much fun playing on the ramparts, fantasizing about days of old, knights in armor, that sort of thing. It's a pity Cromwell blew it up."

Tashum felt a gush of warmth being transduced through Gregory's swirling memories of childhood exuberance. Tashum remembered a similar-looking night. He, too, had memories of Corfe, however, the events occurred before Oliver Cromwell was even born, and they weren't the fantasies of a boy.

"A good memory should stain the mind like good wine," he muttered as he stepped away. Moving forward along the curved rail, he looked across the starboard bow as a shooting star's platinum white tail etched the night sky. He counted the seconds and wondered if his ride back into the Light would be as short?

How true the words of that Parisian poet:

> Time dies in the eyes of a truly interested man.
> Is killed by the words of the poet.
> Murdered by the painter's colours
> Finally assassinated by a true lover's embrace

There was little doubt the endeavors of mankind had helped him pass the hours and years, even unto centuries. Constantly entertained by the built things that came from the minds and hands of humans, it seemed like an endless stream of new invention to Tashum. Had his heavenly brothers learned to construct such wondrous things?

In the latter half of the seventeenth century, Tashum once remarked to Christopher Wren, "Sir, the buildings of your earthly design far outweigh the importance of heavenly creation for one simple reason: heaven's angels won't turn a stone." To which the father of secular architecture replied, "I've had the same problem with my Welsh workers, however, the work still gets done, my good man."

Tashum had been very fond of Sir Christopher Wren. At their first meeting in Paris and later in London they would spend endless nights locked together in architectural debate. He remained fascinated by the scientific mind of the son of a clergyman who secretly was a Freemason and the toast of London society. He had a dangerous weakness for Wren's intellect and would share his secrets, ultimately revealing himself to Wren upon his deathbed. Inevitably, Wren asked about heaven and hell. Tashum could only comfort his friend by telling him that Renaissance painters knew far more about hell than did he. But he was certain heaven could use an architect of Wren's talents. Tashum had a tailored memory; he was standing with Wren gazing at St. Paul's Cathedral, which was bathed in the painter's golden light of a Turner landscape. Of course in reality it was moonlight, and they were quite drunk. Either way, the warm memory of man and his earthly accomplishment was something to smile about.

A gentle shift in the breeze brought a different smile. Fanny was another old weakness. In the years he had traveled fully among mankind, he had watched the dance between men and women. Their ardent display of heat and chill. He laughed whenever he remembered the first time he saw the sex act between the ancients, how he had considered it a kind of laxative. Perhaps it was, after all, for time and time again he had seen a woman's glow transformed after invigorating sex, and the rough edges of the mean man chiseled to a finer point when love and sex worked him into a sleeker being.

As for him, he had never even been tempted again. Not that he hadn't seen women more beautiful, far more loving, and in most respects more desirable than his Fanny. No, the mystery of his love for her was complete. He was as helpless as any mortal when it came to understanding the gravitational pull from the very center of him toward her.

CHAPTER TWELVE

H ello, you've reached the residence of Shelly Green." The recorded American voice continued, "I can't come to the phone right now. Please leave a message after the beep."

Beep . . . "Good morning my dear, this is Robert again, ring me at the hospital when you have a chance. I bet you're in the shower. Lucky soap. I'll try you in a minute."

"Fat chance, Bob! Asshole," echoed a slightly rushed female voice from the adjoining room. "And I want my TV back!"

Shelly stepped through the high doorway into the sitting room, a statuesque long-legged stance, a Stanford girl wrapped in a towel, on a mission. "Where's that damn gum?" she exclaimed as she strolled through the postmodern decor. She stopped at the phone desk. With a tug, the desk drawer was pulled open. The towel wrapped around her head gave way. Long, wet piled hair tumbled out of the towel and down across her face. Then the phone chirped its English ring. Sure it was pest bugging her again—she picked it up and barked into the receiver, "Hello!"

"Shells? It's me," said the soft English female voice, "I was wondering if we could have lunch today?"

"Sorry Fran, I thought you were Bob—lunch, I'd love to—"

"Splendid, I'll see you at Morton's, we can pop round to this new gallery—"

"No-no-no, I meant I'd love to see you but I can't. I'm off to Poole Harbour."

"Poole? Is the navy in?"

"Nothing that exciting," she laughed. "Some eccentric, lives on a boat. He wants some blood work, and he can't come to me, so—"

"Nobody wants blood work, dear. Since when do you go on house calls, or does that bit only apply to rich old codgers?"

"If he's your type, I'll introduce him to you," Shelly smiled. "Trust me, I'm doing this as a favor for an old friend."

"All of your friends are old."

Shelly glanced at the clock. "Oh, shit! Sorry. Got to run."

" 'No shit'? What, you think I'm old?"

"Fran, that's not what I said. I'm late dear, gotta go."

Shelly returned the phone receiver to its zap green cradle. Then she saw it. The stamp-size packet of Nicorette #4 gum was peeking out from under her overstuffed oxblood attaché case.

It was late afternoon in Poole Harbour. A dull gray sky hung over the busy port. *Lofty Vision* wasn't the largest yacht berthed adjacent to *H* pier, but she was the most elegant. Tashum coveted her elegance. If the queen of England had spent a million pounds a year on the well-being of her royal yacht *Britannia*, Tashum would double that amount to keep *Lofty Vision* trim.

Gregory's small desk was crowded with neat stacks of paperwork. He was busy stuffing bonus checks into white envelopes addressed to each of the twenty crew members. Tashum was well known to reward work well done. It was also well known that even if you messed up, you'd receive a bonus check along with the sack. Tashum wasn't sacking anyone as much as he was hedging his bet for any outcome.

Tashum paced the small office. He stopped to look down over Gregory's shoulder. "Good God, man, you're awfully slow at this."

"It's that these sums are so large, they're more in line with severance payment, or winning lottery numbers."

"Large sums of money make you dizzy, don't they?"

"Not really, I don't think profit is a dirty word anymore. I'm just stunned by your generosity, I suppose."

Tashum continued pacing until Gregory had finished running a small damp sponge across the glue on the last envelope and sealed it closed. Tashum looked into Gregory's mind, expecting to hear a mental plea questioning the whereabouts of the envelope addressed to him. But that thought wasn't there. No, Gregory was thinking about bringing Tashum's Bentley out of storage, trying to remember the name of the auto detail shop where he could have it washed and the leather seats soaped in one session.

"Gregory, I know you are quite happy at what you do, but if the world was yours, how would you spend the rest of your life? Give us your wildest dream," he said enthusiastically.

"Anything?"

"Yes, anything."

Gregory paused. His blank expression gave way to sharing his dream.

"Well, sir, I'd rather enjoy having a brass fittings shop. I think possibly in Brighton or California, yes definitely California, Carmel, that would be grand."

"Granted you are brilliant at polishing brass, but surely that's not your wildest dream?"

"Oh, but it is. I've always loved brass."

The simple side of Gregory's character intrigued Tashum. How could someone he'd shown so much to settle for so little? Perhaps Gregory didn't see the offer reflected in the tone of the question from his employer? In any event, Tashum's only wish was to see Gregory happy, and with Tashum's wealth he could play God in that way.

"Well, sir, I'll hand these out to the crew. I know they're all anxious to be ashore."

"How's Ramon reacting to the others going ashore?"

"Well, I haven't seen any bits of glass in my meals, but I'll feel better after they deliver his giant television."

"When is that?"

"Should come sometime tomorrow."

"You may want to eat ashore tonight," Tashum said, teasing.

"Not a bad idea."

"Gregory, remind the crew to stay within two hours' drive of the ship. We may need to make sail on short notice. Oh, and put fresh batteries in the crew's pagers, please."

"I've already seen to it."

Tashum smiled.

Gregory nodded. Tashum held his gaze.

His desire to tell Gregory the truth about himself had been growing with each passing day. All along he wondered if Gregory had simply accepted what he had been told about his employer's skin condition and jaundiced yellow eyes. Years ago, there was a simple lie. Tashum had researched and invented a new tropical disease, a condition called, pigmanocternoitis. Science could explain away most of Tashum's oddities without veering into the fantastic. The cast of their relationship did not require delicate intercourse of a personal nature. For Gregory's own peace of mind he reasoned that Tashum's eccentricities were a product of his enormous wealth. Gregory thought everything in life was balanced. He thought because Tashum had so much wealth in one area, it seemed natural to expect him to be deficient in another part of his life. Gregory was happy to stay as close to the fulcrum as possible—keep it level—keep it simple. More important, Gregory enjoyed his work and felt it was his duty to protect his delicate employer from a world bent on conformity.

The sun had just dipped behind the frontage buildings lining the marina when Gregory headed down the extremely wide gangway that proudly announced the ship's name in large yellow letters appliquéd into the club green canvas sidings.

Gregory noticed the harbor master directing a young woman toward the yacht. He waited at the base of the gangway, thumbing through his pocket agenda book. "Dr. Green, six-thirty," he mumbled.

"Yes, I'm Dr. Green," she said as he looked up at her.

"Hello, I'm Gregory. You'll have to forgive me, I completely forgot that you were coming. Please let me show you aboard."

"That won't be necessary, I'll give Dr. Green the tour," said Tashum in a friendly voice. Gregory followed her raised head and eyeline to Tashum. He was wearing a smoking jacket, standing at the head of the gangway.

"It's Dr. Green, sir."

"Please come aboard, Doctor." Tashum said.

Shelly extended a hand to Gregory, who fumbled the shake.

"It was nice to meet you, Gregory. Now, is that your first or last name?"

"Gregory is my surname. Wynn Gregory."

"It's nice to meet you Wynn. Call me Shelly." She smiled warmly at him, then looked back to Tashum, who was striking a pose leaning against the gangway rail.

Tashum studied her moving anatomy. Natural beauty, an image lifted off a magazine cover. She climbed the gentle incline coming closer to him, now within range of his prying ability.

God he's cute, no doubt rich. I should have packed an overnight bag, sprung from her thoughts and into his mind. He chuckled inwardly.

Tashum extended his hand. She took it. The greeting lingered as he closed his eyes and inhaled her essence. The pheromones danced in his nasal passages. She watched him open his eyes that were disguised by a pair of blue contact lens.

"Dr. Green, I want to thank you for coming so far. My name is Tashum."

"Are you always this dramatic?" slipped out of her mouth as her hand slipped out of his grasp. Tashum smiled at her slight gaffe.

"That's what I like about Americans. You're so direct."

"You mean rude," she smiled. "I'm sorry."

He returned her smile.

"Nice yacht, or is this a small ship?" she said with a glance down *Lofty Vision*'s length.

"That's a gray area. It really depends on whom you're talking to. Let me give you the grand tour. You can decide for yourself," he said with a hand gesture.

After a short tour of the ship, Tashum led her into his private library. He stood back and watched. She was immediately drawn to the walls of hardbound books. She quickly glanced at the nearest section. The books on angels were neatly sorted and sized. Many had bindings printed in Latin and other ancient languages. She recognized John Milton's *Paradise Lost* and Mark Twain's *Letters from Earth* and moved on. Her fingers traced across the volumes of works outlining the written studies of human blood by noted scientists and doctors dating back to William Harvey's theories of blood circulation, published in 1628. By the time her fingers stopped, she was standing before a section dedicated to blood drinkers. Even separated by the width of the room, Tashum could feel the chill run through her. She gathered her thoughts and turned to him. "I don't think you brought me here to talk about mad cow disease," she said lightly.

His smile flattened. "No, I have a serious problem, Doctor."

"Why don't you tell me about it," she said with compassion.

"Doctor, would you please take a seat?"

"Call me Shelly," she said while taking a seat in the wing-back chair. "The doctor thing, gets a little overdone."

"Shelly," he said, smiling.

Tashum had learned to be very careful in the way he revealed himself to those few mortals he had entrusted with his true identity. He untied the robe's silk tie. His muscles flexed, the garment slid off his shoulders and fell to the floor.

Her wide-eyed gaze raced over his body, trying to follow the intricate but faded tattooed patterns that end at the makeup lines on his neck and wrists. Air rushed out of her in a gasp. Finally her eyes stared on his smooth doll-like crotch.

"How do you, ahh—"

"I don't urinate, and sex for all intents and purposes is out of the question."

"But, that's impossible. Is your digestive tract—could you turn around please?"

"And spread them?" his face reflected the indignation in his voice. God, how he dreaded telling humans about his freakish nature. "I have no anus or need of a digestive tract, but you might be interested in these." He bent, twisting at the waist and leaned in toward her. He then took her hand and placed it on his overmuscled back. Her fingers rolled over the raised nubs where his wings had once been attached.

"I had wings once," came out with a slight irony.

"You look organic, how does your body nourish itself?"

"I have a stomach pouch, and a monthly cycle. Each month, I purge the waste of the previous month's meal. It's a rather painful process, but I regurgitate a small black ball. Then I eat a small amount of protein and vegetable matter. My system is very efficient. I don't need much to keep the organic machinery working."

Stone-faced, she caught his gaze. "Incredible," leaked from her mouth. "Is there anything else you can do to blow my mind?"

"Prepare yourself for what hides behind these contact lenses," he warned as his fingers reached up and pried the blue plastic off his yellow eyes.

She sunk deeper into the chair, "Shit. Who are you?"

"I think you mean *what* am I?"

"I'll settle for that."

He bent down and picked up the robe. In the blink of her eye he was dressed, standing across the room, taking a cigar from the rosewood humidor.

"How did he do that?" Her mouth moved but words didn't come out.

Flame erupted from a wooden match struck against the well-worn striking strip. "Do you believe in angels?" he asked, while raising the match to his cigar.

"Angels?" came a stunned reply, "I thought they had wings?"

"As I did once," he said sharply.

"Are you telling me that you're an honest to God angel?"

He kept silent. He had said it once, that was enough. She had eyes, she had touched the nubs.

He tried to hold her gaze but she kept staring at his cigar.

He sensed her hungry need for tobacco. Through billowing smoke he spoke, "Would you care to join me?"

"I'd love a cigar, if that's what you mean."

"Are you sure?" he said as he moved back to her taking the top cigar tray from the humidor with him.

"Look, if you're testing my willpower—"

He raised his hand, "No, it's no test, it's just that I understand it's bloody hard to get off cigarettes. And I don't keep Nicorette gum onboard," he said with a disarming smile.

"Did Hamely Potter tell you that, about my smoking?" she asked as he sat opposite her on the ottoman footrest.

"I know a great deal about you, Shelly Green. That you know Potter is purely coincidental to my interest in you."

She watched him take another cigar from the humidor.

He trimmed the ends and handed it to her.

"I think I'm going to need a drink, too."

"What would you like?"

"Scotch would be great. A double, rocks, or neat."

He struck another match against the bronze bust of Mozart that sat on the fruitwood table off to her left. He swung the flame in front of her face. She moved forward, pushing the cigar into the flame.

Their eyes were locked on one another, not the event.

"Shelly, Potter knows no more about me than he does about you, regarding origins . . . ," he trailed with, "false credentials."

Smoke billowed from her mouth, her eyes grew wide with angst, cheeks blushed red from his words.

"Don't worry, your secret will stay with me as long as mine stay with you." He withdrew the flame.

She lowered the burning cigar, clearly overwhelmed by him, and he knew it.

Tashum needed an edge of dominance. He felt it vital to the working relationship. "Do you still think I'm cute?" he said with a note of humor.

She studied him with eyes dulled by a new revelation of danger. Whatever advantage she had over the alien moments ago was now lost to his intellect. "I see you read minds as well as birth certificates," she said in a defeated tone. "Where do we go from here?"

"I have a very specific question for you." He paused, waiting for her mind to digest what he had fed her and hunger for more. "I need to know how or why my blood kills human bone marrow—"

"What! Tashum, I'm a medical doctor, not a witch doctor."

The amber glow in Tashum's eyes flared brighter at her insult.

"That was rude," she apologized, "I'm sorry—please go on—please."

"I think my blood contains a chemical. I want you to analyze a vile of my blood and isolate the destructive agent."

"May I ask why? And while you're at it, why me?"

"Please, don't cloud your thoughts with questions that you're better off not knowing the answers to. Just do what I ask, and do it quickly and quietly."

"Are you blackmailing me?"

"No, on the contrary, I'm paying you a fortune for your expertise."

She sat back, puffing her cigar the way beginners do. Her mind filled with impossibilities.

Tashum could see the question so clearly burning in her frontal lobe, *He must be giving blood transfusions to humans, but why?*

He sipped his drink.

"Excuse the expression, but aren't angels supposed to have a healing touch?"

"Yes, it's true," he said. "That's the great irony. We have perfect pitch but poisonous blood."

"Pitch? I'm sorry, but I'm not tracking very well with all this—"

She was silenced by his raised hand. "Do you have any cuts or scrapes, any injuries?"

"I knicked my leg shaving."

"Show it to me."

After a moment, she hiked her skirt above the knee. The lamb's wool cloth slid across the surface of youthful skin cracked by clotted blood raised along the eighth-inch-long incision. She glanced up once, as if challenging his sexless state in the face of her slender thigh.

"In my natural form," he straightened with pride, "I am made of liquid light. In my present form," he said, gesturing with his hands, "my light has been frozen, shaped into a rigid skeleton and covered with earthly flesh. My eyes and scarred skin are marks of the Fall. I am nocturnal."

She followed his eyeline to the wound.

"This is hardly worth the effort," he said flatly.

She gently pushed the leading edge of her skirt back down hiding her knee.

"I have a cyst on my shoulder."

"Let's have a look."

She stood and quickly began shedding her lamb's wool jacket and silk blouse. His eyes leveled on her navel. Her flat stomach was so close, he inhaled her essence through flared nostrils. Unnerved, she stepped back.

He sat there a moment with thoughts of Fanny and the same inviting beauty these two women shared. He stood holding her gaze. She stared into his eyes with little idea of what may happen next.

His eyes left hers and he noticed something.

The elegant indentation beneath her collarbone was broken by a protruding lump.

"It's just a fatty tumor. I was going to have it removed next week."

Her eyes snapped closed when his fingers touched her skin and slid up the curve of her arm, stopping midway up her long her neck. His fingers fanned and draped across her pulse. His warmth chilled her.

He smiled at the hard nipples pushing the stretched fabric cups of her sports bra. "I'll save the surgeon some work," he said in a sexy voice, and moved behind her, pushing up against her body. She shivered under his warm breath touching her ear and neck. His arms wrapped around her sculpted shoulders. His opposing hands met at her collarbone, fingers dancing, tapping in circular rotation over and around the lump. In a matter of seconds he'd finished and had stepped back.

A full minute passed before she realized his hands were off her body. She glanced down seeing smooth skin. Her fingers searched but couldn't find a trace of the fatty tumor. When she looked up again, he was standing next to her, offering her a glass of ice-chilled single malt scotch and his bewitching smile.

Tashum thought to answer her most immediate question.

"Harmonics," he said, not quite out of the blue.

"Harmonics," she murmured with a mind full of spinning equations, "reflective resonance." She looked at him with eyes on the verge of discovery. "Yeah?"

"You're on the right track, let me help you along. All living and parts of living things carry a life force, a constant vibratory note, the resonance of life. When organs become damaged, the resonance and harmonics change. The body is literally out of tune with itself."

"I've studied Chinese medicine, and I play the cello. I understand the concept of detuned strings and cross-harmonics," she said with an air of confidence.

"So you understand that the acupuncturist's needles are correcting the organs harmonic resonance through electrical current."

"Yeah, I understand the concept, but we've found it very limited in the West."

"Don't get me wrong. Our healing touch is limited as well, even for my brothers on the other side of the Light."

"What?" she said with an edge, "What did you say—"

He noticed the alarm in her voice. "I'm not the devil!" he scolded.

"I didn't say anything," she said, raising her shoulders.

"No, but you thought it."

For Tashum it always came down to that. It was the inevitable bottom line for a revelation of his kind, the mark of the Fall was the mark of the devil.

*   *   *

Several drinks later, the room was layered in thin planes of ringed cigar smoke. Tashum held out his naked inner arm offering it to Shelly's awaiting syringe.

"This may sting a little."

"Hmm. Go shallow. You don't need a vein."

Her eyes met his. This was the last bridge for her to cross before passing into total commitment to her new patient.

"It's your game, Doctor," he said in a calm, reassuring voice.

The thick amber gel bubbled up as it was drawn up through the needle into the glass syringe. She continued pulling the plunger until the glass was filled with Tashum's honey-clouded blood.

"This is incredible," she said as she withdrew the needle from his arm. "It's phosphorescent. I have so many questions—I don't know where to start."

"I'll answer what I can."

She handed him a cotton ball, but he just smiled, "I'm self-sealing, like an expensive tire."

She rolled her eyes. "Of course you are."

"What else do you need to know?"

"I guess I want to know why you're doing this? I mean, are you trans-fusing humans with your blood?"

He sat silent, staring at glowing mini-electro-volts swimming through his viscous plasma. Unable to find fault with her logic, he admitted softly, "No." He said, looking away, "Maybe a form of redemption comes with the answer, I don't know."

She sunk down beside him. "Do you really need redemption?" she asked, looking up into contemplative eyes.

"Look at me," he said in a voice rising with self-contempt. "Don't you see all things monstrous? Look at me!"

"I am," she said calmly, her eyes taking him in, "And I'm looking at the most amazing thing I've ever seen." She rose into his eyeline. "You're not a monster to me, Tashum."

"No, just a thing?"

"No, I said amazing thing," she smiled into his glare. "I am not afraid of you, whatever you are."

He didn't search for the truth through her eyes but decided to accept her sincerity at face value. "Actually, I prefer amazing thing over angel. It's a lot less confusing." He smiled and handed her the vial. "How long will the tests take?"

"If I get on it, I should have preliminary results in a couple of days."

"Good."

"Under the circumstances, I can't promise anything," she said, snapping shut her medical bag.

"I have confidence in you, Kate."

She froze, her nails gripped into the leather. Slowly, her eyes lifted, rising into his awaiting gaze. "I guess we have no secrets then, do we?" she said, looking into his assured smile.

"I'd rather think of it as tit for tat," he said, holding her gaze. "I keep your secrets, you keep mine."

"Fair enough." She smiled.

CHAPTER THIRTEEN

T ashum read the note describing a winged man and tossed it into the fire. After watching it take flame, his eyes went back to Dickey, who, except for the change in fashion, appeared exactly the same as when he had first spotted him on that beach. Were it not for the anticipation and excitement he felt about Dickey's news, he might have asked more questions about the vampire's life over the years since they had last met.

"... and when I saw this explosion of light, I remembered what you told us so many donkey years ago in Bermuda," Dickey said. "You know about the winged men."

"They're not winged men," said Tashum with eyes rising off the note's ashes.

"Okay, angels."

Tashum stood next to the fireplace in his Kensington townhouse.

Dancing flames pushed wavering shadows across classic seating arrangements and into the far corners. It was a large room with a high, wide ceiling ornately detailed with a raised oval and mural of blue sky painted inside the relief. White rolled moldings capped club green colored walls that were themselves covered by profusely framed oil paintings.

Dickey sat on the hearth looking up at him. He took a short drink from a squat crystal glass half filled with scotch.

"He was one of your kind, no doubt, but . . . ," Dickey continued after another sip, "unlike you and Paladin—after the transformation—his skin was clear, uh, unmarked, and his eyes were a pure, pure blue."

Tashum frowned into his own drink. A hard, unhappy expression took over his features. He turned his back on the fire and stepped away, stopping at the large sepia-tone globe from the Huidekooper house. He gave the painted leather ball a spin. His fingertips dropped and dragged against spinning inertia.

"Why is he so different?" Dickey asked. "Even his blood was clearer than yours and more—what's the word I'm looking for?"

"Phosphorescent," he said without spirit. His finger pressure slowed the globe's rotation.

"Yes, that's exactly it," said Dickey with cheer.

His fingers pressed down and stopped the globe on the eastern seaboard of the United States. He turned, facing Dickey. "In all of this whole wide world, how did you find me?"

"That bloody phone number of yours. That's really quite clever, Tashum."

"How did you get the number?"

"Fanny said she got it from one of her girlfriends."

"Girlfriend?" He smiled. "And who might that be?"

"Don't know, Tashum," he said trying to escape the angel's cold stare. "Honestly, I'd tell you if I knew. Fanny has always kept me away from her friends."

Tashum failed to respond at first. When he did, his voice was deep and ragged. "You said in your letter there were objects, orbs."

Dickey's eye's focused on the angel. "Mmm, orbs—" His gaze went to a point in the distance. The crease deepened between his eyebrows. "Yes, we have them, three of them. They glowed at first, but then they turned dark and—"

"Like the orbs Paladin stole from the Black Knight?"

Dickey shrugged. "I've only heard Fanny talk about them. I wasn't around when all that happened."

Tashum walked toward a fine-legged table, near a pair of restored wing-back chairs and the suit of armor he had danced with so long ago in the Huidekooper house. On the table was a vase filled with exotic flowers. His nose went to a fragrant group of orange petals. He took a long, concentrated whiff of their scents. "Did you feel his presence before you saw him?"

"Good God, no! It shocked the hell out of me." He hesitated. "All I'd felt was that woman's heaving chest and—"

"Enough!" Tashum now turned to the vampire, calming himself with effort. He had no wish to be reminded of their dining habits. "How did you capture him?"

"He seemed willing to come. After Victor's encouragement."

"Victor?"

Dickey smiled weakly. "Oh, yes. I—well, I forgot to tell you about him. He was there, too."

"And who is Victor?" It was one thing to have his old island comrades holding one of his celestial brothers, but the very name of this new vampire made his skin crawl.

"He," Dickey sighed. "He, uh—"

"Tell me in the car." Suddenly he remembered something that had gone right over his head when Dickey first said it. "You said he had clear blood. You didn't bleed him, did you?" Tashum's expression hardened.

Dickey shook his head, averting Tashum's gaze. "Well, I didn't. It's been a fortnight since we nicked him—I haven't fed since then. . . ." The man lowered his head slightly and looked up at the angel, a bedeviled, beseeching look in his eyes. "But you could fix that, Tashum."

"Don't even think about it—and keep your thoughts off my man Gregory. I'm very fond of him." Tashum took a step closer, the heat of the fire reddening his features, the smell of Dickey's lie rising in his nostrils. "Fanny is in on this, I take it."

"Of course. She likes to spend the social season here in London. You know our Fanny."

"Fanny in high society. It's not hard to imagine, at least the nighttime activities."

"She pretends, but she's not really part of it. Society, I mean. We play along with her fantasies of being Sloan Ranger."

The angel stayed his eyes on Dickey, watching him fidget in the chair. A smile slowly spread across his features.

"Is there something else, Dickey?"

"No, not really."

Once Wynn Gregory had settled behind the steering wheel of the Bentley, Tashum called out from the rear, "Number twenty-four Denning Road. Hampstead Heath."

Tashum could see Gregory turning the address over in his mind. The property had celebrity of a negative sort, having once been owned by Aleister Crowley. In the late sixties following Crowley's bizarre death, Fanny bought the old place for a song. Seems nobody in London with any brains wanted to live in Crowley's former residence, lunatic warlock that he was. That was Fanny's innocent story of purchase. Fact was, Fanny wanted it and stopped at nothing to get it, according to Dickey.

The car started, a soft, deep murmur, and Tashum settled back into the comforting embrace of the luxurious leather rear seat.

They sat quiet for the first few minutes. Tashum was looking out the side window as they passed Hyde Park corner. He couldn't help but appreciate the way moonbeams were highlighting the statue crowning the Wellington Arch, "Peace in a Quadriga." The courageous winged lady driving her chariot had always been rather special for him and brought a smile.

Dickey, who had been absorbed in his thoughts, suddenly snapped his head toward Tashum.

"Wait a minute, how'd you get Fanny's address?"

The angel kept his eyes in a dull, relaxed gaze out the wide front windscreen. "I got it from you, Dickey."

"Jesus," the other murmured.

"You read like a brochure."

"Very funny."

"Yes, well, tell me about Victor."

"Why don't you just read it off my mind?"

Tashum had started to but decided he'd rather hear Dickey's version. He didn't want to know all the seamy details, only those important to the moment. "Just tell me."

Dickey took a breath and watched Marble Arch monument speed by the window. Suddenly distracted, he said, "He should have turned onto Oxford Street—"

"Gregory knows the city. You were about to tell me about Victor."

"Victor," he said. "I brought Victor into the family back in the late 1970s. He lived on this small ranch with horses and wild things near Tucson,

Arizona. He was miserable when I met him, terrifying and suicidal. He was facing life in prison for flying drugs up from South America."

"Victor is a pilot?"

"He calls himself one, but it was his penchant for crashing planes that got him nicked. He's still very young, and wicked as hell, but I do enjoy him." He turned to Tashum. "You won't hurt him, will you?"

"What has he done to deserve punishment?"

"Nothing yet." He shrugged. "He just has a way of pissing people off. Fanny thinks just knowing him is social suicide."

Dickey shut Tashum out of his mind and stared at him.

Tashum's eyes narrowed. "I warned you long ago that an attack against any Celestial is an attack against me."

Dickey shrank back into the lush leather.

From a niche in the door panel, Tashum pulled up a cellular telephone and flipped down the mouthpiece. "Call Fanny. Tell her we're on our way and to have our angel friend—does he have a name?"

"Misha."

"Have Misha and the orbs ready."

Dickey's hands fumbled with the phone, his composure evaporating under Tashum's gaze.

"Would you like me to dial it for you?" Tashum asked.

"No, no. I've . . . I'm fine."

A chirping sounded from the wall-mounted phone in the small, dark room. Fanny took the ringing receiver off the hook and placed it next to her ear. Her glowing eyes were trained on the source of a rustling sound across the room.

"Hello," she said in a heavy voice.

She listened for a moment and her mouth curled into a smile as she lowered the receiver.

Her gaze returned to the center of the room falling on the blue-eyed Misha. His arms were drawn up over his head, his hands bound by a rope hanging from the ceiling. His breath arrived unevenly, with effort, his gentle face drained and weak.

She yawned. Slowly she stood up and stretched. She glanced over to a third figure slouched in the corner.

"Come on, Victor," she said. "Get up. Our visitor is on his way."

"What do we do with him?" Victor faked a punch to the angel's mid-section. Misha flinched. Victor laughed, pushed him, causing him to swing back and forth.

"Will you stop playing, Victor? If you break anything—"

"What's your fucking problem, lady?" He picked up a modern blown glass vase. "I don't see what makes this chipmunk crap so valuable."

"It's Chihuly, you idiot, and I like it. That makes it priceless. Just put it down—and carefully. We're going to meet them upstairs. I don't want him to see Misha until the deal has been struck."

She motioned Victor out, glanced at Misha, then closed the door and headed up the stairs.

Victor was a distraction she would rather have done without. Damn Dickey for including this Neanderthal in everything. Not that she blamed her oldest friend. If he felt he needed this companion, then so be it. She had her houses. The old monastery fortress in Morocco and this Crowley house kept her sufficiently occupied, and financially strapped.

Her hand swept along the brocade wallpaper on the stairwell. The first thing Fanny had seen to after moving in was to dismantle every fixture, every lintel, facade, and hearth—to carve out the entire interior of the house into a series of dusty white tombs, completely ridding it of anything that harkened back to anything earlier than last season.

She had purchased the house because of its strange history and reputation. Its magic was the original reason she bought it. She smiled ruefully. Just one of her lures to attract Tashum back into her life. Each year he didn't return for her, she brought in a battalion of decorators, designers, and workmen to utterly recreate interior space, importing new carpets, new furniture, and oil paintings from the hottest young artists of the year, all the trappings she felt would please her angel were spared no expense.

But he never came back for her. Even when she had given up hope, the decorating disease stayed with her. She came to despise anything old and crumbling. History had become, for her, a nuisance. A gloomy reminder of the mortality, the ongoing presence of entropy, the decay from which she had escaped. Gloriously transcended.

How ironic he should finally visit now, when she had run short of cash halfway through this year's redecoration. Her mind's eye saw the room done in soft white with splashes of blue light emphasizing the clean polar crispness.

She paused in the center of a huge parlor painted three-quarters in crimson enamel, with torn sheets of last year's *blanco*-something wallpaper still clinging here and there, some spots fringed all the way to the floor. The place was cluttered with rococo pottery bowls. Peruvian lamps orbited by flitting gray moths cast rambling shadows on soft cashmere carpets, all of which clashed terribly with her new glass tables and Swedish design chairs still in plastic wrap.

"He'll hate it," she murmured. "I should've kept with the organic motif." Her foot was tapping the floor in a nervous tic.

She glanced over at the fireplace aglow with bright orange embers. Her image was perfectly framed in the mirror above the Italian marble mantel.

Fanny's naturally stark white flesh was subtly and expertly hidden under contrasted hues of natural makeup, highlighting the structure of a still beautiful face. She puckered for an imagined *Vogue* photographer and saluted the imaginary gallery of onlookers. Role-playing was second nature for the vampiress; reinvention she had turned into art. She would joke amongst her closest friends that she could put the Ford agency out of business if those two-dimensional, anorexic models ever discovered that they would never lose their glossy looks as vampires.

She pulled an ornate iron frame chair out from the glass-topped dining table, placed a knee on its cushion. Her hand followed her gaze and reached for one of three misshapen, dusty-dark cricket balls bunched together on a silver fruit platter. Turning it, studying its pitted, dull surface a bit further, she took a long inhale off the ivory tip of her cigarette holder.

"What is it about these crusty old things?" she mused.

Victor's voice came from near the door. A cowboy's western twang distorted his consonants. "Betcha them's the balls that old fuck never had."

The corners of her mouth drew down. "Shut your mouth, you cretin."

"I ain't no foreigner," he said, smirking. "I'm American, you know that."

Victor was engrossed with an Egyptian choker necklace. His narrow face and shoulder-length black hair gave him the look of a cheap hypnotist. He tried to make everyone think he was terrifying and mysterious, but Fanny had seen enough punks through the centuries to recognize that overall lack of quality in him.

His fingers darted about the pliable surface of the choker, his large eyes worried and intent. "How's this damn thing work?"

Then he pressed a center gem, and a strawlike needle sprang out from the necklace's inner lining. At the same time, the gem folded down, becoming a spout. The perfect bleeding device.

"This is fuckin' cool!" His voice cracked through his amusement. "You just say, 'Try this on my, dear,' lock it around her purty little neck and start filling your cup. Goddamn! I gotta get me one a them."

She glared up at him. "Victor, put that down. It's not a plaything and it's not yours."

He looked at it once more and, suddenly bored, tossed it to the table, where it clanked on the glass and slid toward Fanny. He flung himself in a seat near her and stared at the orbs—the one in her hand and the other two sitting before her.

"Yeah, well, them balls are *mine*. Put it down, goddamn it!" His jaw tightened as she looked up at him. "See how you like it. Go on, put it down."

She placed the orb back on the table.

"The only reason I'm cuttin' you in on this deal is cuz the little Dickster likes your sorry ass."

"Is that a fact?"

"Fuckin'-A right, it's true, too!" He leaned toward her. "How much you think ole-no-nuts'll give for 'em?"

Fanny took her time before turning toward him. "More money than you've ever seen. But that's not saying much, is it?"

Ignoring her, he picked at his nose, wiggling it side to side, rabbitlike. "I got my eye on a nifty little seaplane—so just remember it's my deal. I do all the talking, cause if he's any kind of man at all, he'd buffalo the shit out of a woman. Especially you."

"About our deal," she said with a shift in enthusiasm. "I think we should split the orbs up. You take one. I'll take the other two, one for me, one for Dickey. That way we can make our own separate deals with Tashum. And you can do whatever you wish with your money."

He gave three squawking laughs, each a different humorless note.

"Three words Fanny, I don't think so."

"Three words? I pick the first three."

"Ok! So it's four," he said, counting his fingers. "This was my idea. Hell, I stole 'em. They're mine! Besides, breaking up a set of anything's bad luck. Didn't your mom ever teach you that?"

"How right you are," broke in a third voice.

Victor spun around. His glare shot to the doorway.

Fanny's startled expression slowly faded into a warm smile of recognition.

Victor left his seat, standing with clenched fists at his sides.

Tashum brushed past Victor and moved to Fanny. She stood and greeted him with a featherweight kiss on each cheek. On her face a genuine expression of enchantment.

Tashum latched on to the treacherous old ring on her third finger, keeping his eyes locked on hers. Touching her cold, hard flesh brought back the pain and the many tender, passionate moments of their distant, murky past.

"Sorry to have barged in like this," he said at last.

"Old lovers needn't knock," she answered softly.

He glanced around the room.

Victor had a curious smile that faded when the angel stared right through him. He spun the straight-back chair around and mounted it.

"Sorry the place is such a mess."

"You've always had interesting taste."

She took his hand, diverting his eyes from the embarrassing decor. "I've missed you, Tashum. Have you missed me?"

"Parts of you I've missed dearly," he whispered.

He glanced at the orbs lying on the glass tabletop—these precious keys, these passage makers home. He wet his lips and he knew she could feel his excitement.

"Give you a real good deal on them things," a voice smirked from the nearby chair.

Slowly Tashum broke his gaze with the orbs and turned.

"You must be Dickey's boy."

Victor rose on bandy legs and extended a hand.

Tashum looked the slim man over, his ridiculous jingling outfit, his sneering grin. The angel turned his back on the young vampire.

Victor withdrew the gesture. "I ain't got no cooties, goddamn it. And I ain't his boy."

Tashum answered over one shoulder, "Perhaps not. But you've got dried blood beneath your nails, and that attracts vermin."

Victor gave his blackened nails a quick glance, then looked back to the towering figure before him. "Yeah, well I got something else you *do* want, and the price just went up!"

"Victor," Dickey chirped from the doorway, "don't be vulgar."

He crossed to Victor and began rearranging the younger vampire's collar, swishing back his hair. Victor responded by drawing closer to Dickey.

"Well, the fucker won't even shake hands! I don't like doing business with people who don't shake yer goddamn hand."

"You are the rudest creature I've ever known," Dickey chastised. "I'd kill you myself if you weren't so damn beautiful." He kissed him on the lips, then lightly pinched his cheek. "Now behave yourself. I'm sure Tashum will be fair with us."

Tashum raised his index finger and pointed at the partially shut door. With eyes sharply focused he spoke, "Open door."

Victor's mouth fell agape as the he watched the slightly ajar door slowly swing wide open, powered by the invisible.

Tashum turned now to Dickey. "Would you please take him out of the room? I'd like a moment alone with Fanny."

Dickey nodded and tugged at Victor's arm. They moved to the door. The black-leather vampire huffed and gave Tashum a narrow-eyed look of disgust. "I didn't know you knew voodoo."

"Voodoo?" Tashum laughed.

"It's mind over matter, you fool!" exclaimed Fanny.

Victor shook with hostility. Dickey followed Victor to the door. He turned and faced Tashum. "Will you be closing the door or shall I?"

"The choice is yours." Tashum smiled.

Dickey grabbed the ornate handle and pulled the door closed behind him.

The door creaked back open and Victor's face peeked around its leading edge. "I'll give yuh ten minutes with the little bitch, no make it eight, she ain't got that much to say about this deal!"

Dickey grabbed Victor by the collar and jerked him into the adjoining room.

Tashum pulled up a chair to sit across the table from her.

"Charming fellow, your new partner."

Fanny blew out a noise of distaste. "He disgusts me."

"But you put up with him."

She drew a deep inhalation on the cigarette. "For Dickey's sake," she said.

He reached across the table and touched her face lightly with the back of his fingers, following a line down her cheek, her jaw, her slender throat.

"I've waited a long time for this," he said.

"So have I, my darling." She seemed to melt under his touch. She reached up for his hand, caressing his fingers in a slow ritual. He gently pulled his hand away.

He picked up first one orb, then the other two, feeling their irregular surface, studying their tiny pits from use after use. Feeling their ancient weight in the palms of his trembling hands, he was reminded of the first time he wore the clothes belonging to someone else.

"What have you done with their owner?" he asked.

Fanny lit another cigarette. "He isn't part of the deal."

"He most certainly is, Fanny. You have no idea what you're dealing with here. And for your sake, he'd better be a virgin."

"No," Fanny snapped. "This isn't your island. You are not in control here!"

"Fanny—"

"Don't threaten me in my house!"

As she spoke, he pulled a blue velvet pouch from his jacket pocket. He opened the small bag and poured glittering diamonds onto the tabletop.

Her face went motionless, her eyes large and staring.

"My stars for yours—Do you remember, Fanny?"

In the adjoining room, a throwing knife spun through the air. With a thud it sank deep into a painted portrait of Fanny. Right between the eyes.

"That's a seventeenth-century oil!" Dickey huffed. "And you've just ruined it!"

"Big fuckin' deal." Grumbling and ranting to himself, Victor walked on his stick legs across the room and wrenched the knife out of the canvass.

"It is a big deal. To her and to me. You'd better hope it can be repaired."

"That cocksucker," Victor complained. "I'm gonna show that scar-faced motherfucking sons-a-bitch who he's dealing with."

At the door, Dickey pulled his ear from the door frame and waved at Victor for silence.

"He didn't make me look stupid in there, did he?"

"No Victor, you're quite good at doing that on your own."

Victor responded with a child's expression of irritation and an upraised middle finger. He held up his knife and took aim at the painting.

Dickey shook his head and pressed his ear again to the crack in the door.

"Dickey said one of your girlfriends had my phone number—"

"That's right," she said, snickering, "and my girlfriend said she'd kill me if I gave you her name."

Tashum watched her strike a stick match on the glass tabletop.

Fanny waved a lit candle over the sparkling mound. She leaned close, examining the diamonds, running a fingernail through them. Her interest drifted back to the orbs. Oily waves of rainbow color scattered and unfolded in the flickering light. They seemed somehow less ordinary now. "All right, we'll throw him in on the deal. Now tell me how these things work," she said, indicating the orbs. "They look used up."

"Fanny, you're dripping wax."

"Don't avoid the question."

Tashum instinctively drew the orbs closer to his body. His antenna picked up troubling messages emanating from deep within her mind.

"Trust me, they're of no use to you," he said. "I'm not even sure they'll work for me."

"But I share your blood." Her expression hardened. "I have the right to know what they are." Her lips drew tightly together as she waited for a reply. When she got none, Fanny continued, "All right, then. You must answer me as a condition of the sale. Surely you understand."

He set the orbs on the table and ran his hands over their surfaces, bumping one against the other, rolling them side to side in a slow rhythm of repetition. Then he noticed the hypnotic effect this was having on Fanny. He kept at it, drawing her in.

Fanny's eyes grew dull, entranced by the orb's faint colors, by the slow back-and-forth movement.

"Just like Paladin," she said in a low voice. "He spent days, weeks playing with those orbs," she said in a slow voice. "It was like he'd taken a new lover."

Tashum continued moving the orbs back and forth, his eyes on her, his energy finding a pinpoint of memory inside her. He began to read her thoughts aloud, "Paladin would set them on the ground, trying one precise triangulated measurement after another, and—"

She glanced up suddenly, her eyes focused again and sharp. She took a drag off her cigarette and glared at him.

Tashum bent forward, thrilled at this revelation. "And what, Fanny? Was he able to make them work? Tell me, damn it!"

Fanny blew a stream of smoke at him. "You want to know about Paladin so badly, tell me what the orbs do."

He corralled the spheres into a triangle. "If set in a certain way, the orbs will open a vortex."

"A vortex?"

"The orbs are my ticket home, Fanny."

"Home? What about Dickey and myself, where are our orbs? Where·is our home?"

"You and Dickey? You must be kidding?" Tashum should have known the hurtful meaning of his words, but his arrogance came through again. "I'm talking about returning to from where I came. It doesn't apply to you."

"But we're family, Tashum. Same blood—how do we get home? Where is our home?"

Tashum stared at her for a moment, not sure exactly what to say. "I can't help you with that. I'm sorry."

"Never quite good enough for you, were we?" She waited for denial that wouldn't come, finally she snapped, "Fuck you! And fuck your tit for tat!" She huffed, "I'll tell you one thing about Paladin for free."

Tashum leaned closer.

"It's ironic that you care so deeply about someone who never mentioned your name in all the years that he and I lived together."

Only now did Tashum realize just how much he'd hurt her by the amount of pain she threw back at him. He seemed to shrink in his frame as she continued.

"Odd, don't you think? Actually it's a bit sad that you can love someone so completely and with such dedication and they don't have a bloody clue—"

He had to stop her. "Fanny," he said softly, shaking his head. "I'm sorry, I know that I've hurt you. I care very deeply about you."

"That's a laugh."

"I have always cared—"

"If you care so much, why did you banish us from your life? Do you know what it was like for someone like me to miss you?" she said in a pleading voice, a tone that took him back hundreds of years to their parting on the bow of the *Merciful*. The sound of a child's heart breaking.

"It wasn't you! It was your needs, your habits, that drove me away."

"Habits. Hmm," she took a breath, composing herself. "You told me once that the difference between eating flesh and drinking blood was only a measure of survival. You and your precious brother have a responsibility to us, Tashum."

"You have to take responsibility for yourself, Fanny. I've searched science and the globe for a possible cure to your situation. I've shown you how to survive without taking life from your own species. And I ask you, since Somers Island—"

She blew smoke at him. "Tashum, it's called Bermuda now."

"All right, since Bermuda, what have you done to curb your appetite?"

She saw the truth in his question and hid the hurt with more accusation. "You infected us with this hell and now you don't give a ruddy damn about leaving us here, like this."

He looked away from her and then back. "I'm truly sorry, Fanny. If I'd known," he said clenching a tight fist.

"If a child asked for poison, would you—" Fanny bit her lower lip. Her expression shifted, the uncaring mask restored. "Silly question, we both know the answer, don't we?"

"I only did what you asked."

She looked away, thinking. "You know, what I had with you pales in comparison to the pleasure Paladin brought me." She began to sing the praises of Paladin—his funny sense of humor and carefree nature—her voice filled with as much admiration as belittlement.

Tashum pulled a checkbook from inside his jacket and with rapid, ornate scribble filled in the amount and his signature. He tugged at the check and handed it to her.

"This is your finder's fee for Misha and the orbs," he announced, and then pushed the pile of diamonds toward her. "And this is for anymore information you are willing to share concerning Paladin."

Her eyes went to the amount without reaction. "Four million pounds— one million for each of the orbs and another million for Misha, is that what you were thinking?"

"Basically, yes. I think that should cover the orbs and Misha."

A raised brow was her only outward reaction.

"Now, about Paladin." His voice lifted with enthusiasm. "Where did you see him last, and what was his condition?" He carefully loaded the orbs into his coat pockets. "Tell me all you remember. I want to know everything."

She folded the check and slipped it into her deep cleavage. Her humorless gaze returned to Tashum. "One deal at a time." Her eyes leveled on him. "This is a nice down payment. But I know how important these orbs are to you bastards and I know how yummy Misha might be—"

"That's a lot of money, Fanny," he said with surprise.

She shrugged a message of big deal. "A pound doesn't buy as much as it used to, Tashum."

"Fanny, four million pounds would fill this room, and in any event, that's all I'm willing to pay you." His voice rang of finality.

Disturbing silence.

His hand reached into an inside pocket withdrawing a dark object. Fanny recoiled defensively.

"It's only a phone," he said, assuring her. "Surely you've heard of them?"

As he punched in the numbers, she stood, moving away from him, her body closing in on itself, her eyes drawn tight at his arrogance.

"Gregory," he said, "meet me at the front door in five minutes."

He pressed a button and then stood, focusing on Fanny's glare.

"I want to see Misha now."

"Do you?" she said, allowing a small ironic smile to play on her face. Idly her thumb rotated the ring on her third finger, firing out the tiny, curved blade. Snapping it out, clicking it back in. "Tashum, the price—the full price—is ten million."

"The check has been written. Let me remind you of the amount." He outstretched a finger and pointed to the plunge in the neckline of her dress. "Come to me, check," he said softly. "Come to me."

The folded check began to emerge from between the glossy mounds of her breasts.

In a flash of movement she was on the table, clutching his finger, digging in with her nails, coming face to face with him, her eyes full of anger and false courage.

"Your cheap carnival tricks may impress creatures like Victor, but don't think they frighten me."

"I'm not trying to frighten anyone. Fanny, you're hurting me."

"Finally, some feeling in this eunuch's body," she said, twisting his finger upward to reveal a glob of golden blood oozing from the broken flesh. Her expression changed, enlivening, and she looked up at him, her eyes asking permission to taste once more.

"You're delusional," he said. "Never again."

She pushed his hand away and swept the diamonds off the table, scattering them across the floor.

"Paladin never refused me," she said, her face filled with bitter memories. "He really loved me. That's the information your diamonds buy!"

Tashum dismissed the idea with a flick of his wrist. "Paladin only made you, then he played with you."

"Don't mistake Paladin for yourself, Tashum," she said, a treacherous sparkle coming to her eyes. "And don't mistake virtue with your self-serving morality and misguided loyalty to heaven." Her laugh was sharp, mocking. "The same heaven that threw you out? What makes you think they'll let you back in? Or that they even want you, just because you want them?"

She stopped, an icicle of pain dislodged from her heart. In her thoughts, Tashum saw a hooded figure bathed in moonlight standing in a the gothic doorway of a church, arms outstretched, coming closer. The image was shattered by a furious mental storm. Fanny glared fire.

"You call us hungry. Our habits repulse you." Her breath came in sharp, ragged spills. "You would feed from my mind as surely as I would feed from your arm. What was it you said a moment ago? Never again? Did you enjoy the little peep show? Yes, that was my first sight of Paladin." She paused for his reaction. "Furthermore, I know about the Druids and their awful wizards. I have seen the magic of flaxen-tangmere and more. I may even know your precious final destiny."

"These orbs are my only destiny," he said. "If you would have been open with me, honest—"

"What? What would you have done? Fed me more? Loved me?" She backed away. Her eyes were piercing, all falsity vanished. "What if I was your destiny, Tashum? And you are throwing me away. For what? To go back? Do you have any idea what awaits you there?" She widened her eyes—

Bam! His brain felt the dull silent explosion as she released a vision for him. The black silhouette of a winged man being absorbed in a flash of bright light. The silence gripped and pierced into his ears.

"Did you see him?" she asked. "Did you hear the silence in heaven?"

"Was that Paladin?"

"These diamonds cover only what I showed you. Have you any more with you?"

Tashum fought back the urge to reach across the table and throttle the little bitch. How dare she hold back information that he wanted so desperately? He fought to hold back his physical strength, but verbally he wished to kill her.

"Do you know what awaits you, Fanny?" Tashum asked in the most hurtful voice he could effect. "I hate to think of *your* destiny. What do you think comes next for a spirit like yours? Do you honestly believe you've been given impunity for your acts of survival? In the final analysis, drinking blood is not quite the same as eating flesh to survive, is it?"

She felt her upper hand slipping away. As usual he was gaining control. "What the hell are you talking about?"

He calmed his breathing. "Think about it." His voice became soft but dedicated. "Surely you understand that these murderous nights can't go on forever?"

"We haven't slipped up yet."

"That's debatable, I'm sure. Point is, you had a beginning, you'll have an end. What comes next, Fanny?"

He held her gaze.

"Think Fanny, remember the night I pulled you from the water? You had drowned. Your eyes had gone out. Did you see a white light? Did you feel surrounded in a sense of joy and well-being?"

She blinked rapidly, her mind playing back the centuries. "Only a cold blackness, but maybe I was only—"

"No, Fanny, you were dead. I revived you."

"No, I don't believe it." She took the cigarette from her mouth with a trembling hand and glanced toward the coals of her fire. "Is there a hell?" she asked in a little girl's voice.

He followed her gaze to the burning coals. "Not like that, dear," he assured her falsely. "It may be a great deal worse," he said, knowing that Fanny feared fire more than hell. "There are things that burn much hotter."

She was flush-faced and quiet. The slight rumble of coals seemed like voices of the damned in her ears. She spent her life avoiding such issues; nothing could make her come undone quicker.

Tashum realized he had gone a bit too far.

Visibly shaken, she started to rise out of her chair.

"Fanny, my advice to you is—

"Shut up!" she commanded through tightened jaw. "You are a vile heartless creature. What have you done to me?"

"Nothing I haven't tried to correct!" he screamed back. "And one other thing, remember my telling you that Paladin and I had once witnessed the birth of lion cubs?"

She raised a brow and glanced at her nails.

He continued, "I never told you the ending of that story. The kittens should have grown up to become consummate killers." He paused. "I witnessed a male lion returned to the pride. He killed and ate the children of his own brother."

"Another fable, or threat?"

"Just a fact, Fanny. The lion acted out of self-preservation. Instinct to protect the well-being of his own children. It was justified."

She whimpered and pulled the check out of her cleavage, waving it at him. "Is this the price of a soul, Tashum?"

Her words broke his heart. He started to go to her, wanted to hold her, but suddenly turned away at the sounds of a commotion from the other room.

The door flung open. "Get off my case! I'll buy her a new painting goddamn it!" Victor followed his voice into the room. He stopped near the fireplace. "Time's up, bitch, now let's talk some turkey."

Tashum ignored the intrusion, returning his gaze to Fanny.

Tears were welling up in her eyes. "Tashum . . ." Her hand went to her open mouth.

"Take care, Fanny," he said, and turned, brushing past Victor.

Victor seized him. "Hey mister, we ain't made no damn deal yet!"

"Fanny made it for you." Tashum pulled free and moved toward the door, where Dickey stood.

"Not so fuckin' fast, asshole!" Victor cried, leaping at Tashum.

Faster than thought, Tashum slipped the throwing knife from Victor's belt and gave it a flick, flashing the blade hard and deep into his leather boot, pinning his foot to the floor. With a strangled cry, Victor dropped.

"You didn't have to do that," Dickey blurted, surprised and visibly angered. He knelt to comfort his shouting, writhing lover, trying to tug the knife out of the boot. "My dear boy—"

Tashum raised a warning hand, "Dickey—leave him there until I've gone. I want him to remember our meeting."

Dickey blinked, as though in a glare of lights, but did as instructed, letting go, leaving the blade where it was and instead wrapped an arm around the struggling, gurgling Victor.

Before leaving, Tashum looked back at Fanny. "Good-bye," he said. "I'm sorry to end like this."

"Our business," she said, weeping, "isn't finished!"

"Unless you have something else to tell me about Paladin, it is. Good-bye," he said with finality.

Victor pushed Dickey aside and reached down, wrenching the knife from his foot with a sharp wail. He staggered to his feet. He waved its bloody tip at the angel.

"You won't get away with this," he screamed, panting and grimacing in pain. "You fuck, you fucking thief!"

Tashum sighed at the sight of this hideous child.

In a delirium and rage, Victor rushed him, knife ready, arms outstretched.

With ease and agility, Tashum slipped out of Victor's path. He grabbed a poker from the fireplace and swung it in a wide arc.

Still in midlunge, the glowing iron rod struck Victor across the face, under the cheekbone, a solid, crunching blow, sizzling a dark brand across his perfect face. Victor tumbled to the floor, and the air filled with the stench of burning flesh.

"Stay, boy!" Tashum said through clenched teeth.

Victor wretched and howled in pain, clutching his face, and Dickey again went to his side, wrapping the younger vampire in a huddling embrace.

Over the sounds of Victor's shrieks, Dickey cursed Tashum with a litany of ancient phrases so wicked and nasty as to burn your ears.

It wasn't Dickey's words that softened Tashum's eyes, expressing his emotional injury—it was his sense of overall failure and the sight of Fanny, with the fight knocked out of her. Clinging to a fragile semblance of dignity, the Fallen Angel walked through the doorway, leaving the vampires with their raving brat.

Tashum took a lit candelabra and descended the steps leaving the third floor. He chased through the gloom of the second floor, where he thought he detected—yes, yes, there it was. A delicate presence, music heard from a distance. Keeping alert, tuning his mind to its odd frequency, he followed down a dim hallway until he came to a door. He paused. This must be it.

Slowly, so as not to raise any alarm, he turned the knob and brought the candles into the room. Their flickering light gleamed on a pair of crystal blue eyes that glanced up full of anxiety, then softened with recognition.

"Misha?" Tashum addressed the man strung up with ropes.

"Help me," the other murmured.

After untying him, with no time for words, Tashum quickly led Misha down the remaining stairway and out the main door. Gregory and the car were waiting. He held the rear door, and Tashum and Misha climbed in.

A scream shattered the stillness. Victor appeared on the front steps of the house. "You're a fucking dead man!"

Gregory turned, facing Victor limping down the steps.

From the backseat, Tashum yelled at Gregory to get in the car.

Gregory hesitated, watching the approaching ghoul, then hurried into the driver's seat. He gunned the engine and veered away from the curb just as a beer bottle flew across the Bentley's windshield. The bottle went smashing against another car parked on the street.

Victor stormed back into the parlor and made straight for the gilt-edged mirror. His fingers pinched and kneaded the black mark on his face.

"Will it scar?" he cried out. "I won't scar, will I?"

Dickey hovered over Victor, making small empathetic noises.

Fanny's eyes were dull and watery as she sleepwalked back from the window. She knelt to retrieve the diamonds. Then she saw it. Tashum's gold business card holder—fallen free in the chaos. But before she could move, Victor snatched the holder and clutched it to his heaving chest.

"He's mine!" Victor said. His head jerking from Dickey to Fanny, a hard, challenging stare. "Maybe you freaks are afraid of that prick—well, I'm not! I want those fucking orbs back."

Fanny held up the check. "He paid us. More than enough for the orbs and the angel."

The pain hit Victor again. He clutched his face, staggered to the window. "He owes me for this, goddamn it." He glanced at his tenderly raised foot. "And look what the fucker did to my boot, I want him bad!"

"Forget about him. After dinner, we'll make plans—a long holiday, someplace warm." Dickey tried to comfort his pet. "Come, you can pick the next one, like I promised."

Victor pushed Dickey away. "Yeah, I already did, and fuckin' Fanny just gave him away!"

"Misha was never ours," Fanny said softly.

"The fuck he wasn't. But don't you worry, missy, I got a head full of ideas that'll turn yer little fuckup right as rain."

Fanny and Dickey looked at one another, their eyes lit by similar hunger.

"Victor's right about one thing—Tashum does owe us more," Fanny said slowly, to Dickey's amazement.

They turned their eyes to Victor, now using the corner of the business card to clean the grime from under his thumbnail.

The three orbs in Tashum's lap, vibrated slightly with the car's motion. London's city lights scanned across his face as the Bentley smoothed through rapid streets and roundabouts.

Tashum held one of the orbs in his closed fist. He could feel the unquestionable living energy, a tiny pulse from deep within its crusty surface. Carefully he placed all three of the orbs back into his pocket. A sparkle of joy rippled through him—he had the tools that could take him home, and learning to use them would be an adventure. The only drawback to his joy was seated next to him.

Misha was leaning forward, his head bobbing from side to side, craning for a look through the front window. In his human form he was a lightskinned man of about twenty-five years, with an eager, youthful face and closed-cropped dark hair. He melded perfectly into his European surroundings.

No scars, no weighty doubts encumbered his innocence. In sharp contrast, Tashum was plotting. "Is heaven still—?" he began.

Misha turned to Tashum. "I need to go to Paddington Hospital." Then he stooped forward to Gregory. "Paddington Hospital, please."

"Hospital?" Tashum said. "What have they done to you?"

Misha sat rigid and concentrated on his own thoughts.

"Hospital, sir?" Gregory asked. He found Tashum in the rearview mirror.

"Yes," Tashum answered, then he looked again to Misha. "Is there anything else?"

Misha glanced down at Tashum's bulging pockets. His mouth fell agape but nothing came out.

Tashum shifted in his seat, a strange sensation filling his face. He saw his reflection in the rearview mirror. His cheeks were flushed red. Gregory caught his eyes for a moment, then looked away.

A single word entered his thoughts, instigating the spread of more warm red color down his neck. A brand-new sensation.

Shame.

Minutes later, the Bentley pulled to the front entrance of the hospital. Gregory got out to open the rear door, but Misha did not wait. He lunged from the backseat and trotted across the wet tarmac toward the glass-fronted hospital entrance.

Tashum stepped from the car onto the street. Through the glass facade he could see Misha at the admittance counter. He heard a sigh, and looked across the Bentley's glossy black roof and saw Gregory, who was visibly shaken.

"Are you all right?" Tashum asked.

Gregory took a breath and nodded. "I suppose I am, sir."

"I should have warned you. Leaving them has always been complicated."

Gregory nodded toward Misha's vacated seat. "Will your friend be staying with us?"

"Don't know."

"Is he ill?"

"I don't have a clue what we're doing here."

Tashum crossed the street, marched up the steps, and entered through two sets of sliding glass doors. Inside, his shoes squeaked on the polished surface of the aging, uneven tiles.

He noticed the floor-and-room directory mounted on a wall. It offered little help.

Then he stopped for a moment and closed his eyes, slowly filling his nostrils with the myriad fragrances of the building. Everything came to him in a rush of images and smells—the death rattle of elderly patients, their staring eyes, the rank odor of disease, the stale scents of cleaning supplies and sterilized equipment, the vibrancy of the newly born and—yes, there it was, traveling across the top of all the others—piccolo notes on an orchestral score, light and airy—the ancient, familiar scent of home. Of Celestials.

Following his nose he moved down a series of corridors and took several flights of stairs before coming to a painted metal door. From the stairwell, he stepped out into the half-light of a patient-care area.

The night nurse looked up from her station, a gray-haired woman from the West Indies. Reflected light turned her glasses into white ovals.

There was the scent—stronger now. His head swiveled, pulled by the aroma.

He sensed the woman watching him with growing uneasiness. He flashed a smile that was unreturned and continued on down the corridor, past several doors.

Tashum stopped finally. Here it was. His face went to a small Plexiglas window set in the door. His breath condensed a white fog on the pane.

Inside, he saw Misha—the other angel was seated at the bedside of a young man, no more than thirty years old, and yet a withered, dying figure. In the dim, orange light, Misha sat with his head bowed. His lips were moving and his breath carried a prayer—a sacred verse for those spirits preparing to pass from this world to the next. A scene of quiet, solemn reverence filled Tashum's eyes. Misha's fingers caressed the other's hand, a small comforting gesture. Through prayer, his entire spirit was connected with the young man, who struggled courageously with his breath, his failing body.

Tashum felt a choking ache rising up in this throat at the sight of an angel going about his work with humble, self-giving compassion.

Misha's head rose, returning Tashum's gaze with a message, *Tashum, this is our real work. This, too, is your calling. . . .*

Enslavement to them, Misha? Tashum responded out of haste. Then he felt guilt over Misha's disappointment. *I didn't mean to be hurtful, only honest.*

Misha turned again to the bedridden man. He coughed, and Misha stroked his forehead, soothing away all fear, all distress.

Tashum's thought energy captured the imagery inside the young man's flickering mind. *A school yard in winter, the reddened face of a smiling young girl, her small mittened hands reaching out for his.*

And in another part of his fading thoughts, the young man heard the angel's prayer, its sweet singing verse, holding back the winds of fear, the terrors of death, cloaking him in peace and joy—preparing him for the journey. Instinctively, Tashum recognized he was hearing only the single voice of Misha and not heaven's choir; missing was the multitude of angelic voices that create the network of celestial communication. Even though the music sounded distilled, the Fallen Angel's ears were filled with the emotion of verse delivered by the truly virtuous, and it was sweet.

Tashum tore himself away from the window. A sob grew in his throat. He could watch no longer, listen no more. He had rejected even the concept of this type of servitude, and yet he was drawn to it. His hands went to his face as the discord vibrated through his frame.

"Sir," came a gentle inquiry behind him.

Tashum kept his back to the woman while he straightened his composure and brushed the tears from his eyes. He cleared his throat and turned to her. "Yes?"

The dark-skinned nurse looked straight into his face, unflinching. "I'm sorry to intrude," she said, "but you look a bit lost."

He took a deep breath, fighting another sob back from the surface.

"Yes," he said. "I'm afraid I am."

"May I help?"

He took a deep breath. "Listen, I want to leave my card for that young man sitting in there." He touched his pockets. His expression dropped when he came up empty handed.

"His name is Misha," the woman said. "He comes here often to comfort the dying."

"So I see. Sorry, but I seem to have misplaced my card holder."

"There's paper and a pen at my desk if you wish to leave a message for him."

"Yes. That'd be fine. I just want to leave my address," Tashum said.

"I'm sorry." A note of genuine concern crossed her face. "Is someone in your family . . . departing?"

"Yes, with any luck," he said with confidence.

"Oh, I see," she said with a puzzled expression.

He followed one step behind her down the corridor. She slowed her gait as they passed a wall-mounted poster advertising a blood donation drive—heroic artwork, recreating the spirit of the Second World War. The woman lingered for a moment, staring at the poster.

Tashum picked up from her that she was struggling within herself about asking him for a donation. The notion struck him as funny. "You don't want my blood, trust me."

"We need all types. How did you know that was what I was thinking?" Her eyes were blinking wildly. "Are you psychic or something?"

"I can't lie," he said, and pointed at the poster.

"Of course," she blushed. "Silly me. Nonetheless, it's good that the art-work caught your attention. I must have passed it a hundred times before I recognized what it was saying. Now I give once a month."

"I'll give a donation of a different kind." Tashum, smiled and pulled out his checkbook.

CHAPTER FOURTEEN

Sunlight filled the curved street as Hamley Potter approached the front steps of his client's grand Kensington House—an English adaptation of the Palladian style set in continuous concave facade of Greek pillars and white stucco.

He tugged at the cuff of his dark, expertly tailored suit, set off with a bright gardenia and a yellow silk tie drawn firmly against his widespread collar. His thinning white hair was combed neatly back, away from his intelligent, broad face, which wore a grin absorbing the brilliance of the morning.

When he rang the bell, the door just swung open.

"Gregory?" he asked, but saw no one. "Hello?"

As the door opened wider, a carpet of white morning sunlight raced across the marble entryway until it stopped at the very tips of burgundy-colored leather shoes.

"Come in, Potter," Tashum said, his face faintly illumined in the floor's reflection. "Gregory's had a rather long night. He's sleeping."

"Hard to imagine Gregory a night owl, but good for him then," Potter answered, stepping through the doorway.

Tashum stayed in the shadows daring not to step forward and greet his friend. The angel had long studied the realationship between the size and shape of doorways and windows and the amount of dangerous light let in by the necessary orifices. It was on an unconscious level that his mind performed the math and told him where to stand. He waited.

Tashum smiled and took Potter's hand in a warm shake, nothing was said.

Moments later, they were in a curtained sitting room lit by a fire and small brass lamps scattered among traditional couches and fruitwood side tables.

Tashum reclined on a long white leather couch and watched as Hamley Potter drew papers out of a black leather case.

"Tashum, that check you made out for four million pounds created quite a stir in my office this morning." Potter leaned forward, handing over the papers. "We filed the disclaimer, but you'll need to sign this release form. It's a bit after the fact, but I recognized your signature on the check as authentic."

"I'm sorry to have used that account. I know you're not a bank, I was just a bit rushed into the transaction."

"No bother."

"Fanny didn't waste any time getting her money."

"It was her solicitor, actually."

"Hmm. Solicitor? I didn't know she had one. What was he like?" Tashum's eyes quickly scanned the three-page document.

"Her solicitor was a woman. Snappy in dress and tone."

"Really? What was her name?"

"Lydia de Flavy, never heard of her."

"Hmm, nor have I." He glanced at the document. "Everything is so complicated these days." He signed and returned the release.

"Yes, well a handshake doesn't mean what it used to."

"You know, Potter, in a bizarre way I didn't mind paying her."

"She got the better of the deal, did she?"

"You know me better than that." He smiled.

"So what did you buy, if I'm not being too personal?"

"No, not at all." Tashum eased back on the couch. "A ticket home—I'm going home, Potter."

Potter's eyebrows raised. "Sorry, but does that mean you've bought a new home and you're going there?"

Tashum chuckled to himself. "I really should speak more clearly. Potter,

I want you to draft a last will and testament for me. Leave the recipients' names blank. I'll fill them in later."

"So you are a mortal after all, just like the rest of us." Potter chuckled. "Looks like I lose the office pool."

"You may lose the wager." He smiled "I promise that you'll gain a great deal by the fact."

"I certainly appreciate the gesture, Tashum, however I seriously doubt I'll outlive you. But then again, I don't want to influence you too much."

Tashum chuckled. "Can you have the document ready by seven tomorrow evening?"

Potter nodded. "This is all a bit sudden isn't it?"

"It's a dangerous world. Surely you've noticed?"

Potter had learned long ago not to challenge Tashum in his avoidance of direct questions he didn't wish to answer. "Well, as usual I don't know what the devil you're talking about."

"I've plans to take my first flight—the first in a very long time."

Potter's eyebrows raised in surprise. "I confess, I've often wondered why you don't fly—given the globe-trotting you do." He wasn't sure about Tashum's sudden change in expression. "Well, who, wouldn't really with a yacht like yours?"

"Truth is, I have a blistering bad case of vertigo. I get violently ill up in the air. I'm hoping I've found a cure."

"I know they've got medicine and therapy for that sort of thing." The lawyer reached under his seat and produced a metal tube. "I read in the paper that a Yorkshire woman is taking flying lessons after years of that debilitating condition."

"Hmm. So—what can you tell me about this warehouse or factory or whatever it is?"

"Before we get started, I want to clear the air about this Malvern business," stated Potter.

"What's to clear? The man's dead, isn't he?"

"Yes, I'm sure the police case is closed." He paused. "There have been nasty innuendos leveled against you by two of Malvern's associates."

"You did pay them, didn't you?"

"What they're saying doesn't have anything do with the money. It's you, Tashum. They think you're more than four hundred years old. Actually they say they can prove it."

"The cheeky bastards. Malvern was hired to find someone who could indeed be that old, but it isn't me." Tashum wouldn't allow Potter to see how really distressed he was by this. "So let's have a look at this building," he said enthusiastically, gesturing at the tube in Potter's hand.

"That's all you've got to say about the situation?"

"Potter, whatever they're saying—they're only words, wicked little stories that no one in their right mind is going to pay any attention to," he said calmly and convincingly. "Let it go. . . . Now show me what you've got there."

Potter scooted blueprints out of the tube and unrolled them. Tashum sat forward, taking in the various elevations and floor plans of the Victorian monolithic structure.

"I share your love for architecture, but I can't imagine why you'd have an interest in this derelict building."

"An old acquaintance mentioned it—sounded interesting."

"Well I suppose there is beauty in function." Potter frowned. "I did manage to find all of the design drawings and specifications. Built in 1880, and it is for sale."

Tashum spent a moment examining the floor plan in detail before turning to the next page. "Splendid. Oh, the survey map, very good. Very good, indeed. I'll want to spend some time with these."

"Yes, well," Potter paused, bewildered at his client's interest. "I feel it's my duty to tell you that the place isn't worth a brass farthing. Even torn down for the property, it's poorly situated on the Thames floodplain."

Tashum was completely absorbed by the survey maps and the building specifications. He didn't respond.

Potter glanced at his wristwatch peeking out from under a white cuff. The unique Audemars Piguet was faceless and difficult for him to read, but the skeleton watch had been a gift from Tashum a distant Christmas past, and he loved it. "I have a doctor's appointment within the hour. Send over the details of your will, and I'll have Matheson take care of the legal end," he said, taking up his briefcase. "Oh, one other thing, Martha found a shop called the Brass Ring in Monterey, California. However the owner claims he has a possible buyer."

"Hmm?" Tashum looked up. "Monterey, is that near Carmel?"

"I believe so, but we may be a bit late—"

"Good, find out more. Make an offer the owner can't refuse."

Potter shook his head and stared down upon the man who never took no for an answer. Tashum was again lost in the building's blueprints. Potter hung there for a minute or two.

"Shoot the moon with this one, Potter. It sounds perfect. I want it."

"Which are you describing, the ruin or the business that has probably already been sold?"

"Well, I should think both."

"I'll look into it." Potter started to say something further, then realized he'd only be speaking to the back of Tashum's down-turned head. Nodding courteously to no one in particular, he made his way out of the house.

The large monitor screen held a computer-graphic recreation of the factory's interior. On screen appeared the amber pyramid housing the winged angel. The depiction hovered just off the factory floor and then slowly rotated, exposing its triangular base and the three orbs. It looked almost as real as the glass window it was modeled after. In a column along one side rows of numerical figures spun in dizzying calculation.

Tashum sat back from the computer screen, satisfied at last with the dimensions and the quality of his formulae. The result after hours of keying in data was glowing before him in hyperreal 3-D animation.

He checked the pyramid's dimensions again. The line segments of the triangular polygons were all equal at thirty-six feet. The figures were guesswork, based solely on the relative size of the glass pyramid scaled to the angel within the artwork. All things drawn relative, the six-foot-tall light being had a wingspan of eighteen feet.

"Perfect. Yes, absolutely perfect." He smiled, and fast-moving fingers added more detail with each keystroke. It almost looked material, as it hovered electronically. Tashum keyed in movement and the angel's wings moved in fluidity set against the scanned representation of the industrial cathedral. With a joystick he guided the animated angel's flight inside the pyramid.

He leaned to one side in his chair and turned toward the real stained-glass window he had taken from the Huidekooper house. It was backlit and now mounted in the far wall. He studied and compared his creation against the real thing.

A quick finger tap on the computer's keyboard for a matching backlit effect was the final touch. On his monitor screen, the intricate image of a three-sided pyramid of amber light came to life. Inside the glorious pyramid, a winged, medieval angel descended. Arms outstretched, his face radiated the glory of the heavens. Tashum's lips mimicked the Latin phrase standing out in bold red letters stretched around the oval art.

But when he repeated, "I am light pure am I" aloud in the English translation, he felt a twinge of guilt that stopped him from saying it a second time.

He swiveled in the chair toward a legal pad resting on an extended writing arm, then flipped past sheets of tightly written mathematical calculations, complex relationships of numbers scrawled in every direction on the page. At last he came to a final page where, among a graffiti of equations, he found a sketch of Earth drawn in relationship to certain key star systems, dotted lines connecting the significant points. A tighter drawing showed the outlines of England in relationship to a series of geometric star alignments. Underlined thickly were, Longitude 0-degrees, 10-minutes, Latitude 50-degrees, 30-minutes=Warehouse.

With an eraser, he began to make rapid changes to a calculation, changing coordinates, reshaping the equation when—

His concentration was broken by the sounds of metal objects rattling together. Looking up, he saw Gregory in the doorway carrying a formal tea tray. His servant looked rested and renewed.

His assistant placed the silver tray on a table and poured a cup, added a tad of milk, stirred once, and presented it to Tashum. He couldn't help but notice the computer screen,

"Sir, is the big experiment on for tonight?"

Tashum inhaled the moist aroma of hot tea, his eyes scanning his numerical endeavors.

"No," Tashum said. "It will be more of a rehearsal."

Gregory glanced at the stained-glass window, then the screen, and whipped his head back to the stained window, mentally drawing the comparison. His eyes came back to a blank screen and Tashum's stare.

"Sorry, didn't mean to pry."

"You'll see the real building later."

"You look tired, sir," he said thoughtfully.

Tashum glanced up at the clock on the computer screen. "Suppose I could use a spine bash."

"You never need more, do you?"

"I only sleep to dream," he said. "But now," he glanced at the stained-glass window, "I may have found the reality of the dream."

An uncertain, quizzical look passed over Gregory. "I see," he said. "Sir—"

Tashum looked up. "Yes, Gregory?"

"This flight you're planning . . ." He wasn't sure how to put it.

"Yes? What is it?"

"I get the feeling . . . you may not return. How will you get along without me?" Gregory's fear for his employer's safety was evident from the man's face. Tashum had many assistants and aides, butlers, private secretary's—the title had varied over the years. But none had served with such cherished or appreciated devotion as the man before him now. Tashum felt a small tinge of regret. All the money in the world weighed less than the slice of shame resting upon his shoulders. He'd been so preoccupied with finally having the orbs in his possession, he hadn't considered the man's feelings about possible job termination.

"Gregory, I'm afraid this is a solo flight."

The answer did not alleviate Gregory's painful questions. "Sir—and don't answer if you feel I shouldn't know—but—where are you going that you won't need me?"

The images jammed together inside Gregory's mind, his voice an insufficient funnel for their release. Scenes from an old movie, an early nineteenth-century scientist sitting in a wild-contrapted chair that took him forward into the future.

It would have been so easy for Tashum to tell the truth. Instinct intervened and told him if he claimed to be an angel, and was going home to heaven, it would only create even more confusion. The truth would leave his friend questioning the years of service and the things he'd seen. With no way to ever prove his knowledge or describe it sufficiently to others, it might lead to disbelief in his own powers of observation and logic. A man like Gregory would suffer under such a burden of truth for the rest of his days.

"Let's just say I have finished my task here in London and will be seeking a new career." He rose, placing a hand on the shorter man's shoulder. "It's a new age. I need to learn how to look after myself. And you, my friend, you need to push your dreams past the needs of others."

"You're not going to tell me all of it, are you, sir?"

"Gregory. Believe only what you have seen."

"When you leave will you be safe. Happy, perhaps?"

"Yes, more than I have been in a long time." He squeezed the gentle man's shoulder.

"I'll be happy for you." Again, those trusting eyes gleamed. Gregory was one of those rare men, the kind of man that the British Empire seemed to create in inexhaustible supply. Gunga Din had nothing on Wynn Gregory.

"Give a shout, when you're ready for the car?"

"I'll do that."

Gregory started out of the room.

"And Gregory?"

He turned. "Yes, sir?"

"Thank you, for the tea."

"You haven't really touched it but my pleasure, sir."

As Gregory cleared the door frame Tashum felt a twinge of guilt. He remembered mentally chastising Dickey for deserting his brother, Vlad. Was he not leaving Gregory the same way? No, he rationalized, they were not brothers, they were of different species, bound by proximity and friendship and not by blood.

Through London's East End, the black Bentley moved in near silence, passing through the deep shadow of abandoned buildings and the feeble light of sputtering over-head lamps. The vintage car turned off the rutted street and onto wide open area grown over with weeds. It rolled to a stop at the side of the huge, darkened factory. With headlamps extinguished the black car lost its shape to the surrounding shadows. Gregory stepped out and opened the rear door.

Tashum exited the car, holding an ornate box in one arm and a lanky piece of survey equipment in the other. He stood there gazing at the bomb-damaged factory. "I want to go in alone."

"Alone?" Gregory asked with a slight quiver.

"Quite, let's put the surveyor's instrument together out here," said Tashum as he kicked open the tripod's legs. "If you'd hand me the transit, please?"

Gregory grabbed the box from the backseat. He took the surveyor's transit from the box and placed on the tripod. He was puzzled as to how to secure the instrument to the legs.

"It screws on from the bottom. It's the big ring." Tashum instructed, "Screw it down, good and snug."

"Are you sure you want to go in there alone?" Gregory asked as he tightened the ring, "Let me carry the transit for you?"

"If you carry the transit, who's left to guard the car?" Tashum said with a light smile. "Would you give me a hand with this, please?" He gestured to the tripod.

Gregory pulled in the tripod's legs and placed the bundle on Tashum's shoulder. Off balance, Tashum struggled for a moment with the cumbersome tripod and the ornate box, then made his way up the wide steps to the entrance of the grim, looming building.

Gregory watched Tashum go inside with lines of apprehension crinkling around his eyes. He thought he saw someone moving in the shadows of another abandoned factory across the way. Only a cat skittered out. Whistling nervously to himself, he took a white pocket square handkerchief from his breast pocket and began polishing the car's flying-B hood ornament

Tashum searched about the interior of the building, peering around mounds of metal garbage, kicking through broken crates, until he stood in the main room's center. It was exactly the way Dickey described it. He put the tripod aside. Next he set down the box and lifted its wooden lid, revealed inside were the three orbs.

He placed one of the orbs on the floor and then placed the surveyor's transit-distance-meter over the sphere, making adjustments in the tripod, aligning the transit until it was level and set directly over the orb.

Taking a second orb he paced off a distance of thirty-six feet, looked back at the first orb, and then placed it on the floor.

He went back to the transit and put his eye to the lens. Adjusting the focus and training tilt and pan, he put the crosshairs on the second orb. Digital numbers across the bottom of the viewer read, 36 feet bearing 0 degrees, 0 minutes, 00 seconds establishing a baseline.

He turned the transit barrel 60 degrees, 0 minutes, 00 seconds and picked a line. The angel paced out what he judged to be the correct distance and as he placed the third orb onto the floor.

The orb began to come to life in his hand, an amber light radiated from its core. Perfectly aligned, the geometry of the horizontal triangle was working.

His heart shook violently inside his body. He looked to the other two—they were glowing hotly. As a test he nudged the orb. The slight movement broke the magic circuitry, and all three orbs lost their glow.

Their glow returned after being realigned.

A stinging wind seemed to roar through Tashum's mind. His entire body trembled as he moved to the middle of this trinity. With arms outstretched and over the machinelike singing of the spheres he called out, "I am light pure am I."

He waited for a blinding flash, for an eruption he thought should engulf him. Tashum looked over at the orbs. The orb's inner light was fading. He felt the opportunity slipping away. *"Ego sum lumen purus sum ego,"* he said in Latin with the hopes the original language might work.

In his louder voice he cried out, "I am light pure am I! I am pure light am I." His words seemed wasted, as the orbs continued to discharge.

He held his position a moment longer, his arms held wide, his eyes squeezed shut, concentrating, willing something to happen, anything.

At last he gave a sharp gasp and let his arms drop. He withdrew a notepad from his pocket and by the dim light eking through the bank of grimy windows, he furiously reread his computations. What mistake could he have made?

A cold wind. A life presence drifted past him.

Tashum saw a translucent figure passing through a moonbeam and disappearing in shadow. The angelic form glided toward the orbs and then circled slowly around the triangle, a silk scarf floating in the air.

Tashum heard his name called from within the chilled breeze. "Yes," he replied.

"Little good are the tools, without the knowledge to use them."

Tashum twisted slowly, following the serpentine path of the spirit. "Mayhem?" he said, his voice faltering. "It is you, isn't it?"

"You know who I am."

"I've come this far, I've followed your leads but—"

"You're close Tashum." The translucent spirit continued to circle the triad of the now dull orbs. "You're very warm, but freezing."

Tashum held out his hands beseechingly. "What am I doing wrong? Please, you must tell me!"

Slowly the dark angel lofted toward the high ceiling, his wings elongated and trailing behind. "What does the Latin script that surrounds the stained-glass window tell you?"

"It's English translation, I am light pure am I."

"Is it one phrase? Is the angel coming or going?" Enormous wings unfolded, great dark sails. Mayhem glanced down. "Don't be so thick." His wings flapped twice and he was gone.

"Mayhem!" he shouted. "May-hem! Don't play this game with me!"

A soft, shuffling sound. Footfalls on broken glass.

Tashum pivoted around, eyes wide.

Gregory approached, apologetically. "Sorry, sir. I thought I heard you call me."

Tashum turned back to the place where the other angel had vanished. After a deep sigh, he moved toward Gregory.

"We're done here for now," he said. He looked to the orbs. They were completely dead.

Five minutes after the Bentley pulled away from the curb in front of the factory, Victor stepped into the street. He was leading a leather-clad figure by a thick chromed chain that was attached to a studded leather neck collar. Victor's date, a street teen, looked emaciated if not diseased.

"Oh, fuck," muttered Victor. He patted himself down until he found the object in a zippered pocket. "Whew, I thought we were fucked for a minute."

"What, master?"

"Shaddup," Victor snarled. "You are fucked." Then he gave the chain a hard tug. "Did I give you permission to speak?"

"No, master." He quivered, awaiting punishment.

Victor swung his boot and kicked the young man's buttocks. The teen groaned without pleasure.

"Fuckin' Fanny, sold us out," he growled. "And guess what? You're part of the payback."

"What?" he asked, gasping for air.

He half dragged his subject across the street. They were quickly absorbed by darkness. Loud, startled moans echoed and faded against the empty buildings.

*   *   *

Later that night, in the computer room, dark but for the lit stained-glass window. It was casting long shadows diffused by a cloud of smoke. Tashum drew on his cigar, exhaling into a large snifter of cognac. He sat back in his favorite chair, gazing at the painted angel. How many times had he done the same, a thousand, he thought, no, closer to ten thousand he finally admitted to himself.

He had long believed the single image and single phrase had two meanings. He thought the painted angel was both descending and ascending, dependent on which side of light you were viewing the depiction from. So simple even a child would have repeated the phrase forward and backward "I am pure light am I," and reversed, "I am light pure am I." That bit he was sure of. Then he realized that the placement of the orbs by his own design, which was based on inner stellar mathematics, was too complex to fit the simplistic nature of the puzzle. Recounting the evening, Mayhem had posed the perfect question: Is the angel coming or going? After more thought, Tashum concluded that he had been wrong about the imagery. The stained-glass window only depicted an angel of Light coming to Earth, and the featured placement of the orbs created a one-way avenue from the Light. Probably depicted as witnessed by some lucky mortal.

In final conclusion, he determined that the orbs required a different configuration to open the vortex for the flight back into the Light.

He leaned closer to the luminous angel until his face was bathed in the reflective glow and his eyes could not focus. He imagined himself wrapped in that Light, and God, how he wanted those wings.

CHAPTER FIFTEEN

Tashum stepped through the doorway into the onetime ballroom. It was still devoid of furniture of any sort, and now aptly called the map room. Tashum walked across the illumined plastic-paneled floor. A huge, backlit map of the world extended from wall to wall. The countries were differentiated by fine-line borders and frontiers laid over natural geographic colored landmarks such as mountain ranges, seas, lakes, deserts, and rivers, a patchwork of softly backlit hues. Of course he could call up cities if he needed by a simple push of a button.

As he moved above this world, delicate shades washed across his features, turquoise as he crossed the Pacific, giving way to the sands of North Africa and finally the deep green of England.

From his lofty point of view he studied the features of the map.

"Let's try the Dartmoor," he murmured.

Tashum pointed the slim black remote control toward Dartmoor and clicked. A dot of red laser light shot from the remote and illuminated an area in southern England.

Then he looked upward toward a vast starry sky reduced to the size of his ceiling. An accurate representation of constellations, the arm of the Milky Way and star clusters, adjusted for that night's sky. As he looked at the numbers scrolling across the LED display on the remote there was a rapid knock at the door.

Without waiting for a reply, the door opened and Gregory rushed in, his hair across his face, his fingers rubbing nervously together.

"Sir, sorry to bother you, but two detectives from Scotland Yard are here to speak with you."

Tashum's placid expression slowly resolved into a worried frown.

"Scotland Yard?"

"Shall I show them into the sitting room?"

Tashum reached for the coatrack. "Um. Yes, yes," throwing on an old-fashioned smoker's jacket. "Tell them I'll be right down," he said, tying the silk waist sash.

Moments later, Tashum stood in the doorway of the sitting room, momentarily pleased by the fact that Gregory had filled the room with large, bright flowers and had a fire going.

The two detectives were seated in the wing-back chairs and both stared into their teacups—a pair of gypsy clairvoyants. The two men in dark suits didn't detect his presence until he stood right before them and uttered a perfunctory greeting.

After introductions, the older of the two, one Inspector Stanton, held up a plastic bag that contained a metallic business card, stained at one edge with blood.

"This is your business card, is it not?" he questioned.

Tashum glanced at the card reading his name and telephone number aloud. His gaze shifted from one investigator to the other. "How did you get this?"

"Let there be no mistake." Stanton's left eyebrow raised bent in the middle. "You do recognize this card to be yours?"

Tashum held his gaze, briefly probing the man's thoughts.

"The card is mine. I don't have a clue whom the blood belongs to."

"We know whom the blood belongs to. And now of course we know the card is yours." He set his tea aside. "I'm hoping the rest will be as simple. We need to know where you were last night."

"Gregory and I were looking at real estate."

Gregory, standing near the fire, nodded in collusion.

"What make of car do you drive?"

"I don't drive, but I own a Bentley."

"Is it black?"

"Yes."

The detectives exchanged glances.

"We'd like to have a look at the tires on your car," Stanton said.

"Inspector," Tashum said, "I'm not shrugging my civil duty. But is that really necessary? I assure you neither I nor my car are involved in murder." Realizing he had spoke too early, Tashum held Stanton's gaze for a few seconds, then he turned to his servant. "Gregory, would you go check my desk drawer and see if my cardholder is there?"

The policemen exchanged another glance as Gregory made his way out of the room.

Stanton said, with a hint of triumph in his voice, "What made you think we were here about a murder?"

"You know how these things wind up in the news."

"Papers haven't run the story yet," remarked the shorter detective with a twisted grin. "That puts you in a queer position."

"Really? How so?"

Stanton gave his partner a disapproving glare and stood up. "We could have come here to talk to you about an auto accident."

"Oh, I see your point, but it's not that sinister. I was only making an educated guess."

"I see," said Stanton as he studied Tashum. "Could you elaborate on that?"

"It's a matter of deduction. Clues. Little things."

"What, like Sherlock bloody Holmes," said the younger of the two detectives. His odd-shaped eyes twinkled under a mat of red, wiry hair that swayed with his head movement.

"Something like that." Tashum smiled. "Plus what you might call a touch of the psychic."

Wilks rolled his eyes. *Bloody wanker!*

"Your mother would wash your mouth out for thinking such thoughts, Detective Wilks."

"Rubbish!" Wilks gawked.

"I think I've made my point."

Stanton held up his hand. "How convenient for you to be able to read people so well," he said. "Perhaps you can use your powers to help us identify this young man."

Gregory reappeared at the doorway empty-handed. "Sorry sir."

"I was afraid of that." Tashum opened his hands in a welcoming gesture. "Gentlemen, I don't know the victim, but I may just know his killer."

"I'm very interested in anything you can tell us that will help with our investigation." Stanton gave Tashum a squinting, mock-intrigued look. "Shall we finish this discussion at the Yard."

"As you wish." Tashum checked his watch. "But I'm on a rather tight schedule. Gregory, ring Potter, tell him I'll be a bit late. Pick me up at the police station at eight." He gave the detectives a questioning look. "We should have finished by then, don't you think?"

"We'll see," Stanton replied in a noncommittal tone. "We'll see."

The gray-walled interrogation room smelled of cigarettes, antiseptic cleaner, and urine. The result of a particularly strenuous questioning earlier that afternoon, Stanton explained as he took off his suit jacket. Without taking his eyes off Tashum, he hung his jacket on a wire hanger and placed it on a wall peg.

By the light of a single hanging lamp, Tashum sat at a long metal table flipping through a stack of glossy black-and-white photos, various angles on a young man sprawled in a cinder patch, rusted fragments of equipment, and segments of iron and steel scattered in the background. Tashum recognized the location as the warehouse. Another photo revealed a long, thin opening in the young man's throat, a hat string line of blood from one ear to the other. Swollen bruises around his eyes and mouth indicated a fierce struggle.

Tashum looked thoughtful for a moment, then picked up a water glass off the table and took a short sip. He glanced up at Stanton. "Odd. Very odd. You found him like this? Out in the open?"

Stanton nodded, taking a sharp inhalation on a cigarette, blowing twin streams of smoke out his nostrils. "Why don't you tell me why it's so odd?"

"It just is, Inspector," he said with disguised eyes leveled on the smoking cop.

The door to the room swung open, and Wilks marched in followed by Davies, who had earlier been introduced as an electronics specialist. He was a dour, red-faced detective with a brown knit tie that stopped at the center of his paunch stomach.

Davies dropped a plastic bag that contained the metallic business card on the table and bent so his face was in Tashum's eye line.

"Right. About your business card. I just got off the line with people at MI6. They tell me the chip that drives the tracking device sandwiched in your card hasn't been licensed to the general public. Where did you get this technology?"

"I invested in its development," Tashum answered coolly. "The application I designed myself."

Stanton coughed a billow of smoke.

"What, in your spare time?" sputtered Wilks.

Tashum nodded, his pale forehead glowing under the single light bulb. "Gamblers, like detectives, need all the help they can get."

"You sound like a man of many talents," Stanton muttered, and gazed at the card. "It just reads Tashum, is their a title or a mister, missing?"

"No, it's complete."

"What is your Christian name?"

"My name is Tashum."

"Like Madonna or Cher?" asked Davies.

"No, like Tashum. I pay British taxes. Look it up."

"Or Beelzebub," Wilks said with hands jammed in his pants pockets.

"We seem to be regressing." Tashum gazed from one to the other without interest. "This has taken longer than I expected. Is my driver waiting for me?"

The detectives exchanged glances.

"No one's waiting for you." Davies moved to the door, as if to block it.

"Hmm, it's not like Gregory to be late." Tashum stood, and pushed away his chair. "I think that about does it. Good hunting, gentlemen."

The other men exchanged a series of glances, a mutual resignation for the time being.

Stanton followed Tashum toward the door and nodded to Davies. The barrel-chested man grudgingly moved to one side and let Tashum pass.

"I want to know a little more about this Victor chap," said Stanton from behind.

Tashum paused with his hand on the door. "I've told you what I know."

"But it's all a bit vague—the way you tell it."

Tashum glanced at the other men, watching him with stony expressions. He looked back to Stanton. "I've only met him once—you might start by checking with the American authorities. The DEA, organizations of that nature."

Wilks brushed back his hair. "You're sure he's a bush pilot."

"Was a pilot. 1970s—I understand he lived or worked on a ranch in Arizona and used it as a base to fly drugs from across the Mexican border. That's all I know." He searched their faces. "I forgot to bring my cellular phone, is there a telephone here I can use?"

"Why don't you just make one," remarked Davies.

Wilks started laughing. "My VCR is broken, think you could fix it for me?"

"The phone is down the hall," muttered Stanton. "Can't miss it, on the left."

Tashum nodded to them, a polite salute, and exited the room.

The detectives let out a series of frustrated sighs and noises. Stanton sucked on the stub of his cigarette and leaned against the wall.

Wilks sat in Tashum's still-warm chair, gazing at the drinking glass.

"Roger, he admitted being at the crime scene." Davies threw up his hands. "And we're going to let him go, just like that? Jesus. Shouldn't we at least fingerprint the git?"

Wilks studied the glass. "What fingerprints? Seems he puts some kind of makeup on his hands that obscures the pattern."

Stanton budged his shoulders away from the wall, straightened, and approached the table. He glared at the smooth ovals Tashum left for prints. Stanton looked up at the other faces around the table.

"There was makeup residue found on the victim, wasn't there?"

"Painted up like a tart," said Wilks.

The uniformed cop confirmed with a sly nod.

"Run a check for a possible match. And those bloody fingerprints we found on the victim, send them to M16, Interpol, and the Americans."

Tashum stood in a hallway filled with Pakistani youths restrained in handcuffs shouting curses into the ceiling, pregnant women conferring with lawyers, and a pair of gilt transvestites covered in scratches and clods of gray mud.

Over the din he counted to himself as the phone rang at the other end, ". . . four, five, six, seven, eight, . . ." In all the years Gregory had been in his employ, the private number had never gone beyond the third ring before being answered.

Tashum hung up and quickly pecked in the digits again, once more with the same result. As he slowly hung up, Stanton appeared out of a cloud of cigarette smoke.

"Need a ride?" asked the inspector in a mocking tone.

Fifteen minutes later, Inspector Stanton leaned forward, the prow of his belly nudging up against the steering wheel of his perfectly restored MGB. He squinted as he tried to make out the house numbers. Tashum gazed dully out the windscreen into the stream of the headlights.

"It's right up here, isn't it?" Stanton asked.

"You found it before," Tashum's voice was smug, "surely you can find it again."

"I get the distinct impression you think this is all some sort of game."

"Inspector, cricket is a game. Life feeding life is something entirely different."

"Life feeding life? What do you mean by that?"

"Just words."

"Am I supposed to read between the lines with you?"

"Here, slow down or you'll miss it."

Stanton slowed the car and pulled to a stop at the curb. "Listen up, mate! I'm not very fond of puzzles or enigmas."

"You're in the wrong line of work."

"Perhaps you are too. Tell me, Tashum, when someone welches on a bet just how far will you go to get your money?"

Tashum's mouth curled into a shallow smile as he chose his words. "There are rules of etiquette; it's rarely a problem."

"Rarely a problem, that's what I'm interested in. I advise you not to leave London."

"Can you tell me why?"

"With your intuitiveness, I'm sure you know."

Tashum noticed a shift in Stanton's accent. "You're not really English, are you?"

"I'm South African," Stanton said with slight unease.

"Some things you can never change." He smiled. "Can you?"

Stanton's eyebrows ran together. "You're a bit of a clever dick for some-one in your position."

"Yes, well thank you very much for the ride. I think I'll be on my way and now, I suppose you'll rush off to a pub and drink yourself legless, like in the films."

"No, Tashum, this is no television program. But you are quickly becom-ing the prime suspect. And prison really is a hard, cold place." He said, hopeful that Tashum's response might reveal something through a jerk or facial tic. "You're a gambler, tell me, in a city of this size what are the odds of us coming up with you?"

"You might have well as been reaching for the stars." Tashum opened the door and leaned out. "Good-bye, Inspector Stanton, or should I just call you Roger now that we're so close?"

"Good-bye is a bit premature I assure you," Stanton mumbled. The car door was barely closed when he slammed the gear lever forward and accel-erated away from the curb. He jerked the steering wheel. The MG veered and nearly collided with a dark-haired young man who ran into the street from behind a parked van. Stanton started to say something but was caught off guard by the bright blue eyes that stared at him, unwavering.

Tashum's footsteps clapped across the marble of the entryway floor. A tele-phone was ringing somewhere deep inside the house. Through contact lenses, his yellow eyes glowed in the darkness—no need to switch on the lights.

His footsteps quickened, then stopped.

His chin lifted and he closed his eyes, picking up the traces of a foreign energy, a fading trail of heat, small crumbs of scent.

"Victor," he muttered.

He rushed into the hallway, the ringing of the phone growing louder with his approach, past the coatroom and into the great hall lit by candles. The ringing stopped as Tashum reached the white phone on the walnut table placed in the shadow of a suit of medieval armor.

He stared at the receiver's gleaming surface, smeared with finger trails of crimson.

The word *blood* leaked from his mouth.

He lurched when the phone rang again. This time Tashum grabbed it and brought it to his ear.

"Hello—Potter, get over here immediately."

He noticed a small, static pool of blood on the table next to the phone. And then a fresh drop splashed. Then another fell and splashed.

He searched for the source and saw blood forming and dripping from the fingers of the armor suit. He sucked in air. "Potter," he said staring at the metal glove, "bring a doctor! Hurry!"

Then he saw it—the ivory handle of a dagger protruding from the dented chest plate. Trembling, he dropped the phone and his fingers went to the visor and fumbled with the mechanism.

He lifted the visor, revealing Gregory's soft, pleading eyes. He was still alive, but barely.

Tashum carefully tugged at the helmet, at last succeeded in freeing it, then gently lifted it away.

"Oh, my God." Tashum choked.

Gregory opened his mouth and a thick bubble of blood emerged. A gurgle emitted from his throat. A wide, cruel gash exposed split skin, severed muscle, and flaps of tissue.

"The orbs . . ." Gregory croaked. "Sorry . . . , Tashum."

Tashum cupped his hands around the back of the Gregory's head and held it upright. "He forced me in—armor."

"Don't speak," he pleaded. "I can read your thoughts—yes, yes I see Victor's signature everywhere here."

Tashum lifted the suit of armor off its mounting and laid it with care on the floor. Kneeling, he placed a soothing palm to his assistant's forehead. The physio-feedback was conclusive.

I'm dying, I've been murdered.

"Yes, Wynn, you . . . you are dying," he whispered. "I'm terribly sorry. You've been such a friend," he paused to brush away the tears filling his eyes. "Please forgive me."

Gregory's eyes were large, pleading for help, pleading for a miracle.

Please . . . not right . . . I don't want to die.

"I know you don't want to die," he said as he undid the leather straps that secured the armor chest plating. "And you're right, it's not fair. You, of all people, didn't deserve this." He gently removed the dagger, the blade grating against ancient iron. Then the hulking metal skin was lifted off his friend.

Gregory's face sagged, and his eyelids drooped heavily, fluttered, then closed.

Tashum's thoughts ran wild searching his intellect for a cure. The damage was too great for his limited touch and science in this case was useless. He struggled to keep the one solution out of his mind, but the idea bubbled up nonetheless.

"There is a way," he whispered urgently. "Do you hear me? Listen to me—Gregory—there is a way!"

A gasping moan came out of the man and for a moment, his eyes opened with effort.

Tashum blinked hard. His mouth was dry and he wiped a hand across his eyes. His gut burned. He shouldn't, he should *not* do this. But how could he let Gregory go? Why should he be suffering like this because of Victor's colossal vanity, enduring this hateful, needless suffering, his future ripped away by the acts of a mad thing? Hunger hadn't driven this disaster, it was the will to kill and Victor's petty emotions at play here. And yet Tashum couldn't help but trace the blame back through himself to Paladin.

The angel twisted his morality and wondered for a moment if humanity really did deserve to be kept safe from human predators. They all seem to carry the killer's gene, buried deep in some, on the surface in others. If any human could handle the hunger it would be Gregory. The angel would help him through the initial terror and bless him with a dark immortality and wealth beyond compare. New rationales supporting what he was thinking kept coming. He imagined Gregory as the polar opposite of Fanny, Dickey, and Victor. A doer of good deeds, a man with a secret.

Tashum rolled up his sleeve, revealing his etched wrist. He stared at this flesh, knowing what he must do. As the blade slid across his wrist a foreign reflective glow appeared on the skin, making his forearm orange and phosphorescent. He looked up in wonder.

A perfectly round sphere floated above Gregory's head. It glowed from some inner light. There before him, his beacon guiding him home, a second orb after almost five hundred years.

He sat for a moment transfixed by the beauty of the thing, the purity of the light radiating softly from its core. And slowly he reached for it, his hand passed through the glorious, delicate hallucination.

"Why come to me now? Do you encourage this act?"

And as gradually as it had appeared, it faded, leaving behind only empty space. He gazed at the place where it had been, perplexed—what was the intended message? Was it indeed a message at all?

But there was no time for these lingering questions.

Turning again to his dying friend he said, "Gregory, I can give you life, immortality even. I can bring you back but it comes with a horrific price. A hunger. A constant desire. And you must swear to me that you will never take a human life to satisfy it. No matter what the circumstance."

Gregory's mouth had come open, grown slack, his eyes rolled into the back of his head.

With his jaw set, Tashum took the dagger and laid the blood-stained cutting edge across his wrist, drawing it evenly back. He ground his teeth together, squeezed his eyes shut, and opened a slit in his flesh. From the thin wound seeped an ooze of liquid, a glowing, gluey stream.

"No Tashum! No, you mustn't!" a voice cried from the far end of the hall.

Tashum glanced over his shoulder and saw Misha crossing the room.

"What are you doing here?"

"I got the note you left at the hospital," said the other angel as he knelt beside Tashum and the dying servant. "Tashum, he doesn't want this. This isn't natural. Let him go. You know it is wrong," Misha insisted, taking Tashum's shoulders and tugging him away. "The orb appeared because it was the wrong thing for you to do. You've been tricked!"

Tashum gave a growl and heaved Misha away, throwing him over a table. "I have to do this!" Tashum cried. "He's my responsibility. This is all my fault."

Misha rose from the floor. "Would you do this out of compassion or your own selfishness, your own guilt?"

Tashum looked down at the blade, still resting on his arm. He swallowed back a jagged, panting note.

"Even if he could keep your ridiculous promise, his spirit will be altered—he would never be the same—and what sort of gift is that?" Misha continued in a damning tone, "Think of Fanny and Dickey!"

Then another voice brought a chill to the room, "Go ahead, do it, Tashum! You won't have a second chance to save your servant!"

Mayhem's wings folded onto his back as his translucent body settled into Napoleon's pose, his stump of a left hand stuffed into his garment while his one good hand held the crystal sword out to one side. There he was, caught in the Light, standing on the hand-hewn block of oak that formed the fireplace mantel.

Tashum's eyes were too filled with grief and confusion to pay any attention to the peacock's arrival. He glanced at his bleeding wrist, then to Gregory's gasping face.

"Should I do it, Mayhem?" he said, keeping his back to him.

Misha drew closer, taking one of Gregory's hands, trying to catch Tashum's gaze. "I share in your pain," he said gently, "your loss is mine, but please don't listen to Mayhem."

"Why not?" came Mayhem's reply. "It wouldn't be the first time, would it Tashum?"

"Don't listen to him, Tashum!" Misha shouted. "You can't do this!"

"Relax, Misha, it's academic now." Tashum sighed.

Gregory's lifeless eyes were staring up into the molded plaster ceiling. Tashum reached down and smoothed them closed.

He groaned. A moan came from somewhere deep inside his body as he caressed his friend's forehead. Tashum rose to his feet. "He's yours now," he said as he brushed past Misha. At the doorway, the forlorn angel looked back at Mayhem. "And you, be gone bad dream," he said in a level tone with clear meaning. He turned and walked away.

Misha bent over Gregory, whispered the sacred verses into his ears, words made from musical cords guiding him toward the brilliant finger of Light.

A snapping of wings came from across the room. Misha glanced up.

The transparent image of Mayhem passed through the air on spread wings. "Misha, this isn't your mission."

"You," Misha whispered. "Why are you interfering with Tashum's journey?"

"His journey?" the spirit chuckled, sinking toward the floor. "How quaint. Do you not think I have bigger things to deal with?"

"Yes, I do. A number of us think you know something about the silence in heaven."

Mayhem swung the sword in an arc out of nervous reaction to the allegation. "Who are the others you're referring to?" His voice grew uneven and demanding. "Who!"

"Those who haven't disappeared."

Mayhem snarled his upper lip. "You, so pure by light? So sad by nature. If I were what you think, you'd be on the list."

Misha recoiled, sprang to his feet, and took on a defensive stance. "I'm warning you to leave Tashum alone!"

"Warning me? From you that's almost funny." Mayhem's wings flared, then fell. His eyes burned bright with rage. He flew toward Misha, blowing through him with cold force, that flattened him to the floor. Mayhem's image darkened and hovered inches above Misha's paralyzed eyes. "I'll be waiting for you." The spirit bared his teeth.

Tashum stood in the doorway of the computer room surveying broken furniture, smashed lamps, his butchered flower bouquet, and the words *FUCK YOU* spray painted across the bank of monitors. He walked gingerly through the carnage—and stopped.

"Ah, dear." He groaned, seeing the shattered stained-glass window. Colored fragments still clung to the frame, while the rest lay in splintered piles.

Tashum tiptoed through the debris to the wall safe, its doors hanging wide open, the contents gone. He slammed the door and turned to his desk, where he noticed the empty cradle for his cellular telephone. Victor had been thorough.

Tashum stepped into the adjoining bathroom. He glanced around and caught his reflection in the mirror. He noticed he had lost a contact lens and removed the other. His yellow eyes were swollen and tired. His makeup was chipped around the edges. He turned on the tap and began scrubbing away the makeup from his face and hands, revealing the intricate, embossed scars that mapped his skin.

Misha stood behind, gazing over his shoulder, sadness clouding the charismatic blue eyes of the Unfallen. Their eyes met in the mirror. So alike but so different, the two sharply contrasted the angelic images gazed at one another. Tashum's washcloth again wiped across his face, taking away small wisps of Max Factor. "You don't have this problem, do you, Misha?"

"We each carry our own angelic mark. Both come with their own dangers," said Misha.

"Would you call this the face of an angel?"

"Yes."

"Give it a break, Misha, look at us. Your looks attract and disarm people, mine terrify and threaten. If we are to be pitted against one another, it's hardly a level playing field."

"In war or games, I am not at odds with you, Tashum."

Tashum continued his washup. "I've got other problems at the moment."

"They really smashed up your home."

Tashum nodded. "They have a talent for destruction." He added, "In this world you get used to nice things being ruined. The cheeky bastard even stole my cell phone."

"Cell phone? I had hoped you'd be thinking about Gregory."

Tashum flinched at the nerve struck and continued to rub the towel against the scars on his face. Too proud to reveal his pain, Tashum changed the subject, "Where do these human spirits go when they die?"

Fighting the urge to give his brother comfort with knowledge that is rightfully his, Misha could only bite his lip and look down at his hands, clasped in front of him. "I cannot tell you, Tashum, but I think you know."

Tashum looked up and snorted "Can't, or won't? There's a big difference, you know."

"It's not my wish."

"Not your wish? What, are you sworn to some sort of oath that keeps you from communicating with the fallen?"

Misha didn't respond.

"Is heaven really that regulated?"

Misha bowed his head. "No."

"Misha, if you are as good as I think you are. How can you possibly deny me the answers I need so desperately?"

"You've seen my work. That should be enough."

"I've seen you comfort the dying, how do you decide who gets comforted? I mean logistically speaking there must more humans dying every day than there are angels in existence."

"We work on both sides of the Light. No human truly dies alone."

"Even villains?"

"Even villains."

"I have killed men. My hand still weakens with the thought of it."

"Your actions were witnessed and the spirits of those men were reclaimed."

"But I was there! I didn't sense any presence from the Light. I never have!" Tashum caught his own reflection in the mirror. "I sensed grief over my act of murder, but if it's not final, if the spirit recycles, why should it hurt me so badly?"

Misha sat on the cool white edge of the bathtub. "Think of what you are, where you came from." Misha then took a breath. "Tashum, I must get home. I need your help."

"Pardon me if I don't jump," Tashum said, "but I've spent forty thousand years stranded here."

"I know."

"No, you don't. You know nothing of linear time. Forty thousand years, maybe more, I've been searching for answers, searching for a way back. And you sit here worried about overstaying, what a few days?"

Misha drew closer. "When you fully earn your redemption, your orbs will be revealed to you in more than just a vision."

"I was never given any orbs," he said "And redemption? Redemption from what? We were all given free will with little mention of consequence!"

"I'm sorry for you and the others like you." Misha lowered his head. These were words he had heard before from angels on both sides of the Light during the argument that had ultimately seen Tashum banished.

Tashum watched Misha wrestling with the dilemma of whether or not to tell him the truth about the orbs. For a brief moment he looked into Misha's mind. The mind probe uncovered not the communication network he remembered as being thickly layered and held together by the thoughts and messages from the millions of angels ruling the heavens. Instead, Misha's mind was fragmented and fearfully unclear, murky with questions of great mystery. Something had happened in the year 1430. Whatever the event, the result seemed to be a silence in heaven and missing angels.

I can show you no more. Misha blinked and the mental connection was broken.

"What exactly did the vampires do to you?" Tashum asked, looking for a cause of the angel's delusions.

"It's not important," he said with downcast eyes.

"Oh, but it is important. It's a matter of pride."

"Pride is a dangerous emotion," he said sadly. "Please, will you just give me my orbs?"

Tashum, hesitated. "Unless you tell me about the orbs, you'll never get them back. I'm quite serious."

Misha's mouth opened and the words fell out. "After the Fall, all angels were given a set of celestial orbs. They allow us to break dimensional barriers, to pass back and forth between the visible and invisible worlds."

"Yes I figured that much out."

"Through an act of selflessness your orbs are waiting to be claimed."

"But, I've done good deeds. I've even seen a visionary orb, but never the real thing." Tashum blushed, embarrassed at the shallow, pitiful sound of his entreaty.

"Your orbs are inside you, lost perhaps within you, but there nonetheless." Misha turned away, his jaws working silently over his hidden, internal argument. "You can't use mine." His voice broke from frustration. "You have to earn your own."

"Did Mayhem earn his return back into the Light?"

"No, I'm sure he didn't."

"If he borrowed a set of orbs, so can I." Tashum walked out of the bathroom and into the computer room.

"Tashum," Misha hurried after him. "I need them back now."

"We're on my schedule now, Misha."

Misha shook his head and spilled his guts. "The orbs can only exist in this dimension for one cycle of the moon. My orbs are at the end of their thirty-day cycle."

"What?"

"Everything in the physical world decays and is recycled back through nature. The energy it takes to break through the barriers decays as well. At sunrise two days from now, my orbs will be absorbed back into the fabric of the universe if not used."

"Can any Celestial pass through the vortex set by the orbs?"

"Yes, technically, but you can't use mine, Tashum!"

A grin developed on Tashum's mouth. "So you're stranded here like me if you don't use them in the next seventy-two hours?"

"Something like that."

"If I went through the vortex first could I get them back to you?"

Misha winced. "No, I don't think they work that way."

An intercom buzzed.

Tashum kept his eyes on Misha a moment longer, then went to a black panel on the wall, where he pushed a button.

"Yes?" he said, speaking into a small mic.

"Tashum," Hamley Potter's voice came out of the speaker, "it's me, Potter. Dr. Blake and I are half an hour away—"

"Yes, Potter, thank Dr. Blake, but as it turns out he won't be needed. Let yourself in. Meet me in the main parlor when you arrive." He released the wall button. Tashum leaned against the wall with a new sense of urgency coursing through his being.

Misha eyed him closely. "Why didn't you use my orbs when you had the chance?"

Tashum kept his eyes down, pretending to study a broken bust of Marco Polo. He reached down and picked up the jagged clay nose.

"You had them overnight," Misha continued. "You could have used them." Misha stared, openmouthed. "You don't know how the orbs work, do you?"

Tashum shook his head slowly. "No, not all of it."

"That's why you're still here. You would have used them, without a thought to me."

Tashum felt the stab of Misha's words. "I would have tried to get them back to you—somehow."

Misha glanced around the wreckage in the room. "Where are my orbs, Tashum?"

"Gone." Tashum sighed, dropping what was left of Marco Polo. "Stolen."

Misha's cheeks flushed red. "Tashum, I need to get them back—will you help me?"

Tashum's eyes looked away, and he weighed his options against his abilities. "I know how to get them back. And you know how to use them," he said slowly. "Maybe we can work something out. An arrangement."

"I've already divulged more than I have a right to," he turned away. "I've shamed myself—"

"No, Misha," he said softly, "I reached in and took information from you." Tashum stepped forward placing his hand on Misha's shoulder. "You've done nothing wrong, and from my point of view neither have I."

"I can't tell you anything more." He swept Tashum's hand from his shoulder and faced him. "Only one of us will be able to return to the Light."

"Only one?" said Tashum in a competitive tone.

"Only one," Misha said with a slight nod.

"Life down here has always been a gamble, Misha. You learn to play the cards as they're dealt." His eyes wavered and then narrowed. "You learn to start again when you lose."

CHAPTER SIXTEEN

A huge moon appeared over Poole Harbour, white and chalky, its soft light giving shape to the seaplane tethered alongside the short pier. The Grumman G-44 Widgeon sat heavy in the water, half submerged, her boat-shaped fuselage was a sleek outline. Her overhead wings and white paint reminded Dickey of a swan.

"Victor was right. It does look better in the water, don't you think?" Dickey commented as he closed the boot lid of his older Ford Cortina. He latched onto two of the three suitcases resting on the curb and followed after Fanny.

Fanny crossed the narrow road and stopped on the landing atop a flight of steps that led from the roadway down the incline to the remote pier. She briefly studied Victor's dream machine. "It's a flying boat any way you look at it, in fact it appears it might sink." She added in a dismissive tone, "And those folded wing tips completely spoil any lines that lame duck might have had."

"Silly girl, it's the extra fuel tanks what weigh her down." He stopped next to her. "And the wing tips when folded down like that are floats, keep her balanced on the sea."

"Well they still look ridiculous." She glanced back at the car. "You will go back for my other bag, won't you?"

"Only if you promise not to blow the wind out of Victor's sails. He's very proud of this plane, and we need to build his confidence."

"I suppose you're right, considering he's our pilot."

Dickey glanced at his wristwatch. "He should be here any time."

"You should have gone with him."

"I hate explosives, you know that."

"Dickey, why is it that you hate everything difficult except Victor?"

The little seaplane's twin engines droned and surged as it skimmed the cresting cobalt blue waves in Poole Harbour. Her wing-tip pontoons pounded the shallow waves into white spray, and her wings then lifted her into the air.

At the cockpit controls, Victor let out a whooping cowpoke's cry of excitement. He held the yoke with the rigor of riding a champion steer.

Grinning, he looked to Dickey in the seat next to him, then swiveled to Fanny in the seat behind him. His teeth on full display, his eyes as bright as a marquee. "Ain't she sweet?"

"Reel in your tongue before it dries out and falls off," Fanny said from the shadows. "And while you're at it, fly the plane."

"She might have a point," added Dickey as they pitched to port.

"Just remember it's up to me," Victor declared, and showed her his hands weren't on the yoke. "Look ma, no hands."

"I'd hate to see you wreck your new toy," Fanny said with little concern. She glanced at her upturned cuffed hand. "Dickey, where's my nail file?"

Dickey grabbed for the yoke—

Victor took control. "Don't never do that!" he scolded, slapping at Dickey's shoulder. "I was flyin' her with my knees. Man, you coulda fuckin' kilt us all." He raised a fist in a mocking blow. "Jesus, that was dumb."

Once fully airborne, Victor turned the yoke and swung the plane into a sharp, banking turn.

Beside him, Dickey extended the antenna on a handheld remote control device.

As the plane veered, Fanny was jostled in her seat and scrambled to steady Tashum's ornate box holding the orbs. "I thought you knew how to fly."

"What the fuck do you think I'm doin'?" said Victor as his eyes scanned the marina below. He shouted to Dickey, "You see that piece a shit, yet?"

Dickey's eyes were pressed to the starboard side window, searching piers, flanked by sailboats and yachts bobbing in their slips.

"There it is!" Fanny called out.

"I spy with my little eye something that goes boom," Victor said.

Dickey's eyes blinked, and a look of remorse crossed his features. *"Lofty Vision,"* he read, emblazoned across the yacht's transom.

"Jesus H—" Victor hee-hawed. "That's a dumb fucking name for a boat. You with me on this one?"

"I suppose," said Dickey with a lack of enthusiasm.

"Well don't get too excited." Victor wiggled his eyebrows. "Let's put that bitch outta her misery."

The plane made another wide arc around the far end of the marina, rising, then diving, leveling off just above the rippling water surface. She picked up speed across open water. As they closed in on their target, Victor pulled back on the wheel, and the nose of the plane lifted toward the heavens.

"How much of the explosive did you plant?" Fanny asked, noticing their slight altitude.

"Just enough," Victor said. "Get ready, Dickster, one, two, three, bombs away!" Victor called out. "Push the button! Push it! Push it!"

"Seems a shame," Dickey said, "destroying something so beautiful."

"Victor, we're too low," she said with alarm.

"Fuck you," Victor replied. "Dickey, push the goddamn button."

Dickey's head turned farther, watching the yacht being passed over.

"Victor! Pull up!" she screamed.

"Now!" Victor shrieked. "Push it, you dumb fuck."

From behind, Fanny lunged forward. Victor pushed Fanny away from the controls, forcing her back into her seat. His fist pounded Dickey's finger onto the button.

"We had better be high enough!" she screamed.

Victor jerked back the yoke.

The initial energy pulse of the percussive blast rocked the plane, and pieces of bulleting debris pelted its outer skin. Bright orange fire bubbles lofted into the air. The huge balloon of flame rose up all around the plane's windows. The vampires screamed as the nose plunged into the center of the tumultuous inferno. Victor guided them through the hell and into wide, open night sky.

"Yeowza!" Victor panted. "We were a little low."

When he realized they were unscathed, Dickey searched the sea below to catch a final glimpse of the burning wreckage of Tashum's once proud yacht. A massive funnel of smoke towered into the air. Flames and glowing embers littered the marina.

Victor giggled and hooted, let out a raucous rebel yell.

Fanny turned from the window and settled back. "One piece at a time," she murmured.

Dickey twisted in his seat and looked back to her for reassurance. "Fanny—"

"Don't worry, Dickey," she said with a half smile. "It'll be all right."

His eyes lowered, and he produced a weak smile.

Victor was still in the midst of his own wild celebration. "Now that's what I call a lofty fuckin' vision!"

The plane continued to rise, skirting out from under dissipating clouds, then swooped down, chasing its shadow over a shimmering moonlit sea.

Hamley Potter stood before the fire in the study, stirring coals with an iron poker. He wore a dark olive pullover and dark slacks.

Tashum sat in a wing-back chair, legs sprawled, staring into the churning, winking fire. He drew softly on a cigar, holding the smoke in his mouth and releasing it slowly. "It's been a rough night, Potter," he said as he dusted an ash off the black silk of his coat sleeve.

"I'm sorry to be the one to tell you," Potter said, returning the poker to the rack. He sat on the hearth. "I thought perhaps you'd received a call or seen it on television. It was everywhere."

"No. I'm not listed. And television—" He shook his head. "Well, I suppose I should pay more attention."

"BBC-1 showed what was left of her as she disappeared into the water. Burned right down to the waterline. Thank God most of your crew weren't aboard at the time. Unfortunately they found three bodies. It was bloody awful."

"My yacht can be replaced, but they were good men." Tashum surged out of the chair, puffing on the cigar and pacing before the fire.

"They stole the orbs for more money," he said, voicing his thoughts. "They killed Gregory to hurt me. And now they've burned my yacht to keep me from following them."

"Tashum, what are you—?"

"The cheeky bastard even nicked one of my cell phones," he said without paying any attention to Potter.

"What are you—?"

"The only thing I don't understand is the dead boy."

Potter shifted. "What the devil are you on about? What orbs? What dead boy?"

Finally he glanced at Potter. "Vampires. A trio of them. And they've stolen something I must get back."

"Did . . ." Potter shook his head as if to free his ears of water. "Did you say vampires?"

"You really should do something about your, hearing, Potter," he said in an attempt at covering his slippage of thought into words. A clinking of porcelain cups and saucers caused Potter to turn toward the door. Misha entered the room bearing a tray with tea things.

"If you didn't say vampires, what did you say?"

"Potter," Tashum said with a hand gesture, "I want to introduce you to Misha. He's taking over for Gregory. Misha, just put those things here on the table."

Potter nodded to Misha, mumbling a greeting, then turned to Tashum. "Good God, man, that was awfully damn quick. I hope I'm not that dispensable to you."

"Nobody that I call a friend is dispensable."

With dawn spreading hints of neon in the east, Victor's seaplane made a tight, curling turn at the edge of an enormous desert land mass. The yellow cliff that rose out of the black water was capped with a monolithic structure. The silhouetted square turrets of the medieval fortress framing the pinking sky. The dim light of daybreak shown through the small round-topped windows and dusted high stone walls here and there. A dark figure carried a torch. He crossed the pillared balcony and hurried up a flight of steps that wrapped around the crenelated tower. From his high vantage overlooking the sheer drop to the sea he waved the torch—a signal.

In gentle descent the plane's wing tips folded down, her fuselage lightly splashed the wave tops, then dropped its weight fully and skipped across the choppy water, plowing the surface and sending a wake of waves against the base of the cliff. Its engines reduced, the winged vehicle motored into a small protected cove in the shadow of the crumbling fortress.

The plane pulled up to a wooden slip, where a man in flowing white-and-black Berber garb threw a line and scampered to one of the wing tips, mooring the plane to its resting place.

Two other Arab men in similar garments emerged from a nearby cave entrance, cut centuries ago into the yellow rock. Automatic machine guns hung from their shoulders. They took up guard positions on both sides of the cavern entrance. One smoked a dark brown cigarette. The other picked his teeth with the small blade of his knife.

Dickey, Fanny, and Victor in turn jumped out of the plane carrying small travel bags. Fanny took the lead, and they made their way across the dock and up a sloped path cut into the cliff side. The two guards snapped to attention with the vampire's approach. Fanny nodded to them, *"Bonjour, Ali Maisara."* She smiled at the man smoking. He returned the greeting with a smile and a nod. She looked to the other unfamiliar Berber face, *"Bonjour, Je m'appelle, Fanny. Comment vous appelez-vous?"*

He said his name was "Yusuf Ibn Bashfin" and he bowed his head. She quickly introduced them to Dickey and Victor and then entered the cavern.

Inside the cave the trio was met by a young Arab holding a torch.

"Tio!" Fanny smiled, wrapping an arm around him.

The dark-skinned youth returned a discreet, shy smile of his own. He turned, and they followed the glow of his torchlight dancing in the bevels and facets of the chiseled ceiling.

"Smells like piss in here," Victor barked, looking all around the walls of the passageway.

"Shut up, Victor," Dickey gasped tiredly. "Don't mind him, Fanny."

"For once he's telling the truth," she said.

"What the hell is this place?" Victor asked her. "I thought you hated old shit."

"It's called history," Dickey corrected.

"Old shit," Victor maintained.

"Some memories are worth keeping intact and others better off forgotten," Fanny said with a sidelong glance to Dickey.

"What's that supposed to mean?" asked Victor.

"You wouldn't understand," Dickey cut in, "sweet bird of youth."

"You know I don't get that poetry shit." Victor groaned.

"It wouldn't hurt you to pick up a book once in a while," Dickey sneered.

"Don't encourage him, he'd only use it as a weapon," said Fanny, teasing.

"Haaaay, that ain't a bad idea, pitchin' books like horseshoes. I'm pretty good at that, you know."

"I was only kidding, Victor," she said dryly.

"Oh, I knew that, so was I," Victor said dusting off the insult.

The four turned down a bend in the passage and then up an endless flight of steps that channeled them into a large, airy open room with a vaulted ceiling held up by limestone pillars. At the far end was a wide, unobstructed vista of the Moroccan coastal waters. Warming, predawn light illuminated long gauzy curtains gently swaying between the solid pillars.

From an adjoining room, a darkly tanned Moroccan man appeared under the arched door. He carried a silver tray bearing porcelain cups and a silver carafe of coffee. He had bright gray eyes set above high cheekbones and perfect, glossy skin.

"*Bonjour, Samir,*" Fanny said, with an expression of warm delight. "*Je vous présente, Dickey et Victor.*"

"*Bonjour, Samir,* good to see you," said Dickey.

Victor merely winked at Samir.

"*Enchanté.*" Samir nodded and smiled graciously.

Fanny turned to Dickey and Victor. "Tio will show you to your rooms." She then smiled at Tio. "*Merci, Tio.*"

"All right," Victor said, turning and following Tio. "I could use me a little shut eye. How 'bout you, pops?"

"You need a bath," Dickey answered.

"Don't gimme that old line."

Their querulous voices diminished as Tio led them through a series of arches and down the corridor.

Fanny set down the wooden box and, with outstretched arms, yawned happily and spun around in full circles, drinking in the grandeur of her crumbling desert palace.

"Madam Matar," Samir said, placing the coffee tray on a table, "we must discuss your unpaid bills."

She stopped in midpirouette and frowned in his direction. Ecstasy cut short.

"Surely we can discuss it later." Then a look of tired fulfillment again took hold of her. "But first draw me a warm bath. I feel dirty."

He dipped his head in an obedient nod.

She took his hand, her perfect, scarlet lips curling in ripe anticipation.

"It will be my pleasure, madame," he said. "Is it still thirty-seven degrees Celsius? Your bath water, I mean."

"What a memory, Samir, and your English is much improved."

"Thank you, I still prefer French," he said with pride.

"*Naturellement.*" She smiled. "*Je ne veux pas vous faire de la peine.* But please speak English around my guests."

"*Et avec ça, madam?*"

"Yes, there is something else," she paused, turning away. Her palms came together, her hands rubbing back and forth under her delicate nose. "There are two metal boxes hidden in the rear of the plane." She turned back to him. "I want you, and only you, to fetch them for me."

He held her gaze, and slowly lowered his eyes. . . .

CHAPTER SEVENTEEN

Stanton sipped at his steaming coffee in little spurts. The object of his attention was the auto section of the *Exchange & Mart*. The trade rag was laid out before him on a neatly kept metal framed desk. With his pen he made a large circle around the listing: LOTUS ELAN, ROADSTER, 1967, B.R.G., TAN LEATHER, RESTORED CONDITION, TEL: 0606 47915.

The latch on the office door clicked, and in burst Detective Wilks. "Roger!" he exclaimed.

"You're here awfully early," Stanton grumbled, pulling his mind back to police matters.

"We've got a match," Wilks sputtered and ran his fingers through his unruly hair. "The makeup residue found on the victim matches what we found on Tashum's drinking glass." He bent low over the desk. "Max Factor base and toner."

Stanton twisted his mouth to one side. "Can't you buy that at any corner shop?"

"Wouldn't know, would I? But I'm telling you it's the same stuff," he said, and then he noticed the circled auto advertisement. "You know what Lotus stands for don't you?"

Stanton crossed his arms. "I give up, what?"

"Lots-of-Trouble-Usually-Serious," he said, and laughed.

"Very clever." Stanton nodded. "Any news on the fingerprints? And this Victor fellow?"

Wilks scratched at the back of his neck and shook his head. "Still waiting. I've just—I've got this strong feeling Tashum's our killer."

Stanton leaned back in his chair with a chorus of squawks. "Now you're psychic, too?"

"Come on, Roger. What are you waiting on?"

"Let's interview his alibi. That Gregory chap. I also want to check the tire tread on Tashum's Bentley against the tire tracks at the warehouse. On second thought let's bring them both in for a chat."

"Right on it," Wilks said, hammering the door shut behind him.

"Hang on, hang on, wait for me, damn it!" Stanton complained and rose from the chair. He slugged down the last bit of coffee and grabbed his jacket off the door hook.

Deep beneath the Kensington House, the air was chilled and damp, smelling of earth and ancient plaster. Tashum and Misha had labored for an hour, replacing uniquely cut stones back into the puzzle work of a foundry wall. Tashum stopped for a moment, gazing through the odd-shaped opening.

Inside the secret room lay the remains of several bodies draped in yellowing cloths resting on traditional crypt stones. Now Gregory's body was added to this collection. He lay in peaceful stillness, covered in a new white sheet.

"He was a good friend," Tashum said softly.

"And the others?" Misha asked.

"Time has taken many good companions," he replied. "Every friendship ends in tragedy."

"Tashum, death is just the conclusion of physical life."

Tashum shrugged. "They move on, while I remain behind. Immortal."

"Immortal . . ." Misha repeated. "You've mentioned that before."

Tashum rested a stone in place. "What?"

"Just the way you used the word."

Tashum stopped and turned to the other, trying to understand the implication in his tone.

Misha continued, "Immortality means never dying, correct?"

Tashum shook his head. "Of course it does."

"Celestials can die. You know that."

"I've been speared, stabbed, shot, even drowned. I haven't died yet. I'm pretty sure you're wrong."

Misha studied Tashum for a few seconds before coming to a decision. "Have you ever been to the Antiquities Shoppe in Paris?"

"What antiquities shop in Paris?" Tashum asked.

"The only one with the skeletal remains of an angel?"

"Rubbish," Tashum said with an incredulous glance.

"You know that I can't lie to you."

"No, I don't know that." Tashum knew he wasn't lying, but how could such a thing exist? "I've got to see this," he said in a dismissive tone. "Show it to me and I'll show you a fake."

"Tashum, it's real."

"As real as the orbs?" he teased.

Misha's eyes were suddenly full of conflict. He stood quiet as Tashum went back to work tamping the earthen fill between the stones with his trowel. Misha slowly followed suit, picked up another stone, and nestled it carefully among the others. Tashum bent to retrieve another cut block.

A buzzer rang from the floor above. Rang again. And again—a long insistent ranting.

"I'd better see who that is," Tashum said, rubbing grit from his hands.

After climbing several sets of stairs, he came to a small room filled with electronic security equipment, just off the entryway; the one room that Victor didn't make himself at home in. Tashum looked into a black-and-white surveillance screen built into a gray console. He wiggled the small joystick. On the monitor image panned the front steps, he could see Inspector Stanton and Detective Wilks heading up a small army of uniformed officers.

The buzzer continued buzzing.

"Yes," Tashum spoke into a microphone.

Outside Stanton looked directly into the lens of the motorized camera and held up a sheet of paper that wavered unreadable in the morning breeze.

"This is a warrant to search and arrest those on the premise. You must open this door immediately."

Misha stepped behind Tashum and glanced over his shoulder. "What's this? What's going on?"

Tashum stared into the screen, then paced away. "I told them who killed the young man," he complained. He glanced back at the screen, at the collection of dour faces. "I've got to get a few things—meet me in the library. Go! I'll be along."

On the front steps, Wilks continued to press the buzzer. "Open up!" he shouted.

Stanton stepped back, waiting. He checked his wristwatch, then he pointed at the two bobbies closest to the door. "Break it down."

The two officers lifted up a heavy steel battering ram. With one at the head of the implement and another at the rear, the two charged at the door, giving it a tremendous slam. The heavyset door jolted in its frame, but held. The men backed up and rammed it again. This time a split opened down the center. They backed up again and repeated the battering, and the door began to rock loose in its frame. On the fifth blow, the ram exploded through the center of the door. Splinters of wood flew into the entryway.

Tashum was carrying a small attaché bag when he flashed into the library with such speed that left brief lags of his image hanging in the air. He stopped at a tall panel of books towering to the ceiling. He beckoned to Misha to hurry behind. They glanced backward, hearing the door as it finally succumbed to the battering ram. Immediately shouts and commands of the police echoed throughout the house, followed by sounds of running feet, doors opening and closing, shattering glass.

Tashum pulled out a thick green volume from the shelf and the floor-to-ceiling bookcase slid to one side, revealing a secret passage. He shoved Misha ahead of him into the opening, and both disappeared as the disguised door closed behind them. They were safely in darkness before a bobby appeared in the far doorway.

The officer quickly searched about the room and carefully picked his way around over turned couches, smashed lamps, and books scattered on the floor. His eyes were drawn to a slashed and ruined gold-framed painting hanging over the small fireplace: a scene painted in oil depicted an angel watching a sunrise. He gave his whistle a blow, realizing that this century-old work had the face of their suspect.

"Hey, guv!" he shouted to Stanton, who directed the search from the hallway. "Inspector Stanton!"

"Yes, what is it?" Stanton answered.

"You got to see this, sir," he said, pointing at the art piece. "It's him."

"I want the real thing, not a painting!" he barked.

Wilks stepped into the room with his eyes trained on the floor. He walked past Stanton without a word.

"Wilks, what are you doing?"

"Following these dusty tracks," he said as he followed the faint outline of shoes across the marble flooring and onto a deep marroon carpet. The trail ended at the bookcase.

Tashum stopped for a moment and slipped the contacts out of his eyes, allowing them to glow—lamps in the darkness.

"Misha, this is where we part company," he whispered. "Through there," pointing to a small door on their right, "will get you to the street. Take this bag to Hamley Potter's office at fifty-five Tottenham Court Road. Tell him I'll be there as soon as possible."

Muffled shouts of the police came through the secret chamber door.

"Why can't we go together?"

Tashum could feel his insecurity. "Trust in me."

"Can I trust you, Tashum?" Misha asked.

"We're partners now, aren't we? We need each other. Go on."

Misha stepped to the small wooden door. With his hand on the door latch, he glanced back. Tashum gave him a confident wave and waited until Misha had gone. Then he moved at a quick jog to the left down an ancient, packed-earth passageway, hunching here and there where the ceiling dipped low. He looked back many times to see if the police had discovered his escape. Each time he was satisfied that the tunnel remained empty of blue uniforms.

Wait. He stopped for a moment. Listening. There were footfalls now. Creeping along behind him in the gloom, moving lightly, skillful, predatory. Tashum peered forward—there wasn't far to go now. The vibration and rumble at the far end grew louder. He began running. He knew this passage better than any pursuer. At his full speed he covered the last stretch, coming to a modern metal door. The rumbling outside was heavy. He could feel strong vibrations in the still, moist air. He could hear the following footsteps gaining on him. "Impossible!" He slipped through the unlocked door, shut it, and passed into a lit tiled passage.

Tashum sprinted one hundred yards down the endless corridor before falling against the next door. Quickly he popped his contacts back in and then felt along the top of the doorjamb until his desperate fingers found the key. With a trembling hand he plunged the key into the lock and stepped through the doorway, just as he heard the door at the far end scraping open.

He emerged into the back end of a fast-food vendor in a London tube station. Early morning passengers milled about, drinking tea, smoking cigarettes, and reading half-folded newspapers.

The young Asian man looked up from the cash register and nodded at Tashum. The angel gave a grim smile and shouldered his way through the crush of commuters.

The tracks were empty and people milled about, anticipating the next train. Tashum glanced all around the long stretch of the underground platform taking in the huge, curved billboards on the far side of the tracks, and on his side, the hundreds of faces.

At one end of the platform he saw a pair of bobbies strolling through the crowd, their faces busily searching the streams of people.

Then one of them looked straight at him. He glared from the bottom rim of his domed helmet and held Tashum with his unblinking eyes. Then he nudged his partner and spoke into a radio mic mounted on one shoulder.

Tashum turned his back to them, then glanced back. They were pushing their way in his direction. He joined a stream of people, and very gradually he shrunk his height to match those around him by bending his knees, which were hidden by the length of his overcoat. He ducked behind a man holding a large folded-out map and merged into a flow of people moving in the opposite direction. When he passed by the pursuing bobbies he glanced away, striking up a conversation with the woman walking next to him. Once behind the bobbies he turned around and followed them until they were flagged by a troubled traveler. Tashum stopped, careful to shadow their movement, careful to keep to their backs and out of their eyeline. He pretended to tie a shoe as they answered the old man's questions.

Tashum figured he could easily play cat and mouse until a suitable train came along. He glanced at the face of his watch peeking out from under his shirt cuff. In a few minutes his train would follow on the heels of the express. All he had to do was hold their prospective position.

At the far end of the platform, a third officer appeared out of the crowd. Through a hole in the crowd he caught a glimpse of Tashum kneeling down. Tashum raised his head and met the officer's stare. The contact lasted but a second before the hole in the crowd closed. When it opened again, Tashum was gone.

The bobby's solid body plowed through the throngs of waiting passengers, a hunter's intent in his eyes. A fellow officer joined his side and called in a radio alarm.

The two bobbies Tashum had been eluding left the little old man and restarted their search.

Tashum was on the move. His working space was shrinking, and the secondary avenues of escape were being cut off in quick succession by pairs of eager policemen.

"This way," a familiar voice said. "Hurry, Tashum!"

Tashum whirled around.

Misha stood there and tugged on his coat sleeve. "Come on," Misha urged. "This way."

"What are you doing here?" Tashum barked as they started a brisk walk.

"They found your secret door."

They crossed the platform toward a wide set of railed stairs leading up in the direction of the exit gates.

"Misha I can't go out in the daylight!"

"Well you can't stay here."

The bobbies shouted at them from the floor of the platform. Misha stopped and looked down at them.

"Don't look at them! Keep moving, Misha."

Dodging through the rivers of humanity, the two angels made their way to the top of the stairs and followed the curved landing around to the left, taking another set. All the way, Misha offered words of help and encouragement that seemed very patronizing to one who was well practiced at the art of stealth.

"There's enough shade on the street. You'll be fine."

"I'm not exactly new at this, you know. When we're on the street you'll need to shield me until we cross the road into the shade."

At the top of the stairs they bent left again, hurrying along a catwalk that hung high over the train tracks. On the wall, a painted arrow pointed to the city streets.

They were going to make it. They were halfway across the suspended walkway—

At the far end of the walk, four more uniformed men appeared. It took them only a second to recognize him. They slowed, spread out. Waiting.

Tashum's pace slowed to a stop. At a glance he counted an even dozen adversaries.

"Come on," Misha said, pulling him to the guardrail.

"What, jump? No—no, I can't do that. I'd rather face them."

"If you choose to fight, we'll never get the orbs back."

He looked beyond Misha to the four policemen marching in step with batons at the ready. In the other direction he watched eight bobbies clear the stairs and form ranks.

As he looked over the edge of the guardrail, a rush of nausea seeped through him. The dark, greasy tracks some thirty feet below seemed to jump up and fall away. "Vertigo," he whispered, suddenly desperate and ill.

Below them, a train roared out of the tunnel. The express train sent shockwaves of noise and wind through the subterranean station. He was mesmerized by the blur of speeding train cars beneath them. A knot of sickness swelled in this throat. His legs began to buckle, and the world swirled around him in a fray of nightmarish images.

Misha climbed and perched himself on the rail. "On three," he said.

"I can't. I'll fight them!"

"With what?" In what appeared as amazing ease, Misha lifted Tashum to the edge of the rail. "You've got nothing left."

"Hey there!" shouted one of the bobbies with outstretched arms, lunging, his fingers clasping Tashum's overcoat—

"Three!" Misha cried, pulled Tashum with him. Tashum slipped out of his coat, leaving it in the firm grasp of three bobbies.

Tashum felt himself dropping through empty space, plunging toward the tops of the rocking train cars whizzing beneath their feet.

Tashum let out an anguished cry and closed his eyes.

Together, they hit the metal roof of the last car. Tashum's head slammed against the hard surface, and his eyes popped open. He watched in a daze as everything—the catwalk, the shouting, angry policemen, the brilliant lights of the station—slid from view with sickening speed, and then it was dark.

For a moment it was all he could do to remain conscious. The pain in his head blossomed into a white flare.

"Tashum!" Misha shouted.

Misha's warm hand gripped his tightly. The soft flesh of his fingers sent signals of strength and comfort. "Look at me," he insisted. "Tashum, get up— we're not out of this yet."

"I can't, I'm too dizzy," Tashum answered, his eyes crossing.

The cold metal of the car felt good against his face, the steady rocking was bringing on waves of blessed unconsciousness.

"You can do it, Tashum," Misha encouraged.

"Let me lie here, just a bit longer, let me—"

In a swift, powerful move Misha flipped him around. Now Tashum was staring up at the soot-blackened ceiling, at air shafts singing past at short intervals.

"Look—up ahead," Misha said.

Tashum swiveled about, his eyes blinking into the wind. He saw the train's lead car plunging out of the tunnel and into hard, blinding daylight.

"God, no!" Tashum cried. Suddenly a survival electrobolt shocked through his body.

"Take my hand," Misha said.

He took it.

"Hold tight!" the other howled. And his hand shot up, waiting for something in the air shaft. He grabbed at it.

Tashum felt his body snap taut and then swing free as the train vanished beneath him. He looked up to see Misha holding the bottom rung of a ladder welded to the metal lining of the shaft.

The tunnel went silent. The only sounds were Misha's hard, panting grunts as he struggled to keep his hold on the rung. Tashum's feet dangled inches above the angled beam of sunlight flooding in through the tunnel's open mouth.

"I don't have the strength, let go of my hand—"

"You're not serious!" Tashum exclaimed. "My feet are warming up as it is!"

"No! Listen," Misha croaked, "climb over me. Let go of my hand and climb over me."

From deep inside the blackness of the subway tunnel, Tashum heard the roar of another oncoming train.

"Now!" Misha said.

Holding back waves of illness, Tashum clambered up Misha's body, grabbing a belt loop, a shoulder. Then he grasped the cold, hard metal rung and pulled himself up into the shaft. Hand over hand he continued up into the shaft.

The roar of the other train filled his head. He dared not look down.

At last he came to a small cement chamber with a metal grate for a ceiling, a space lit by a dim blue safety light.

Breathing heavily, Misha scrambled up the ladder rungs and joined him.

Tashum laid back on the floor. Above, through the metal grated ceiling, he could make out the underbelly of a car and sounds of the London street.

"Thank you." Tashum breathed. "I'm a bit rusty at being chased."

"I was there. Glad I could help," Misha said, crouching beside him.

"That was you following me in the tunnel, wasn't it?"

The other angel nodded. "I came out on the street and went to your front door. They thought I was your gardener. I saw they had found the secret of the bookshelf, and I wanted to warn you. So I—"

"I'm not an injured bird. How did you know I'd be at the tube station."

"I knew about your escape route," he answered with a curious intonation sure to pique Tashum's interest.

"You spy on us from the invisible world, don't you?"

"We're not supposed to."

"Misha, you're no better at following instructions than I am." He gazed at the ceiling. After a few minutes of reflection, he said, "I guess I owe you one."

Misha's young, innocent face framed a tender smile. "For my work you owe me nothing."

"You like being a hero, don't you?" Tashum asked with a trace of bitterness in his voice. "Helping out where you can. Being a servant."

Misha faltered, uncertain how to respond.

"I can't do it, you know," Tashum said, his breathing coming in more regular rhythms. "It's not who I am. I don't understand—the joy of being last in line, the joy of waiting on others hand and foot. I can't see myself traipsing around the universe in search of those more needy than myself— it's just not my nature." He sat up and leaned back against the wall. "I suppose you see it as some kind of Taoist expression—water-being-more-resilient-than-stone sort of thing."

"I see it the way it is." Misha's face was troubled, his Persian-blue eyes filled with uncertainty. "It's the only way to restore balance in this world. In the universe."

"What order? I've seen only chaos on Earth. And from you I sense there is chaos in heaven."

"Tashum, I—"

Tashum glanced around. "Where's the bag I gave you?"

"I must have left it on top of the train. I'm sorry. I'll make it up to you."

Tashum shook his head. "No, don't worry about it. Nothing's lost that can't be replaced."

"Like your makeup?" Misha asked, with a small half-smile.

Tashum nodded. "Among other things," he said, ignoring the other's amusement. "Hmm. We need Potter." His eyes lifted. The car that had been parked directly overhead was gone, its undercarriage replaced by a sliver of morning sky. "I can't go out into that daylight," he complained.

Misha walked toward the other end of the space and examined the bottom side of the grate. His reaching fingers traced the steel bars. "If you can wait until dark?" He clenched the bars. "I think I can pry it open."

"You could, or you could pull that lever." Tashum nodded toward a red metal pull lever mounted on the cement wall.

"Don't look so surprised." Tashum smiled. "I don't always travel first class."

Misha chuckled. "No, but first class suits you."

"You still need to get over to Potter's office." Tashum stood and pulled the lever. The grate rotated upward. "I've never told Potter the truth about me. So don't go into the details of what's happened. Tell him to bring my travel bags. He'll know what you mean. Be back here at sunset."

"Will you be all right?"

"I'm immortal, Misha," he said firmly. "Of course I'll be all right."

Misha wouldn't argue the point. He simply lowered his eyes.

"Now go. Oh, and one other thing. You'll need to get a passport photo of yourself."

Misha returned a quizzical look. "What?"

"Don't worry, Potter will take care of it for you. Now go."

He pushed Misha up the rungs of the ladder. When Misha stood on the street, Tashum reached for the lever again, bringing the grate shut with a metallic thud.

*   *   *

Tashum patiently waited for sunset. He felt alone but for his thoughts. It seemed the two of them were lashed together—he and Misha. Misha knew how to use the orbs. Tashum knew who had them and how to get them back. An uneasy, unwelcome partnership had been formed between them—a partnership that in the best case scenario would result in one winner and one loser. However, given the time frame, there was greater probability that both would lose.

There was slight comfort in the latter of the two outcomes for one small reason—he hadn't found Paladin. If already in the Light, Paladin surely would have come to him as Mayhem had. Paladin would have come to his rescue as would be the reverse. Unless he were to believe Fanny's claim that Paladin had lost love for him. Impossible. In his heart, he felt Paladin was still here, somewhere on Earth. In a strange way, he still felt lashed to Paladin. He had often felt his brother calling to him from some remote place. A whisper in the night. A shadow on a rooftop. All these years Tashum had watched for his brother—often without realizing it. On the crowded street in Venice, an art gallery opening in New York, at the ballet in Moscow—in these densely peopled places, he'd often discovered himself searching the faces in crowds for that other familiar face.

As they had held each other during the fall, so, too, might they cling together in their redemption. If such a thing as redemption existed. The gambler calculated the odds to be nonexistent, to be pure fantasy, taken from some other angel's wish list. After forty thousand years, to solve the mystery surrounding Paladin in forty-eight hours, with no new leads, was indeed pure fantasy. He accepted the notion that once back in the Light he could find Paladin wherever he was. Reality checked in, and beneath his wrinkled brow and pensive eyes, "I need those orbs!" burst out through his clenched teeth.

Night was falling on the Tottenham Court Road address when the posh glass-and-brass door swung inward. Potter led Misha out of the office building and down the steps. Misha was carrying two large attaché cases and followed Potter's brisk pace into the private parking garage.

"I'm sorry, Potter, I wish I could tell you more about the situation."

They stopped at the Jaguar XJ-12 sedan parked in its boldly marked space. Potter moved to the driver's door and held up a hand. "I learned a long time ago that I didn't need to know all of Tashum's secrets. After these recent events my ignorant bliss may have just been shot in the ass, as the Americans say."

Tashum awoke from a half-sleep and looked around his cement cell. The only light filtering through the teeth of the grate was artificial now. He crept to the edge and peered upward, cautiously.

Night had finally come. Tashum, in fluid motion, emerged up through the hole and was on the sidewalk of a boutique-filled street.

An elderly woman in a plastic scarf stood holding a small dog. She stared at the man who had appeared out of nowhere. He greeted her blank expression with a smile and gentlemanly nod before stepping into the recess of a storefront entrance. From this nook in the long line of shops he watched for Potter without being so visible.

He checked his watch and showed his back to the small police van as it rolled slowly past his location. Through the storefront glass he could see Potter's Jaguar turn onto the road from a side street.

Potter's Jaguar traveling in the opposite direction passed the police van. Tashum rushed into the street and hailed him to a stop.

The Jaguar slowed to a stop, and Tashum reached for the back door handle. Once inside, he nodded to Misha and twisted around, looking out the back window as the brake lights flashed on the police van.

"Drive, Potter, drive!"

Potter glanced back in the rearview and hit the accelerator. "Drive where?"

"We're going to Ascona, Switzerland, via Paris."

"Paris? Switzerland?" Potter's eyebrows flattened. "You know I don't have a change of clothes."

"No bother. Besides, Potter, you're the only man I know who keeps fresh underneaths and a pressed shirt in the emergency kit of his car."

Tashum glanced at the two attaché cases filling the seat next to him. Both were custom made of black leather with small, gold latches and the letter *T* discreetly monogrammed below the handles. Identical in shape and appearance except for one tiny detail that only Tashum knew. He chose the case of his interest, spun the tumblers on the alphanumerical combination lock, and opened its lid. He, pulled out a rainbow bundle of foreign currencies and passports. He thumbed through the different nationalities and identities. "Yes," he said to Potter, "I've thought it all out. We'll put your car on the Chunnel train and then on to Paris, and from there we'll take the Train à Grande Vitesse, to Geneva."

"The what?" asked Potter.

"The bullet train."

"That's what I thought you said, but you don't understand. I was under the impression that the two of you were up to something, but I'm simply not prepared to go abroad—"

"Life is full of surprises, Potter. Misha, did you get a passport photo?"

"Yes." Misha nodded.

"Good. What nationality would you prefer?"

Misha raised his shoulders and hands, not knowing.

"I think you're Canadian," said Tashum, handing him a passport.

"What the devil are you talking about?" Potter demanded. "I can't just leave for Switzerland like that. I've got a business to run."

"I'm your number one client." Tashum glanced back again to be sure they were not being followed. "And I need your services in Switzerland. Besides, you've never seen my diamond collection."

"I don't need to see your diamond collection."

"Quit complaining. The mountain air will do you good." Tashum placed the money stack back in the attaché case.

"Why the bloody hell don't you just fly there?"

"Potter, please," he said disdainfully with a raised eyebrow.

"Vertigo, I know. But you said you were about to fly somewhere. Couldn't you—?"

Tashum and Misha exchanged a serious look.

You know only one can go!

So you've said, Misha.

Potter realized he wasn't going to get an answer. He plotted their way through mounting traffic. He sighed. "Well I hope you've at least booked us into decent hotels."

"Don't worry," Tashum said. "If my plan works," he glanced at Misha, "well, I'm sure you won't be too terribly disappointed, let me put it that way."

Misha slumped in his seat, his arms folded tight.

*　　*　　*

Several detectives and other uniformed officers milled about the destroyed computer room in the Kensington house, searching file cabinets, picking through broken glass. Upstairs, investigators lifted up the floor panels of the global map system searching for evidence. The entire house was be being picked over. A fingerprint expert brushed at the computer keyboard. A photographer held up a camera, stood back from a graffiti-sprayed wall, and gave the room a sudden flash.

Inspector Stanton winced at the bright light and turned toward the computer station.

Wilks entered the room, carrying a wire-bound notebook. He crossed to Stanton.

"Well?" Stanton said.

"Well. We've got a suit of armor full of blood." Wilks fumbled in an inside pocket and held up a dagger in a plastic evidence bag. "And the blood-stained weapon."

"Anything to go along with the blood?"

"No body yet. . . . Roger, why would Tashum do this to his own place?"

"We don't know he did, do we?"

"He's twisted sick. I just know it."

Stanton calmly examined the dagger. "If not sick, certainly eccentric. The only toilet in the house is in the butler's quarters."

"You having trouble with your bowels again, Roger?" Wilks grinned.

Stanton shot him a look, then gestured to the computer. "Get someone in here to turn this thing on."

Wilks placed the bag back in his pocket and maneuvered around the fingerprint tech. He leaned over the console hitting the on button. The bank of monitor screens lit up, glorifying the painted graffiti with backlit brilliance.

"If you had kids, you'd know how these things work."

"I still want an expert. We don't know what he's capable of."

Another flash filled the room. This time it was not the photographer. All eyes went to the curtainless window to see new rain falling through the streetlamps outside. A moment later came the rumble of thunder.

"Hey, Stanton, look at this." Wilks motioned him over.

"What'd you find?"

Wilks held up the building specifications. "Recognize the street address?"

Stanton's bushy brows ran together as he took the drawing from Wilks. "Store this with the other evidence," he said, and handed it back.

"I told you it was him." Wilks beamed. "Too bad you let him go."

Stanton wanted to chastise his underling, but Wilks was correct. He had let him go. "It gives you another opportunity to be a hero," he said coldly.

"When I catch him will you keep him?"

"Just do your job, Detective."

One of the bobbies who had chased after Tashum in the tube station entered the room carrying the bag Misha left on the rooftop of the train.

"Inspector Stanton," in a working class brogue, " 'E left this on the train."

Stanton took the leather bag from the bobby. "Have you given the sketch artist details of Tashum's accomplice?"

"No sir?"

"Be a good lad."

Near Folkestone lashing rain streamed out of the black sky, pelting the long lines of slow-moving cars and canvas-covered lorries. Inching through this traffic jam was Potter's Jaguar.

Potter turned on the wipers. The blades whipped back sheets of water only to be blanketed again almost instantaneously. The windshield was a blur of red taillights and blinking overhead signs warning of traffic delays.

"What's the bloody use of a bloody Chunnel train if you can't even get onto it?" Potter muttered with impatience. "We ought to have taken the ferry."

"In this storm?" Tashum murmured from the seat next to him, somewhat distracted, his ear to the car phone. "Once we're in the Chunnel you'll be happy." Then he spoke into the receiver, "Yes, that's right. My account number is T-1-19-8-21-13-FA . . . correct. I'm requesting a satellite trace on the following mobile transponder codes: group GBL-003B through 009 Zed. Could you repeat that for me, please? Correct, I'll ring you later for the results."

He placed the phone back into its console cradle. Tashum returned to typing something into a laptop computer. He turned and looked in back to see Misha sleeping in perfect serenity. He glanced to Potter and nodded toward the backseat.

"I like him better when he's sleeping," he said.

Potter glanced in the rearview and smiled warily.

"Where do you suppose those murderous scoundrels are hiding?"

"Using a little vampire logic I—"

"Must you insist on calling them vampires? I find it terribly distracting and frankly growing more bizarre by the minute."

"Potter, I know you didn't study vampires at Eton. But they do exist. And these particular vampires are bent on destroying everything I own or care about."

Distracted by the slow-moving traffic, Tashum's words seemed to be going over Potter's head. "I saw Nelly once," he said in a daydream. "At least, I think it was her."

"Point in case, Potter. Vampires are as elusive as the Loch Ness monster."

The traffic eased forward about three feet and stopped.

"Christ," Potter muttered. "Of course you're just using this vampire thing metaphorically."

"Did I say that?"

"No, but you have a funny way of putting things. Comparing Nelly and vampires, it's a bit like chalk and cheese."

Tashum, not one to beat dead horses, smiled at him. "My guess is they're in Morocco. The Ramadan Festival is coming up, and Fanny has a thing for young brown men. So does Dickey, for that matter." He smiled to himself. "In any event, if they have kept the remainder of my business cards," his eyes narrowed, "I should be able to confirm their location with the global tracking system."

"How the devil did you ever get involved with these people?"

"The odds were against it, but it happened anyway," he said, his eyes lowering back to the glowing screen.

"Call it fate," Misha said from behind.

Tashum froze in mid-keystroke.

"You know, I heard someone say on the radio once that if you believe in angels you had better believe in vampires . . . ," Potter faltered, recalling the rest of the message.

Misha went on to complete Potter's thought, ". . . because good and evil are mirrored images of one another, having once split from the same core. Each having disciples, angels and vampires, troubadours and demons, voices and spirits."

Tashum glanced over his shoulder—Misha was staring back.

"That's spot on," Potter exclaimed. "You must have heard the same program. Do you remember what that woman's name was?"

"No," said Misha. "I just recall it was a program about vampire hunters."

"I thought the woman claimed to be an angel," Potter said.

"Hmm, something like that."

"Perhaps I should tune in more often," Tashum said, turning back to his laptop computer.

"I don't know, Tashum, the whole thing sounded a bit dotty."

"I'm sure it did," mumbled Tashum.

Slowly the hulking shapes outside the window began moving. Soon they'd be loaded onto the train and whizzing through a concrete tube laid beneath the mud silts of the English Channel. For Tashum, this engineering feat represented yet another example for taking the word *impossible* out of the dictionary, or at least relaxing its acute meaning.

"Tashum?" Potter giggled. "Be an angel, hand me my wallet and passport out of the glove box."

Tashum's comic head jerk and startled facial expression brought a chuckle from the other two. Tashum composed his slightly discombobulated state with a smile. "How do you know I'm not the vampire?" Tashum added in jest.

"If you were the vampire, that would make me Rennfield, wouldn't it?"

"Could be a good role for you, Potter," said Tashum, teasing.

"What, me, eating spiders? I think not."

All three were laughing when they reached the tollbooth.

CHAPTER EIGHTEEN

The moon straight up illuminated the protected cove in a bath of wan gray. Dickey wrapped in a large, warm towel stepped out of the cave and back onto the narrow wooden dock. Nearby the seaplane bobbed in its slip. Its nearest wing-tip pontoon knocked with lazy insistence against the pier post, somewhat irritating the vampire. He puffed on a brown hand-rolled cigarette bummed from one of the guards standing just inside the cave. Smoke rose off the tip and spun slowly around his head in the soft, warm breeze. He noticed Victor's towel draped across the handrail and scratched his head, wondering where his lover had gone off to.

Hearing a tumble of small stones overhead, Dickey moved back several steps, his eyebrows tugging together in a look of worry. Chips of rock clattered to the wooden deck just inches from where he stood.

Far above he could make out a figure, clad only in a Speedo bathing suit, recklessly climbing the corner of a tall square-faced tower. The climber stepped out onto a horizontal lintel of stone that spanned the face of the tower. He crept along the narrow jagged ledge, leaping over holes in its length.

"Victor, you're much too high," Dickey called out in a raspy voice.

For a moment Victor stopped in midascent and shouted back, "Too high! Ain't no such word."

Dickey shook his head. "There is such a word," he muttered to himself. "You idiot."

Victor leaned flat against the unstable wall of limestone rock. He kept creeping upward, his fingers finding crumbling holds, his toes touched here and there locating niches, knocking loose small avalanches of stone. After a few scrambling moments he came to a *meurtrière*, a tall, narrow slit in the wall, a medieval invention to protect archers, allowing them to shower arrows upon any enemy approaching by sea. Here he rested for a moment, his gaze fixed on the glow coming from the window above. He carefully turned and faced the water far, far below—Dickey looked no bigger than a pebble.

Victor was balanced on a flat stone cantilevered out over emptiness. He thumped his chest, letting out a Tarzan yodel. Pleased with this performance and with his ability to still frighten Dickey, who worried down below, he advanced, lizardlike, up the rock wall. As he moved farther up, the strong winds tugged at him, filling his ears with a ghostly hiss. His fingers clawed the ledge of the slender lancet window, and he pulled his face up into view.

Inside, standing motionless before a large gold-framed mirror, Fanny admired the white nude perfection of her body. She fingered a leather pouch hanging between her breasts while Samir approached from behind and draped a long white satin cloth over her shoulders. She reached up and took his hand, still gazing into the mirror, drinking in the sight of his dark hand against the whiteness of her body. Samir moved around and pulled the robe closed in front, his hands brushing against the fullness of her breasts.

"Nice tits," Victor chirped.

Fanny's head snapped to right in time to see the pale, leering face at her window.

Victor giggled and raised a waving hand. "I ain't shitin' yuh, you got nice tits—" His toehold gave way, then his hand swept free of the stone frame—his face froze, and he vanished from the window.

"Such a fool," Fanny said with a curse and hurried to the ledge.

On the dock, Dickey watched with enlarged eyes, his mouth open, losing the cigarette.

Victor plummeted hundreds of feet, letting out a shrill, startling howl. His arms and legs spread, waving wildly.

Dickey saw silhouetted a black star against the soft underbelly of moonlit clouds. In contrast, Fanny watched a flying squirrel leaping to its death.

He was facedown, gaining control, arms drawing together with tightly clenched fists leading the dive.

Both his elders were quite surprised with what grace Victor entered the water.

Rings of water spread out from his point of impact.

Dickey scrambled to the end of the dock, his hands to his mouth, calling out for Victor.

A moment later Victor's face erupted out of the waves.

"Told you I could do it," he sputtered. His face and hands were flush, dotted with broken capillaries.

"You idiot!" Dickey shouted, threw down his towel, and stalked away toward the cave entrance. "You goddamn idiot."

Dickey hurried through the torchlight of the cave and up the wide stairs cut into the rock, making promises to himself, once and for all to rein in his pretty, young creation. He marched straight through the main sail-domed pavilion, stepping lightly on the Persian tile that chilled his bare feet. On through another rounded doorway, into the adjoining gallery. His following shadow was created by moonlight creeping in through rows of windows that faced the sea. He passed numerous doors before stopping at the chamber he shared with Victor. Dickey loved this room. He had history here. It was the only domain where he felt truly safe.

The room was wide and tall, the walls covered in faded murals of Moorish horsemen riding into battle. One cavalryman painted in a flowing crimson robe led the charge wielding a curved saber. It was this beautifully brave Berber warrior he saw in Victor the night in which they met. As Dickey stood gazing at the painted images, he cursed his own lack of restraint. Fanny had warned against this fascination with Victor. And now Dickey damned her name. She could have been more forceful in her objection. She could have finished him off herself.

When he and Fanny went on their Wild West Blood Tasting Tour in the mid-seventies, neither had any idea that they'd be bringing home this cowboy Lolita with the sex drive of a fruit fly and the moral sense of a bottom-feeding catfish.

And the appetite of his psychopathic waif! Dickey should have realized, after watching him at a ranch barbecue in west Texas. In some sort of macho display, Victor scarfed down what appeared to be half a heifer, but he was wasteful, never finishing what he had on his plate before going back for more.

He would take but a single bite from a plate filled with steak before throwing the succulent meat on the fire just to watch the fat sizzle and pop. To Dickey's disappointment, the physiological and radical change from solid food to liquid dietary requirements had not affected Victor's wasteful nature.

Dickey flopped on the canopied bed draped with blue silk and mosquito netting. He sighed, having to admit that as much as Victor assaulted his taste and refinement, which Dickey had honed over several hundred years of European life, he could no more imagine his existence without the boyish criminal than he could do without Fanny.

He wadded his towel and yanked on the woven horsehair bell pull. He paced from wall to wall until Samir arrived, bowing and courteous.

"Dress me," he said, undoing the waist belt of his terrycloth robe.

"As you wish," Samir replied, and went to a huge wooden armoire at one end of the room.

Dickey quickly undressed, leaving his robe and swimsuit in a pile. He sat naked on the wooden bench at the dressing table and glared into the mirror. He watched Samir's reflected image backing out of the closet, his arms loaded with a stack of folded Egyptian cotton cloth.

"Candles all round would be nice," Dickey said in a friendlier voice.

"Of course," Samir answered. He placed the clothing at the edge of the bed and went around the room lighting numerous fat candles placed in elaborate iron candelabras and others spilling down ornate wall sconces.

With the chamber illuminated in bright golden hues, Dickey again turned his attention to the mirror, gazing with keen dissatisfaction at his features. He resented not having been born with Victor's or Fanny's natural beauty. He despised the oval and ordinary features imprisoned in the awful truth of the mirror. He whisked open the top of a box filled with makeup and began slathering on a base of European flesh tones. When half of his face was covered he stared at himself in worse humor. Gazing at Samir, he had a sudden change of heart.

"This is Morocco, after all," he muttered. And he began mixing bases, applying a far richer, darker bronze coloration.

Victor appeared in the doorway, dripping wet, grinning as though he'd just won a gold at the Olympic games.

"Did I scare yuh?" He teased Dickey's mirrored reflection.

Dickey frowned and continued patting his face with base color.

Samir unfolded the soft white garment for Dickey's approval.

Victor grabbed it and slithered into what turned out to be a tunic. He then pulled a red sash off a chair and wrapped it around his waist, scuttling toward Dickey, swinging one end of the sash—now his pretend sword.

"Hmm, that fits you rather nicely. Now why don't you join me and we'll do your face," said Dickey patting the open space next to him.

Victor caught Samir's reflection in the mirror. "Sorry, Samir, don't go takin' it personal," he said, then looked to Dickey, "but Dickster, I don't want to be no sand nigger."

"Oh, I suppose you were thinking of going out as what, Lawrence of Arabia?"

"He got killed didn't he?"

"Yes, a long time ago."

"Some gal told me once I looked kinda like Peter O'Toole," he said, resting his hands on Dickey's shoulders.

"She couldn't have been more wrong." he said, holding Victor's reflected gaze. "A young Dirk Bogarde. Actually, right now you resemble Montgomery Clift, after his accident."

"Who?"

"Before your time, I guess."

Quietly, to be kept from Samir, he leaned into Dickey's ear asking if he still thought of him as the world's greatest lover.

Dickey flashed a smile of supreme insincerity.

Samir approached again with another nearly identical tunic.

Dickey stood and allowed the Moroccan to slip it over his head and wrap a wide, black sash around his waist. All the while Dickey said to Victor, "You can pretend to be whomever you wish. But never forget you are my boy."

"I ain't yer boy!"

"Oh damn!" cried Dickey as he noticed makeup stains around the stand-up collar of the tunic. "Samir, why did you let me apply my makeup first?"

Samir helped Dickey out of the stained garment. "Sorry, but you did not ask me." Samir backed away in his servitude manner.

"I'm no one's boy," Victor announced for Samir's ears, while playfully doing battle with the air, swinging his sash with imagined heroic displays of swordsmanship. "So when do we get to do some water skiin'? I ain't even seen Fanny's ski boat yet."

Dickey sat at the table again, looked at his makeup job, and sighed. Disheartened. "There is no ski boat, and you're far from the world's greatest lover."

"No boat, huh? Well fuck fire, ain't that a change in the weather." Victor thought about it and turned to the mirror. "So who's better at doin' it?"

Dickey frowned, and his head bobbed side to side in a gesture of indecision. "I don't know, I just know it's not you."

From the doorway Samir spoke up, asking if there was anything else they needed at the moment besides a fresh tunic. Dickey suggested apparel that opened in the front so he could finish his makeup. When waved off, Samir bowed his head and left the room.

Victor watched him go and then swiveled back around to Dickey. "You ever done Samir?"

"No, he's Fanny's." He saw the appraising hunger in Victor's gaze. "And she feels it's impolite to eat the help."

"She does him though, right?"

"Yes, I suppose, but she once told me that Tashum is the best lover in the world."

"That dickless wonder?" Victor scoffed and threw himself on the bed. "No way!"

"Tashum is very sensual. Beyond physical, perhaps spiritual."

"A lover's gotta have something where it counts," Victor said, grabbing his own crotch and growling.

"Try a little higher, Victor. Maybe up around the heart region."

"God, you're boring—you're old, old, old and boring, boring, boring— I'm hungry." Victor rolled over and over on the bed until he fell off the far end. Then he straightened up, glaring into the mirror. "I'm fuckin' hungry, and I want to go water skiin', goddamn it!"

"Please come over here and help me with this makeup," Dickey said, tossing down his canister of base and glaring at a too-dark mudpie face. "We'll go out in a bit and find us a couple of nice gay Arab boys as an appetizer. How does 'swish-kabob' strike your fancy?"

"I'd rather have another angel cocktail." Victor smacked his lips. "Mmmmm-mmm, that Misha was tasty."

"You should get him out of your mind." He dabbed again, then wiped at the right side of his face.

"Yuh know, I bet them two are hooked up."

"Tashum's going to be very angry, but as long as we have his precious orbs—"

"Yeah, well, fuck him, remember—this time we get what we want, not just what Fanny thinks is enough." Victor leaned closer to the mirror, ran a finger down his marred cheek. "I stole 'em twice, I don't wanna do it a third time."

"This isn't a game, Victor."

"Sure it is." Victor moved Dickey away from his focus in the mirror. "You gotta admit this is the perfect place to domesticate blue eyes."

"You'll be lucky to ever see Misha again."

"I say we hang him in a closet and put spigots in his wrists." Victor slapped Dickey's back. "Ha, we'll open one of them fuckin' soda fountains."

"Now look what you've done!" Dickey said as he looked at his smeared makeup. "I'll never get this right. Will you help me?"

"Goddamn it—I'm bored with this stupid old place," Victor snapped. "I'm hungry, I'm bored, and you look like giant turd. I'm outa here."

Victor swept out of the room, leaving Dickey to towel off and start again.

Dickey pranced into the pavilion. He confidently shuffled to the rhythm of the sitar music and glanced briefly at the musicians before his flowing robe went aflame as he passed between two raging fire pots. He stomped on the robe's tail, killing the flame. Hoping no one noticed, he carried on crossing the great open space to the deep recess in the opposing wall.

Victor and Fanny were perched on a mountain of large, worn velvet cushions neatly scattered around a towering hookah pipe. Dickey joined them, hoping they hadn't noticed what started out as a cool move.

"Graceful entrance Dickey," Fanny said, teasing.

"Wanna toke?" Victor said, offering the mouthpiece of the ornate silver-and-cloth-wrapped hose stemming from the bulbous water pipe. "Hey, come on, dude."

Dickey waved him off with a limp wrist.

"It's good shit, man."

Fanny threw a frown toward Victor.

"Hey, I was just sayin' you got some good shit, don't get pissed off." His eyes bulged. "Hey, lets start flyin' this stuff—I know guys who'd buy it—"

"Victor, shut up. Listen to the music!" she said in between draws off her own mouthpiece.

They turned their attention to a collection of Moroccan musicians playing antique stringed instruments and tapping out polyrhythms on a variety of native drums.

On cue, a belly dancer appeared at the top of the landing, dressed in colorful silks and gold coins strung together. In a flow of intoxicating movement she danced down the short flight of broad steps. With the lightness of a feather she twirled toward them. Her smooth mocha stomach surging and sucking in, snake arms writhing, jangling her adornments of coinage and jewelry. The music grew louder and more insistent. A mesmerizing rhythm rose up around them. The dancer moved more wildly, her generous breasts rose and fell, her ample hips shimmered, her body took on inhuman, vaporous contours.

Dickey turned and saw Victor staring at her with ravenous eyes.

She moved closer and closer to the three, swirling through the smoke from the pipe.

Victor suddenly lunged with teeth bared, a wolf snarl in his throat. He was on her in a flash, pinning her to the floor, his wide-sprung eyes gazed on her long brown naked throat.

The music stopped, instruments clanging to the floor. The musicians watched in disbelief. Then in a flicker of movement, Fanny was on top of Victor and effortlessly tossed him aside.

Samir rushed in and helped the dancer to her feet.

Fanny waited until Samir had ushered the musicians out of the room before moving back to Victor. With the toughness of iron, her hand clamped around his throat.

"We dine in town later, never here," she whispered firmly. "Never here."

All air cut off, Victor could only stare bug-eyed and nod.

"So you do understand me?" she asked.

He nodded vigorously, and she released him.

Victor scooted away, staying close to the floor. He was unusually subdued, out of character. With fear in his eyes he glanced over to Dickey.

"I've tried to teach you the enjoyment of foreplay, my boy. But you just won't listen," said Dickey as he stood and stretched, having enjoyed the entire performance. "I for one am ready to see the town."

Fanny looked past Dickey and saw Samir reappear at his station by the entry arch. She bent and grabbed Victor by the crotch he gave a strangled yodel.

"This isn't London, you insect. They're just primitive enough here to believe that our kind exists. That makes it more dangerous—and I like it here. The last thing I want is to wake up some evening and have my castle surrounded by torch-bearing Berbers."

"Jesus, Fanny." He rubbed at his sore crotch. "I think you nearly tore off my equipment."

Her tone lowered, mocking, soothing. "When that happens, you and Tashum will finally have something in common."

Dickey chuckled and walked toward the main entry.

She followed, but after a few steps she stopped and turned. "Coming, Victor? I was under the impression you were hungry."

The moon hung in the uppermost part of the sky, a silver opening at the top of a deep blue well.

Bathed in her beauty below, three figures misshapen by flowing robes drove their horses hard up an inclined ridge of slipping sand. The thin-layered top crust broke and slid away beneath galloping horse hooves. They climbed high along the ridge. It curved to the right, and their speed increased with the leveling of steepness. They were atop this wavy sand mountain. Their horse's legs stretched in fluid unison, pounding, pushing, carrying their riders smoothly across the rippling surface until they were reined in to a standstill at a promontory point.

The three hooded riders sat atop their snorting mounts.

Fanny threw back her hood and dismounted. "There it is," she said, shoving a molasses treat into her horse's mouth.

"Don't look like much from up here," complained Victor. "Coulda stayed home."

"Yes, well, we couldn't have you doing the band, could we?" Dickey continued, "Besides I thought you would enjoy the ride."

Fanny gave the nugget treats to all three horses before remounting.

For the longest while they gazed down from their sandstone perch studying the sparkling festival lights of the small North African town. Fanny explained the tableau of flat roofs and the layout of ancient, winding streets.
She suggested a meeting place, as she wished to hunt solo. Dickey agreed
and promised to keep a leash on Victor.

Fanny gave a long delicious moan, her nose discerning the air rising from
the town. "If you concentrate, you can taste their aroma on the breeze."

"You'll have to teach me how you do that," Dickey said.

"Visualize what you know is there."

"Moroccan red, my favorite wine," Dickey joked.

"You two sniff the air all you want. I'm going to find the drive through
for some takeout." Victor straightened in his saddle and backed his horse off
the small sandstone plateau. His red lips opened into a long cruel gash of a
smile, and he let out a cackling spate of laughter. With a whoop, he kicked
his horse, bounding forward, plunging down over the sand cornice, the horse
stretched out into thin air. Victor lay back against the horse's rump loin, and
with one hand holding the rein and the other clenched around the root of
the horse's tail, he masterfully stayed in the saddle. They hit the sand running. He continued kicking and kicking his steed, his high, cowboy shout
trailing away.

"Yippee-yi-oh-cayeh."

Fanny watched his attack on the slope and she turned to Dickey. "Victor
worries me."

"He's a worrisome boy."

"No—I'm saying he's out of control. You've got to watch him." She
stood in the saddle to better see his progress down the slope. "And if you
don't get him under control, I'm going to do something."

Dickey kicked his horse. "Whatever you say, mum." And he followed
Victor's tracks.

Fanny watched as Dickey's horse dug in and refused the twenty-foot
leap. Dickey was thrown forward and flew over the horse's head. She hated
herself for laughing, but she could not help herself. "It's not your night, is
it?" she laughed.

Dickey stood on shaky legs, brushing the sand particles off his face and
out of the folds of his loose attire. "How did Victor make it look so bloody
easy?"

She could still see Victor, a small moving dot on the outskirts of the town. "With him, it's always luck."

Dickey climbed back up the slope and remounted his horse.

"I feel a complete twit."

"You've never been good in sand, Dickey." She smiled.

Together they rode farther down the ridge to a safer jumping-off point.

For a moment, as she rode out ahead, she thought she could hear Paladin's voice in her ear, urging her forward, as he did when he taught her how to ride, standing in the stirrup, Cossack-style, centuries before.

"Paladin, I've done what you asked me to do," she whispered to the wind in her face. "I don't know why you've asked me to betray someone who loves you so dearly. But I have done what you asked. Don't you betray me."

CHAPTER NINETEEN

Connections

Tashum glanced up in time to see the large green highway sign:

N-17 PARIS—EXIT 10 KM

Potter rubbed tired eyes and hunched forward over the steering wheel, stretching cramped vertebrae.

Tashum kept his attention on the cell phone at his ear. Suddenly he jolted forward. "How—? What do you mean, I've been denied access? This is ludicrous—you—no—just listen to me—No! I will not hold the line!"

He stabbed a button on the phone and stared forward. "Damn police!"

Potter looked over at him. "Why would the police shut down your account at the satellite communications company?"

"Did I say that?"

"You know, Tashum, that's only the beginning. Once they start to unravel your financial network, they'll seize all of your accounts."

"I don't need a bloody dissertation on the ruthless pursuit of the police."

"I beg your pardon, but I've got something at stake here as well."

"Point well taken, Potter. I am sorry." He replaced the telephone in its holder. "What you don't know can't hurt you. You are innocently accompanying me to assist in a delicate business transaction. Period."

"It's not really that simple though, is it?"

"It can be, if that is all you know."

Potter shook his head with dissatisfaction.

"Tashum, how will you find them now?" Misha asked softly from the backseat.

Tashum quietly shut down the laptop computer, then he turned it back on. "Cheer up, everyone. The last hand hasn't been dealt yet."

Potter gave him a quizzical glance.

Moonbeams raked the mud walls and ancient ruins partially buried by drifting sands that formed the town's western perimeter. In the long shadows two tethered horses tossed their heads and made small, impatient snorting and stomping sounds.

Dickey ignored them, his eyes on the shimmering stars, his voice tinged with laughter.

"So at any rate, the prince says, 'They didn't like the fox hat in Twixton,' and the queen says, 'Of course they wouldn't like the fox hat, in Twixton they're the Fox Preservation Society, you silly sod!' and the prince says, 'Well you told me to wear the fox hat!' And she replies, 'No! I did not—I said, 'Twixton, where the fuck's that? Not Twixton, wear the fox hat!' "

Fanny chuckled and rubbed at a spray of blood on her clothing. She pulled the cloth to her mouth and licked it.

"Tashum told me that one," Dickey continued. "When we were driving over to your house."

"Now he's telling jokes," she replied, sighing. The smile drained from her features. "He's come a long way since we found him on that beach in Bermuda."

He jerked with surprise. "Fanny, with all due respect, he found us on that beach."

"That's right." She smiled as if holding back some big secret.

Dickey knew her smile was masking something else. He lay back on the rooftop of the ruined house, where they'd stopped to rest and enjoy the afterglow of a particularly fruitful evening feed.

"We may have gone a little too far this time. He'll try to destroy us now, you know," he said, and swatted at a fly. "If I had only kept Victor on his leash that night. I hate to think of what Victor might have done to Tashum's home."

"Then don't. Think about it, I mean."

"I can't help but. I mean, everything would have been fine. He'd have his orbs and we'd have the money."

"We still have the money and his orbs." Fanny sat up. "Dickey, I goaded Victor into stealing the orbs again."

"You what?" He turned. "Why on earth—?"

She sighed. "My pride was hurt, I suppose. He seemed more interested in the orbs than in me."

"But why did you let him have them in the first place?"

"To see him again. You may not understand this, but just looking at him makes me remember."

"You hated that island, Fanny. It was a god-awful place."

She looked down at her hands. "We really were naughty, you and I. We might have ruined it for ourselves."

"Might have?"

"It's Victor he's really angry with. He could never stay truly angry at us, you know that."

"But Victor's really an innocent in all this, Fanny."

"*Innocent* is a word not associable with Victor."

"I generally agree with you on issues of Victor's behavior, but not this time." Dickey scraped a bit of blood from his thumbnail, trying to keep the fear from his voice, the love. "That silly boy has this romantic idea that we'll just ride off into the sunset like Butch Cassidy and the Sundance Kid, keeping one step ahead of Sheriff Tashum and the posse."

"Tell Victor to watch the rest of the movie. They didn't ride off into the sunset, they met their end—and there's nothing romantic about that. There's nothing romantic about being hunted, period, or have you forgotten?"

"But that's my point, Fanny. He really doesn't understand, and that means we've used him. We gave him this disease without the details—"

"You gave him the disease." She sat up, animated now. "Dickey, you and I, and even Victor, for that matter, share this curse from these Fallen Angels."

"They gave us life, Fanny. Don't forget—"

"They gave us life! That's right, and they may have obliterated our souls in the process." She waved off a slow-moving fly.

"Our souls? Fanny, what does that mean?"

"I'm not really sure, but Tashum hinted at it—"

"Stop it!" He shivered. "I don't want to know."

"The worst bit is they don't give a damn about what they've done," she said, ignoring his fear. "Our bond must be to one another, to this . . ." She held up a blood-smeared hand. "It must be with each other that we go forward, break the old bonds. And that gives us the right"—she paused, her eyes flashed in all directions, building nerve—"to take everything Tashum holds precious, and then some—"

Dickey turned and watched her face for a moment, a dawning realization. "Christ, you're still in love with him."

"No, no. You're wrong," she said, drawing her knees close to her body. "I loathe Tashum. I hate him, everything about him, everything he touches."

"He used to touch you."

"Used to. That was a long time ago, Dickey. Time empties love, changes it. Kills it."

"Don't try to make me believe that," he said. "You still care for him. Love's opposite isn't hate, it's indifference."

"Don't feign poetry, Dickey. It doesn't suit you."

"No, I don't suppose it does—"

"Freedom is ours for the taking."

"Fanny, we're as free as birds, always have been."

"I'm talking about freedom from these dark angels! They put their curse on us and now we have to break loose from them. Can't you see that? I'm so sick and tired of his judging us, turning up his nose at our needs. Needs he forced upon us. No, we have to break away. The same way children have to break free from their parents."

"Fanny, they can read our thoughts."

"They need to find us first."

"We can't hide from them—they can't be killed—we can be."

"What makes you think they can't be killed?"

"They can't. I've seen Tashum wounded before—on, on that beach. He was shot, remember? Why are you smiling?"

Fanny faced him, moving to her haunches, an expression of threatening contentment on her face. "We should get back. Where's Victor?"

Inspector Stanton drank a two-bag cup of tea, Irish Breakfast, courtesy of their missing host. He needed to stay awake, keep on top of it. He had let him go once. He felt the fool now. This case was big and growing. Contents from the leather bag found in the tube tunnel connected Tashum to the mysterious suicide of private investigator Malvern. A ledger found in the bag recorded Malvern's day rate at two thousand pounds a day plus a discretionary fund of limitless monies. Why was Tashum paying so much money to find someone who had been dead for more than four hundred years? He couldn't imagine. He sat there, pondering. What would be the thread that sewed all these events together?

Perhaps his old friend Malvern had stumbled onto some kind of cult. Why else would the name *Paladin* be carved into the kitchen countertop of Malvern's London home?

Richard Malvern had apparently fallen asleep in a warm bath after lopping off the tip of his right index finger with a kitchen knife. He bled himself to death in warm water. No explanatory note, just the word *mayhem* above the kitchen door painted in his own blood and the name *Paladin* carved by the very knife that severed his finger tip. Why didn't he just shoot himself the way most men do?

In his perverse way, Stanton loved the excitement that came attached to this kind of intellectual chase. It was the closest thing to sex he'd ever encountered, a notion he kept privately to himself.

Stanton slapped the ledger's cover closed as he rose from Tashum's antique desk. "Pickney," he called out.

Detective Pickney raised a hand, signaling Stanton to come over to the computer console.

"Did you see the inside of Malvern's flat?" Stanton asked as he joined the two men huddled at the computer workstation. The man scrubbing away spray paint from the computer monitor looked up at Stanton.

"Yeah, Becker called me round to Malvern's place to look at his electronics—Roger, you've got to see this," added Pickney with excitement. "Welcome to the twilight zone."

Roger Stanton put down the cup and stood over the shoulder of the young technician, staring at a computer screen free of spray paint.

The large screen filled with blocks of color that slowly resolved into the image of an Arizona state driver's license. On the left side was a color photo of a young Victor Mann with a crooked, smirky grin. Long black hair, narrow, deeply tanned pretty-boy features.

Stanton felt his tweed jacket for his glasses, wrestling them onto his face. "What year does that say?"

"Nineteen seventy one," answered the blond technician, typing a series of commands into the computer keyboard.

"Where did this come from? I don't believe it—how did you do that?"

"I didn't! The bloody machine's got a mind of its own. Or someone is accessing the computer via modem. Whatever the reason, I'm locked out."

"I want a definitive answer." He pointed a stabbing index finger. "Where is that coming from?"

"Inspector, I think we've got something here," said a familiar voice entering the room.

Stanton turned to see his red-haired colleague, Detective Wilks, holding up a small portable TV with a built-in VCR.

"What's that for?" Stanton frowned.

Wilks found an electrical outlet and plugged in the unit. He turned it on and slipped the cassette into the VCR slot. "This is the tape they had on Sky News. Some bloke at Poole was videotaping his boat for insurance purposes when the explosion happened."

Stanton and others gathered around the TV.

The handheld camera panned the length of a sleek white sailboat. Suddenly the screen whitened and the speakers belched out the clamor of the explosion farther down the dock. The image jostled violently and for a moment the screen was filled with zigs and zags of color and images. Voices could be heard shouting, and as the cameraman regained his footing and backed away from his own vessel, a seaplane whizzed by. The camera panned, following the low-flying plane as it veered and nosed sharply upward, chased by a ball of flame.

Wilks hit the pause button and froze the plane in midflight. A series of numbers and letters near the tail appeared, blurred but visible.

"We got the registration," Wilks said, turning to Stanton.

"And?"

"It was just purchased by one Victor Black. Paid cash," answered Wilks, a broad grin spreading over his face. "Cash for an airplane? That's our drug boy, all right. I'll wager Victor and Tashum have some sort of feud going on."

"Wilks, we don't have evidence to suggest that."

"Typical of drug runners," said Wilks. "Remember the Orlandos?"

"For God's sake, stay focused, Wilks," moaned Stanton. "Now then," he addressed the group, "Victor Mann changed his name to Black. At the moment, Victor Black is as important a catch as Tashum." Stanton speculated as he looked across the faces of his men. "Get this information to MI5 and Interpol. He's not likely to have gotten off to America. Yet."

"Doubt it," said the middle-aged detective standing next to Wilks. "We drew a grid of the possible sites he could have flown to without refilling his fuel tanks—Iceland to North Africa, Monaco, Sweden—"

"That far?" Stanton interrupted. "Are you certain?"

"The particulars indicate that the plane was fitted out with extra tanks. She has that sort of range."

"Stay on it."

Stanton whirled back around to the computer, where Victor's image still glowed on the screen. "Anything yet on a trace?"

"Not yet. My guess is our caller is using a cellular phone modem."

"I want to know who that person is. Keep working on it."

"Yes, sir."

Stanton took another sip, smiled. One way or the other, they were going to come out of this stink smelling like roses. All the evidence pointed to this Tashum chap, a wonderful, enigmatic mystery man who would have the tabloids singing for months. The known evidence was circumstantial but on the surface damning. Based on past investigations Stanton would have normally considered Wilks's theory very plausible. Victor-Mann-Black appeared to fit the profile of a petty thief and overall loser. He could have very easily been Tashum's connection to the world of drugs or even prostitution. There were two things known with certainty, first was what started out as a single homicide just increased to five, with the additional deaths of the four crew members aboard Tashum's yacht. The second known fact was he had let Tashum go. Stanton was lengthening his reach with the inclusion of Interpol and the U.S. Drug Enforcement Agency, although he had no intention of letting anyone else but himself capture Tashum and, now, Victor.

Stanton's thought was broken by the commotion of other uniformed cops rushing into the room.

"Inspector Stanton," said the flush-faced officer.

"Yes."

"Sir, we're going to need help with this one."

"Why is that?"

"Because we've just found fifty-six bodies in the cellar, sir."

*   *   *

As Misha passed through the doors of the Paris train station a sharp wind laced by streamers of fog tugged at the ticket envelope in his hands. For a moment, he thought he might have lost one. In a pool of hazy streetlight, he pried open the envelope and checked inside. Three tickets to Geneva— good.

He walked quickly through the rows of parked cars, finally stopped at the Jaguar.

Potter was still behind the wheel. His seat was leaned back, and the man was napping, head turned, mouth slightly agape.

In the next seat, Tashum's face was illuminated by the glow off his laptop screen. His fingers moved rapidly over the keyboard. When Misha opened the door and peered in, he was startled to see Victor's image on the computer monitor screen.

"You recognize this lost soul, don't you?" Tashum asked.

"Yes." Misha rubbed his wrists.

With the press of a button, the screen went blank and Tashum disconnected the car phone computer modem.

"The train to Geneva leaves in two hours," Misha said, handing the ticket envelope forward.

Tashum glanced over a shoulder. "Good, we'll let Potter sleep. I want to see this proof of our mortality that you promised." He took the ticket envelope off Misha's fingers. "Where is this Antiquities Shoppe?"

"It's in Sainte-Germaine. We'd have to leave now to make it back in time."

"Hmm, maybe we should just head on to Ascona. There's a lot I have yet to do."

"Tashum, you need to see this. We can take the Metro to within walking distance."

Tashum's curiosity couldn't resist. He allowed himself to be pulled to the Metro.

Once inside the depot he paid for the tokens, then followed the signs to the platform.

Onboard the train they were seated facing one another. Misha grinned, catching Tashum's eye.

"What's so funny?" asked Tashum.

"I was just thinking back on our last train ride. The look on your face when you wanted to take a nap—"

"Well, I'm glad you found that amusing. I really do prefer riding on the inside of trains." Tashum smiled.

The wave of warm humor washed over them, followed by a slight stab of pain. He'd forgotten what it was like to play with his celestial brothers. He did miss them.

Long after the laughter died, the Metro car was still rocking side to side, clattering through the dark tunnel buried beneath Parisian streets. Passengers crammed together in the seats while others stood holding to center poles and straps overhead. The train began a series of tugging jolts, its speed decreasing as it entered the artificial light of an underground platform.

Moments later, Tashum and Misha emerged with a thin stream of late-night passengers up the steps to street level. A motorcycle roared past, its wind pulling at them. Misha glanced up and down Boulevard Sainte-Michel, taking his bearings off Notre Dame's twin towers standing off to his right, and the distant Tour-Eiffel to his left. "I'm afraid we got off too early," he said. "The shop is over there, somewhere." He pointed over his shoulder.

"Are you sure we've got time for this?" asked Tashum.

"If we hurry," he said, pulling on Tashum's dark cashmere coat sleeve.

Misha led Tashum down the sidewalk, past a series of dimly lit storefronts, most of which were already closed for the night.

Rising fog off the River Seine crept through the damp streets, diffusing the orange streetlamps and hiding their armature, giving an illusion of low-slung stars on the wane. Tashum was reminded of the floating orbs, and it was all he could do to keep up with Misha's fast pace down bent streets that ran through asymmetrical intersections—through alleys that ended at a door, through doors that opened onto streets. It seemed a maddening maze cloaked in vaporous gray.

They turned down a narrow street lined with small shops with apartments above. The fog seemed to melt from around them as they stepped forward into the light of a rectangular display window set squarely into a facade in need of plaster and paint.

"This is it," Misha said, nodding to a glimmering display.

Tashum's awestruck face appeared before him reflected on the glass. "What on Earth?"

Beyond his reflection, Tashum saw a full life-size headless crystal skel-

eton brilliantly refracting light. Silently, he stepped closer to the display window. The skeleton gave the appearance of human form, but even at a glance
there were fewer bones. A single shaft instead of two connected the hand
and elbow, likewise the lower leg was a large tibia with no smaller fibula
attached.

"It—it can't be what it appears to be. We are immortal, impervious to
death in the flesh."

"Look closer," Misha murmured.

Tashum's eyes took in the crystal bone works, the arms, the shimmering
spine, winged pelvis. Flashes of blue and red sparkled where the halogen
floor light struck its many surfaces. Then he saw it. Protruding from the back
of the shoulder, rising above the broad scapula—crystal wing nubs. His
breathing grew harsh, his eyes fixed on the luminous ribcage.

One of the ribs was chipped—missing a large pear-shaped section.

A dry, hard noise emitted from his throat. His brain shrank from the
arising thought. His swimming gaze tilted down past the torso, down the leg
bones, to an oval brass plaque at the base that read:

THE FALLEN PALADIN
I am light pure am I.

"No . . . ," Tashum was trembling. "No, it can't . . ."

His hands pressed to the cold glass, his face a mask of terror. The missing
piece of rib. His mind reeled, his memory exploded. He was tumbling again
through a dark cloud, clutching his brother angel. More than forty thousand
years ago—that blast of lightning—and then his brother was gone. Crying
out, clutching a large black-rimmed wound in his side as a chunk of his
crystal rib spun away into—

"Paladin!" he screamed, pounding the glass. "Oh my brother! My Paladin—oh, God no! Not him!"

A wave of thick sickness passed through him. A lump swelled in his
chest, his vision grew dim. A heavy moan convulsed from deep within him,
and he doubled over and collapsed into Misha's arms. He shook violently as
Misha tried to keep him upright.

"Paladin," Tashum sobbed. "My brother."

Misha took him under the arms, helped Tashum to his feet. His eyes
rolled toward the radiant remains, but he couldn't bear to look again. He

turned and buried his face in Misha's chest. Uncontrolled sobs spilled out of his shaking frame. His legs collapsed. Misha sank to the wet pavement with him.

"I'm sorry Tashum, I'm so sorry, the name plaque is new. I had never put it together before. I knew it was an angel, but I wouldn't have brought you here like this had I known that it was Paladin."

"Don't say that!"

Through the fog came a woman's sudden giggling laugh. Misha rose up slightly, looking over the hood of a parked car, seeing a man and woman arm-in-arm laughing as they crossed the street. He thought they were Americans. Not with them but tagging along behind them, a familiar face, framed by short spiked hair, a waif of a girl in her late teens. She appeared unbathed, a street urchin by dress.

"Sasha?" crept from Misha's mouth as he stood and recognized her fully.

Tashum, oblivious to everything but his grief, crawled back toward the window.

"That's not one of us, tell me it's not true . . . ," Tashum cried in a voice of delirium. "Do you hear me! Tell me it's not a Celestial!"

"What other creature do you know of that has a crystalline bone structure?"

"It's man-made, I tell you," Tashum sputtered. "It's a fake!"

Tashum was too preoccupied to notice the approaching footsteps.

The attractive couple stopped at the inset shop door. Sasha nudged past them. She tested the locked door handle, rattling the door, pushing, trying to make it open. The couple stepped back from the ruckus.

"Sasha," Misha said with a smile.

The palms of her hands slapped against the glass door panels—

"*Allez-vous-en!*" cried Tashum. "*Partez!*"

The man returned Misha's smile and nudged his companion. "Come on, honey, let's come back when they're open," he said with a Midwestern accent.

Her eyes were glued on the skeleton. "It's incredible, Jack," she said, her hand clutching a trinket hanging from her necklace.

"Go away! Leave us, now!" flooded from Tashum's frustration.

"Look, we didn't mean to bother you," he said, taking his companion's hand.

Sasha seemed mesmerized, stoned. She brushed past Tashum and leaned up against the window, palms flat against the glass, her breath condensing on glass, her angelic blue eyes gazing at Paladin.

Without looking, Tashum pushed her hand away from his. "Leave us be!" he shouted at her. "This isn't a circus sideshow! Take her away!"

The man frowned at the outburst. "Sorry, but she's not with us." The American pulled on his companion's arm. "Come on, honey," he said as they receded into the fog. "I swear, even the drunks in this city have an attitude."

"They're French, Jack," she said. "They can't help themselves."

Misha watched them move on down the street, vanishing into the veils of swirling whiteness. Then he turned back to Tashum, slumped against the window, and the young woman still standing there.

"Sasha, are you with them?" he asked, his hand reaching out to touch her.

She flinched away from his touch. Her eyes were wild and confused. She mouthed the name *Sasha* but did so as if it were foreign to her.

Misha tried to look into her eyes, read her confusion, but her movement was too frantic, and he saw nothing. "Sasha, do you need help?" he asked with great concern.

Too troubled to speak, she twitched like so many lost souls living on the streets. Misha reached for her. Both hands grabbed her shoulders. She broke away from his grip, turned, showing him one last puzzled look before sprinting off into the fog.

After a moment of gazing into empty fog, Misha returned his attention to Tashum. "We had better leave," he said gently.

Tashum looked up, catching his own beatup image reflected in the glass. He rotated away from the troubling images and sat with his back to the window. His vacant eyes staring out into nothingness. A crater was opening inside him, filled with an ugly emptiness. "Paladin gone? Killed?" Tashum hastily wiped at his tears. "Then he's in heaven, right?"

"I've never seen him." Misha shook his head. "If that is Paladin's skeleton, I don't know what happened to him, or his spirit."

"Angels can . . . this can happen to angels?" Tashum asked, his head tilting back, bumping against the window. "His flesh gone? His head? Butchered like an animal!"

"We are not immortal," Misha said sadly.

"But I've heard him," Tashum whimpered. "He cried out to me from some distant place."

"Are you sure it was Paladin and not Mayhem?" he said with caution.

"It was Mayhem." Tashum stared into the swirling fog, his voice resigned. "A spirit appeared to me on the island. An angel, I-I think. I'm sure it was Mayhem." Tashum tore a hand across his face, clearing the wetness from his eyes. "He said to me, 'Your forsaken brother calls to you—join him.' "

"Join him?" Misha questioned with suspicion.

"Yes—don't you see? Join him. Put him back together! Oh, God! All this time, all these years—dead, dead, dead—torn apart."

" 'Join him,' could also mean something else," Misha warned.

"What?"

"I'm not sure, but trust me when I tell you that Mayhem is the universal joker. Take heed with his lead."

Misha bent over him, pushing the disheveled hair from his face.

"If this can happen to Paladin," Tashum whimpered, "it can happen to any of us?"

"To you," Misha said.

"Yes, to me," he admitted at last.

Suddenly it was cold. Very cold. Tashum pulled his knees close to his chest. All heat seemed to leak out of his body at once. He reached for Misha, pulling him close for warmth.

"Nothing lives forever, Tashum."

"But I've done!" he answered. "I have lived for hundreds, even tens of thousands of years. I've been shot and stabbed, I've fallen from bridges, I've had coaches collapse on me, car wrecks—for God's sake, I fell out of the sky. And I lived."

Tashum's grief was being overshadowed by sudden anger. He raised his right hand, the murderous hand that had taken life and just stared at it, seeing it as not a part of himself but as an object, a tool for destruction. His thoughts drifted back to his brother. How could this have happened to him? What black magic could kill an angel? Why Paladin? Speaking aloud these questions, Tashum was freeing himself of truths he'd etched in stone. Had it not been for the pain, it might have been a comfort to know he had a choice in his existence. But it was his precious brother, Paladin, whose demise was being spoken of. And that called for vengeance.

"I—I don't have an answer. I'm sorry, Tashum." Misha hugged his shoulder.

Tashum's worried gaze watched the billows of fog pass by the light from the window. He saw little spots of radiance in the fog, sparkles from the hideous skeleton inside.

"Is it possible, then, that he's not in heaven?" Tashum disengaged himself from Misha and rose with effort, steadying himself against the glass. For a long moment he stared with unbelieving eyes at the skeleton.

"He's Fallen, just as you are," Misha said. "What happens in the case of an unredeemed death, I can't say."

"You can! And you should!"

"No—I'm telling you, I don't know. I don't have all the knowledge."

"Why would his skeleton stay behind? And where is his head?"

"Tashum, I don't have answers for any of your questions."

"No, perhaps you don't, but I know who does." Tashum's voice was sharp, his jaw muscles tight. "My dearest, thieving, lying Fanny."

Fanny pushed the grooming brush in long even swaths across the horse's withers, gliding down the valley in the back to the swell of the haunch. The combing action left a smooth trail that broadened with each pass of the brush.

"Fanny," Dickey's voice echoed in the fort's mud-walled barn.

Her eyes raised from her work. Through the sway in her horse's back she could see him in the next stall floundering with a similar soft-bristle brush. "Let it glide across the horse's back," she said. "Try long, smooth strokes."

The brush squirted out of his grasp, falling to the fresh straw bedding. "I really do feel the twit," he said bending down to fetch the brush.

"Hold it loose in your hand, like I showed you."

He pushed the brush the length of his arm before it slipped out of his hand and fell a second time. "Could you do it for me?" he smiled. "Please. I'm just no good at it. Never was, you remember—"

"All right," she moaned, "but only if you clean the tack."

"Saddles or bridles?"

"All of it. That's fair, I do the horses, you do the leather."

"Deal!" He stepped away from the mare. "I much prefer saddle soap to horsehair." He lit a hand-rolled cigarette and watched her labor.

*   *   *

Misha stood at the door of the Jaguar listening to Potter's raucous snores and watching his eyes swim under their lids. After a moment, he opened the door and placed a hand on the sleeper's shoulder.

"It's time to go," he said softly.

Potter shuffled about, yawning. "Just resting my eyes," he said.

Tashum stood in front of the Jaguar watching the night sky. There was a stillness about him that hid a fiery place of silent anger from which he struggled to emerge. He couldn't shake off visions of death, the dreams he once had of Paladin standing in the center of whirling fire were now supported by his brother's remains. He glanced at Misha helping Potter out of the car. "Misha would you bring my travel cases, please?"

"I'll need to get my bag out of the boot," added Potter.

"Misha will take care of it, Potter."

"He'll need help with them," Potter mumbled, and blinked his watery, bleary eyes.

"No, he doesn't, he's quite capable."

Tashum led Potter and Misha through the crowded platform past a sleek new bullet train with the initials TGV painted on its sides. A uniformed porter came to Misha's aid, insisting on shouldering the bags.

Tashum climbed aboard the first-class car and moved to a booth table. His hands rubbed lightly across the stiff white cloth, straightening crooked seams—his fingers shivered to a stop when he thought of Gregory doing the same. He wondered if there was a way to make it all right. Through the window he watched Misha chatting with the porter, patting him on the arm, surrendering all of his money in a tip and doing so with a smile and warm cheer.

"*Oui, oui—*" said a voice nearby. "*Alors—*"

Tashum glanced toward a French-speaking passenger at the next table, a man in a trim, dark suit speaking into a cell phone. The slim, black instrument bore the letters TGV.

"Cell phones, awful invention," complained Potter as he sat next to Tashum. "You can't get away from the bloody things."

Tashum's expression lit up. He snapped his fingers at the car waiter. The energetic man in crisp whites moved to their table. He gave them the once over.

"Let me guess?" he said in English. "Tea?"

"Good observation, however, I was thinking more along the lines of a cell phone, the brandy list, and, can I smoke a cigar in here?"

"Tashum, I don't think you're allowed," Potter chided.

The waiter bowed slightly. "Sir, you are in first class. *Pas de problème*"

"*Quelle chance.*" Tashum smiled. "I'd like to see what you have from Cuba?"

"Of course." He glanced at the Englishman. "And you, sir?"

"Just tea for me," Potter said. "Something good and black."

"Cream?"

"Just a touch."

When the server had gone, Potter leaned toward Tashum. "There's an advantage to wearing English clothes when traveling abroad."

"Potter, you might as well have a Union Jack painted across your forehead."

Two thin steel blades clashed together—whipped apart and clashed again. The opposing figures lunged toward each other and separated.

Dickey caught his breath, brought the foil's blade to his face, his eyes darting, then he charged Fanny again.

At the top of a high, crenelated wall overlooking the sea, the two vampires clashed again in sharp, flashing movements. Two ghosts, their flowing Berber robes flit through the salt-tinged breeze. Their dance took them up and over the domed roof of the great pavilion. Fanny slid down the shallow incline of a flying buttress on steady feet. Dickey followed chase with a little less grace. They had traversed the fort, replacing their seascape backdrop with one of the desert.

The foils crossed and retreated, slapped together again. They circled each other, pounced simultaneously, foils locked together at the hilts, face to face.

Dickey gritted his teeth, holding off defeat. "You're much better at this than I remember."

"I don't suppose you get much practice at this with Victor." Fanny eyed him intently. "He has made you soft."

She flicked her wrist and his foil shot skyward. Dickey leaped straight up, catching the sword in midflight. As his feet touched the ramparts, her blade swished up between his legs, its tip catching him in his groin. Then it slipped up his body carving a delicate incision in his clothing from crotch to chin.

She pulled the blade away.

"Checkmate," Fanny said, smiling.

Dickey looked down, opening his robe to find his flesh undamaged.

"You're too . . . bloody good at that," he said, forcing a swallow down a dry throat.

"Remember, Dickey, leaping is easy. It's always the landing that kills."

He nodded and saluted her with a wave of his foil.

Through an arched doorway, Samir appeared with a battered leather suitcase. He glided down a flight of battle damaged steps and joined them. As he approached, Fanny could hear the muted sound of a telephone ringing from inside the travel bag.

"What are you doing with Victor's suitcase?"

"Madam Matar, the suitcase, it is ringing."

Fanny shot Dickey a troubled glance. "So I hear." She turned back to Samir. "Open it."

Samir placed the suitcase on the rooftop and popped up the lid. Inside he dug through wadded, unwashed clothes and various objects bearing Tashum's embossed name: a calculator, a letter opener in a leather case. He located the phone wrapped inside a monogrammed towel.

"Well, well. Victor stole Tashum's phone, too. Go ahead, answer it." She glanced at Dickey with a false grin. "Wouldn't it be a giggle if it was you know who."

"Hardly a giggle," perceived Dickey with downcast expression.

"*Bon jour?*" Samir said into the phone.

"Who is it?" Fanny asked impatiently.

Samir held out the instrument. "He would not give his name. But he wishes to speak to you."

Dickey trembled. "Fanny—it's Tashum! I know it's him."

"Get a hold of yourself." Fanny refused to look at him, taking the phone and in a low, composed voice said, "*Bon jour?*"

"Fanny," said the familiar voice on the phone.

She jerked the phone away from her ear. Though she had expected to hear his voice, it still startled her. Slowly she brought it back to her ear.

"Isn't modern technology amazing? I'm so glad we live in a time when no one is more than a phone call away," said Tashum's digital voice.

"You and your toys, Tashum. So clever."

"Yes, well, you know why I'm calling."

"No, as a matter of fact, I don't." Her wide eyes stared hard at the stone flooring. "I thought you'd be in your precious heaven by now or wherever the hell you were going."

Tashum took a deep breath. "I enjoy a good game, but you went too far when you killed Gregory."

"Gregory?" She paced to the ledge and stared out across desert sands. "How awful, I really had no idea—"

"Drop it, Fanny. I want the orbs back, and quick."

She spun around and pointed at Tashum's cigarette holder. Dickey grabbed it from the suitcase.

"Well, I'm glad to see that we've got your full attention." Dickey gave her a cigarette. "But as for quick, I don't think we can possibly see you before . . . " She paused as he cuffed his lighter and flame ignited the cigarette tip. "Realistically, I'd say sometime next week." Smoke poured from her nostrils.

"Tomorrow, Fanny. That's how long you have. We do it tomorrow or the whole deal is off."

She giggled. "All those years, you couldn't stand the sight of us, now so impetuous. What's a girl to think?"

"You've got something to lose now, too. Your little stunt brought Scotland Yard into the game."

At the mention of the British police, she pushed away from the wall, stalking quickly along its edge until it became a corner. She looked out over the main gate and the desert road.

"Scotland Yard?" she said in a broken voice. She cleared her throat and continued, "Tashum, what are you talking about? You know I have a . . . distaste for the police. Why would you call them? I . . . " She paused, hearing commotion down in the courtyard. She could see Victor talking to a collapsed horse. He tugged on the reins, and when the unresponsive animal refused to rise, Victor threw off his hat and kicked the sand with a shout. As she watched, he drew a pistol from his belt.

Fanny turned away from the scene, fighting to keep her concentration on the conversation. "I thought you, of all people, would want to keep this within the family."

She jumped at the sound of a gunshot. Trembling, she fled the edge of the wall, fighting to keep her mind on Tashum.

"Scotland Yard came to me," Tashum said, "with a bloodied business card and questions. Tell Victor the police are on to him, as I am on to you. I'm giving you one last chance, Fanny. I want—"

Her face hardened with anger. "You want? Try asking what I want! It's a seller's market, Tashum! You don't make the demands, we do!"

"What would you like now? I'd sign over the London house, but it's been pretty much destroyed. Oh, there's the yacht, but it seems to have developed a fairly significant leak. As for money, all my accounts are frozen because of your messy stunt in London."

"Stop accusing me of something that Dickey's American monkey did. I never would have hurt Gregory."

"What do you want, Fanny?"

She took a slow, deep breath trying to think it through. "Where are you Tashum? Let's start with that."

"Nice try, but get serious."

"I was—"

"Fanny!" he warned.

"All right! I want the rest of your diamond collection, Tashum." Her lips drew into thin snarl. "And I mean all of it this time."

"You're so predictable, Fanny," Tashum answered her venom with calm. "Fine. As you wish, the rest of the diamonds are yours. But you'll have to meet me in Ascona tomorrow, before Interpol finds out about them, as well. I'll be waiting in the bar at the Hotel Splendideo at midnight tomorrow. I'm sure you can catch a plane."

"Switzerland, hmm, I don't think so. I was thinking more—"

"You want the diamonds? They're in Ascona. Thanks to Victor, we've got no choice, we're all a bit hot right now. So be careful."

Her eyes raced back and forth, she took another drag from her cigarette. "All right, Tashum. See you in the bar."

"Oh, and Fanny?"

"Yes, Tashum?"

"Don't forget to bring the orbs."

The phone clicked in her ear, and Fanny lowered it slowly.

"That son of a bitch." She spat. "Always the last word. Always thinks he's in control." She gave Dickey a long, piercing stare. "I promise you, he will be put to sleep faster than a rabid dog at the RSPCA."

"What?" Dickey asked.

"You heard me."

"What else did he say? How did he find us?"

"Dickey, you've always been slow. Don't be stupid as well. Your boy may have ruined this whole deal for us. Go get packed. We're going to Ascona. Sunset tomorrow."

Fanny turned again to the parapet and shouted down into the courtyard. "Victor—is that my horse lying out there?"

Victor turned an unsteady head, still drunk with Moroccan blood, his clothing wet and saturated in dark red stains.

"Let me check the brand fer yuh." He made a show of looking closely at the horse's rump. "Yep, looks like the Pentagram *M* to me." He curled his upper lip into an Elvis sneer. "I guess I run the fuckin' legs off the sorry-ass bastard."

Fanny gripped the stone of the wall. "You'll not leave my horse lying out there like that!" she commanded.

"Ah shit, Fanny," he wheedled. "I was just kidding. Listen to me now, don't go losing it. I thought he picked up a stone, but the poor sons-a-bitch had a broke leg. Surprised the shit outa me. I'm sorry, okay?"

Her deadly stare from the high wall slowly peeled the smirk off Victor's face.

"One damn fine ride. You oughta had left the nuts on this one—"

"Shut up!"

"Hell, Fanny, I'll get yuh another one, somewhere."

When she vanished, he knew he'd had it.

"Ah, fuck," he grumbled and kicked the sand.

"Victor," said Dickey from the wall, "you'd better come inside."

"Uh-oh . . ."

She met him in the pavilion, a long, black bullwhip slithered above her head. Victor felt the razor sting before he heard the sound. The blow sent him rolling. The whip cracked again and again, and Victor dove for cover under an end table. Fanny kicked the table away and pinned his arm to the floor with her foot. She unleashed a furious volley of blows, the long thin whip forming a whistling **S** in the air. A crisp snap—the cutting leather opened his face with ragged slash. Each stripe evoked fresh yelps and sobbing howls.

At last, Fanny let him loose, still hovering above him. "Those are my horses, and this is my house. I love them both."

"Fanny!" Dickey cried out, his hands to his mouth. "It wasn't his fault. He put the creature out of its misery! For once in his miserable life he did the right thing, goddamn it!"

She slapped Victor again and again with the whip until he cowered on the floor, mewling and frightened. He rose up on his knees, pleading with her.

"I love horses! I'm fuckin' sorry." He wept, his body convulsing, blood coursing down his torn face. "Fanny, please, I'm beggin' you."

"You don't know the meaning of sorry," she snapped. Her arm rose. "But I will teach you how to beg."

Another lash ripped a gaping gash diagonally across his neck. Another sliced across his chest. Quaking and wailing, he fell again to the floor.

Dickey flashed across the room, catching Fanny's wrist in the midst of a fresh assault, their faces inches apart.

"He was just healing from the lashing Tashum gave him," he said calmly. "I'd hate to see any permanent damage.

"When he knows his place, I may slow down."

"Fanny, granted he's a fuckup, but he wouldn't have intentionally hurt your horse."

Her arm jerked away, and she wound up for another swing. Again, Dickey caught her arm. His other hand cupped her face.

"Goddamn it, Fanny. Think for a moment. It's not him you're really mad at."

Her eyes seared into his, giving Victor time to scurry on hands and knees across the floor and wrap himself around Dickey's legs for shelter.

She dropped the whip and broke away from Dickey's grip. She moved to a table and removed a cigarette from a filigreed gold box, slipped it into a long, ivory holder, lit up, and draped herself across a zebra-skin couch.

Dickey bent and ran his hand through Victor's hair, comforting his wounded pup.

"Victor." Fanny's voice was almost friendly. "Tashum mentioned something about a business card. And that the police were on to you. What have you been up to?"

Dickey helped Victor to his feet and pulled his long black hair away from his face wounds, cringing at the bloodied disfigurement.

"She really fucked me up, didn't she?" Victor panted through cut lips, his face a hideous mangle of flesh.

"Answer her," Dickey said in stern reply. "What is this all about?"

"I—" Victor began in a contrite whine, "I took one a them cards Tashum dropped at Fanny's place and left it in the hand of a party boy. After I slit his throat, of course."

A stream of smoke billowed out of Fanny's mouth. "And his body? Did you hide it?"

Victor looked to her, then to Dickey, and weakly shook his head no.

Dickey blinked, his features growing rigid. He stepped away from Victor's hunched-over pose. "You didn't hide the body?"

"Fuck no! I wanted the sons-a-bitch to be found."

"Victor—" she was cut off.

"What's the big fuckin' deal? That dickless prick pissed me off. You told me to go after him. Remember them words, Fanny?"

"I told you to get the orbs back. Not play the Terminator." She shook her head, glancing at Dickey. "It appears he went a bit mad at Tashum's house. He killed Gregory."

"Oh, dear," lamented Dickey.

Victor looked through his fallen hair, from one to the other. "It ain't like we don't go out and do this kinda shit every night a the week."

Fanny shook her head. "You know the rules about hiding bodies and involving the police."

Dickey whirled around in a dance of frustration, shouting out his anger. He turned and faced Victor again. "Let me get this straight." His finger raised. "On your own, you tried to frame Tashum for murder? That's it, isn't it?"

"Purty much. Yep."

"God, you're so stupid. Tashum was so right. You really were a bad experiment."

Victor held out his arms in a posture of supplication. "I don't get it? Why am I always the bad guy?"

"Because you're an idiot." Fanny stubbed out her cigarette. "Go wash your face, Victor. Then get some sleep. I want the plane fueled and ready by sundown tomorrow. We're six hours from Ascona," she said before turning to leave, "and you need to get us there by midnight."

Dickey watched her glide up broad flat steps worn uneven from routine, and up on to the torchlit mezzanine. "Fanny," he said gently as she disappeared behind the trunk of a potted palm tree. Reappearing, framed beneath the fingers of luminous green leaf, she looked innocently appealing, and dangerously seductive at the same time.

"Yes, Dickey, what is it?" a mother's soothing voice.

"Nothing, I . . . I was just wondering where you were off to?"

"You should come with me." She smiled, then ducked back into the flickering torchlight. Dickey stood there watching her until she was swallowed by the medieval cavernous architecture, amazed as ever by her chameleon nature and emotional abilities. He glanced down at Victor. "Thank God you're not a woman," he muttered, then followed after her.

Mayhem, afraid to venture closer chose to observe Paladin's skeletal remains from the rooftop across the street from the Antiquities Shoppe. He crouched down and let his wings trail out behind him. Even through quick-moving wisps of fog Paladin's skeleton appeared more impressive than he remembered it being. It worried the spirit that the shopkeeper had chosen to display an artifact that could be interpreted as a warning to any Celestial whose eyes should see it. He tried to think of better days with Paladin, but in the end their noble adventure led to this heartbreaking spectacle.

Suddenly he felt something beyond remorse, a vibration that spread through his crystalline shape. Then he heard their voices, a siren wail delivered by three messengers. He was surrounded by their song. He leaped to his feet snapped his wings taught, and lifted off the roof shingles. His vision scanned the invisible world. All around him the tiny strands of light that hang suspended in the ether were rigid and vibrating. He realized that he was at the center of triangulation with a voice at each point. They were vectoring in on him. The tickling vibration was turning to pain.

And then he saw a thin silhouette. It was approaching at eye level on a spread wings set in a glide.

He had to spin around to see all three silver-winged, angels of Light. Their mouths were stretched open and distorted, resembling the bell of a trumpet. They were armed with only their song. Each messenger carried a different note of the mystical chord that was undoing Mayhem on a cellular level.

He clutched the handle of his sword and felt an overall weakness in his hand. His entire being was suddenly constricting under the pressure and pelting of the sound waves. The harmonic electrification surged to the level that shriveled the tips of his wings. He screamed, and when he couldn't take much more he summoned his power, flapped his wings, and relied upon their ability to get him to the neutral safety of Notre Dame's cellar.

CHAPTER TWENTY

Deep inside the fortress, Fanny stepped through a small earthen doorway that had been hidden by a tapestry. She took a torch from the corroded iron wall bracket and handed it to Dickey. She took a second torch for herself. He lit both oiled rags with his Zippo lighter. As light filled the tight space, he could smell the sea and feel its dank presence.

"Where exactly are we, Fanny?" he asked as he carefully made his way down broken steps to the landing where she was waiting.

"What I want to show you is down here," she said, tugging on a thick wooden door that opened to a flight of stairs clinging to a curved wall, winding down and disappearing into an enormity of darkness.

"That crashing sound?" he said, as he swept the flaming torch across the open gorge. But the weak light from his torch could not reach the seamingly bottomless pit. "It is just the sea down there, isn't it?"

"What were you expecting?" asked the face of innocence.

They descended down spiraling stairs laid with flat stones cantilevered out from the curvature of circular walls. Revenant veils of cobwebs hung about crumbling masonry work and adjoining doorways. On the landings, rusted chains and manacles dangled from the damp limestone.

"Is this what I think it is?" he asked.

"If you think it's a dungeon, then you're right," she said. "Lucky ones were chained high. Those chained farther down rarely made it past high tide."

"Hard to say who was really the luckier," he said as he dusted a centipede from his shoulder.

Ducking through a low doorway, Fanny led him into a rectangular cell. The wall to his left featured large cut stone slabs married to natural rock formations, which gave him a clue as to where he was. On the eastern approach to the fort he had long noticed a low-lying belt of masonry that seemed far below the fort's aggressive foundation and completely inaccessible due to the wraparound nature of the cove.

Dickey swung his torch around, then stopped. He stared with uncertainty at the dark stain on the wall farthest from where he stood.

Fanny looked to him, catching his curiosity before following his gaze. For an endless moment neither of them spoke. In their silence, the drone of light surf, trickle of water seeping through the walls, and the faint sizzle of burning torches filled their ears.

Slowly Dickey approached the wall, his torch illuminating a tall, noble gray outline of an angel silhouetted in charcoal. His wings spread, his arms held up shielding his face.

"My God," Dickey whispered, studying the features of the face, the stature of the drawing, "is that Paladin?"

"His last moment on Earth—my sweet Paladin." She stood back, hands on her hips, head cocked. "He doesn't look as fierce as you probably remember him."

Dickey stared hard at the wall, torchlight flickering across his figure. "He has wings."

"Only for a spilt second."

"How was it drawn?"

"It's not a drawing." She paused, under a wrinkled forehead. "The Black Knight." Her body sagged under the weight of the memory. "I warned Paladin away from him—but all he could talk about was his home beyond the stars. Here, hold this," Fanny said, giving him her torch.

Fanny produced a small knife from the folds in her robe. She began to scrape bits of the charcoal off the image, letting the dust fall into a small glass vial.

"It's him." His gaze traced the lines and contours of the burned image. His face heavy, numb. "Why've you never told me about this?"

"I . . . couldn't," she admitted.

"All this time, I was sure Paladin was alive!" Dickey turned swiftly, facing her, his lips trembling. "You said he abandoned us—that we'd see him again. But this? He's bloody well dead, isn't he?" He stepped back completely stunned.

"Hmm, quite." She stopped scraping. "Dickey," she said with her eyes lowered, "Paladin trusted me and what I had with him—"

"What you had? Well what about me? He saved me, too! He gave me his blood, he gave me this life." Dickey lifted his hands to his face. "Fanny— you had no right," he said, tears spilling onto his hands, his voice shattering. "He was my father, too! I loved him, too!" His hand moved gently toward Paladin's image, one last touch, connection—

"You should have known better than to steal from him!" she barked.

His hand quickly jerked back. "Stealing from Paladin was like taking sand from the desert. Why did he even care? He always got what he wanted. And more."

"Dickey—when you were sent away, things happened, terrible things. I've never shared with you. Paladin forbade it. You have to understand that. Believe me when I say that I understand what he meant to you, but—"

"You could have prepared me," he said, sinking to his knees. "This," gesturing to the blackened image. "This is worse than showing me a corpse." A dark splinter shown in his eyes as they narrowed. "You should have told me about this, Fanny," he said in a lower gravelly voice.

She flashed her winning smile to no effect on his dark expression.

"I'm sorry." She bent and kissed his wet face. He slowly softened under her gaze.

"I always thought . . . ," he sighed, shaking his head in disbelief, "I always thought that one night we'd be sitting in a Parisian café, or coming out of some L.A. moviehouse, and there he'd be. Just as tall and amazing as ever. I thought angels—if anything in this world—went on forever."

"What's more disappointing, knowing that he's dead or thinking that he doesn't love you?" Fanny asked, as her finger traced an outlined wing.

"They're both rotten," he said, rising to stand.

She turned her back on the visage to face Dickey.

"Paladin banished you in 1429. That same year the French dauphin was crowned Charles VII, and the Christians drove us out of Orleans. Paladin had letters of introduction from Philip Augustus, but they were of little help." She paused. Her face seemed to ripple in the flickering light. "For two years we traveled through Spain, and then Paladin brought our little coven here."

"Who was left in the coven?"

"Lydia left shortly after you did. Pasquel, Doreen, Nabid, Paladin and me, and the servants. We had been here barely a fortnight, maybe longer, when the Black Knight," her jaw tightened, "he led a band of Moorish cavalry against us." Her eyes flared. "They caught us sleeping. It took three days to butcher everyone, and then they came to me—Paladin howled with grief. Only then did he give the Black Knight what he wanted, and in exchange they spared me."

"What was it, Fanny, what did he want?"

"A set of orbs." She paused for his stunned reaction. "Paladin somehow had swindled them away from him."

"Orbs again. So Paladin was as crazy about them as well." Dickey mustered the courage and finally touched the ashen image. "Was the Black Knight the same as Paladin and Tashum?"

"I don't know, I never saw his face. He came to us when we were still in Spain. Paladin was elated and entertained him for days." She paused holding the memory. "And then out of the blue, Paladin told us he was going back France. Something terrible had happened there, but he wouldn't say what." She paused, dusting her memory bank. "It involved that weirdo Timean and Joan of Arc, but I never really knew—"

"Forget the history lesson, Fanny, what about Paladin?"

"You know who you're starting to sound like?" she snapped.

"Sorry. Please go on."

"Once the Black Knight had the orbs back, his men tied Paladin to this wall and I-I was tied over there." Her eyes burned with the memory. "Throughout the night, they painted Paladin with a paste of camel urine and dung mixed with a powder they got from a Druid monk. Something called flaxen-tangmere."

Dickey's eyes followed her gaze to a sealed window set high up on the back wall.

"At sunrise they opened that window." She winced. "When the daylight hit him, a brilliant flash swept the room. It permanently blinded the Moors. I was in the corner," she pointed to the other side of the room, "protected by shadows. I saw his wings, Dickey, and then," with a hard swallow, "as

Paladin's flesh was blown from his bones I saw him with wings. He was all lit up and looked like he was made of glass."

"God almighty . . . ," Dickey lowered his head.

"The death blow came when the Black Knight swung his sword and cut off Paladin's crystal skull." Her face sagged with anguish. "Paladin's light left his glass shell in strands of stringyness. I could feel the bundle's warmth and watched the light fibers being sucked into something invisible."

"What's stringy light?"

"I don't know how else to describe light that didn't mix; it stayed in stringy strands."

"Hmm. How did you ever escape?"

"The Black Knight kept his word to Paladin. He took the skull, collected the orbs, and left me there without a word."

"What about his blinded men?"

"Well, those he didn't cut down on his way out he left stumbling around in their misery. It was horrifying the way they groped at me." Her upper lip curled into a sneer. "I killed the rest of them myself when I broke free."

"Jesus, Fanny, I had no idea you'd been through so much."

"How could you?" She held up the vial filled with gray dust and gave it a shake. "This was all that was left of—"

"What happened to Paladin's skeleton?"

"I sold it," she said with ease.

"No, you did not."

"Hmm, I did."

"God, you're cold."

"It runs in the family." She smiled, shaking the vial. "I had no choice."

"So that's flaxen-tangmere. I thought it was just some kind of incense, you know, fairy dust."

"Incense, fairy dust." She snickered. "I'm hoping there's enough left."

"Enough left for what? What are you planning?"

She ignored the question and continued to scrape more of the charcoal.

"Fanny." He placed a hand on her shoulder. "I don't feel so bad about being banished by Paladin. He was a thief, too, wasn't he?"

"Not like you, Dickey."

He shrugged his round shoulders. "You know, all these years I thought you two had some kind of falling out. You know, like with Tashum. Something too hurtful to discuss."

"Paladin appreciated his creation. He wouldn't have left me." She looked deep into his eyes. "Us . . ."

"Angels can die?" Dickey questioned with wonder.

"It's worse than any human death," she said. "And horribly beautiful at the same time. You should have seen the colors." She looked at the vial, then up at her longtime companion. "Dickey, we must strike first."

"What does that mean?"

"I plan to put Tashum to sleep," she stated with confidence.

"Fanny!" he exclaimed, backing away.

"Don't worry Dickey." She paused, noticing Dickey's sudden change in expression. "I know that look, what is it?"

"If . . . ," he faltered, building courage. "If we have the power," his eyes lifted, holding her gaze, "why not just kill him?"

Fanny quivered at his words, so cold, so precise, so final. She took his face in her hands and kissed him. Her voice broke, as though a sob were rising in her throat. And she stared at him with large, glistening eyes. "Dickey, the price for my life was a vow made to Paladin."

Dickey followed her eyes to the outline on the wall.

"Even in London," she continued, "I knew that we would stand in Tashum's way. But now I realize that—that Tashum knew something I didn't. Something even Paladin didn't understand about all of it."

Dickey eyed her closely. The whirling, in-and-out tale of love and not love, mortality and immortality, spun in his head.

"What, Fanny?"

She took the time to stroke his hair. "We're soulless, you and I."

"If that's true," he winced, struggling to make the rational connection, "then we don't exist except down here on Earth."

"Maybe."

"Then we owe nothing to anyone. None of that karma business that Paladin threatened us with. No soul, no credits, no debts. Right?"

"I suppose, in a queer way." She smiled.

Dickey's face relaxed from the mental strain of thinking so hard.

"To him, we're a hideous mistake," she added.

"We're the rotten children he wished he never had."

"I saw that when he left us. Dickey, I thought he loved us, and I would have sacrificed anything for him. His kind want only one thing—to return to their celestial womb. This world for them is a prison, and you and I are just fellow inmates. You should have seen Paladin when he thought—for a single day—that he really could return. I knew I'd lost him . . . I thought things were different with Tashum. We shared incredible sensations, far beyond anything physical . . . I thought it would last forever, that I could train him," she said. Her voice rose with bitterness, "Of course, I was a fool to believe such things. A bigger fool to believe them twice."

"You love him, and yet you hate him for wanting to leave you," Dickey said. "That's the real reason for this, isn't it?"

She broke the embrace and stepped away. She closed her eyes and her hands went to her face, rubbing it wearily. "I have to," she said finally. "If I didn't love him and hate him, I couldn't do what Paladin asked of me. Paladin saw the future, you know."

"You mean he knew his destiny? About all this?"

"The vision made him go crazy, screeching something about a silence in heaven. It was very bizarre. Very sad. I hated seeing him so troubled."

"That's their bloody problem, isn't it?" Dickey said.

"Yes, it's a party that we're not invited to." Fanny reached out for him and they clung to each other at the foot of the black angel, neither voicing their thoughts, neither expressing the immense, unspeakable conspiracy blossoming within.

CHAPTER TWENTY-ONE

Throughout the night the trio was jostled about in the relative comfort of their small first-class compartment. Their fast train snaked its way through the Swiss Alps, speeding along on twin rails laid in deep glacier-gouged alpine valleys whistling through a series of tunnels that burrowed through miles of solid granite with Swiss precision.

Belinzonia to Locarno was the last leg of the rail journey. They would follow the Fume Ticino, through wide glacier-cut valleys where the river eventually drains into Lago Maggiore.

In their private compartment, Potter was the only one sleeping, pacified by the trains gentle rocking motion. His head was resting in Misha's lap, his body prone on the straight-backed bench settee. Misha's eyes were peacefully closed.

Tashum sat across from them, his mood less serene. He checked his Rolex, quickly calculating that they had one hour, fifty-seven minutes until the sunrise. He estimated another thirty minutes on the train before disembarking in Locarno. Add to that a fifteen-minute car ride from the rail station, across the Fume Maggia delta and into Ascona.

"Plenty of time," he said to no one in particular.

His smile flattened when his gaze went back to Misha. A single word entered his mind: *Betrayal*. Was it fair? Of course not. His carefully orchestrated rationales for stealing from someone so pure were playing the opening strains of a discordant inner aria.

Tashum jerked his head away, afraid that his fellow angel's eyes would open and see his self-disgust. He wanted to get away from him, leave behind this gentle, unblinking source of self-doubt. He felt so close to his desire and yet so far from ever being able to enjoy it. Even if he could escape back into the light, what would he find there? Could he fix this colossal mess he was leaving behind on Earth from a place in heaven?.

Misha's soft voice brought him out of the cycle of awful thoughts.

"Tashum, Potter is dreaming that he's a dog. He just lifted his leg on his mother's handbag," Misha said with an impish grin. Misha radiated goodness through his big eyes, through his boyish looks, through the innocence in his very being.

Tashum nodded without really hearing Misha's words, he was so caught up in the startling realization he was in the presence of an angel unsullied by the Fall. Misha embodied the type of being that had captured the imagination and hearts of humans. How ironic that Tashum and his fallen comrades had been the chosen ones to walk amongst mankind.

"We are only separated by our experience, Tashum," Misha said softly.

"No, we're different," he replied blankly. "I mean not just physically." Tashum's blinding anguish was paramount. "But in all ways."

Misha's face filled with compassion. "Take my hand, brother."

Tashum shook his head, waving him off. "I don't dare."

"Why?"

Tashum looked away, avoiding even his own eyes in the reflective glass. "Because, to do so would mean to lose."

Tashum's home in Ascona sat on a prominent raised point separated from the lake's rocky shoreline only by the Via Moscia. It featured a commanding view over Lago Maggiore, encompassing her quaint waterfront and the curvaceous Italian buildings lining the Piazza G. Motta and Via Albarelle.

Hotel Villa Splendideo had set the standard of quality for the *Reilais & Château Guide*, but for reasons known only to the hotel's management, the villa had remained unlisted anywhere. Not a private haunt, just a well-kept Swiss secret for those willing to shell out twelve hundred Swiss Francs a night for the basics. The suites were quite a bit more.

The Mercedes limousine made a hard right turn off the via Moscia and onto the long brick-surfaced drive that was perfectly flanked by beds of orange azaleas mixed with blue rhododendron, with small palm trees interspersed. Her cut stone facade rose up five stories, capped by a Roman-tiled mansard roof.

By the time Tashum, Misha and Potter were stepping through the Splendideo's main entrance, her normally off-white plastered exterior was tainted a faint pink with the coming of a new day.

Tashum led Potter across the airy lobby subdivided by squares of posh cream-colored leather seating and broad green-leafed plants, set against large Roman arched windows. They stopped at the check-in counter, where they were greeted warmly by the night manager, a small dedicated man wearing a blue suit. *"Buon giorno—"*

"Buon giorno, do you take Barclays here?" Potter asked.

"No, Potter, it's strictly cash here," Tashum interjected.

"But—"

"No buts, I'll take care of it my friend." He turned to the awaiting manager. *"Mi chiamo Tashum,"* he said and hand gestured toward Potter. *"Questo é il signor, Potter."*

"Yes sir, we've been expecting you. We have three suites on the top floor, facing the lake. It's always a pleasure to have you here," replied the manager with an Oxford accent.

"Thank you, Manfred. It's always good to be here," he said, reading the man's name off his lapel pin.

Tashum noticed a flyer attached to a brass plaque on the counter advertising the opening of a new restaurant Grotto Splendideo.

"Finally doing something with the old escape route, are you?" Tashum smiled while looking at the artist's rendering of a subterranean dining room, featuring a skylight directly over a large natural pool of water.

"Right sir. You'll see it from your suite, at least the glass ceiling."

"What, did they roof the old sinkhole?"

"Yes, that's right, they enlarged the cave. They've done it all up rather posh."

"Looks fun, don't you think Potter?"

"Bed sounds like fun right now."

"How about you, Misha?" Tashum glanced over his shoulder. Misha was gone. Haphazardly, he stepped away from the counter to look down the wide corridor leading to the bar and elevator lifts. He didn't notice the hard line of sunlight seeping across the high polished granite floor. He stepped out from behind a stout carved pillar. *Whapp!* A bolt of sunlight reflected from the floor-to-ceiling gilded wall mirror, a reflection of the great orange ball itself, ran head long into his face.

An invisible fist knocked him to the floor, and just as fast, he was back on his feet standing upright next to Potter.

"What the devil?" asked Potter in bewilderment. He visually remeasured the twenty-foot distance covered in a heartbeat. "How did you do that?"

Tashum didn't reply, acting as if nothing had happened.

Potter scratched his head and seemed too tired to even try to make sense of it.

The clerk acted, very discreetly, as if nothing had happened. "Shall I give you all three keys, sir?" he asked in a soft voice.

"Hmm, yes. Well I'm not sure where my other travel companion has run off too."

"I don't think he even came in with us, did he?" offered Potter.

"Perhaps he's enjoying the lake. It is quite beautiful this time of morning. I'll show him to his room when he returns."

"Yes, that will be fine."

Tashum took two of the keys offered on a silver tray.

"I'll ring a bell man."

"No, don't bother I know the way. I'll show Mr. Potter to his room," he said, taking Potter by the shoulder.

"Very well, sir. I'll have your luggage brought round to your room."

Tashum used Potter as a shield against the sun's horizontal rays flooding in through a wall of glass windows. Dispersed by plants and furniture a patchwork of danger lay ahead. They walked the gauntlet without Potter ever suspecting he had a role in any heroics. Tashum's constant twitching and flinching seemed normal for a man drunk with sleep deprivation. Ducking into an enclosed corridor, Tashum released Potter's arm and moved ahead to the double elevators lining the left wall.

Fanny hadn't slept well. Her hair was a wad of baled straw, smeared makeup streaked her face, and swollen eyes that had cried all night begged for rest. By candlelight in an otherwise dark room, she gazed at her ragged appearance

in the large vanity mirror. There was only one cure. Trembling fingers slid a
pair of dark movie star sunglasses up the sharp bridge of her nose.

She sat naked at her vanity desk carefully placing a well-tailored cigar
into a pocket-size silver humidor. Then she leaned over a pile of Paladin's
ash spread across a small drug mirror.

Her index and middle finger pulled the plunger almost out of the syringe. The ash was sucked in through the needle's point and swirled into dust
inside the glass tube.

"Paladin, my darling, is this what you saw when you looked into the
future? Is this the way you wanted me to keep Tashum on Earth?" she asked
in very shaky voice, "I can only do this out of my love for you." Her mouth
vowed as her hand rammed the needle deep into the length of a brown-
leafed Corona cigar. Slowly, the plunger depressed, pushing the ash back
down the glass tube and through the needle. Carefully she withdrew the
needle until the syringe was empty.

Through the closed door she heard Dickey's muted voice call her name.
She looked up, seeing the door reflected in the mirror. His feet cast twin
shadows in the strip of light sneaking in through the gap along the bottom
edge of the crude wooden door. "Fanny, are you awake, my dear?"

With tears forming under the sleek Italian black rims, she replied in a
choppy voice, "No, I'm sleeping. Whatever it is, can't it wait?"

"Sorry. We'll take it up later. Sweet dreams."

In the mirror she watched his feet flicker the light as he walked away.
Her eyes lowered back to the laced cigar resting on her fingertips.

The elevator doors split open. Stanton and Shelly Green were suddenly face-
to-face, bumping into each other. His breath fogged her tortoise-rimmed
glasses, an embarrassing moment made worse by his hand brushing against
her breast and her hand landing on his gun, holstered beneath his long cream-
colored overcoat.

"I beg your pardon, I'm terribly sorry," said Stanton. His cheeks blushed
red. He stepped back and smiled. "Sorry." She nodded and quietly slipped
around his bulk.

Her distressed expression stuck in his mind. He sensed it was there before their meeting. He watched her slim figure hustle down the marbled
corridor. She marched past an assortment of broad-leafed potted trees that

reached high for the skylights cut into the eighteenth-century vaulted ceiling. He wondered which of several upscale office fronts was her destination. It wasn't until she stopped at a set of bold framed glass doors that his thoughts changed from a male appreciation to a cop's suspicion. He withdrew his hand from the leading edge of the elevator door, allowing the doors to close and leave without him.

As she crossed the threshold into Potter's outer office, Shelly glanced back over her shoulder. Stanton was staring back. They held each other's gaze for a brief moment, and with a fling of her hair, she disappeared behind the highly polished doorjamb.

The elevator doors split open again, and two buttoned-up executive types navigated past Stanton. He stood there looking into the awaiting lift, paused, then took another look at Potter's office door. His hands on autopilot searched his pockets, coming up with a packet of Silk Cut cigarettes.

"Excuse me, but smoking is not appreciated on this floor," barked a voice from behind him. He froze, intimidated by the snappy upper-class bite in her diction. *Ball cutter* came to mind.

The middle-aged woman with short-cut hair, wearing a dark gray businessman's suit, stepped past him into the lift. She had a snooty expression that spoke before her mouth did, "And you won't be smoking on the lift, either."

"Of course not," he said, stepping back as the doors swooshed closed.

He lit his cigarette and focused on Potter's office door.

Martha hurried Shelly into Potter's private office, quickly closing the heavy oak door behind them.

"Where's Hamley?"

"I don't know. All hell's broke loose—the police were just here."

"I think I just met one of them at the elevator. What did they want?"

Martha gravitated to the executive desk that owned the room. She sat in Potter's chair as Shelly plopped down on the corner of the desktop.

"You've seen the splash headings, haven't you?" Martha blushed.

"I saw it on TV, that's why I'm here." She paused. "But why were they here?"

"Inspector Stanton said they wanted to confirm Ham's appointment times and dates that were registered in Tashum's journals and appointment book." Martha's long face grew longer. "What has Ham got us into?"

"Damn," moaned Shelly.

"Sorry?"

"They'll find my name in there, as well," she said, feeling the weight of the layered lies. Her made-up life was balanced by fact and fiction, and a police investigation into her past would shift the fulcrum. The truth would ruin her career. Her model-perfect face became oddly animated. "Have you ever met Tashum?"

"Hmm, several times, always at night. I simply can't imagine Ham being involved with a mass murderer." She shivered. "And poor Tashum."

"So you don't buy it, either? I mean, Tashum being a killer?"

"Well, he is a bit odd." Martha shrank back from Shelly's stare.

"That's not a crime. Do you think Hamley is with Tashum?"

"Don't know. Ham left a message on the phone machine, saying that he was taking a few days off in seclusion but didn't mention Tashum."

Shelly suddenly seemed preoccupied. "I've really got to get back to the lab." Her facial beauty reshaped into a frown. "I need to get a message to Tashum. When you contact Hamely have him pass it on—"

"But—"

"It's a very simple message. Ammonia."

Martha wasn't used to such drama. Her mouth hung agape.

"Write it down if you need to. It's very important."

"Ammonia? That's it?"

"Actually, it's a lot more complex, but Tashum will understand." Shelly slipped off the desktop and crossed to the door. "I'll check back later," she said as she left the room.

Stanton was choking down street-vendor coffee outside the posh business address. In midsip, he saw her. He awkwardly ducked behind one of the newer glass phone kiosks. She shuffled down the steps without noticing his jerky actions and walked away down the sidewalk.

Weaving in and out of pedestrians of all shapes and colors, Stanton followed her in his coffee-stained trenchcoat. She led him south on Marylebone High Street. It was several blocks underfoot before she turned left onto New Cavendish Street.

Then they turned left again onto the smaller Westmoor. Midway down the tree-lined street, she entered a brick building identified by a small brass plaque mounted next to the main door.

Stanton's cigarette dangled from his lower lip as he stared at the brass plaque: THE ROYAL HOSPITAL OF BLOOD SCIENCE.

In a bathtub fit for a king, Tashum leaned back, inhaling the fragrance rising off the steamy surface. He sank deeper into soothing bathwater made frothy by a secret Swiss blend of herbs and lanolin, precious oils for the body. Even his netherworldly skin gladly soaked up the herbal drug. Sleep. His eyelids fluttered closed, restless at first, but settling fast. Sighs of relaxation and visions of heaven on earth passed through his mind. If he could just hold that thought and shut all else out.

The sun had climbed above the mountains, warming the alpine air. The radiant heat felt good against his face. From where he stood, Misha could look across the placid ice-cold waters of Lago Maggiore. He could see the grand spectacle of the Splendideo, nestled among the pastel colors and soft renaissance structures of the small New Age town.

As pastoral as it was, his thoughts, his worries, his hope centered around Tashum. He sensed a hidden danger to any further meeting with the band of vampires, but Tashum needed guidance and he would face that danger to help his brother. His skin grew clammy at the thought of them drinking from him, their maniacal eyes burning with a hunger he'd never seen in any human. He couldn't imagine Tashum alone on an island with them, willingly feeding them. Loving them. They were killers, bold survivors of death, not geniuses, but cunning, nonetheless. He was reminded of rats and their almost supernatural ability to survive.

Misha turned from the lake, hiking a smooth dirt path that twisted around the bases of ancient pine trees. The shaded path traversed the forest's sharp incline. Misha was winded after a long sprint to the top of the ridge. He sat on a boulder and looked across the lush green meadow. At the far end of this opening in the trees, Misha could see what he'd come for: a small stone church with a sagging slate roof and stone steeple holding aloft an iron cross.

He felt the soothing energy of the dirt beneath his feet, the warmth of solitude and contemplation of countless mortals. He knew this chapel to be a meeting place for immortals as well. There were many of these secret meeting places hidden from the troubling mystery in heaven, but this was Misha's favorite.

He walked through grass and leaves, hearing only the crackle beneath his feet. He remembered a time before the Silence, when he stood on this very ground and with just a harmonic thought, he had summoned the voices of a thousand angels, creating a miracle in the ears of desperate villagers gathered here.

He passed through the open front door into the stone-and-timber chapel. Small, it housed six rows of wooden pews separated by a narrow aisle. The pews faced an elaborate carved oak pulpit at the far wall. The Gospel wall murals he had witnessed being painted in 1356 were now faded and barely visible. He moved down the narrow aisle toward the pulpit, taking a seat on the front pew. The wood was scarred with scrapes and indentations, worn smooth by visitors from heaven and Earth.

He lowered his head and began to pray. *I call on the celestial light of a cosmic Christ to surround and protect me.* Over and over, in constant repetition, he continued, *I call on the celestial light of a cosmic Christ to surround and protect me.* A melodic chorus was being created by an overlapping echo effect as the message layered itself into a symphonic blend.

After bathing, Tashum had been confronted by an indignant Potter wanting to know how an Armani suit that he had not ordered or been fitted for was waiting for him when he awoke. Tashum explained that while Potter had been sleeping, the morning maid had taken his measurements from his worn clothes hanging in the bathroom. Nothing to get excited about, after all, it was only off-the-rack shopping. In contrast, Tashum's measurements were kept on hand by tailors around the world. His new olive green suit fit like a glove. Misha was odd man out. He couldn't be fitted or his size even guessed at. He had simply disappeared.

Tashum sat silently watching the finger of smoke being pulled from the tip of his cigar, away from the crystal ashtray, rising up into the draft and set aswirl by the slow moving blades of the overhead fan.

Across a linen-covered table dressed with a midday meal for one, Potter was vigorously pushing a heavy silver knife and fork across the ornate china plate, creating a loud clanking in the otherwise quiet suite.

"Are you sure I can just march in there and clear out your safe-deposit boxes?" he asked in between mouthfuls of risotto smeared across the back of his fork. When Tashum didn't answer, he finished chewing and washed it down with sip of Pinot Noir, he re-posed the question, "About your diamonds—"

"Sorry, what was that?"

"Are you all right? You seem distracted, not that you don't have a great deal to be distracted by, but nonetheless—"

"I was thinking about Gregory's love for risotto. He had exquisite table manners . . . ," he paused, "among other things."

"He was a good man. You'll miss him, Tashum."

"That's an understatement, I assure you."

"I take it you've lost interest in purchasing that brass shop in California?"

Tashum tightened up. "That's one dream I should have delivered on," he continued under a buckled forehead and grievous expression. "I blew it, should have seen this coming. . . ."

"It was out of your control, Tashum. Had you been there they'd probably have killed you as well," he said with fatherly firmness. "It wasn't your fault. You're not to blame here." He took another bite and watched Tashum's wrinkled expression smooth.

Tashum was glancing down at the Rolex watch that Gregory had given to him two Christmases past.

Potter didn't know the significance of the watch and was eager to get on with more pressing subjects. "Now how exactly am I supposed to retrieve your diamonds?"

"Peter Carcanni at the Swiss Union Bank is expecting you at three this afternoon."

"Just like that, over the phone?"

"Hmm, just like that."

"Rather a special arrangement, isn't it? I mean, your not having to be there?"

"No, not at all, besides, you know that my life revolves around special arrangements. Eccentric—isn't that how you describe me?"

"When the Oxford-Cambridge Dictionary is redone, I'm expecting to see your photograph next to that word," he said with a slight chuckle.

Tashum didn't respond. His mind was filled with thoughts of unfinished business set against a ticking clock with a closing chime. "Have you seen Misha? I'm more than a bit concerned about him."

"No, I haven't. What, does he think he's on holiday? I mean, he is your new valet, isn't he?"

"Not quite." Tashum leaned closer to his friend, looming over his ashtray and glass of lemon-lime gazosa. "As of tomorrow, Misha will become my sole beneficiary."

"Tashum, have you lost your mind?" Potter shot back in frustration. "Where is it you think you're going that you won't need money? There is no such place, Tashum."

Tashum held his gaze, waiting for the flush to empty from his cheeks and the roundness to return to his green eyes.

"You'll become the executor of my estate, no restrictions, increase your fees as you need to, as you want to. You can play with my wealth as you wish, and for that, I want Misha looked after, as you've done for me. No doubt he'll need more in terms of business guidance—"

"Why not just give it all to him?" Potter's face soured. "Would save us all a great deal of trouble!"

"Because, Potter, you love what you do, and unlike you and I, Misha would give it all away to the poor and dying."

"You really are mad! Tashum, I'm terribly worried about you—"

"Perhaps it's time that you knew the truth about me."

"No." His expression became hard, more serious. "Under these mysterious circumstances I hope you understand that ignorance is bliss . . . I have a professional reputation to consider."

Tashum looked deep into the eyes of his friend, beyond the green color bands where he saw this morning's *Daily Telegraph* headline—KENSINGTON SERIAL KILLER ON THE LOOSE. The probe stopped there. Tashum didn't want to know, he would not gamble. They had been friends for a long time. If Potter's thoughts about their friendship had changed and was anything less after this speculated newsprint, Tashum didn't want to know. Only if Potter questioned him would they ever speak of it.

"So be it. I understand fully, my friend, and you are right. You've merely accompanied me here to conduct my business. I can only hope that as a last request, you will look after Misha for as long as he needs your help."

"In the insanity of the moment, it's the least I can do for you," he said with a nod.

"You are a man of your word. Is it your word that you give me?"

"Yes, as long as Misha needs me, I will be there for him."

"Good," Tashum said, relaxing back into his chair.

Misha's eyes were tightly shut, his lips were fluttering, spitting out his symphonic plea, *I call on the celestial light of a cosmic Christ to surround and protect me.* He overlaid and built up the wail into crescendo.

"Misha," said a voice in a soothing tone rising above his melody.

Misha's eyes sprung open, straight up into a set of large almond-shaped pools of iridescent blue. "Geicai," he said warmly.

To be seen as a vision for her angelic brother wearing the missionary flesh of man, she had positioned herself in the direct beam of late afternoon sun that pierced the glass and flooded in through three tall gothic arched windows flanking the nave.

Misha saw her shape shifting from her commissioned Oriental female features to the neutrality of her natural angelic glory, a sexless, raceless, winged light being, a Celestial caught in the diagonal beam of sunlight. Elegantly pointed wings of light held her translucent humanoid image several feet off the stone floor. Blue eyes and fluid smile looked down upon him.

"I've not called for help for myself, but out of fear for our sister Sasha. In Paris I saw her in the flesh, but she did not know me. She was wild and confused."

"She's not alone. I saw Felcon in Beijing. He was dazed in the same way. And Mingguy I found naked and enslaved in Jakarta, completely lost to herself. And what about the others who have just gone missing? What is happening to us, Misha?"

Misha's thoughts darkened. "Mayhem has the sword of banishment."

"But it's never been used, has it?" she asked.

He raised a bushy brow, cocking his head.

"You don't believe—?"

"What else would explain this amnesia that has befallen our brothers and sisters? Could this be why the Voice—"

"No! That is unthinkable! Stop it, please. These negative thoughts will drive me away."

"I'm sorry, but what should I do? There is no guidance without the Voice," he said flatly.

"We are individuals now—"

"Geicai," he said, placing his hands together, the human signal for prayer, "I may be marooned here for quite awhile."

"A selfless act would bring your orbs back even if Tashum did use them," she reassured.

"I understand that, but Tashum doesn't." He clasped his hands tighter. "He must earn his redemption without the gambler's cold calculations! Look at the trouble Mayhem has caused by sneaking back into the Light. Imagine the chaos with two dark angels and no Voice to give guidance." His shoulders drooped with a heavy realization. "Without the Voice we may as well be blind and deaf to each other."

"Mayhem is in great pain. He is a soul alone." She drifted closer. "He will need the love of the universe to ever truly be home. His wounds will require more love than we have given all the other Fallen upon their return. . . . And you must be patient with Tashum. He, too, must decide for himself."

"I'm doing the best I can."

"My precious Misha, you must use your best nature to overcome these adversities," she said in a comforting tone. "Let me help." She floated down, spreading her wings, enveloping him in her warm glow. "Let me warm you, brother, let me dissolve your doubts."

Misha gave himself over to the embrace of his invisible sister.

The sun had just dropped into the sea, leaving behind a dull ambient haze, when Dickey and Victor emerged from the cave's entrance.

"Victor are you sure? This isn't a time for bravado." Dickey was looking for a grain of truth as he followed his lover across the wooden dock.

"It's simple math, thirteen hundred miles, give 'er take a few, this baby cruises at three hundred sixty knots. We'll be a little tight on fuel, but yeah, I'll plop this sucker on your little lake, whad you call it, Margarita?"

"No Victor, Maggiore, Lake Maggiore, Lago Maggiore," he said in perfect Italian.

"Like margarine?"

"You're hopeless. God knows how you can fly an airplane."

"No, now I wanna get this right, yuh say it's Logo Majorine?"

"Close enough, just don't try and impress Fanny."

"I still wanna know who fuckin' died and made her king?"

From her tower window, Fanny was watching them standing next to the tethered seaplane. She stepped away from the window. Her expression hardened when her eyes focused on the last tarot card Samir had flipped faceup. The death card was staring back at her from the desktop.

"The card represents change, madame," he said, looking up at her, batting his big brown eyes. "It's only a game, madame."

"We both know better, don't we, Samir."

He bowed his head in sad agreement.

"I will miss this place, and you," she said softly, extending her hand. *"Je dois partir demain."* She kissed his hand. *"Tu me manqueras."*

He rose from his chair and moved toward her. Taking her hand, he knelt. *"Tu m'aimes?"*

"Samir, I want you to know how important you've been to me, but you don't want my love." She pulled him to his feet. Their eyes met, and she spoke softly into his ear, *"Je ne t'oublierai jamais."* A tiny kiss.

Through her fingertips draped across his wrist pulse, she could feel the liquid of her desire and could have bled him so easily. His eyes showed he half expected it, and those thoughts started her engine. She dropped his hand. Her hands slid up and grabbed his shoulders, holding him at arms length.

For Fanny, bloodlust and sexual prowl shared the same set of emotional buildup and release mechanisms. With him, she had always been extremely mindful not to kill her dark-skinned pleasure. A game, an exotic danger that up until now she had managed to keep in check.

He would tempt fate, remaining subservient to her will to the last command. Held in her gaze, the willing victim stood there, his mind wide open, arms hanging at his side.

She was pulling him close, her thumb rotating her deadly ring, *Too easy. No! Not him!* sprang into her mind. Fanny froze, took a deep breath, forcing the buildup of sensations back down between her legs, that second hunger that had never been truly satisfied after Tashum. When the last quiver shook through her shell, she spoke in a soft voice, "You're too fine a lover to have

such awful thoughts." She leaned in, kissing his cheek. "I need you, Samir."
Her eyes drifted away from his, focusing on the black figure of death staring
back with red eyes. It was her card. . . .

Misha walked to the edge of the churchyard and gazed down over a pine
forest. He could see the twinkling lights of Ascona flowing back from the
waterfront and rising up into the hills on which the village was built. It was
a vision of peace now, but in a few hours he knew things could change.

The wind increased. He decided to walk straight into it, around the lake
toward the hotel. He knew Tashum was going to try to get him out of the
way, probably requesting he leave with Potter. Tashum wouldn't jeopardize
Potter's safety by detaining him too long. So a long walk was the answer.
The journey would give him time to pray.

A rosy-cheeked woman peeked around the doorjamb. "Sorry to interrupt,
but I've been ringing for three minutes. Have you got your buzzer turned
off?"

Shelly looked up from her work and watched the pear-shaped secretary
waddle over to the desk. "How would you even know, dear?" she said, looking at Shelly's desk, which was buried beneath unorganized piles of paperwork. "Dr. Green, this intercom panel is not a storage shelf," she chastised
while removing a stack of reports off the small electronic box. She flipped
the on button. "There, now you'll know when someone rings you up."

"I'm very busy, Ms. Carlton, can't we do this some other time?"

"This is the fifth time he's called and the first time that you've been
here. Would you please speak to the man?"

Shelly looked past Ms. Carlton to a figure in the doorway. Her eyes
narrowed on the man she had bumped into earlier. "Who are you?"

"Inspector Stanton, Scotland Yard. Sounds rather important," he said,
glancing and gesturing at the phone on her desk. "I can wait."

"Go on, Shells, line five," the receptionist said, waiting for Shelly to
make the move.

"Detective, I'm extremely busy."

"Inspector," he corrected. "Inspector Stanton."

Under the pressure of his gaze, Shelly crossed to her desk.

"Well, I've done my bit," said the older woman as she turned and stepped out into the corridor.

Shelly couldn't mask her discomfort. This Stanton didn't just watch, he seemed to record her every nuance. Her index finger stabbed blinking button number 5. She brought the receiver to her ear. "Dr. Green here." She turned, trying to conceal her response to the voice on the other end. Her expression gave it away—he lunged, slapping the speakerphone button on the phone's base.

"What was that click?" asked Tashum through the speakerphone.

"It's a policeman, turning on the speakerphone," she said in a calm warning.

"Tashum, Inspector Stanton here, I've been looking for you. Actually, the world is searching for you. We have a very large problem here—"

"Damn it, Inspector!" Tashum barked. "I'm one of the victims, not the perpetrator of these crimes."

"We would like to talk to you about that—"

"I told you what I know, now get off the line! I need to speak privately with Dr. Green!"

"No, sorry, I can't do that quite yet. Lets see, you told us about Victor, but there have been some rather grizzly discoveries in your cellar that are cause for further discussion. Where exactly are you?"

"My servants have always been part of my family. As such I take complete care of them—"

"Just one large extended family, how convenient for you."

"It's not a matter of convenience."

"It must be difficult for a man like you to lose your driver. Why don't you let me send a car around to pick you up?"

"Shelly, are you still there?"

She nodded her head.

"He can't see you! Speak to him," Stanton ordered gruffly.

"Yes, I'm here, Tashum."

"What do you want from her, Tashum?"

"It's really none of your business, Inspector."

"Oh, but it is. You see, I've laid claim on you. It's only a matter of time."

"Sorry to disappoint you—Shelly, my time is up, destroy the vial."

"Ammonia!" she screamed. "It's ammonia, Tashum!"

Stanton ripped the phone receiver out of her hand, only to hear Tashum breaking the teleconnection. Dial tone. He placed the old-fashioned receiver back into the cradle.

"Ammonia vial? What was that all about?" he demanded.

Shelly pursed her lips, crossed her arms, stood there a moment, weighing choices. On one hand she had a cop who could ruin her career, possibly put her in jail. On the other hand, she held secrets of a being unique to human history. No contest.

"Like he said, it's *none* of your business."

"I see. Ever been to Tashum's Kensington home?"

"No. We have a professional relationship," she said, slipping back down into her chair.

"I suppose you think you can invoke some sort of physician-patient confidentiality?"

"Yes, I think that applies here."

"Ordinarily I might accept that professional ethic except for one small detail. You're not a doctor are you, Kate? You do prefer that over Cathy, I'm told."

She folded her hands in her lap to keep them from shaking. She was practiced at the deceit of self-reinvention, of primary deception. She knew it couldn't last. Somehow, in some way, she would pay for her past, and tonight her past walked in through the door. "I've never seen the inside of Scotland Yard," she murmured.

She refused to look up, though she knew Stanton was studying her. Legal types rarely accept the old victim-of-circumstance plea. No doubt the FBI report had described Catherine (Kate) Green as a promising intern at Stanford Medical School until an experimental act crossed the lines of ethics and she was stripped of her career. Was there any way to explain to a man like Stanton just how difficult it had been to shake off the baggage of what she had been born into, then reconstruct the lost pieces of a broken life into wholeness with no visible seams?

"You may never see the inside of the Yard, if you help me," he said as he offered her a cigarette from the red Dunhill box.

Their eyes met.

"I'm trying to quit."

He nodded, and pushed the cigarette pack closer. She extended her hand.

"Isn't aiding and abetting a reformed smoker against some sort of law?" she asked as she withdrew a cigarette from the pack.

"The suspension of certain investigatory procedures is wholly at the discretion of the lead investigator," he said, holding a lighter.

"That hardly answered my question." She inhaled deeply and let the smoke drift from her nose. "Smoking really should be illegal."

"Someday it probably will be, though I doubt that would stop you." He grinned. "Now, why don't you tell me about ammonia."

"Ammonia. Never would have ever guessed," Tashum said to no one. He slipped the cellular phone into the slanted pocket of his silky white dinner jacket. "Did you hear that?" he asked the night sky. "I've got cleaning fluid coursing through my veins."

Tashum gazed out over the moon polished water. The Splendideo's rooftop garden was a wonderful place to sit under the stars and soak in the rich fragrances of the gardener's efforts. From his nook in the corner of the parapet he let his eyes wander. Everywhere he looked he found a memory, across the Maggia River Delta he could see the lights of Locarno, which brought with it images of Chamberlain, Briand, and Stresemann, signing the Locarno Pact of 1925. He rotated, away from the night view. His gaze took in the large stone table against the far wall, where he remembered sipping tea with Isadora Duncan so many years before. Tashum loved this arty mountain community that, "existed, so close to heaven yet with all the earthly convenience of the Splendideo," to use Duncan's words.

He felt an increasing sense of closure, for if he had his way, this place where he stood would be his departure point back into heaven. He would light the night sky with his flight.

He had the diamonds, and if things went as planned, Potter and Misha would be safely out of harm's way, safe in Italy by the time Fanny and Dickey arrived here. Delightful images of pleasures past and future, suddenly darkened considerably with thoughts of them—compounded by the realization that he still didn't know how to fully activate the orbs. The placement of the orbs had to be as simple as the phrase itself. But how?

Tashum glanced at his watch and noticed he had somehow put it on backward when he dressed. He removed it, turning the face around straight. "Nine thirty-six, much better."

Better than your chances. Much better.

"Mayhem?" Tashum asked, having felt the message as much as heard it. "Are you here?"

From behind, Mayhem blew hot breath across Tashum's left ear. Tashum's head slowly rotated to the left. They were eye to eye. Tashum knew he was there but couldn't see him. He started shortening his own focal lengths, by de-focusing on distant points, blurring out each consecutive background until his vision became a Picasso-esque blur of shape and design. He trained his vision to the molecular structure of the air itself. It was in that narrow bandwidth of perceptible light that he found Mayhem's thin face.

"For someone who can run like the wind," said the spirit, "you've been awfully slow to pick up this trick."

"And you've been of no help at all."

"What you have in mind is very dangerous," he said, looking past Tashum.

"You worried for me—that's a bit of a stretch, isn't it?"

"I have problems of my own," he said, his eyes growing large, his expression twisted.

Tashum witnessed the unfurling of Mayhem's enormous wings. Suddenly Mayhem was gone. Tashum searched other focal lengths but could not find him, nor the cause of his panicked departure. His eyes were still relaxing when he noticed a dark figure walking toward him. "Misha?" he asked, adjusting the visual. "Is it you?"

"Nope, sorry, it's just me," Manfred said. He stepped next to Tashum. "Good evening, sir."

"Good evening, Manfred. Were you looking for me?"

"No, no. One of the guests complained of a broken deck chair up here. I thought I'd see to it."

"Over there." Tashum pointed to an area beyond the seating arrangements to a wide open spot for sun gazers. "It's the one on the end," he said pointing to the lineup of reclining lounges.

"Oh yes, I'll have it fixed in the morning."

"It's been that way for years, you know," he said softly.

"Years? About time we got it fixed, I'd think."

"Manfred, that chair was broken when Winston Churchill dropped into it a bit too hard."

"Really?" He gleamed. "Churchill here?"

"Hmm, just after the war. Your predecessor used to tell, with Sir Winston's blessing, of course, a very funny story about the incident. I'm surprised you've never heard it." He paused. "Might be a pity to lose it. The artifact, I mean," he said gesturing toward the chair.

"Right. Well I suppose some things are better off left unfixed," he said, looking up into Tashum's smile. "Would you mind terribly telling the story to me? I'm rather new here and, well, would you mind?"

Tashum couldn't refuse the man's enthusiasm. "It would be my pleasure. I wasn't here mind you, but the way Alfonzo told it . . ." And so he began. . . .

CHAPTER TWENTY-TWO

The twin engined seaplane hummed through the cloud-flecked atmosphere.

"Where are we?" Fanny, a picture of elegance asked from her rear seat. She wore a round pillbox hat; its soft ermine fur rustled in the forced-air ventilation. A matching ermine coat was draped over her shoulders, its openness revealing perfectly cleaved breasts held tightly together by a black sequined gown. "Did you hear me?" Fanny asked again.

"Sardinia or Corsica," Victor said, throwing his head back, looking at her upside down. "I kinda lost track of my latitude, or somethin'."

She flicked her middle finger off her thumb, thumping him right between the eyes.

"Ouch!" He jerked the steering yoke, jostling them as the wings teetered. "You shouldn't never fuck with the pilot."

He glanced over the instrument panel, his eyes targeting again the blinking red light on the fuel gauge.

Fanny leaned forward, following Victor's eye line to the flashes of red. "What's that light, Victor?"

"Baby's thirsty."

"Are we out of fuel? You said we'd make it," Dickey bemoaned from the copilot's seat. "Damn it, Victor."

"Yeah, well, we're flying against the wind, pops. It's been pushin' us backward and sideways."

"But you should have known that and figured on it!"

"Whoa! Hold on here. I said I'd get you to Ascona by midnight, I never said nothin' about gettin' there on one tank. Of course one of yuh could bail, you know, lighten the load a little."

"You're probably the heaviest, Victor," Fanny said, frowning. "Unfortunately we need you, at the moment."

"Ha-ha," he replied. "You bet you fuckin' need me," he continued in a barely audible mumble, "need me more than I need you, that's for fuckin' sure".

"Victor," she said in a catty voice, "do you think you could replace the word *fuck*, with something like 'friggin',' or possibly—"

"Like fudge?" he laughed. "Oh, fudge! Nope, Fanny, it just don't carry the same weight—"

"Shut up, Victor! What are we going to do?" Dickey asked, twitching about in his seat.

"Well, duh, we stop for fuel." He laughed and slapped Dickey's arm. "No biggy."

"Oh, Victor, you could piss off the pope," Dickey huffed.

"How critical is it, Victor?"

"Ah, I was just shitin' you guys. Fanny, what do you see out the starboard side?"

She looked left.

"No, no other side, left side is port," he said as he dipped the right wing. "That's the northwest coast of Corsica, them lights I figure must be Calvi. I loved that name. I bet that's geek for cow?"

She could see the mountainous island clearly framed by the rectangular window. "Dickey and I sailed from Monaco to Calvi once. Do you remember, Dickey?" she asked warmly.

"Mmm, I suppose I do."

"You had a smashing time, surely you remember, umm what was his name, come on you must remember, lets see there was Paladin, you, myself, oh, God, what was his name, the Persian fellow?"

"The good old days with Paladin are over, Fanny," he said with a tad of sarcasm.

"Everything but memories." Fanny's smile flattened. She leaned close to him. "They were good days, as I recall." Then she turned to Victor. "We need special fuel. Can you get it in Calvi?"

"Chill, lady, we got enough jack to get us to Idyland."

"Presumably you mean Italy."

"Imperia, Alassio, Albenga, maybe go on as far as Savona before fillin' 'er up. Then we'll wing it up to Ascona on Lago Maggiore."

Victor's perfect pronunciation of the Italian port towns impressed both Dickey and Fanny into a momentary silence.

"Been watching travelogue programs?" she teased.

"Even a loser can't be wrong all the time," Victor said in a humble tone.

This softer, more human side of the creature took Fanny by uncomfortable surprise. She had no sympathy for him at all, but as she slipped out of the green glow of the dashboard and nestled back into her ermine cocoon, she could not help but see a glimmer of what Dickey was trying to mine out of his lover. Hardly mineable ore, in her opinion, but it seemed enough for Dickey's simple needs.

She loved flying. The list of dangers involved only heightened her desire to partake in the winged adventure. She found it so easy to sleep with the hum of twin rotary engines working like a hypnotic drug. Within minutes Fanny's dreams and fears were dissipating, temporarily suspended within her hypnotic state.

Twenty minutes later the Italian coastline filled the horizon. Victor and Dickey now wore radio headsets. Victor turned a small frequency knob on the radio, while Dickey monitored air and ground chatter.

"Any good shit, man?" Victor asked with a slight edginess.

"Don't turn the dial so quickly," complained Dickey, "I'm a bit rusty with Italian, I need time to translate."

"Dude, we need to get down, now."

"Do they take credit cards for that?" asked Fanny's incoherent voice as she awoke with the plane's sharp change in altitude and weightless descent.

"We got cash, Fanny!" Victor's eyes bulged. "Don't we, Fanny? Where the fuck's the money?"

Fanny sat quiet.

"You did bring it, didn't you?" asked Dickey with alarm.

The swath of moonlight revealed the lower half of Fanny's stone-still face. "We'd have been fools to bring that much money. Besides, we need something to go home to."

"What are you saying, dear?" asked Dickey.

"I'm saying, don't worry."

"What! Did you leave our dough with them sand niggers of yers?"

"The money is in a safe place, Victor."

"How much did you bring?" questioned Dickey.

"Enough, Dickey, enough. We'll use plastic if we need to."

"Put away yer American Express, this one's on me, Israeli Express." Victor grinned and reached down beside his seat pulling up a snubbed-barreled Uzi. "Never fly without it." He laughed, waving the gun around. "I don't know why you guys bother with all them stolen credit cards. Shit, man, there ain't no waiting with this sucker."

"Put that down before you hurt someone!"

Victor waved the gun at Fanny. "Like you?" he said, and pushed the barrel to within inches of her face. "You scared?"

She coolly stared back and said nothing.

"Do as she said! Put the gun down." Dickey's voice cracked with anger. He reached over and lowered Victor's arm. "Fly the plane."

"I got the safety on, fer Chrissakes. I was just teasing her."

Fanny and Dickey had a long contemplative eye exchange.

Tashum's knuckle rapped three times against Potter's door. He heard Potter's muted voice call him in. He entered Potter's suite, closing the door behind him.

Potter was seated at the fruitwood desk. He lowered the phone receiver from his ear, waving Tashum deeper into the room.

Tashum glanced around the richly appointed suite. His eyes stopped on a large television housed in a tall armoire. The volume was turned down, but onscreen three circus jugglers were tossing flaming torches to each other, creating a solid arc of flame.

"Pour yourself a drink. It's Martha," Potter said, referring to his phone call, "the bar is over there."

"I know where it is," Tashum replied, taking his eyes off the TV.

"Right," said Potter before getting back into his phone conversation. "Sorry, please continue with what you were saying."

Tashum strolled past the leather seating and coffee table arrangement. He stopped at the three-sided alcove bar. It was lined with mirrors and pro-

fessionally stocked with liquors in decanted crystal bottles, identified by platinum tags. He reached for the single malt scotch. When he reached for a
tumbler, through tiers of crystal glassware, he saw the TV screen reflected
in the mirrors. The image was being refracted and bounced into multi-images
from the angled mirrors. He glanced up, and the illusion was made complete
by light sweeping across the alcove's mirrored ceiling. His mind was sent
spinning by the images of televised light. The jugglers by their three-point
positioning had created a circle within a triangle. Tashum's fingers relaxed
their grip on the tumbler.

Potter's pen was jotting down the word *ammonia* onto Splendideo sta-
tionery when the crystal crashed. He spun in his seat to see Tashum standing
over a pile of broken glass, staring blankly at the TV.

"Martha, I really need to get off the line, I'll ring you later," he finished
quickly and returned the receiver to it's cradle.

"Tashum, are you all right?"

"It can't be that simple," he mumbled.

"Are you aware you've dropped your glass?"

Tashum's thoughts were miles and years away, deep in the past a memory of the soft juggling stones given to him by Shrug and later etched and
monogrammed by Fanny. She had teased him about becoming proficient at
juggling, telling him about Paladin's efforts to gain the dexterity of the sport.

Potter couldn't fathom his friend's lost look. "Hmm." He cleared his
voice. "Tashum, Martha just told me that the police came round to my office
today. I'm afraid it sounds very serious."

Tashum looked his way, his thoughts shifting from wonderment to danger. "Yes, I know."

"How could you possibly know that?" he asked with a raised voice.

The prosecutor's tone drove a chill through Tashum. He didn't dare look
into the eyes of his friend. He could feel the stress creeping beneath the old
man's skin as it was.

"Well? Are you going to answer my question?"

"I spoke with Dr. Green earlier. It was a simple deduction after that."

"Then you know the meaning of ammonia? What sort of cryptic message
is that?"

"You are better off not knowing."

"You haven't got that poor young woman involved in all of this, have
you?"

Tashum shook his head slowly. "She did some research for me, that's all. The police coming to her was routine, just like they came to your office."

"I would hate to see her career damaged through any association with this . . . situation. I'm sure I don't need to elaborate."

"It was accidental, Potter."

"Accidental!" Potter exploded. "How does one, or should I say fifty-six people, get accidentally planted in a burial mausoleum hidden in your cellar?"

"I've never hired people with families, and when they die I bury them. There have been fifty-seven, actually."

"Fifty-seven! How do you explain something like that?"

"I just told you, my friend."

"No! You just told me there are more bodies! Do you know how bad this sounds? The British press will turn you into a monster. They're going to crucify you. You're facing ruin! Prison!"

Tashum just stood rooted to the spot, looking at the floor. After a brief silence he asked, "Are you finished?"

Potter's heat cooled fast. "I've known you for a very long time, and I apologize for raising my voice—"

"Forget it, Potter. It's I who owe the round of apologies for the present situation. I didn't plan it this way."

"Do you believe you can simply disappear?"

"I hope to."

"The world isn't as large as it once was. You can't really hide anymore." He looked into Tashum's eyes. "If they want you, they'll find you."

"I'm a gambler by nature," he replied in a failed attempt to lift the mood.

"Come with me back to London. We can hide you out until I have secured a topflight criminal defense team. You can certainly afford the best—"

"Please," he groaned, "I have no intention of ever dignifying any form of criminal charges surrounding Victor's activities. As for the mausoleum, that's my business."

"Have you listened to anything I've just said to you?"

Tashum glanced at his wristwatch. "Potter, we need to finish our business. Where are the documents?"

Potter shook his head, then leaned over and pulled a thick document from the leather folds of his attaché case.

"You don't really have to do this, you know, I already have your power of attorney."

"Now you'll have more." He grinned. "Power without having to be my attorney."

"You do understand what you're doing to Misha, don't you?" He plopped it square on the desk, rose from his chair, gesturing for Tashum to take his place. "You're sending him from complete obscurity to becoming possibly one of the wealthiest men on earth—"

"I'm not that rich, am I?" he asked, sinking into the chair.

"The pope might have more money—"

"With his vow of poverty, little good it does him," he said with a grin. "Who else?"

"We added it up one day. Actually, it took two days—"

"We?"

"Yes, Martha and myself."

"That was a bit dodgy."

"No, no it was donkey's years ago. I lied, I said something about secret ledgers of the Royal Family. I thought she'd laugh me out of the building. Last time I tried fibbing to her."

"Clever lady. So she knows. I mean, she's all right with it?"

"I'm not exactly sure what you mean. But she thought your fortune was all tickety-boo." He paused, with a frown. "But this other business has her terribly shook up."

"The allegations are ridiculous." Tashum glanced at the contract packets of ownership. "My pen or yours?"

"Use mine, the ink in your pen may just disappear," he said as he handed a gold pen to Tashum. "I don't doubt for a minute that you are completely innocent of what's being said."

Tashum locked his gaze. "Thank you, my friend. That means a great deal to me."

Potter nodded with a stiff upper lip.

Tashum sped through the top pages, unceremoniously leaving his signature on ten of the pages. Finished, he stood and returned Potter's pen. "There, it's all done. Here's a hearty congratulations on your new executorship." He threw his arm around Potter's shoulder, pushing them toward the door. "There is a chauffeur-driven car waiting for you downstairs, I'll meet you there shortly."

"You seem awfully cheery for someone who has just given away the world. Please don't tell me that it feels like a weight lifted off your shoulders."

Tashum smiled, thinking of the wondrous weight of wings.

"I don't know what to think about Misha. Of course he'll need to sign documents of registration as well." Potter paused. "Are you sure about all of this, Tashum?"

The wingless angel nodded. "Quite." He guided Potter to the door. "Don't worry about Misha, I'm sure he'll be in touch."

"He'd be a fool not to claim what you've given to him."

"It's not a gift as much as it is a trade."

The plane swooped low, over a relaxed sea swell. She banked to port, swinging level into the wind, her hull descending, skimming the smooth surface, then slowing, her weight settled into the water. At a crawl, the plane motored up the inlet toward a grouping of dingy wooden buildings set around a long, drooping pier and seaplane docking and ramp area. At the far end was a fuel pump bathed in stark white light cast from the overhead hooded bulb.

From inside the plane it appeared no one was around, but there was a light in the window of the single-story marina building adjacent to the fuel pump.

"See anyone?" asked Dickey.

"Looks good, you ready?"

They were closing in on the floating dock. Victor pulled a lever and watched the wing-tip floats fold back into the wing. Next he reversed the engines, and on his signal Dickey opened the side window. In Dickey's hand was a coil of rope attached to a small grappling hook.

"Why don't you just put the wheels down and drive up the ramp?" asked Fanny as she leaned forward.

"While you were sleeping we decided it would be safer this way," Dickey said as he leaned out the window.

"Come on, Dickster, we're runnin' outa dock. Fling that pup!"

Dickey flung the hook and bundle of rope. As the wad unfurled and sailed away from the plane, Victor leaned across him, grabbing the rope's tail.

"Jesus, Dickster, you gotta hang on to this end."

The four-fingered hook hit the wooden plank on the dock's landing and skittered across a row of planks until one of its fingers found a groove and dug in. The rope was suddenly drawn taught.

Victor shut down flight systems while Dickey tugged on the rope, pulling the plane closer to the dock.

Minutes later the seaplane was berthed parallel to the dock, lashed bow and stern to a thick pier post rising up out of the water.

Victor glanced around. The hoist and work area was empty. He thought about stealing parts off the only other visible seaplane parked outside a hangar and quickly descided he didn't want to sully his hands with grease. He walked to a large fuel tank mounted on a metal frame. He knocked on the tank's shiny drum and was satisfied to hear a dull thudding in response.

"Is it aviation fuel?" Dickey called out in a muffled voice from behind.

"It sure as shit ain't diesel. We'll need a key," he said, slapping the large padlock.

He beckoned to Dickey, and the two of the them approached the wooden building. Dickey read the painted signs for Victor and told him that they were about to knock off a general store. As they slipped up onto the porch they heard a man's voice singing loudly off-key to a pop song blaring from the radio.

When they burst in, they startled a fat white-haired man behind the counter of the small, general supply shop. He stopped in midharmony, his eyes widening in anger at them, their weapons.

"*Che cose fai!*" the man shouted at the two. He stood, knocking a stool aside.

Victor leaned against the doorjamb, took off his cool shades. "Hey there, Pavarotti," he said.

"*Via! Va via!*" the man shouted over the noise of the radio, gesturing them out of his building with one hand, reaching under the counter with the other.

Victor ran across the room and caught the man's large wrist, his pink, flabby hand clutching a small cheap-looking automatic pistol. He squeezed the man's wrist until he dropped the small gun.

"*Che cosa desidera?*" he asked of Victor.

"Dig this, a twenty-two. Did yuh hear that, Dickster? He thought he'd scare me with a Saturday night special."

"No, that isn't what he said. He wants to know what you like." Dickey was holding his Beretta and finished screwing the silencer onto the barrel as he moved toward them. *"La benzina, per favore,"* he said in a friendly voice.

"Quanta nevuole?"

"La chiave, per favore."

The man pointed to the key ring hanging off a nail.

"Grazie," Dickey said. He looked at Victor. "Is there anything you need to know about filling the tanks?"

"No."

"You feel like Italian tonight?" Dickey said flatly.

On the radio, a hyperactive chattering deejay suddenly replaced the hit parade, with an irritating effect on Victor. "Dickey—the radio! Kill it!" Victor screamed. "Foreign shit makes me fuckin' crazed!"

Dickey leaned back and let out a silent burst of gunfire, punching the radio through a window, scattering a cloud of canned goods, posters on the wall, and odd pieces of paper.

In the deadly silence that followed, Victor stared at the man, watching his lower lip begin to tremble. Sweat formed around his eyes. Slowly he nosed the tip of the Uzi into the man's mouth.

"Pavarotti wanna cracker?" he said, then pulled the trigger and—*ra-ta-ta-ta-ta-ta-tat*—splashed the back wall with something resembling a wash of bloody oysters. Victor followed the man's fall to the floor.

Dickey's face was speckled with blood. "You idiot!" he yelled. He holstered his gun and walked to the wash basin behind the deli counter. He began washing up.

A commotion of voices swelled outside.

Victor looked up over the counter. Dickey lowered the towel from his face and swiveled around to see two more younger workmen standing in the doorway.

Dickey let a volley of bullets fly, firing at near point-blank range into the men. They staggered back, one against the other, and collapsed, where they lay motionless.

"I've got the key, let's go!" Dickey commanded.

Victor took one last draw on the ragged blood vessel. He leped over the counter and followed Dickey to the door. In the shade of the doorway, Victor's blood-covered hands struggled to get a wallet out of the victim's pockets.

"Come on!" Dickey shouted, and walked away from the building.

"Hold your pants on," he complained as he whipped out his knife. A single pass, a practiced slash, cut the wallet free from the twisted pant pocket. "Hey, nice leather," he said. Blood dripped from his chin as he stroked through the bills folded inside. "Aw, fuck it, I'll count it later."

Victor joined Dickey at the fuel tank. In moments they had removed the padlock and had the hose connected to the plane's petcock in the fuselage, and fuel was draining into the tank. Dickey caught Victor gazing at himself in the highly reflective surface of the fuel tank.

"Shit man. With all this blood on me and my face all fucked up, I look like something out of a freak show," Victor said while raising his fists in a mock boxing match with his reflection.

"The object is to get the blood on the inside of your body."

"Ha-ha, very funny."

"What did you expect? You damn near had the gun in his mouth."

They could hear the sound of a truck, gears grinding, tires dropping into potholes. It was stopping behind the building from which they had just come.

"I'll take care of this," Victor said, and left Dickey at the tank.

"Victor, wash up while you're at it." Dickey called to him, "And be careful."

"Is everything all right out there?" asked Fanny through the plane's side window.

"Everything is fine."

"Dickey, can he go anywhere without shooting up the place?"

"Give it a rest, old girl." Dickey leaned back away from the petrol fumes. "He's crude, but you have to admit he's efficient."

"If you say so," she said, disappearing from the window.

A moment later Dickey heard shouts on the far side of the building and two pistol shots, followed by a burst of automatic gunfire. He stood quiet vigil until Victor's unmistakable shape appeared out of the darkness.

Victor was back, limping.

"Fucker winged me," he complained.

Dickey glanced down at a bloody spot on Victor's leather pant leg. "You all right?"

"Just a nick. What's with these guys and their dinky little popguns?"

"We're almost full," said Dickey with an ear pressed to the side of the plane's tank.

"The sucker's got a fuel gauge you know."

Minutes later, Victor disengaged the hose and let it drop to the wooden dock. Reddish fuel poured from its nozzle, soaking into the wood, leaving an expanding rainbow in the water underneath.

Back in the plane, Victor pushed a starter button and brought the engines back to life. In quick succession the port and starboard propeller blades were blurred by their spin speed.

Dickey pushed the plane away from the dock and leaped into the loading door in the plane's port side. Hunched over, he walked forward through the narrow aisle, avoiding Fanny's teasing stare, and took his seat next to Victor.

"That went well," Fanny mocked. "Did you two leave anybody alive?"

Victor's smile was half grimace.

The plane taxied away from the dock. Victor popped open his side window and pushed the Uzi's barrel through the opening. A barrage of bullets blazed out of the weapon—Dickey and Fanny shouted at him, covering their ears—until they heard an explosion rock the air around them. Throttles forward, and the plane lifted into the sky. They looked down to see fire and burning debris scattered across a wide area, pieces of dock floating free.

Inside the store, now filled with smoke, a tiny surveillance camera continued to record the evening's events.

"Well, I guess this is it," Tashum said, as he and Potter walked the last few feet to the awaiting Mercedes limousine. They both sensed a certain finality, a sadness that simultaneously stopped them. They gazed at one another and quickly looked away. It was awkward. Neither knew exactly how to end such a long-standing business interest or the deep love, unique to both of their experiences. Potter was restricted to his gentry. Tashum couldn't just leap into his arms, and he didn't want to. "It's not easy saying good-bye, is it?" Tashum asked.

"No, it isn't. Especially under these circumstances."

The tall uniformed chauffeur swung the rear door open.

Potter tugged his arm, pulling him aside. "Tashum it's not too late—"

"Potter, please—"

"No, let me finish. As a solicitor I'm not allowed to participate in unlawful practices. The bar particularly frowns upon harboring fugitives, but I've heard that Brazil has favorable extradition laws for a man in your situation."

"Thanks for the tip," he said with a trace of a smile.

"You wouldn't even consider it, would you?"

"No, Buenos Aires perhaps. Rio may be the perfect place for Misha, or even for you if things don't bode well in London." His grin growing.

"That's not funny." Potter shook with a mixture of grief and anger. "Tashum, you're incorrigible."

"I know how it must seem, Potter," he leaned closer, "but I'm very fond of you."

"And I, you, Tashum."

"One other thing—I think it's time you paid a bit more attention to Martha. She'd make a whole man out of you."

"You're a fine one to be giving advice about women," he said with schoolboy sulk. "I suppose next you'll be explaining cricket to me."

"I will miss you."

"I'm going to enjoy the rest." Potter's sulk covered his rising emotion.

"Godspeed, my friend."

Tashum took him in his arms, a short embrace, one last close-up look, just long enough to print an ever lasting impression for each of the other.

Potter tore away and stepped into the car. The door closed, and he was hidden behind German steel and tinted glass.

As the chauffeur returned to the driver's side, Tashum gently rapped on the side glass. "Potter," Tashum said as the window sank into the door, "someday, if things don't work out—if my plan fails—I may need a loan."

Potter smiled back. "Good, that's a start, my boy."

They were both smiling now, with the repairs started on the tiny piece of damage done to their friendship. They held each other's gaze in warm fellowship until the limousine carried him away.

Tashum stayed on for a moment, glanced at his watch, almost savoring the contentment of knowing that Potter would be safe in Italy at the bottom of the hour.

In and out of shadow, Misha strolled down a narrow and steeply twisted street flanked both left and right by Italian-influenced dwellings. From a second-story veranda, a folk melody lifted the serenity. He could feel as much as hear the vibratory response of the plucked acoustic guitar strings. He chuckled at the tickle in his ribs, brought on by the standing wave of a slightly detuned *A* string. Held by song, he stopped. As he swayed with the rhythm he looked up, seeing a swath of stars between the two- and three-story buildings. For a brief moment he studied the stars respective location to one another. He might as well have been reading the face of a clock. He had plenty of time, the Splendideo was only twelve minutes away, and the vampires weren't due for another forty minutes. The angel took a deep breath, and when he exhaled he blew away all thoughts of the vile creatures.

Eventually he continued on, comically moving his arms, toying with his long shadow cast by a particularly bright moon on a particularly clear night. Misha's shadow was headless and handless. Had the angel been naked, there would have been no shadow at all. Driven by his amusement, the image moved across the cobblestones like a dancing coat and pair of trousers. He envisioned the rendered characters from his favorite film, Disney's *Fantasia*, and tonight he was the artist. . . .

Led by its own crisp shadow, the seaplane shot across the open waters toward the lights of the crescent-shaped town on Lago Maggiore's northern shore.

Victor had used his drug-running skills to get them this far. Just south of Milan, he ducked below Italian air-control radar nets by dropping right down on the deck, humming along just thirty inches above the flowing waters of the Ticino River. Visual detection was a given danger, but safer in that it took more time for the authorities to process and react to. The Ticino River's headwaters formed in Switzerland. It flowed into Lago Maggiore from the north and out into Italy from the lake's most southerly tip. Victor had simply followed the river north from Pavia. Easy during the day, but it took a pirate's eye at night. He didn't mind burning bridges, he wouldn't come back this way. Italy had been a piece of cake because of the romantic nature of Italians. Even Victor figured that in Switzerland he wouldn't have that advantage. He'll cross that bridge when he knocks it down.

Fanny searched the horizon ahead. Somewhere in that twinkling light display was Tashum. A wave of anxiety coursed through her, and momentarily she wanted to turn the plane around and head back to the safety of her desert fort. Forget this deal. They had money. She had kept her vow once already and that was enough, she reasoned. Then she thought about the rapidity at which that money would be eaten by her unpaid bills.

*   *   *

The plane skimmed the lake surface, sending up a spray, then settled into the alpine water and began its taxi toward the dock, a quarter of a mile, dead ahead.

Victor glanced down at a digital clock on the instrument panel: 11:35 P.M.

He grinned. "Damn, I'm good. I want you two doubting dotties to check it out. We're a half hour early." He raised a finger, wagging it first at Dickey and then at Fanny in back. "I told yuh, this plane was worth every fuckin' penny I put down on her."

"As I recall, we all threw in money," she said.

"Fanny, you didn't want no part of it. I 'bout busted a gut laughin' when you asked that sales guy if we could lease."

Dickey nodded, admitting, "You were right, she's a fine machine. Well done, Victor."

Fanny leaned forward. Her hand reached around Victor, sliding under his leather jacket, her manicured nails slid across his bare chest. "Yes, you'll make a good chauffeur when you grow up." Her nails formed a cat's clamp, dug in over his heart.

Victor felt an involuntary shiver as her nails released their grip. "Hey, that woulda been kinda sexy 'cept it stung a little."

"Sometimes love hurts," she said without thinking.

Dickey noticed her head resting on Victor's shoulder and gazed at her with the most curious of expressions and a tinge of jealousy. "Fanny?"

Fanny glanced at Dickey with dreamy eyes, and then jerked away from Victor as if she was waking up next to a snake. "Now, the Splendideo is across the street from the municipal dock," she blurted out.

CHAPTER TWENTY-THREE

The Price of Betrayal

Tashum sat in the bar at the Splendideo Royal. He drew on a long cigar, lifted a snifter of cognac, and exhaled a rolling plume of smoke into it. He watched the smoke curl up lazily inside, and then he took a drink.

"Hey, would you turn that up?" asked an American of the bartender.

The bartender nodded and picked up a remote control, increasing the volume on the television.

Tashum turned to the TV screen, where he saw an attractive woman with a CNN microphone standing in the light of an overhead lamp. Behind her was a furious activity of flashing blue police lights, red ambulance lights, and men in official uniforms moving back and forth through a scene of chaos. A box across the bottom of the screen read: LIVE GENOA, ITALY.

The correspondent adjusted her earpiece and raised the mic. "Italian authorities are telling us that two men and possibly a third person were caught on videotape killing the depot owner and stealing aviation fuel for a seaplane." The correspondent paused, checking her notes. "A gun battle erupted, killing three and seriously wounding two other people. The perpetrators managed to escape in their seaplane, but not before blowing up this dockside fuel tank over here," she said, pointing as the cameraman widened the camera's aperture to include the flaming debris. "Their identities are not yet known to CNN, nor are their whereabouts known at this time.

Authorities here are said to be in contact with the British police, suggesting a possible link with the bombing of a luxury yacht in Great Britain that killed four. Details are still coming in, and we'll stay on the scene until more is known. Reporting live near Genoa, this is Elena Palumbo for CNN World News."

With a nod from the American, the bartender lowered the volume on the television.

Tashum gazed into his drink. "A seaplane. I should have guessed."

He swirled the remaining amber liquid in his glass and finished it off. He stood, straightening his colorful Hermes tie.

The ornate clock behind the bar read 11:45 P.M.

The plane bobbed in the dark water as Fanny stood on the dock holding a bowline. Her attention was fixed on the golden lights beaming from the Splendideo.

Dickey finished securing the stern line and moved to her. He took the line from her grasp and tied it to the dock.

"Victor is trouble," Fanny said firmly. "I don't want him in on this part of it."

Dickey nodded in agreement.

Inside the plane, Victor finished shutting down the flight systems, flipping a series of switches as the propellers chugged to a halt. He pulled a small mirror out of an equipment bag and studied the whip wounds on his face. Refreshed by his drink at the dock in Genoa, there was only one cut under his eye that was still open. Reaching up he pressed two sides of a long gash together and watched, sick at heart, as they spread back apart.

"That bitch," he moaned.

He glanced up and saw Fanny and Dickey conferring. Then he noticed the ornate box sitting beside him. Slowly a grin came to his face as he lifted the lid and stared inside at the orbs.

A moment later Dickey stuck his head in the side window. "Victor—"

"Let me guess, Queenie wants me to stay here with the horses?" Victor said. "This sucks."

"That's right, Sundance, or is it Charles Lindbergh now?" he said with a half smile, which wasn't returned. "Well, someone's got to watch the plane, don't they? Would you please hand over the orbs?"

Victor shoved the box at him. "It's still my deal," he said, spitting venom. "And it won't be over until I get my say with Tashum, goddamn it."

Dickey sensed trouble. He studied Victor carefully, waiting. With a growl Victor reached across the seat and slammed the widow closed. Dickey lingered a moment before moving back toward Fanny.

"Is he staying?" Fanny asked as Dickey stepped next to her.

"Yes, but he's not happy about it."

"Victor's happiness is your department," she said, moving up the dock toward the hotel.

Dickey followed on her heels. "It wouldn't hurt to be nice to him once in a while," he whined.

"I think it would be terribly painful," she said, sneering. "I can't be bothered."

The lobby of the Splendideo was a spacious cavern of pastels and buff-colored sandstone. On one wall a wide, smooth band of water cascaded quietly down terraces of reddish marble. In the center of the room on a white marble floor stood a large round mahogany table with four carved lion's paw feet. The centerpiece was an enormous arrangement of tropical flowers with exotic names and fragrances. Tashum inhaled deeply, soaking in the multitude of delicate scents. This was one thing he would miss—the amazing smell of flowers. With each minute ticking away his time on Earth, he was starting to realize there were a great many earthly things he would genuinely miss.

When he turned around, Dickey and Fanny had entered the high glass doors held open by a blue-suited doorman.

The sight of him sniffing the flowers brought a smile to Fanny's face. She kept her eyes trained on him and seemed to glide across the floor without her feet ever taking steps. Dickey followed behind her, almost resembling the trailing servant, holding the box.

Tashum met the vampires in the center of the lobby. He returned Fanny's hopeful gaze with a deadly stare. "You're early."

"I try to be punctual."

"Punctual means on time."

"I said, I try." She flashed her smile.

"New tailor, Fanny?" he jabbed as his gaze fell on her cramped breasts.

"I know how you like things packaged, Tashum."

"What were you thinking, Fanny? That maybe I would take you back, in spite of everything?"

Her eyes narrowed and her face took on an expression of uncertainty, then sneering cynicism. "A girl can dream, can't she?"

"At your age darling," Tashum said, teasing, "you're no girl."

"And you're not a very good host," she shot back.

"I'd offer you a drink in the bar, but from what I've just seen on CNN, you must be quite full." He glanced past her to Dickey. "You're awfully sheepish tonight."

Dickey started to say something, but the words wouldn't come. He looked to Fanny for protection.

Fanny shrugged her shoulders. "CNN?" She blinked repeatedly. "Television, you say?"

"Yes. It seems that having Scotland Yard after you wasn't enough, you had to invite the whole world to this little party. I suggest we finish this quickly."

Dickey stepped forward, too anxious to speak at first. He showed Tashum the box. "Sorry about the phone. I've got that as well, if you want it back—"

"Yes, well, why don't we go to my room," Tashum said while sticking a tiny white rose from the flower arrangement to the glittering brooch on her pillbox hat. "I prefer that we have show-and-tell in private." He stood back admiring the addition. "That gown's a bit snug. Have you put on weight?"

Her nose twitched once before she buried the rest of her humiliation behind an angry mask.

In the seaplane, Victor sat in the near dark humming a quiet, small pleased-with-himself ditty. He held up one of the orbs into the ambient light. Then he held all three to the light.

"And then Victor became very, very rich and lived happily ever after," he said, snickering to himself. "Yep. Rich, rich, rich."

The sound of helicopter blades broke into his reverie. Off to his left, about a hundred yards away, he saw a beam of light sweep the lakeshore promenade and pass over Misha.

"Yum, yum, yum fuckin' yum," he screeched at the same time fumbling the orbs, spilling them into the floorboards where they knocked together and spread out. One rolled under the seat. The other two rolled farther back. All out of his reach.

"Oh, piss," he muttered, casting his hand around in the darkness. "Fuck 'em!"

A beam of hot white light washed over the cockpit. With covered eyes, he hunched forward, his head snapping this way and that, searching the air above.

The beam of light swung around the lake, a brilliant finger of God coming back toward the seaplane.

Victor froze. The light was sweeping closer.

"Oh, fuck," he cried, making a desperate scramble for the door. He burst out of the plane. Suddenly the entire world was a blinding light. Victor stood in the center of the search beam, his hair flying around his face, lake water sprayed in all directions. The military helicopter stopped its drifting and hovered directly over him.

A voice boomed from above. "Halt!"

"Open now," said Tashum.

Fanny's eyes sprang open. She stood in the main room of Tashum's suite, bedazzled at the sparkling waterfall of flawless blue-and-white diamonds cascading from a large metal box and onto a black velvet cloth loosely draped over the length of the dining table.

Tashum emptied the metal box of the last gem and stepped back.

A small rush of wind escaped her lips.

For a moment the room was silent except for the street sounds of cars and the pulsating blades of a helicopter.

Tashum's eyes drifted from Fanny, who was transfixed on the radiant hills of gems, to Dickey, still clutching the box of orbs and avoiding the angel's eye contact.

"Dickey, why so nervous?" Tashum asked.

Dickey glanced up for an instant and then away.

Tashum turned to Fanny.

"This is incredible," she exclaimed, and with a giggle added, "do you remember once comparing diamonds to the droppings of a pig?"

He nodded. "And I remember you once thinking they were stars."

"Maybe they're just the tears of angels." She held his gaze, careful not to let him in. She blinked hard. "But it's not all that you have, is it?" she asked, batting her eyes. "Did I tell you, we want everything?" Her voice was now cold and firm. "Everything!"

Tashum could only offer an incredulous stare.

From a pocket, she produced her cigarette case and ivory holder. Slowly, with her eyes still on the diamonds, she twisted a cigarette into the holder. Too much pressure. The cigarette snapped off flush with the holder. "Damn it!" she cursed with slight embarrassment.

"Fanny, my other holdings would require you to have solicitors and bank accounts. Not quite your style, dear."

"Piss off, I want it all. Dickey, fix this." She pushed the cigarette and holder into Dickey's hands, already full with the box.

Dickey cursed her under his breath, as he crossed the room to the alcove bar.

When Fanny turned back to Tashum, he was ready. "All I can give is already there on the table. The rest is spoken for," Tashum said. "The gems' market value must certainly exceed fifty million pounds—"

She rose a finger. "Did you say spoken for?"

"It's really none of your business—"

"Oh, but it is, and knowing you, I bet you've offered Misha a deal he couldn't refuse . . . at our expense."

Tashum approached her. "My best advice is take the diamonds and run. Victor has left a trail that leads right to you." He looked to Dickey. "And you."

"We've been chased before," she said with confidence.

"Not like this, Fanny."

"Will you be chasing us?" Her eyes ran the length of his body.

"I'm going back to the Light, Fanny. I give you my word, even after all your treachery, you won't see me again."

Fanny looked up at him, her lips compressed. "That's awfully big of you, Tashum." With a bit more sarcasm and a cocked smile she added, "You shouldn't make promises that you can't keep."

"I hope you use at least some of the money these diamonds will bring to research your condition—"

"What!" she exclaimed. "I think we know damn well what we are."

"Fanny, Paladin didn't save you from death—he inadvertently murdered your souls with his blood—"

"Stop it!" She cringed, cupping her ears. "I don't want to know!"

Dickey dropped the ice pick he'd been using to clean the cigarette holder, and rushed back to Fanny's side. "Is it true, Tashum?"

"Yes," answered Tashum. "I can't be certain but I think so."

For an instant her veneer seemed to crack. She glanced at wild-eyed Dickey, and then with effort she produced a tough, angry voice. "How dare you frighten Dickey when you really don't know anything about us."

"I'm not frightened, Fanny," chimed Dickey. "I think we're lucky that way. I mean think about it."

Tashum was struck silent.

"I'm not quite as thrilled as he is," she said.

"Fanny, there is a chemical in our blood, its properties are probably similar to ammonia. Whatever it is, it killed your bone marrow's ability to produce its own blood—"

"I don't give a damn about how it works, what's your point?" she demanded.

"I guess," he said with voice full of disappointment, "the point is, just be careful, enjoy what you have while you have it. This may very well be your last incarnation. I hope you make the most of it."

"The whole lot of us?" asked Dickey the simpleton.

"It's not an invitation to a blood orgy, Dickey," Tashum scolded. "Now if you don't mind, let's get back to the business at hand." With his gaze taking in both of them, he said, "I want you out of here, the sooner the better."

She stared hard at him for a long moment. Her mouth moved in a quiver. She silenced it with her hand pressed against her lips. "All right, we have a deal," she said unevenly.

"Good," Tashum said.

Dickey half smiled, not sure if they'd won or lost. "Fanny, I've fixed your holder."

"Thank you," she said softly. "Keep it for me."

"Perhaps we could seal the deal with a drink, Tashum." Dickey smiled.

"I didn't think to order champagne. But if there is something in the alcove bar that suits you, please drink it."

"That's not really what I had in mind," he gushed. "You know—"

"What, one for the road?" Tashum snorted. "I don't think so."

"Dickey, Dickey, Dickey." Fanny chuckled. "You really are too much." She pulled a silver case from her pocket. Her thumb pushed the latch, and the lid popped open.

Tashum's eyes lit up.

"If not a drink, how about a cigar?" she said. "I meant to give these to you in London, but things didn't quite work out."

Tashum accepted the gift and chose one from the case. His fingers rolled it, then a quick sniff. "Cohiba, number six," he said, taking the cutter and trimming the ends.

Dickey flashed a confused look—she returned a sly smile.

"These really are my favorite," continued Tashum. "I had a chance once to invest . . . ," he paused, realizing he had missed something between them.

"You were saying?" said Fanny, extending her silver lighter, flicking a flame to life.

"It was nothing. Just another story."

"Well stay cheered, we are celebrating, right?" she smiled.

Holding her gaze, "Recent events are hardly worth celebrating," he remarked, bending to Fanny's outstretched lighter, he lowered the cigar into the flame and a billow of smoke came from his lips. "But I thank you for the gesture of cigars nonetheless."

She watched with a satisfied grin.

"Mmm, this is deliciously fresh," he said, then extended the case to Dickey. "Care to join me?"

Dickey took a step back, shaking his head.

"Once upon a time, Tashum, I would have joined you anywhere, for anything," Fanny said, trying to pry his mind off Dickey.

Tashum's eyes stayed on Dickey. "You're not begging off for health reasons, surely." He inhaled again.

"Go ahead, Dickey," Fanny said, smiling. "If Tashum's willing to share, don't be rude."

Dickey watched the stream of exhaled smoke. He stared at the coal of the cigar and mumbled an incoherent excuse, shaking his head.

Tashum glanced at the cigar with raised brow.

"Well," Fanny said. "If he won't join you, I certainly will."

Tashum turned to her. Her fingers reached for a cigar in the case. Instead, Tashum quickly handed her the cigar he had been smoking.

She looked up at him, hesitating.

"Go ahead, make sure it suits you, before we light a second," he said gently.

She took it. "Always the gentleman." Raised a brow. "Is this proper etiquette?"

"Waste not, want not. Fanny," he said as she took a shallow draw.

"I vaguely remember Freud talking about cigars," she toyed. A plume uncoiled out of her mouth. She blew it his way. "Something about how its size and shape makes a man feel about himself." Her love-injured eyes were on him, her mouth set and defiant. "You know, the sense of power all men carry between their legs. Then again maybe you don't know."

Tashum held her wicked gaze, his expression softened. When he spoke, his words slurred out. "Not . . . thish . . . time . . . round, F-Fannnnn." His eyes crossed with blurred vision. "Fannnee!"

Her gaze sharpened.

His strength began to dissolve. His legs gave way, and he staggered backward, catching himself. His eyes watered and lost focus. He looked from Dickey back to her, to the cigar, then back to her. Always back to her.

"Fanny, you all right?" asked Dickey.

She took a step toward him, tears forming in her eyes, "Tashum, please," she moved closer.

"Wha's . . . wron' . . . me?" He slumped.

She took him by the shirt, held him upright. "Tashum? Tashum."

His eyes focused slowly through a strained wince. "F-Fannneee?"

Dickey shot a look to Fanny: "He's a mess—are you sure you're all right?"

"I was careful." She extinguished the cigar in a snifter of brandy and threw his arm over her shoulder, helping him to the sofa. Both stumbled across the coffee table and fell onto the leather couch.

"Jesus, Fanny, did you kill him?" asked her excited partner. "I can't believe he went for it."

Tashum was sprawled. Fanny struggled against dead weight to sit him upright. She was leaning over him, his face pinched in her hands. "Tashum, we can't go home, and neither can you."

Her words came to him in nightmarish distortion, and echoed through a mind drunk on something that had turned highly tuned muscle to soft rubber.

"W-w-why?" he pleaded, clutching her sleeve with only the strength of a small child.

They watched him lie there, slipping away, a shrinking of former stature.

Fanny fought the maternal urge rising within her. She balanced her desire to take and keep and love him forever with the reality of their situation and the hopeless nature of her betrayal. She stayed close until he was stone still.

"Is he dead, yet?" Dickey asked nervously, watching her rise to her feet. "Tell me he's dead."

"No, I didn't kill him, and we had better be the hell out of here when he wakes up." She tugged his limp arm, pulling him back into an upright position.

Tashum was bewildered. Their eyes met, a silent message passed between them.

Why, Fanny?

Paladin saw the future. You're not supposed to go back.

Why not?

I don't know. Paladin didn't tell me.

The three of them were startled by the sound of a loud banging on the door.

Another terrible racket on the door, then it crashed open. Victor stumbled in, his face wet, his hair twisted and stringy.

"They're all over the fuckin' place," he shouted. His arms flapped wildly, sending water droplets flying. Water drained from his clothing and left wet footprints with every step. He brushed past them and took a place by the window, peering out. Panting and wild-eyed.

"Who, Victor? Who?" Dickey asked.

"How the fuck should I know? I don't sign their paychecks." Lake water drained from his clothes, forming puddles at his feet. "They got big guns is all I can tell yuh."

"What happened to you!" Dickey asked, looking at his wet clothing.

"I been swimmin', what do you think? If I hadn't seen that grotto entrance I woulda never—"

The room trembled with the low approach of a helicopter, its search beam flooded the window. Victor ducked behind the long drapes.

"Oooorbs—gimmmme orrrbbssss," Tashum bellowed.

Victor noticed Tashum hunched over like so many of his drunk victims. "What the fuck's wrong with him?"

Fanny opened her mouth to protest, but Dickey intruded to defuse the situation. "Victor, the diamonds!" He pointed to the table in the adjoining room. "A third of those gems are yours, my boy."

Victor's eyes were trained on Tashum. His thoughts were running wild.

"Quick, Victor, lets get them loaded up and get out of here."

Victor glanced to his left. Just a few steps away were more diamonds than he ever thought existed. He licked his lips. "Only a third huh? What's that work out to?"

"We'll work that out later, Victor," said Fanny.

"That's always been the problem with this outfit," he snorted. "But yuh gotta admit it, we're lucky," he said, turning his Cheshire cat smile back on Tashum. "Luckier than you."

"Victor, would you please get the diamonds?"

Victor danced his way over to the sofa and seating arrangement.

Fanny lowered Tashum's head against the high-backed cushion, and stood to meet him. "You were not invited here, do as Dickey told you."

"Yuh know, Fanny, we ain't in one of your houses or your fort, so don't think you can just push me around."

"She didn't mean it that way, Victor."

"Sure as shit sounded that way to me, Pops."

"Fanny, what should I do with the orbs?" asked Dickey.

She paused to think. "Give Tashum one of them, and let's get the hell out of here." She pointed a finger at Victor. "After tonight, we're finished Victor."

"We can finish it now if yuh want," he said, wild-eyed.

Her eyes flared. Her body began to coil back, taking a stance.

"Victor! Where are the orbs?" Dickey screamed as he looked into the empty box.

The vampires traded looks, and one by one they looked toward Tashum's outrage. He struggled to stand. "Viccer!"

Victor pushed Fanny aside, leaped up onto the coffee table, and swung out a leg in a karate kick. The stacked heel of his cowboy boot connected with a hard thud under Tashum's jaw. The forceful kick lifted Tashum's body off the sofa, and as he sank back down, another boot caught him behind

the ear. His head snapped to one side as he rolled over the armrest and off
the end of the sofa.

Fanny leaped up. Victor cold cocked her with a short left jab. She fell
backward, crashing into a flower-filled vase, tipping over an end table, and
tumbling to the floor. "Goddamn! That felt good!" he screamed.

Victor turned to Dickey. "You want some of this old man?"

Dickey was torn by loyalty. "I guess I'll see to the diamonds myself."

"Good fuckin' idea, cause I got something to settle with dickless. Kinda
funny, ain't it, Dickey and Dickless, my two rich uncles," he laughed. "Now
where the fuck was I?" he said as he leaped over a chair, then knelt down,
pulling Tashum up by the hair. "You're much more fun when you're all
fucked up." He giggled as the blade of his knife was laid across Tashum's
throat.

"Victor, no! Don't do it!" screamed Fanny. "No!"

Victor withdrew the blade. He followed Tashum's helpless eyes to
Fanny. "Still fuckin' soft on each other, ain't yuh?"

From her knees she pleaded with him. "No, I'm not, but if you drink
his blood you'll die, just like he is." She continued her lie, "He'll be dead by
sunrise."

"No shit?" He searched her eyes, "Fucker's dyin', huh?"

Fanny rose to her feet. She glanced at Dickey. His raised brow told her
that he wouldn't interfere. He looked away and continued loading the diamonds into a leather flight bag. "Victor," she said calmly, collecting her
thoughts, "I-I think I've been wrong about you. Um, we need the plane and
we need you to fly it."

"Right on both counts, but first it's payback." He stood erect, looked
around the room, and found the fireplace. "You wanna help out little lady,
build me a fire—"

"Victor, we don't have time—"

"We'll make fuckin' time!" he screamed.

"She's right, Victor, we need to leave now," said Dickey as he zipped
closed the bulging flight bag.

"I gotta gut this fucker first!" he said. "Gimme that blow poker off the
fireplace, go on, Fanny, get it."

"Let him go, Victor!" she screamed.

Tashum struggled with the strength of a small boy.

Victor dropped him, and after a series of bone-crushing kicks, he had pushed Tashum across the room. Tashum would rise to his knees only to be pummeled back down again.

They were all screaming at one another, and with each blow Tashum muttered, "Punk!" That word fueled Victor's vengeful passion. Fanny leaped onto Victor's back, pounding the back of his head with her fists. He staggered around, reached back, and found the scruff of her neck. He dropped a shoulder and flung her into the adjoining guest bathroom. He rushed to the fireplace and ripped the blow poker from its rack.

Tashum's face was slightly distorted by broken cheek- and jawbones. He grabbed the window frame and tried to pull himself to his feet.

Victor rushed him with the blow poker. "See how tough you are when I got the weapon!" he screamed as the first blow caught Tashum's midsection. Tashum doubled over and then was lifted by an uppercut blow. He stumbled back, up against the window's glass.

Victor leaped straight up and delivered a double-footed mule kick, both boots driven hard against the angel's chest.

Propelled by inertia, Tashum's feet lifted off the floor. His body flew backward with a greater force than the window's tinsel strength could withstand.

Tashum barely heard the breaking glass over Fanny's shrill scream. Pushed through breaking shards of glass, he was falling, caught in gravity's grip. His arms flailed, fingers desperately trying to grab the window frame. The last thing he saw in his line of vision was Misha's terrified face standing in the doorway to his suite. "Nooooo!" His scream trailed off, as he fell.

Tumbling through the air, the nauseating physical sensations of vertigo mixed with the sedative effect of flaxen-tangmere, coursed through his body until he was helpless. The words of the champion alpine skier Jean-Claude Killy sprung into his drugged mind, *To recover from a fall always keep your feet below your head*, but he wasn't wearing skis, and there was no ski slope, only the glassed skylight over the sinkhole rushing up at him. How odd it looked to him, this dim bluish light rising up through panes of glass covering the irregular-shaped hole set in the lush green lawn.

Five seconds later, Tashum's head led the fall. He pulled in his arms, shielding his eyes. He curled his body, and it rotated. His shoulder and left side would make contact.

The metal-webbed frame holding the glass panels moaned as it broke apart. The angel rode the collapsing framework and crashing glass down twenty-some feet into the subterranean room. The fall ended with a sobering plunge into a large pool of iridescent blue lake-chilled water. A huge plume of water splashed the chiseled stone of the grotto and shot up out of the sinkhole, wetting the lawn in a sudden downpour.

Fanny was at the window, eyes tilted down. Her gloved hand rose and covered her mouth with a hush. "Tashum!" She could see his silhouetted body floating lifeless in the backlit water. "Damn you, Victor!"

"He only did what you didn't have the nerve to do," Dickey said coldly. "Fanny, look who's here."

"I never wanted to physically hurt him!" she said, turning to see Misha standing a few steps away. "Misha?"

"Fuckin' amazing! Just when you need a hostage, dinner shows up," goofed Victor.

"No, you had it right the first time, hostage," she said with chilling calculation.

Misha tried to flee. He made it out into the hall before Victor dove, flying prone, his knife leading the charge. The knife blade sliced through Misha's denim cuff and cotton sock, filleting ankle flesh, severing the Achilles tendon. The sinew snapped, the foot went lame. He collapsed to his right, hitting the carpet. Like a hungry cat, Victor grabbed a leg and climbed his way up Misha's body until he was looming over him, eye to eye. He then licked Misha's clear blood off the blade while holding his gaze.

An olive-skinned maid stepped into the hall from Potter's suite. She dropped her cleaning tools at the sight of Victor pouncing Misha.

A single gunshot rang out.

Victor held back his knife, looking up in time to see the maid bounce backward off the wall and hit the floor, dead.

Dickey lowered his smoking pistol. "Cuff him and bring him along," he said, moving out of the doorway.

"Wanna come live with us? Sure you do." Victor croaked, then stood, wrestling the chrome handcuffs off the shoulder epaulet of his biker's jacket. "I hope these babies didn't rust," he mumbled.

Dickey watched, almost mystified by Misha's simple magic.

The angel pinched the raw white ends of his severed tendon together and when his fingers had finished a curious little dance, the tendon looked new, and the dead foot moved. Then the angel looked up, catching his gaze. Dickey felt the words *This is so wrong* enter his mind.

Misha's eyes dimmed as the handcuff was hooked and snapped closed on his left wrist. The sister cuff, Victor loosely closed on his own wrist. Chained together, Victor pulled him to his feet.

Fanny entered the hall carrying the flight bag bulging with diamonds. She winced slightly seeing Misha standing on one foot, the other tenderly raised. She herself felt wounded by her trespasses of trust and the violations against these angels. There was little relief in knowing she had done precisely what Paladin had demanded she do. The ashen flaxen-tangmere had worked, and Victor's intervention, as vicious and tasteless as it was, ensured that Tashum would remain earthbound, for what reason she knew not. But that was always the problem with these angels, it was always a test of faith with no proof of purpose. She had done her bit, and as a consequence she found the world allied against her.

"We need that plane!" she stated firmly. "Where is your gun, Victor?"

"I don't know. I lost it in the lake."

"You'll need more than a knife for what we're stepping into."

"Let me show you how this works," he huffed, holding the knife at Misha's throat. "Those pussies ain't gonna blast yer ass when yuh got a hostage. Simple math, Fanny."

Bobbing in the water, facedown, Tashum lay still. He was concentrating on his broken facial bones. A punctured lung made breathing hardly worth the effort, and his shattered left arm and leg made movement painfully difficult, if at all possible. The lacerations were too numerous to count. Most were gelling to closure, but a few of the deeper glass gouges were hemorrhaging, leaving amber slicks floating and swirling around his outstretched limbs. The more serious wounds, the compound fractures, didn't reset or realign themselves as much as they melted in a fluid way, refashioning the bones to their former shape and function. It was an eerie feeling, an irritating itch deep within that begged for rubbing relief but could never be scratched. Tashum had never fully become accustomed to the regenerative sensation of healing, however he fully appreciated its final resolve.

He opened his eyes to a filtered blue underwater world as the harmonics of his own crystalline skeleton hummed a healing and repairing message through his earthly body. The vibration transmitted beyond his body, created ripples in the otherwise smooth liquid surface of the grotto pool.

He drifted in the gentle current controlled by the subtle but constant movement of Lago Maggiore's tide. Then he saw it, resting on the natural rock bottom of the grotto's inlet waters. Within arm's reach was Victor's Uzi. Seeing the gun brought back the mental image of Misha standing in the doorway. The horrific possibilities hurt far beyond any physical pain he felt.

"I wanna march through the front door this time, hell, we gotta shield," bragged Victor, raising and waving Misha's chained wrist along with his own.

Fanny took her eyes off the declining red digital numbers flashing on the readout window above the sealed elevator door. "Forget it, Victor—we get a car in the parking garage—"

"Fanny," Dickey said, noticing the slowing motion in their descent. "I think that we're stopping a floor early," he warned as he pulled the Beretta 9-milimeter pistol from his trouser waistband.

"Damn it!" she replied. Seeing the big red *L* in the readout window, she vigorously, repeatedly punched the parking garage button on the shiny panel.

The doors swooshed open.

The vampires were face-to-face with three policemen and a pair of heavily armed soldiers dressed in battle fatigues. There was a moment of stunned silence from both groups, each sizing up the other.

Dickey raised his pistol at lightning speed. Victor pushed Misha out in front of him, slapping his knife's eight-inch blade across his throat. The soldiers reacted, leveling the barrels of their M-16 rifles, loosely aimed in their direction. The policemen reached for their holstered pistols. A third soldier arrived on the scene. He flipped the safety switch on his automatic shotgun and took aim.

"Sorry, wrong floor. Going down." Fanny smiled as her hand punched the close-door button.

The doors began to slide closed when Dickey fired through the shrinking gap at the policeman lunging for the elevator control panel on the corridor wall.

The report from the returned fire into the enclosed elevator compartment was deafening. Bullets ricocheted around the polished brass and walnut paneling, remarkably not finding a target before embedding themselves into the rich wood.

As Fanny hit the panel of button commands, a tightly spread patter of shotgun pellets chewed away part of the door frame and indirectly struck her midriff, throwing her back as the doors sucked closed.

"You stupid bitch you hit the wrong fucking button!" screamed Victor as they watched the floor numbers increasing and he stepped out from behind his protective shield screaming "Fuck." He pounded the parking garage button and repeated his favorite word so fast his tongue sounded like a valve stuck in a flutter.

She slid down the back wall to a seated position on the floor.

Victor pried open the control panel and started fiddling with wires. "We want a direct trip," he mumbled.

Dickey stuffed a fresh clip of bullets into the butt of his pistol. His eyes narrowed, following the smeared blood trail that led down the wall to Fanny. She was staring at her blood-stained white gloves. Then he noticed the warmth of his own blood trickling into his eye and felt the sting of a grazed forehead. "Are we all right, Fanny?" His voice deepened with concern, "How bad is it?" he said, kneeling down to her.

"I'll be all right, but I think he killed my ermine coat," she said with false courage and a pained smile. "Have a look."

He winced, seeing the bloody baseball-sized hole in the fur. He gently slipped the coat off her shoulders and quickly removed his lamb's wool scarf from around his neck, then stuffed it in the fist-sized wound.

"All right!" Victor said, feeling the elevator descending. "Whoa-daddy-oh," he said, chuckling. He glanced down at them. "You guys look like you could use a drink." He smirked. "I tell yuh, yuh gotta get one of these lucky charms." Again he raised Misha's wrist cuffed to his own.

"We let him go on the dock," she said looking into Misha's eyes.

"In his fuckin' dreams! Hey, your lipstick's runnin'," he said, teasingly.

She brought a gloved finger to the corner of her mouth. The white silk turned crimson from the red trickle.

Victor laughed. "What's more important now, good looks or good taste?"

Dickey shot Victor a very nasty glare, then looked up to Misha. "Misha, can you help her?" Dickey pleaded with the angel. "Please."

Misha swallowed hard, and looked away, a tear forming in his eye, and self-guilt forming in his gut. Her pain called out for his touch, and only higher reason could keep him from giving it. He had a flash, and for a glimmer in time he felt the guilt of their creation and understood the pity bestowed upon them by Tashum and Paladin.

"Dickey, it's all right, I'm not going to bleed to death."

"Yuh see there, she'll get over that. Hey 'member that fuckin' time we was in—"

Dickey leaped up—slapped Victor with the back of his hand. "How dare you!"

A sudden hush, as the motion of descent stopped and the elevator door swooshed open.

They looked out into the parking garage expecting danger, but it was silent except for the muted noise of sirens and vehicles outside on the street level. Then a BMW-5 series station wagon came wheeling around the corner, a man and woman arguing heatedly in the front seat.

Dickey was suddenly in front of their car. He stood firm and waved the gun, demanding they stop.

"Kacke! Ich kann nicht verstehn," screamed the agitated German while slamming on the brake pedal.

"What bit don't you understand, old boy," he asked, clicking back the gun's hammer now just inches from the driver's round face.

"Ahh, Englander, vhat do you vant?"

"Please tell your wife to get out of the car, one of my friends is in need of her help. Verstehn?"

Sweat droplets uniformly appeared across the fat German's face. "Yahh, Ich verstehn," he said in a resigned tone.

Dickey glanced inside the vehicle and saw two pretty little girls sitting glumly in the back. "Picture perfect!" He smiled and then called out to Victor, ordering him to bring Misha to the car.

Tashum's eyes were empty, defeated. He shut them tight, closing out completely the underwater artificial blue light. It would take days, perhaps a week, to regain his full strength. He felt too damaged, too depressed, to stop them. By sifting through his anger he was burying his self-disgust under the layered actions of others. It was so easy to hate Fanny and her friends or to blame poor-luck Misha for his present situation. This would mark the second time that Goody Two-shoes had bumbled his way into their grasp. Tashum had saved him once, though his motive was secondary to the act. He recognized that being his brother's keeper was instinctive, but hardly a full-time job. Nonetheless, Misha's recapture was inconceivable, and equally as puzzling was this nagging question of why an army of light beings didn't come to Misha's rescue. Surely they were watching from their invisible world?

Tashum opened his eyes, finding the strap to Victor's weapon floating toward him, daring him to stay involved.

The BMW bounded up the parking garage ramp, making a hard right hairpin turn, tires squealing.

"Mein vife? Umm, wird sie sich wieder erholen?"

"You'll get her back if you—Beeilen Sie sich!" said Dickey indicating drive faster.

Parked cars and cement supports flashed past the windows. The German hit the brakes and slid around another blind corner. Three soldiers jogging down the corkscrew ramp scattered—one hitting the hood, rolling up the windshield, and disappearing from view. Victor leaned out the rear window, grabbing an M-16 right out of the hands of a young unsuspecting soldier.

Dickey's foot pinned the German's foot to the gas pedal and pushed it to the floor. The Beemer raced down a long aisle of parked vehicles. In the backseat, Victor played with his new toy. "It'll do, but it ain't no fuckin' match for an Ak-47."

"Victor! There are children here," Fanny scolded, leaning over Misha, who separated the two vampires. Terrified by Victor, the young girls were clinging to Fanny, who was now wearing their mother's long black woolen coat. She nestled them as if they were hers.

"Fuck . . . oops, pardon my French." Victor sneered. "Hey you're kinda cute," he said, and winked at the older girl.

"Keep your mind out of the gutter!" Fanny warned.

The car flew up a steep ramp and emerged through an arch into the night.

The driver hit the brakes and put the car into a skid. They came to a stop adjacent to the main lobby entrance. His wide eyes counted a dozen or more as he scanned the small groups of soldiers and policemen stationed in the lobby, at the entrance, surrounding the grounds, and marching up the drive.

Dickey saw the same dangers. Then he saw the German about to hit the horn and scream for help. He was prematurely silenced by the barrel of

Dickey's Beretta firmly lodged in the flabby folds under his chin.

"Getenzie out," Dickey whispered into his ear.

"Meine dotters," the German murmured. "Take mein auto, und der money," he pleaded, "not meine dotters." He had tears in his eyes. "Please, not mein dotters."

"Victor, you had better drive," Fanny murmured.

Victor turned the key and quickly slipped Misha's free wrist into the cuff he had been wearing. Misha's wrists tested the handcuff chain with a tug. "Yuh wanna play with my gun, little girl?"

"Get out!" warned Fanny.

Victor kicked open the back door, slipped out, opened the driver's door, rolled the German out onto the stone pavement, slipped behind the wheel, and slammed his foot down on the accelerator. The friction between spinning rubber and pavement screamed the car's tires sending the BMW fishtailing down the drive.

In their wake a desperate father alerted everyone within shouting distance of the kidnappings.

The top of the drive was S-curved, and Victor guided the car deftly, swinging sideways, correcting and thundering down the long, sweeping right-hand curve toward the boulevard.

"Watch it," Dickey said.

A small group of young pedestrians scattered out of the way.

Then an ambulance's flashing red lights appeared rounding the bend. The red-and-white vehicle was roaring up the drive, with a police car trailing close behind.

Victor slammed the brakes and yanked the wheel. The BMW sideswiped the ambulance and the trailing police car rear-ended the ambulance with a dull thud. Victor spun the wheel left, then right, aiming at the tight opening between the granite embankment and the two vehicles.

Amid shouts and screams and wailing sirens, Victor slammed his foot on the accelerator and persisted in squeezing past the wreckage. Pieces of the smashed car rattled against the tires. He kept the engine at top revs, its nose pointed toward the boulevard and the docks on the farside.

A gunshot shattered the back window, and Fanny ducked. She pulled the children's heads down under her protective arms and then whirled around, squint-eyed. "We have children in here!" she shouted out the ragged window.

"Hostages!" added Victor. "Bambino hostages!" He slammed the car's accelerator to the floor. "Hang on to them kids, Fanny!" he called out, gripping the steering wheel tighter. "They're as good as gold."

They flew into the road depression. The BMW's coil springs flattened, and the station wagon bottomed out with a hideous scrapping sound. The whole car sank down on its wheels and heeled over as Victor gunned it through the intersection. They crossed onto the boulevard sliding sideways, moving against the traffic light. Horns blared, as surprised and angry motorists cleared an opening, allowing the BMW to narrowly slip through.

The mild current floated Tashum the short distance through the inlet cave to the mouth of the grotto. He began treading water once out in the open under the stars. Gone was his shredded shirt and jacket, shoes kicked off, his makeup washed away. But for trousers, he was naked. His overmuscled shoulders and wing nubs supported the Uzi strapped to his back. His dilated owl-shaped eyes were trained on the action, the snarled traffic, the BMW jumping the curb, and racing down the pedestrian promenade toward the dock and the seaplane. It was all happening no more than a hundred yards away. He began a slow breaststroke across dark water. He was following in the wake of the forty-foot Swiss Navy patrol boat motoring with slow caution toward the dock.

Soldiers and policemen took up shooter's positions behind the vehicles scattered on the dock, and cars parked along the boulevard.

Victor guided the car through the vehicles, holding his breath.

The sweep of the patrol boat's searchlight lit the angry faces of the soldiers, policemen, and onlookers, but it settled on the BMW now stopped—a brief standoff with a small Swiss armored personnel carrier blocking its path to the dock's end.

The patrol boat's 10-k beam of blinding brilliance was instant pain to the vampires. They shielded their eyes in absolute misery. Dickey shielded Victor's eyes with his arm.

Victor slipped on his sunglasses and squirmed up through the open sunroof. His upper body leaned against the roof, and he took aim on the blinding lamp. A steady stream of bullets from his M-16 tumbled through the air, extinguishing the burning beam with a popping sizzle. Victor quickly slithered back into the driver's seat.

In the side-door mirror, Dickey noticed a man in a black bodysuit creeping alongside the car. "Fanny, just outside your door," he said with quiet calm.

Fanny opened the door, and swung the four year old off her lap, gently holding her vertical by the arms for the masked officer to see. *"Bella bambina."* She smiled.

The soldier lowered his pistol. "What do you plan to do with her?" he asked in very plain English.

"I'll give her and her sister back to their parents as soon as you move that armored car."

He removed his black woolen head cover, rising higher on his haunches. With a wave he signaled the armored vehicle to back away. That gesture started negotiations. "Now it's your turn," said the thick-necked professional.

But before he could finish, Victor spun smoke from the rear tires. Fanny stretched, leaning out. "Tit for tat. Take care of her!" The little girl was hanging from her extended arms. The commando lurched forward, dropped his gun, and grabbed the precious little girl as Fanny released her. He pulled the toddler close into the safety of his chest as he rolled across the pavement, away from the car.

Fanny didn't take her eyes off them until the commando came upright and she could see the little girl's mother and father break the newly formed police line to claim their little girl.

Fanny felt Misha's eyes on her and recognized that her own were filled with the same genuine concern for the children. She wiped the bloody spittle she had coughed up, evidence of the wounds hidden beneath her borrowed coat, wounds that she instinctively knew the angel could heal with the ease of touch. But instead of turning to him for help, she comforted the remaining six-year-old hostage with promises of all the cool stuff her parents would give her after the ride in the car was over. Fanny spoke German with a Bavarian accent and spoke it to Vollkommenheit.

Dickey sharply sucked in air, bracing against the dash, as the car was running out of dock. "Victor!"

Victor skidded the car to a stop a foot or two from the rail. "I hate these fuckin' ABS brakes. Shit, man! I thought we were goin' in the drink—"

"All right, listen up," Fanny said. "Victor, get in the plane—get it warmed up—"

Victor craned his neck to see her. "I ain't goin' out there with no protection! Forget that shit right now."

"He's right, Fanny. We should move together, I see sharpshooters out on the street."

"Sharpshooters don't spook me as much as them twin fifty-cal deck guns on that patrol boat," Victor said, running his fingers through his tangled hair. "Them fuckers will rip yuh up."

"Can we outrun the boat?" Dickey asked.

"Nope, they'll pen us in, but we ain't got no choice."

"What would Butch and Sundance do, Victor?" Fanny asked ironically.

"Come out fuckin' shootin'," he said, gritting his teeth, pumping himself up. "I'll ram them cocksuckers if they make me! Goddamn it." He slapped his fist into the palm of his hand. "Might take a few more hits. Shit, we got blood," he said, looking at Misha. "Don't we?"

Suddenly the little girl began screaming, kicking, and crying. Fanny pushed her away after being bitten on the shoulder and hand.

Victor freaked, pulled out his knife and threatened the child. "Shut the fuck up, you little munchkin! Do you—"

"Victor! Put that down!" screamed Dickey and Fanny in unison.

Misha gently clasped his chained hands around her small, quivering right hand. The calming effect was immediate. She looked into his big round eyes and cherubic smile, then settled next to Misha, burying her nose into his side, shutting out her captor's faces.

"We have you surrounded," blared from the megaphone. "You must surrender the child and your other hostage immediately."

Victor pounded the steering wheel with both fists, venting frustration with incoherent phrases. "This ain't Bolivia," he chanted over and over, his new mantra.

"At least they recognized Misha as a hostage, that's in our favor" said Dickey as he flipped the safety switch on his hand gun.

"We're dead unless we act smart." Fanny surveyed the buildup of enemy forces. She estimated their numbers in the high thirties. Any form of retreat or escape by land was impossible. The patrol boat was positioning itself to thwart a water escape by blocking the seaplane's taxi path. The word *"fuck"* floated off her breath. "We need to make a move. The odds aren't going to improve."

Dickey's eyes were locating the enemy. His lips were still counting them when he replied, "It's now or never." Then he looked at Victor. "You ready, Sundance?"

Victor cracked his knuckles, then snickered "Let's boogie, Butch."

Misha clutched the little girl closer to his body.

Standing on the patrol boat's transom, Tashum could see the backsides of two Swiss naval officers through the open rear door of the raised pilot house.

Tashum stayed low and moved along her port side. At her beam, he stopped just under the side windows of the bridge. Sneaking a peek around the front of the deckhouse, he saw two sailors were gathered around the pedestal-mounted twin-barreled canister-fed machine gun. He overheard them saying the helicopter was refueling and when it returned they would make their advance.

He leaned back against the steel deckhouse, then he noticed the row of half a dozen smoke screen and flare-launch tubes set in angled racks welded to the deck and deckhouse wall. He crouched for a closer look. At the base of each tube hung a short pull chain and a red cardboard warning label. He jerked his head when he heard one of the seaplane's motors kicking over, then rumbling to life. After the first rotary engine ran smooth, a second engine's electric starter was engaged. Tashum was on the backside of the patrol boat, away from the action, and couldn't see the dock, but his ears told him it was time to move.

His fingers quickly unscrewed the metal caps and removed them from the six tubes. Each was packed with a different color and type of powdered pellet. A firm tug on each of the chains triggered the firing mechanisms. Tashum turned and ran aft.

The mortarlike devices shot flares high into the night sky and spewed huge plumes of red, green, and gray. Smoke engulfed the forward deck with choking fumes. The cloud drifted back, cloaking the entire vessel.

Victor was wearing his radio headset. Off the plane's port bow he could see the red-and-white flares erupting through the thick expanding cloud of smoke.

"Could you tell us your name?" asked a male voice from a radio speaker on the dash.

"Damn, looks like yer navy's got a little problem," he replied into his headset mic.

"We want to work this out." The negotiator's radio voice continued in a friendly Italian-accented sort of way. "If you could tell us more about your intent, it would help us improve the situation."

"The sit-u-ation will improve when we fly out of here, so if you'd just clear the way, we'll just mosey on down the road."

"What you fail to understand is that I can't let you go that easily. If you'd please shut down your plane's motors—"

"Cain't hear yuh, cheese face!"

During the onboard confusion, Tashum rounded up the four crew members and sequestered them below deck, locked behind the metal door of the munitions room. The radioman was missing, but there wasn't time for a thorough search.

Tashum climbed the companionway ladder and entered the pilothouse. He went right for the radio operator's desk. He picked up the operator's headset. He heard Victor's voice cursing the hostage negotiator.

Dickey unclipped the oval-shaped carabiners releasing the plane's tail from the shoreline. He walked forward, dragging the tetherline, then joined Fanny at the fuselage side door.

She was sitting in the oval-shaped opening, shielded by Misha and the girl standing before her on the dock's edge. In her left hand she was holding a dog's lead that was attached to Misha's handcuffs, in her right was the Beretta pistol trained on the girl.

"We're warmed up," Victor yelled from the pilot's seat.

Dickey took the gun and Misha's lead strap from Fanny, who crawled deeper inside the fuselage.

Dickey took her spot, crouching in the doorway. "Give me the girl," he said to Misha. "Hand her to me."

Misha kept his back to him. "But you said—"

"Did you hear me! Give me the girl!"

"Fanny said we stay here—"

"I will kill her right now!"

Misha looked back over his shoulder. "I can't let you have her."

"Victor, hit the throttle when you hear the shot!" He pulled back the gun's hammer.

Three commandos had taken up positions behind the BMW.

A fourth commando whispered orders over a radio headset as he crouched behind a trash bin. They took aim. Fingers pressured triggers. Cries of "Please don't shoot her!" were heard from two of them. The third mumbled something else more threatening and steadied his aim.

Misha went down on one knee. He whispered into the girl's ear. As soon as Dickey became an open target, a single shot came from the rifle's muzzle steadied over the hood of the car. Two more sniper shots followed.

Dickey collapsed and rose a bloody arm, finding the girl in his shaky gun sights.

Misha pushed the girl in the direction of a commando, who was now running toward the plane. Misha then spun and jumped in the open door and onto Dickey, wrestling him for the gun.

Victor kicked left rudder, slapped the throttle bars forward, and the plane rotated away from the dock.

Immediately dozens of soldiers and policemen blitzed the dock.

"Target the pilot!" an officer cried to his sharpshooters.

The assortment of bullets chipped glass and pinged new holes in the fuselage but missed their target through the highly reflective windows.

Shot from mortars on the boulevard, three grappling hooks aimed at the fleeing seaplane flew overhead, their rope tails arcing high over the dock. Two of the hooks missed and flew wide to the right then splashed into the water. The third hook's barbed talons shattered the glass canopy above Victor's head, its metal fingers digging into the canopy frame. It was pulling against their forward motion, tearing at the subframe. Victor pulled back the throttle bars, then neutralized the spinning propellers. He jumped up through the gaping hole with knife in hand, but before he could cut the nylon tether, the knife was shot out of his grip. Bullets chased him back into the pilot's seat. "Someone's gotta cut that fucking line," he screamed, holding a mangled right hand.

Dickey finished hog-tying Misha's ankles to his handcuffs, and Fanny handed him Victor's knife that had fallen at her feet. He crawled to the door. He could see the limp line hanging just outside the door. He glanced back at Fanny for support.

"It's up to you," she said, picking up the M-16.

He flung open the door and leaned out, swinging the knife.

She fired the rifle for effect more than accuracy.

Return fire peppered the area around the door with a concentrated lethal burst from more than fifty guns. Bullets pounded Dickey flat against the curvature of the fuselage. His watery eyes saw the frayed end of the tether.

The plane was free. Fanny grabbed his belt and pulled him inside.

"Go, Victor, go!" he croaked.

The port engine revved. The plane continued making a U-turn. As her nose rotated away from the dock, her tail swung into the gunner's sights, and the gunfire suddenly stopped faster than it started.

Victor monitored the emergency frequency and listened as the negotiator inside the armored car unwittingly told those standing around the open door that the objective was now for the navy to detain them. If that failed, they would track them in the air, back across the Italian frontier, where the authorities don't mind public executions.

"You gotta hear this shit," he said, turning on the cabin speakers.

Misha hunched down against the bulkhead, watching Fanny cuddle Dickey, both wounded beyond natural human recovery. He blanched at the sensation of their fear, and their love for one another touched him in ways he never thought possible. . . . But as his instinctive feelings of compassion rose, so did his sense of duty to the Light. He would not intervene. To keep his healing hands off, he had to bite his lip this time.

"Victor, are you still alive?" asked a cynical but familiar voice over the radio. "If you want to survive, listen to me very carefully."

Complete surprise registered on the faces of the angel and the vampires when Tashum's voice came from the radio speaker.

Through a bullet-riddled windshield, Victor looked across fifty yards of open water. "Fuck me!" Victor said as he studied the boat's position. He realized that whatever course he chose, he could never get airborne before the boat's speed would cut him off. "You're supposed to be dead, you double-crossing asshole!"

"I presume that is a yes. Do exactly as I say," he demanded in his strict tone.

Then the negotiator broke in, "This is a classified operation. Whoever you are, you are not cleared to be using this frequency."

"Victor, I'm in control of the boat. Come alongside, you've got something that belongs to me."

"Victor, where are the orbs?" Fanny yelled.

Victor suddenly smiled with the realization Tashum couldn't drive the boat and use her guns at the same time. "All right," he said, "no fuckin' around. I get what I want, you get what I give yuh."

"Something like that, Victor."

Tashum thought Victor was incapable of following instructions, even if it meant saving his own life. He devised a plan as he quickly dressed, putting on a high-neck sweater he found hanging in the captain's locker. He heard the sailors rustling on the deck below, but he couldn't leave the helm. He had to watch Victor's approach very carefully and to counteract his every move to keep them from slipping past—ram the plane, if necessary.

Surprisingly, Victor chose a true course, coming alongside as close as the wingspan would allow.

Standing at the ship's beam, Tashum held Victor's gun at his side. He tried to raise Victor's gaze, but Victor wouldn't play. From the corner of his eye, he saw the fuselage door open. He turned to see Misha in the opening.

Dickey was fumbling with the key, trying to unlock the handcuffs. Then he saw Fanny's face pressed against the passenger window. Even separated by twenty feet of water, he could see the tears rolling off her cheek and the apologetic eyes, willing to speak at last.

"For a dead man, you look pretty alive to me," Victor yelled with punkish sarcasm. "Felt good gettin' a piece of you!"

"Show me the orbs!" he shouted back.

"Come and get 'em. Lets see yuh walk on water."

Sudden footsteps on the forward deck caused Tashum to spin and run forward along the curved rail. Then he heard gunfire from the seaplane, and her engine's roar. The sailors were loose and armed. Pistol and automatic rifle fire seemed to be erupting all over the boat.

Tashum started running aft. Flashes of muzzle fire spit from the cockpit and the side door of the plane as it began pulling away. Victor was cutting across the boat's stern to keep out of reach of the twin fifties on her bow.

The tip of the port wing rubbed and scraped along the boat's aft lifelines. It barely cleared the transom when Tashum made his leap. He struggled with the twelve-foot span. He looked human in the effort such was his weakness. His chest cracked against the sharp trailing edge of the aileron, fingers slapped the smooth metal surface searching for anything to grab. A length of nylon grappling rope was slithered across the plane's top surface in the building wind. Through the stinging spray he spotted the grappling hook embedded in the roof. He reached for the flailing rope, but it slithered away. He felt himself slipping and tried to stop his slide, but the wing surface was too slick, and he felt himself falling into churning water. He had given up when he was saved by the strength of a single forearm and a clutching hand that stopped his fall.

The plane picked up speed. The hull pounded the surface, pelting the angels with sheets of lake water. Tashum locked arms with Misha and was lifted from the water.

Misha pulled him deeper into the fuselage until Tashum's bare feet were no longer dangling in the wind-driven spray. They lay next to one another, catching their breath in the cargo space behind the two rows of split seating.

The hard thump of pounding water ended as the wings took lift.

Fanny's eyes were dazed. She was slumped sideways in her seat. She had three new unattended wounds in her shoulder, hip, and thigh. In her bloody grip she held Dickey's Beretta.

Dickey curled into a fetal position and lay in the aisle between the seats. His head rested on the pillow Fanny had placed there for him—his body was leaking badly from a dozen uncovered wounds.

"Dickey, are you dead?" Fanny's voice was a horrified whisper. "You're not dea—"

"I can't bear to move." His voice scratched through wheezing lungs. "I . . . don't think I can."

"Hang in there, Dickster," Victor called over his shoulder. "We're almost out of this shit." Victor muscled the damaged yoke with his one good hand. The plane banked to starboard in continued ascent.

Dickey whispered through a grimace of a smile, "Wake me for cocktails, will you?"

"Did yeah hear that, Misha?" cried Victor.

Tashum's eyes sprung open. His face was flat against the floorboards. He could see two of the orbs lodged in the lower framework of Fanny's seat. One was within reach.

Tashum thrust an arm forward, his spread fingers falling toward it— slapping the floor as that orb was snatched away.

His head jerked. He watched Misha reel in the orb.

Tashum's outstretched hand shifted focus. Through his eyes he commanded the second orb from its resting place just beyond his fingertips.

Misha watched, somewhat mystified, as Tashum's will rocked the orb back and forth. With each rotation it rolled farther from its resting place and closer to his grasp, until his fingers could rake it in.

Tashum and Misha exchanged stubborn glares.

"Are we really going to make it?" asked Fanny coming out of her delirium.

"Hell, yeah, they just reported that fuckin' chopper was refueling in Locarno. We got clear skies," he said, before switching off the transponders and radio. The cockpit became blacker than the surrounding moonlit night.

"What did you do that for?" asked Fanny, somewhat startled.

"With any luck, we'll disappear in them lights over there." He pointed to the twinkling village lights of Vira on the opposing shoreline.

Fanny looked out the side window and then forward, squinting. "Victor, are we flying in the right direction?"

"Any direction's the right direction. I figure, I'll keep her down on the deck, swing out, and make a beeline around that mountain. 'Less of course you got some better idea."

"At the moment I'm fresh out of ideas."

"Just a little disappearin' trick I picked up in 'Nam."

"Victor, you weren't in Vietnam," choked Dickey.

"Yuh, well the sons-a-bitch that taught me to fly was," he muttered with a crazed smile. "I wonder what old Mikey would do? Probably 'bout the same I reckon."

While Victor schemed against the imminent arrival of the helicopter, two Harrier fighter jets were being cleared from their mountain hangars. At the same time, a platoon of highly trained Swiss Guard boarded two Aloette helicopters at their base near Geneva. Dragged from their beds, high officials on both sides of the Swiss-Italian border were activating their respective military response to the threat of possible terrorist activity. Containment was the word most heard. Whitehall was notified of the situation by the assistant deputy at their embassy in Geneva. MI-6 notified the CIA and requested a link transmission of the IBX-1 spy photographs presently being taken by their satellite as it passed over the region.

Victor flinched when a hand landed on his shoulder.

"We found two, where's the other orb?" asked Tashum, looming behind him.

Victor startled and shied away. "Jesus! You're like a bad case of VD! Where the fuck did you come from?"

"Where is it?" Tashum said as he laid hands onto Victor's shoulders.

"Hey, how the fuck should I know? Gotta be here somewhere."

Tashum's fingers dug deeper into the flesh around Victor's clavicle. "The orb?"

"Ouch! Goddamn it! Don't fuck with the pilot, dude!"

"Why are we headed out over open water?" Tashum asked, getting his bearings.

"Just a little trick—"

"It won't trick anybody, it's costing us time—"

"Don't never tell me how to fly my plane!"

"Do you see those flashing beacons?"

Victor squinted to his right.

Tashum pointed. "No, off your port wing? Those beacons aren't stationary," he said, restraining the escalating urge to pummel the jackal.

"Fuck! It's that goddamn whirlybird, fuck 'em, I gotta mile lead on the bastard." He pulled back on the yoke with a slight turn, banking the plane to the right.

Tashum felt a wave of nausea spread through his body. He closed his eyes and turned away from the windshield. Misha's touch had accelerated his healing, but there was no cure for his vertigo.

Fanny's weak hand tugged at Tashum's sweater sleeve.

Tashum checked his anger, backed away from Victor. He knelt next to Fanny. His eyes roamed the length of her broken body.

Misha rummaged through the plane's first-aid kit. He tossed a roll of gauze to Tashum and turned to Dickey with a second roll of white cotton.

Dickey's eyes rolled upward. "I'd be better served if you just stuffed my bloody clothes into my mouth," he whispered.

Misha nodded. "If you wish," said the angel as he peeled a torn strip of red-wet oxford cloth from the vampire's chest. The blood staining his fingers had a mesmerizing effect.

Tashum lifted the bloody cloth from his brother's fingertips. "This isn't your work, Misha," he said with compassion as he lowered the saturated cloth onto Dickey's awaiting swollen tongue.

Misha scurried to the back of the plane and started to scrub the blood off his fingers.

Tashum could feel Fanny's weak grip on his sweater. He continued wrapping her shoulder wound with gauze.

"Bermuda," she whispered.

"Bermuda?"

"I need you now like I needed you then," she continued in a faint voice, supported by pleading eyes. "I'm bleeding to death, Tashum. Dickey, too."

"We'll find a farm—"

"No animals," she choked. "I need you, Ta . . ." Each cough was filling her mouth with a flood of blood. Her eyes closed and for warmth and strength she fell into his chest.

As Tashum held her, he could sense the penetrating stare from the back of the plane. He looked into gloom. Barely visible was his brother, tucked between travel bags.

Misha opened his mind's eye, allowing Tashum to eavesdrop on his inner struggle.

They are my brother's children, just as blinded by fear and hunger as any other creature on this world. And just as deserving of comfort and guidance in death. Perhaps more so because they were strange-birthed by celestial blood. When they should have passed on into the Light, were they not transformed by the vicious serum from angelic veins of the Fallen? An experiment gone bad, surely. But must the guinea pig be punished for the mistakes of the experimenter? Can we deny these children the very comfort of threshold experience that we so willingly bestow on hero and villain alike? Is there no forgiveness for the children of my brothers? If not, then how do we forgive ourselves for their abandonment?

On a cellular level, Tashum could feel Misha's torment over this issue of intolerance of aberrations in nature's garden. For centuries Tashum had internalized this argument, and if it weren't so painful for his brother to struggle with, it might have been comforting to see another Celestial twist a gut over these issues of responsibility and abandonment.

"Tashum, could you ever forgive me?" she asked.

He stroked her hair but kept his eyes on Misha. "I think so, Fanny."

"I forgive you, Tashum."

"I'm not worthy of your forgiveness, Fanny—"

"Don't hate me for loving your brother."

"I could never do that—"

She silenced him with a raised finger on his lips, her stony eyes gazing up into his. How she loved being in his arms, where she felt safe in a cradle of strength that had never weakened. She was focussed only on the moment and not her injuries or situation.

Misha gave it a hard thought. He studied the quivering vampire stretched out on the floor, so apparent was the shock he knew to be the final stage of any dying animal. He had never witnessed the death of a demon. Actually, Misha knew no more about the true condition of a vampire's soul than did Tashum. He wondered if Tashum was right; that their souls had migrated and the body was kept alive by blood and the semi-immortal spark of an angel, a fume of a spirit. Methodically, he rationalized, even if they were predatory nonhuman machines, they existed in the flesh and as such they needed help in this transitional period—or in their case, dissipation from something to nothing. . . .

With a nod to Tashum he scooted forward, extending his hand, warm angelic fingers feeling cold vampiric fingers for the first time, his touch soothed Dickey's tremor.

Victor suddenly screamed, and the plane went topsy-turvy up on its wing, tumbling angels and vampires into a heap pressed against the side windows.

Tashum recognized the whine of jet turbines. He glimpsed blurred profiles of two Harrier jump jets streaking past the window. At incredible speed they skimmed the lake surface. Within a heartbeat, the birds of prey had disappeared behind a veil of darkness.

Victor regained control. He leveled her wings, throttled up, and made for the river-cut canyon half a mile off the starboard wing. "Where the fuck did they come from? You fuckers better say yore prayers, cuz when they come back, we're fuckin' dead."

Tashum realized the fighters were flying west to east, across the width of the lake. "Relax, Victor. They won't be back," Tashum assured, while helping Fanny back into her seat. "That was just a message. They want you to know, it's their game—"

"Yeah, what the fuck you know about military shit?"

"We just crossed the Italian frontier, and the Swiss won't leave their airspace—"

"Yeah, yeah, yeah." He glanced back into the cabin. Dickey lay in a nest of blankets. Misha leaned over him, dressing his wounds with earthly gauze. "Hey! You be careful with my old man, I'll kick your ass." And then a new thought. "Dude, about time you started servin' drinks, ain't it?"

"That's enough, Victor," Tashum scolded.

"I don't wanna die dry." He grinned.

"He's a cruel joker, don't listen," Fanny said to Misha through a hacking cough.

"Fanny, you'd take it if he offered it." Victor belched.

"Victor," chimed Dickey, "did you feed the cat?"

His off-the-wall question silenced the group.

"Yes, the cat's been fed," Fanny told her tender lie with practiced ease.

"We don't have a cat," Victor said to himself. "Dickster! You all right?" he asked with genuine concern. "Hey, talk to me. Hey! Butch, don't go noddin' off."

"He needs to be quiet," offered Misha.

"Just don't let him go to sleep till he's fed, hear me?"

Misha nodded. "Yes, I understand."

"Fanny, we found two of the orbs. Do you know where the third is?" Tashum asked, wrapping the blanket around her shoulders.

She held his gaze, wondering how much she had to give before he gave what she so desperately needed in return. "I really don't know. Here in the plane somewhere."

Tashum leaned forward, spreading his hand across Victor's leather-clad shoulder. He spoke quietly into Victor's ear, "Victor, the sun will rise in thirty-two minutes. I don't know what your plans are, but Misha and I need to be on the ground."

"You know where the door is."

"You don't have to actually stop. You know your stall speed, we'll jump near the shore."

"I was shittin' yuh, man."

"I'm not shitting anyone."

Victor thought about it. "Yeah all right. I reckon we're pretty even-Steven."

"Not quite. We're short one orb."

"Hey, gotta be under the seats rollin' around somewhere. I was juggling 'em and the sons-a-bitches got away from me."

Tashum jerked his head around to catch Misha's reaction to what Victor had just said about juggling the orbs—Misha's mouth and expression drooped.

Tashum held his gaze. "That's it, isn't it? Juggling," Tashum said, and awaited a response. Misha's silence gave him his answer.

"So, like, whada yuh do with them things?" Victor asked as if they were old buddies. "I'm kinda interested in all this angel shit—ain't we related somehow?"

"Just fly the plane," he said, squeezing a little pain into the boy's shoulder.

Tashum moved and settled next to Fanny. "In Bermuda, the stones, the juggling—they were clues, weren't they?"

She batted her eyes once in slow surrender. "After you touched me that night in the clearing," she said reaching up and gently running the back of her hand down his cheek, "I was torn between a vow to your brother and my love for you. I'm so cold, Tashum." She moaned. "I kept my promise to Paladin. I'm sorry Tashum."

Tashum drew the blanket tighter around her shoulders, and blew hot breath onto her clasped hands. He pulled her close. Her eyes closed against his chest.

Victor was still fixated on the fighter planes. "Them pricks come outa nowhere. Asshole almost hit us." He glanced over his shoulder. "I'm glad to see you're so damn lovey-dovey back there, how's 'bout a little help lookin' out fer them jet jocks?"

"Victor, can you turn on a light?" asked Misha.

"Fuck no, they'll see us. Jesus! Just whose side you on?"

"I promise you they know where—" Tashum gasped as he looked over Victor's shoulder to see that they were already flying over trees. "I told you to drop us near the shore!"

"Hey, I'm captain of the ship, and the captain says yer comin' with us. At least till we get to the next lake—"

"You bloody fool, there is no lake," Tashum chastised.

"Wrong! I saw it on the map. We'll follow this here river up the canyon, up over some falls, and plop her down into the lake."

"Victor, there is no lake!"

"Don't fuck with me, I seen it on the map!"

"Lago Lugano lies to the east, we're flying west."

Victor pounded his index finger on the small plastic-coated reference map. "It's right there, you fucking asshole!"

Tashum studied the map. "I beg your pardon, you're right. There is a high alpine lake whose waters run into the Toce River, but this isn't the Toce, you fool—"

"I'm a tellin' yuh it is!"

"Victor, if it were the Toce, we would have flown over Verbanca. I didn't see any lights—"

"I'm bettin' yer wrong."

"You're betting more than you own!"

"So!"

"He's got us this far, hasn't he, Fanny?" Dickey said quietly in a wheezing voice.

She looked over at him with loving eyes, and merely smiled.

"He's a good pilot."

"That's right, and I know there's a fuckin' lake . . ." Victor said, hoping Tashum was wrong.

Tashum sighed. "You're the pilot."

For the next few minutes there was peace in the cabin. Dickey was in a state of happy delirium. Fanny had pushed reality aside, and started in with her, "Do you remember" stories about their many escapades. She had arranged the tales, and normally delivered them as a richly orchestrated travelogue, but tonight's versions were disjointed and incoherent. Her brain was starved for oxygenated blood, and she kept dosing off in midsentence. Tashum and Misha politely listened to Fanny while they searched for the missing orb.

Tashum fought back the nausea of vertigo while grilling Victor about a possible snow landing. It required his complete concentration to deal with the vicious clown in control of their destiny.

"Yuh know, Tashum, I'm about half glad that poison they fed yuh didn't work. You got some good ideas."

"Just put her down when you can," Tashum said.

"You wait and see. I'll set her down in that lake."

Fanny blinked hard, trying to clear her vision. In the distance she could make out the flashing beacons of a helicopter in pursuit.

"No," she murmured. A semblance of her survival instinct was returning. "They're coming." She moaned. "You'd better get us the hell out of here."

Victor turned in his seat, his head bobbing up and down, catching a glimpse of the pursuers.

Dickey let out a low groan. "Fanny—" he whimpered.

"Hold on," she said, touching his hand, brushing at the paste of blood drooling from his mouth. "Hold on, my darling." She looked to the pilot. "Victor, we've got to find a place to land."

"Yeah, yeah. First we gotta burn off some a this fuel."

"There is no time for that!" Tashum remarked, turning away from the window.

"Hey—I don't know what kinda landing we're gonna have. If we burn off some gas, we got a better chance with the rough stuff. Trust me you don't wanna go up in a ball a flame!"

"At least you're not looking for an imaginary lake," Tashum heeded.

"Yeah, well, I'm gonna prove you wrong on that little deal, too. There is a fuckin' lake, you just fuckin' wait and see."

"Tashum, don't argue with him." Fanny leaned back, her hand going to the wound in her side. "Hold me, my prince," she murmured in a voice too weak for his ears.

Misha sat quiet as the level of tension increased around him. He now held two orbs, and was eyeing the one Tashum held in his left hand.

Tashum's eyes were crossed with frustration. His vertigo couldn't bear this bird's-eye view. He quickly turned away from the windshield, refocused, and noticed the missing orb now resting in Misha's lap.

Once again the angels locked eyes.

The seaplane glided through the narrowing canyon, walls of alpine forest looming up on both sides. The wide band of the river below was shrinking to a wild, tumbling stream.

Victor was concentrating on the high granite ridge rising ahead of them. His tongue flicked out and licked his lips. He blinked repeatedly, his lips moving, speaking silent instructions to himself.

Fanny craned forward. "I don't see any lake, Victor."

"If we can just get over this ridge, you'll see it. It's there! And don't you nonbelievers contradict me, neither."

He pulled back on the yoke and one of the plane's engines sputtered. The plane began jerking and bucking as the second engine backfired and plumed light gray smoke.

"Them fuckin' Idy's sold us bad gas!" bitched Victor. "It'll pass, no biggy." No sooner said, and the engines resummed their healthy purr.

"Can you get us over the ridge?" Tashum asked.

"Fuck if I know, already got the pig goosed!" He slapped at the throttle bars and struggled with the yoke. "Come on, bitch, climb, damn it!"

Fanny blew out a breath and leaned back. She looked to Dickey, lying motionless, his mouth hanging open, his lips jiggling with each shudder of the plane. The yellow light in his eyes had faded. She spread her arms down around him, putting her face next to his, caressing him.

"Fanny," he slowly looked to her, "did we get away?"

She clenched her eyes tight. "You're in Italy now, and you're very rich. . . ."

"There is a lake, isn't there?"

"I hope so." She kissed him softly, and rose up with great hope that he was right. She exchanged half-smiles with Tashum.

The plane careened toward the smaller waterfall, the lowest point in the ridge.

"It's too fuckin' high," Victor breathed. He pressed his teeth together. "Come on, baby," he said pulling back the yoke, easing up the plane's wavering nose.

Tashum's eyes were trained forward. The waterfall filled the windshield and as it grew larger, the crest of the falls continued to rise and fall within the windshield's frame.

Tashum reached from behind and latched on to the yoke, pulling it just a tad closer to Victor's chest.

Catching updraft at the last possible second, the nose section rose slightly. Turbulent air threw up a spray of water as the front of the plane cleared the cresting waterfall by inches.

Through the streamers of water running down the windscreen, the moonlit Matterhorn, dressed in glistening snow, materialized before them. Victor's river of escape led to glacial runoff and boulder fields sat where Victor's lake should have been.

Victor let out a disappointed sigh. "Well, double fuck me!"

Fanny's hopeful expectations of finding the lake faded with her breath. Dickey strained to look forward. "Beautiful, isn't it?"

Fanny patted Dickey's shoulder, concealing her fear. "Yes, Dickey, the Matterhorn is very beautiful tonight." Her hopeless eyes found Tashum's grim expression.

As the tail cleared the falls, the entire plane yawed to one side. The port wing dipped and clipped the mound of an uprooted pine tree. The wing tip float lost it's retractable strut, folded, and snagged a rock protruding from the water. A violent shudder popped open the fuselage door. Inertia sucked Misha out through the doorway. He tumbled a dozen-odd feet into the fast-moving stream.

The port propeller whipped the water as its wing planted itself in the stream, now a pivot point. The live starboard propeller drove the action, spinning the plane. The port wing collapsed upon itself. The tail section caught in the stream's flow spun the seaplane 180 degrees, directing it back toward the lip of the waterfall.

All eyes were trained forward. From the top of the world they were looking down. They could see the helicopter that had been shadowing their climb up the steep canyon. The grand view lasted only a brief second before they dropped and were engulfed by cascading water, plummeting, toward certain destruction. Uncontrollable screams filled the interior.

A jagged rock ripped through the undercarriage of the fuselage, a buzz saw tearing up through the flooring, gutting the plane's belly, leaving a trail of guns and diamonds and metal chunks of the twisted body falling into the water. Among this debris, an orb flew through the air, landing with a splash into the shallow stream. Fanny and Tashum were thrown across Dickey. Her head smashed through the side window. Victor was plastered to the ceiling. Dickey was thrown forward, landing in the copilot's seat.

Tumbling out of control, the seaplane started breaking apart. The starboard wing was shorn away by passing rocks. The engine and spinning propeller spiraled off into the night. A tree limb exploded through the front windshield and stabbed into the cockpit, pushing through the length of the plane. Then the tail section snapped off by a passing tree, where it hung for a moment among shattered branches before it dropped. Tashum fell with it.

Inside the wingless, tailless fuselage, everything was spinning. Dickey was now pinned to a seat, impaled by the tree limb. The diamonds seemed to hang weightless, floating. Fanny was whipped and tumbled, smashed against one side of the interior, then thrown to the other.

With a metallic shriek, the left side of the cockpit tore away. Victor, strapped in his seat, vanished with it.

Fanny was thrown free, launched into the darkness.

In a fireworks burst, the diamonds sprayed out of the severed fuselage, glittering in the moonlight.

The fuselage continued its self-destructing fall, sparking against each rock it hit until being stopped by trees.

At the base of the waterfall, the twisted metal hulk creaked and moaned as it settled into the boulder field at the water's edge. After the booming echo had spread down the canyon, the silence of nature returned.

In the boulders above the bulk of the plane, Fanny lay sprawled across a flat rock. From where her head lay, her eyes pivoted upward, seeing Victor, unconscious and still strapped to his seat, dangling from a tree limb.

From a rock perch at the top of the waterfall, Misha peered over the edge. He could see Tashum was stranded, clinging to a wet rock overhang some twenty feet below his position.

Tashum was contemplating the eighty-foot drop when he heard Misha's voice, over the air-buffeting sound of the approaching helicopter. He looked up. Misha was holding one of the orbs. Tashum smiled, and raised a hand holding a second orb. "We've got ten minutes," he called out, pointing up to the purple hues of a new day forming.

"Will you give me that orb?"

"Will you get me off this rock?"

The helicopter hovered over the wreckage. Its powerful beam of light swept the boulder field.

Tashum recognized the bell ranger's markings as belonging to the Italian army. They were looking for a place to land, no doubt calling for reinforcements. He had to get off the rock face before they found a suitable opening.

Tashum ducked as the helicopter passed over him and continued on upstream.

Misha reappeared, hanging a long droopy pine bough down toward Tashum—six feet short, he would have to climb higher to make the grab.

After a weary effort, Victor managed to open his seat belt and drop out of the tree. He free fell twenty feet and landed on a half-felled tree. He slid on his butt down the leaning tree and tumbled to the ground. When he stood, he did so on wobbly legs and held out his arms for balance. He danced over the moss-covered rocks and stumbled to the remains of the plane. He winced at what he saw through a gaping hole in the metal.

"I'm fucked up, but you're dead, man," he said with little care. "The Dickster killed by a tree. Who woulda ever thunk?"

Dickey hung forward, a tree limb was embedded in his chest, impaling him to his seat. His dying eyes opened slowly and looked at Victor for several moments before any signs of recognition came to him.

"Drink from me, Victor," Dickey said with sincerity, "take what life I have left. Save yourself, boy."

"I ain't a boy and I'm gonna drink something better than you." He glanced around the debris. "Where's my fucking gun?"

Dickey's head swayed forward and hung off his neck. A tear rolled down his cheek.

Victor's forehead crinkled when he heard the whacking sound of helicopter blades returning. He scurried for cover among the foliage and piled boulders.

The helicopter moved above the scattered debris. It hovered and circled for some time, its searchlight again scanning the area in diminishing circles.

Through the trees, Victor could see it hovering like a fat target. Searching for his gun, he glanced farther downstream. He thought he saw several figures disappear and reappear as they moved through the boulder field.

Under a rock overhang, Fanny pushed herself up into the small space in response to the beam of light that touched down around the mouth of her shallow cave, only inches from her feet.

Misha and Tashum were together, hidden in the rocks at the crest of the waterfall, looking down on the spinning rotor blades. They could see sudden spurts, muzzle flashes down in the darkly shaded trees. The Bell Ranger, in a dramatic maneuver, lifted up and over them. Now trailing smoke she flew farther upstream.

"Victor?" murmured Misha.

"They do love their guns." Tashum straightened and turned around. He saw the silver thread of daylight outlining the rugged shape of the Matterhorn's south slope. "Come on, we've only got a few minutes." Tashum could feel energy building up in the orb he held so tightly. "Something is happening with the orb."

"Mine too," said Misha. "We're about to lose them."

"The third one must be here somewhere."

They continued to slosh around in knee-deep water, searching the rocky stream bottom for the missing orb.

Crawling out of her small cave, Fanny could see Tashum and Misha wading through water on the shelf high above.

She started to ease back into her overhang when, in the running water, she spied an object rolling about in the stream. She leaned over as far as her wounds would allow, and dropped a quivering hand to retrieve it. An orb. She ran her hands over its warm surface. Clutching it, she brought it close to her chest. Again she looked up to the angels whose only concern was the object resting next to her bosom.

She cried out in vain, her small voice lost to the continuous roar of tumbling water. Victor heard her cries and was rushing over to her, leaping from boulder to boulder, his Uzi tightly gripped.

Determined beyond her injuries, she started to move. Her bloody fingers dug into the granite and pulled. With one arm she was dragging her useless legs and by fits and starts she crawled toward the rock wall. As she started inching her way up, Victor's hand latched on to her ankle. She gasped as he pulled her down. Her body peeled off the rock face and crashed down upon him, both falling flat against a granite slab.

"Whatcha got there?" he asked, rising to his feet.

"They need it, Victor," she exhaled in a choppy voice.

"You're just gonna give it to 'em? What about us?"

"It's over, Victor, do the right thing," she said, searching for a morsel of goodness in him. "I don't have the strength. Take the orb up to them," she pleaded, and held it out for him to take.

He snatched it out of her hand, they exchanged eye contact. Each saw only the blackness within the other.

"Thanks, Fanny. Now I'm about to save your sorry ass," he said firmly. "You can thank me later, just remember, from now on, it's you and me doll face." Then he pulled the gun's cocking lever. "This will get their attention."

Tashum bolted upright at the sound of Victor's Uzi spitting bullets into the air. He looked at Misha. Both angels splashed through the water to a vantage point where they could see Victor holding the orb above his head.

Tashum took in the scene, sized up his options, and turned, cramming his orb into Misha's gut. "Stay here!"

"But Tashum—"

"You can come to me from the other side. I know things aren't right at home. Promise me that you'll come to me when I call."

"If I hear your voice, I will come."

"No! Make a promise to me that you will honor!"

"If I hear your voice, I swear I will answer your call."

"I believe you will, Misha."

A quick embrace followed. Tashum tore away from his brother.

Like a skier, he slid down the narrow goat path, his feet gliding over loose rocks. Leaning back into the hill, his dragging arms helped negotiate the switchback turns. Thirty seconds was all it took.

Victor watched Tashum pick himself up off the ground. "I told yuh I would get his attention."

The flesh on Tashum's hands was raw. Scraped knees shown through shredded trouser legs. "I need the orb, Victor!" he shouted.

"Damn, that was pretty good, but it's Misha's *clear* blood I wanted."

"Victor, please!" pleaded Fanny. "Give it to him!"

"Let me handle this, Fanny!" he said pointing his weapon at her. "I'm the boss now, Fanny." He sneered at Tashum. "I really prefer your buddy Misha—but hell, we're all family, I'll—we'll", he gestured toward Fanny, "Yeah we'll settle for you." He smiled at her dour expression. "Just lookin' out fer yuh, honey."

"Give me the orb!" the angel demanded.

"Don't get pissy with me!"

"Give me the orb!" he commanded with an outstretched hand.

"On your fuckin' knees and open a vein!" screamed the vampire. "I suck you, then you suck me!" He was holding his crotch.

"That bloody well tears it!" Tashum conjured up all of his strength. He sent forward a fist that crashed into Victor's face, covering his delicate features, driving the bridge of his nose and bits of cheekbone deep into his brain. Victor's feet swept out from under him as he fell backward.

The orb catapulted from his flailing arm, flew skyward.

Tashum leaped up for it. As he flew through the air tracking the orbs trajectory, he could see Misha and the reaching rays of first light blanketing surrounding mountain peaks. The light was racing toward him. Tashum abandoned all thought of himself. Devoid of all emotion, his wounded life force was completely focused on seeing his brother returned to the Light. Nothing had ever meant more. He was using his powers to cheat the physical laws of movement. When he'd reached the apex of his superhuman leap, he gathered his powers to push beyond. The air around him began to split and waver. The orb was suddenly off his fingertips, and then in his hand. In midair, some thirty feet off the ground, he spun, pulled his arm back, and pitched the now-glowing orb toward Misha.

Misha tossed the two glowing orbs into the air. The Latin phrase that had first appeared in the stained-glass window rolled off Misha's lips, "I am light pure am I." Misha spoke in perfect time with Tashum's perfect throw. The orb slapped loudly into Misha's raised palm, and the third joined the other two in juggled orbit.

An eerie phosphorescent, three-dimensional glow filled the circumference of the arcing orbs. The shimmering ball of light engulfed Misha in a platinum brilliance, hued amber, and so bright that it made pale and dimmed radiant light from the encroaching sun.

Then a pyramid of light appeared, its sharp straight lines angled and tied together at tangent points, inside the dimensional ball. Misha's Earth body crumbled away from his crystalline light being.

Tashum's last image before his power faded and he dropped back to Earth was the unfolding of Misha's elegant wings. It was a vision that he had searched for but had always eluded him: an angel, in the morning light. Tashum expected to see the angel take flight the way he and Paladin would launch themselves away. But Misha's thin image just simply evaporated.

Tashum felt great strain in his ankles and knees when he landed hard next to Fanny. He looked up. Misha was truly gone, and the birds were singing. He glanced over at Victor's body. The young vampire lay faceup, dim eyes gazed up at the fading stars. His hands were twitching in weird robotic movements.

"Tashum, you had better leave," Fanny warned in a worn-out voice.

Tashum glanced to the wreckage planted at the base of tall pines. He could see Dickey's lifeless arm and shoulder surrounded by twisted metal.

"Tashum . . . I . . . " She collapsed.

Tashum scooped her up into his arms as the first broom of sunlight swept toward them. He flinched as it hit his back. He tried to protect her as best he could from the burning sting. He stumbled, almost lost her. He struggled through the blinding light, making his way across the series of broad flat rocks, into the thin shade of a pine bough. He frantically searched the rocks for suitable shelter. Then he heard his name being called by a familiar voice.

"Mayhem? Is it you?"

"Hurry," cried the spirit from the shadow of a small opening in the rock formation. "Tashum, Tashum—"

He put a fix on the voice and carried Fanny across the uneven footing to an opening in the rocks. The entrance was short and tight. Bending over with her weight was difficult, but after a few steps the cave's mouth opened into an eight-foot ceiling. Tashum stumbled, falling, dropping Fanny gently to the coolness of the cave floor. They both lay there, the dark soothed their solar burn. Tashum rolled up onto his side and watched the last flicker in her eye. Her eyes were as dim as they were the first night they met in Bermuda.

"Well?" asked the spirit, "Are you just going to let her go?" Mayhem's translucent shape hopped down from his stone perch. He stood over Fanny.

Tashum rose to his knees and leaned over Fanny. He lifted her up into his arms. In her eyes all the arguments and shields were gone. She invited him in, no tit for tat, no want for blood, no terms for surrender. None of the barriers waited in ambush. Instead, he saw in her mind's eye the death card that Samir had drawn for her. And beyond those heavy locked gates once impregnable, but now thrown wide open, the bare flicker of her final life force.

Then a truth, even if expected, pierced his heart; her shell was empty of any light. A spark of life borrowed from living blood, but the soul had vacated.

Tashum's mind went spinning, dizzy with the final realization. He regretted having told Fanny something that, at the time, he was only guessing at. He had always held a glimmer of hope that Fanny's condition was purely physiological in nature. Angelic blood had simply killed her body's ability to produce its own most precious fluid. Cause and effect. Possibly there was some broken process that could be physically corrected—like a disease being run out of the body by induced chemistry. He had always held the hope her body would be cured of this illness. He felt she was not responsible for what she was, only what she had become. He wondered if her karmic baggage would be dealt with through the reincarnation process. But to actually find no soul struck a death blow to his own spirit.

"What exactly were you expecting?" Mayhem asked as he sifted through Tashum's thoughts.

"Mayhem, she has, no soul—" he said through tears.

"You knew that, you even told her that."

"I was hurt and I wanted to hurt her, I lied. How could I have known? She never let me in where I could have seen the difference for myself."

"Don't you feel you owe her something?"

"More than something." Tashum gently laid her down and stroked her hair. They gazed into each other's eyes. The sound of a helicopter chattering in the distance filled the silence. She raised a tired smile.

"You said you loved me," she said, through swollen, bleeding lips. "That's all I've ever wanted to hear."

He bent over her, tears falling onto her torn clothing. "Fanny—oh God, I'm so sorry, so sorry. This is my fault, all of it. All those years . . . I—I don't know if I can fix what Paladin and I have done to you."

The light in her eyes began its final fade. Tashum pulled her close, holding her weak body as if it were too precious to give up.

"Tashum . . ." She breathed. "Paladin said Earth exists to heal the wounds of heaven."

"You said Paladin saw the future. Did he see this moment?"

"He only told me," her breath failing, "you couldn't go back."

"Why? Tell me why, Fanny."

"His diary . . ." Her jaw fell slack. "You love me."

"Yes, yes, you must have known my love for you," he said, his forehead touching hers, his breath going into her mouth. "Where is Paladin's diary? Please, Fanny. Maybe the answer to your situation is in his writing. Where is his diary, Fanny?"

Her body quivered against his, her teeth chattering. She nestled closer. "I'm not ready for hell," she said in a dreamy whisper.

"Fanny, dearest Fanny. There is no hell—it's only a word." He let her slip from his arms and tore off his sweater. With trembling fingers he took her hand, wrestling the old ring off her third finger.

"My sweet darling," he said, "I've always denied this, I've always sworn myself against it, but I know I have responsibility for you. I've ignored it, I tried to buy my way out of it—no more. No more!"

He turned the ring and the small, curved blade snapped out, he held it over his wrist.

"Don't hesitate this time." Mayhem's voice echoed through the cave. "Gregory might be here right now if—"

"Stop it!" Tashum barked as he realized that there were no illusionary orb this time, as there had been every other time he commenced to share his blood and pass the disease. He felt a new power within himself, an invisible force pushing the blade away from his flesh.

He looked into her eyes, trying to find the words of the hero turning his back on the needy. She waited for words and actions that didn't come and rewarded him with a brief smile and then she closed her eyes forever.

"You're a fool, Tashum. She was the best thing that ever happened to you. Even a pet doesn't give that much unconditional love."

Tashum's tears were immediate. He pulled her close and buried his face in her hair, holding her as if it might make a difference. His sobs came from his gut, rattling through his entire frame. Her death didn't produce the lightness of being he had felt with Gregory's passing. Over the centuries Tashum had noted that humans lose body weight at the moment of death and he determined that the soul carries weight. This revelation began with the death of Shrug, the first human he'd ever known. This was a physical phenomenon that could be measured. The cause of death was always irrelevant. This migration seemed as constant and cyclical as the sunrise. But not for Fanny. Buckets of tears poured out of him.

In profound silence, he rocked back and forth, hugging her slack, lifeless body. He cupped her face in his hands, kissed her eyes and lips. Weeping, he could not catch his breath.

He sat staring at nothing for what seemed hours, though it was only minutes. His mind was blank. No humans. No vampires. No Light.

From out of the darkness behind, he felt a chilled, soft breeze pushed by Mayhem's impatient wings.

"Mayhem." He started to stand. "Why have you been leading me away from redemption?"

"What? You mean the vampires? Well they add a little excitement, don't they?" Mayhem whispered through the cool cave air.

"Mayhem, don't you understand what we've done?"

"Don't be so hard on yourself. Their souls returned to the universal fabric the day Paladin killed them. On the other hand, you've just seen the last sparkle of Paladin slip away."

Tashum shook his head and inhaled deeply. He looked back to the spirit. "So much death everywhere," he moaned.

"What lives dies."

"I saw Paladin's skeleton in Paris. Where did his spirit go?"

Mayhem glided toward Tashum and rested on a jutting rock. "I love the City of Light," he said with a sly flavor. "And Tashum, I told you before, Paladin is waiting for you. No one else can bring him back from his oblivion."

"He's not in the Light though, is he?"

Mayhem studied Tashum's anguished expression. "No," he finally admitted, "and he can't return unless he is whole again." Mayhem paused. "And until he's put back together, neither can you."

Tashum's eyes slid back and forth. His ears pricked up at Mayhem's threatening tone of voice. "Why do you want to keep me here?"

"I just told you. Redemption is free, but it's rarely easy."

"Is that what you meant all those years ago, when you said I should join him?"

"A play on words, to avoid speaking of forbidden knowledge."

"But it was you in my dreams speaking to me wasn't it?"

Mayhem started to agree but caught himself and fell silent.

"Admit it. Tell me it was you," Tashum said.

"Let's just say Paladin spoke through me."

Tashum shifted, letting Fanny's body slip gradually back to the earth. "Is Paladin's situation a question of his redemption?"

"No, more one of treachery."

"Is he in great pain?"

"Burning." Mayhem's smile spreads across his tattooed face. "He's waiting for your rescue."

Tashum stood, blinking, his mouth hardening. "Who could do such a thing to him? And for what reason?"

"Paladin's killer is a vile, evil spirit. A worse experiment than even your vampires."

"Is he the mysterious Black Knight?"

"Who knows . . ." The question changed Mayhem's expression. His image flickered.

"You are the Black Knight, aren't you? Tell me the truth!" demanded Tashum.

"Paladin was a brother to us all." He fluttered a few yards away. "He must be avenged. And you are the avenger."

"Don't leave me—not yet, please," Tashum begged.

Mayhem turned back to face him. "I was in Paris that night. I saw your hysteria when confronted with Paladin's skeleton."

"You get around, don't you, Mayhem?"

"How dare you speak to me with such arrogance! What makes you think I didn't have the same reaction? I loved Paladin just as much as you do."

Tashum nodded slowly. "I'm sure you did," he said, his jaw going to one side. "Please accept my apology." He unfocused his eyes, searching for the right focal length and a glimpse of the spirit.

Mayhem thought he was smiling in a way that Tashum could not see. "I think I understand your frustration. You've been down there a lot longer than I was." He drifted closer, spoke in a lower whisper still. "Revenge must be yours. In the name of Paladin, you must kill the Parisian shopkeeper."

With growing suspicion, Tashum's eyes slid the length of Mayhem's image. "Kill the—that's an odd command, especially coming from someone with wings."

"Not really." Mayhem held up an arm that was missing a hand. "I would do it myself, but for certain unfortunate limitations." He leaned forward. "Do it, Tashum. And I will help you make Paladin whole again."

"Do you know where his missing skull is?"

"You do your job, I'll do mine. Tit for tat, isn't that the way you put it?"

Tashum nodded. "Tit for tat, I've learned better."

"Don't change the rules now, not at the close of the game."

"Game? Misha was concerned about something he called the silence in heaven. Is that the game?"

A visible chill ran through Mayhem. He clutched the sword tighter. He quickly composed himself. "You'll find out. Some things are better experienced than described."

They both turned toward the hushed commotion of soldiers at the cave's entrance.

"Tashum," Mayhem said quickly. "You must leave this place. Come, I will show you the way."

Tashum stood unmoving. "In the past you've never helped me. Why start now, Mayhem?"

"I won't beg you," Mayhem said coldly. His pale image moved toward the back of the cave. "Tashum, follow my voice. It's the only way out."

Tashum looked back to the opening, weighing his options. The sound of chopper blades pulsated the air outside the cave. He knelt next to Fanny's body and kissed her forehead.

"Until we meet again, Fanny," he whispered. "I will always love you."

Mayhem sank into the darkness. "Tashum, you haven't much time left, hurry! Do or die!"

Tashum stood and gave Fanny one final look. He then realized that he

wouldn't recognize her spirit reincarnated, as he had never known the original. Another moment passed. The soldiers' voices were louder. He turned
and quickly followed after Mayhem, going deeper into the cave.

Tashum had disappeared into the gloom seconds before thin laser beams
of red light appeared, flashing, crisscrossing, searching for targets.

A single pin light washed across Fanny's body. Instantaneously, three red
laser dots appeared on her profiled face.

Three black-faced commandos took up positions around her body.

For hours, the spirit led Tashum into a maze of small, tight dank passages,
diagonal gaps between granite and quartz strata, sometimes horizontal, where
Tashum would flatten onto his belly and pull himself by the strength of his
fingertips. For Mayhem, twisting around the roots of these mountains presented little problem. He could pass through granite the way that water flows
through a sponge.

Eventually, the precarious route brought them into the spectacle of nature's frozen architecture in the form of an ice cave, a deep chasm once filled
with glacial ice, made hollow by time, made blue by the noonday sun directly
overhead.

"How much farther, Mayhem?"

"How far do you wish to go?"

"I think you understand my commitment." Suddenly Tashum felt a
thrust of air.

Mayhem's wings pumped a second time. He drew the sword from his
belt in midflight. His wings held him hovering inches from the ice ceiling.
His demon eyes trained upward.

"Mayhem, are you with me?" asked Tashum, squinting his eyes, focusing,
unfocusing searching for a trace of his new partner.

Through the ceiling of the thick ice, Mayhem watched the soles of celestial feet walking above. The rippled image came closer to him. The obscured figure was almost overhead. He tightened his grip on the hilt and held
the sword, ready to thrust. A second pair of feet touched down in the path
of the first. Mayhem held perfectly still, dialing in their conversation. From
their greeting, he recognized the voices of Misha and Geicai, but in the blink
of an eye, they were both gone.

After the anxious moment faded, he relaxed the sword and began a circular glide. His eyes never left Tashum during the descent.

"Tashum, we have several hours before the sun sets. This would be a good place to spend it," Mayhem said before evaporating in the blue shadows.

Tashum had no idea what had just taken place overhead, and with little argument, he agreed to stay sedentary. He needed to reflect upon the events of the past seventy-two hours. He needed to analyze the cracks in the foundation of his belief system, sift through the rubble of his own dreams, and understand the rhythm and the resultant effect his pursuit had pushed upon the lives of those he loved and stranger alike.

He looked at his hands, remembering, knowing fully what they were capable of, and then he began to dream of what they might build. Tashum wrestled with the meaning of the visionary orbs nonappearance over Fanny when he was ready to share of himself. His heart knew the answer. The orbs were already within him. His orbs had been unconsciously claimed and were unceremoniously absorbed into his crystalline skeleton during the only unselfish and truly pure moment of his entire earthly experience. When the commitment to send Misha home was acted upon, he had earned his orbs. They came wrapped in their own working knowledge, and the only thing keeping him on earth at this point was the will to use them through another act of selflessness and self-sacrifice.

He thought about Mayhem and the odd request the spirit had made. And Misha's hints of confusion and mystery surrounding the silence in heaven. Tashum's survival instinct and streetwise sensibilities, honed through experience, told him they were connected. Fanny mentioned that Paladin had been struck by lightning while crossing the Serengeti plain and had seen the future. But why he wanted Tashum kept here on Earth was unclear.

There was only one final conclusion; Paladin wanted rescue.

Tashum felt the confluent flood of destiny and desire, of hope and despair, pushing him with great force into league with a partner who may be the devil himself. In any event, he was once again on the run from humanity and searching for truth.

Afterglow

At home in her Battersea loft, Shelly was packing a hard-shelled suitcase with her science books layered between folded lamb's wool sweaters and denim pants. She tamped out a safe spot in the center of the suitcase and placed a small wooden box in it. She stood back, shook her head, and removed the box. She set it aside and began stacking her well-worn Brooks Brothers shirts in neat rows until the suitcase appeared to be overflowing.

A few minutes later she stood by the bay window overlooking the Thames. The river's slow-moving waters were reflecting the gray morning. She took something from the wooden box and gave it a shake. She opened her fist and held the vial of amber blood between her thumb and index finger.

Up against the morning light the liquid was alive with volcanic churn. Thread-thin electrical fibers, minibolts of life, appeared and disappeared in the viscous plasma as she rotated its host vial. It was magical, and she chuckled, thinking about her youth in Jackson Hole, Wyoming, and the lava lamp that had mesmerized her pot-smoking parents throughout the long winters there.

Hamley Potter sat lightly silhouetted against a large bay window set deep into the thick wall. Outside, a soft rain was keeping things wet. He made a slight adjustment to his yellow silk tie and gazed across his large walnut desk at Inspector Stanton, who was lifting up his cheap umbrella from the back of the client's chair.

"If you hurry to your car you won't need that," said Potter with impatience. "It's barely a drizzle."

"I always prepare for the worst."

"I suppose that's wise in your line of work."

Stanton looked past Potter to the weather outside. He spoke without looking at the solicitor. "As I was saying, witnesses place you in Italy at the time of the chase. As far as I can tell, no laws were broken before you left Ascona."

"Inspector, if I had been aware of what was going to happen, I would have dragged my former client along with me."

"You have a legal mind, I think you know where we stand." Stanton leaned against the doorjamb. "You said former client. Has Tashum sacked you?"

"No, not quite."

"And you've spoken with him since?"

"No, no. You're not putting this together correctly. We ended our association that night." He sighed and leaned back in his chair. "Inspector, if I knew where he was, I'd tell you, as I'm ethically bound to do."

Stanton studied him.

"Now, if you don't mind, I have work to get back to."

Stanton turned to go, stopped, and looked back. "There was one other thing. I'm curious. How long have you known Shelly Green?"

Potter's composure shrank a little. "I don't know, really—"

"A rough guess should work for now, a year, two, three, four, ten—"

"I get the point." Potter leaned forward over his high-polished desk. "I believe it was at Claridages, high tea. Three or four years ago." He gazed into Stanton's probing glare. "Look, I really don't recall much more than that."

"How, exactly, did you meet?" noting Potter's unease. "I'm interested to know if she introduced herself to you, or did you make the first move? That's all."

"I see, well, as I recall, Dr. Green and I met at the buffet table."

"Did she introduce herself as a doctor?"

"I don't recall. She had taken the last blueberry tart, and when she saw my disappointment, she offered it to me. Actually, the tart was for Martha, but that's immaterial, I suppose, to your inquiry?"

"No, not at all, I'm trying to paint a picture."

"Hmm, well I'm sorry I can't add more color."

"You knew more than you thought you did. That gives us texture for the painting."

"Inspector Stanton, this is all very interesting, but I must ask you to leave, I'm terribly busy."

Stanton slyly nodded. "I bet you are, busy I mean." He glanced around Potter's posh private office. "Do you have many clients like Tashum?"

"I'm not sure what you mean by that," he replied with a face taking on color.

Stanton smiled. "Thank you, Mr. Potter." He turned and crossed to the solid wooden door.

"Stanton," Potter called out after the detective, "you may need your umbrella, after all."

Stanton thought he heard a warning in his vocal tone. He looked back to Potter sitting against rain-stained windows. "If Tashum contacts you," he said, "or you happen to remember anything more, be sure to give us a ring."

"Yes, yes, yes." Potter waved him off as he picked up the chirping desk phone. He waited, watching Stanton leave.

Stanton disappeared behind the closing door.

"Potter here . . . Wouldn't give his name? How rude." His eyebrows twitched. "Go ahead, put him through anyway." Potter picked up his gold pen and drew doodle squares on a notepad as he spoke "Hello." His eyes squeezed closed, "Tashum!" he choked, sucking in air. "Wait, wait. Slow down, you want me to meet you where?" Excitable fingers jotted down an unreadable meeting place. His shoulders rounded and sagged, and as he listened to the Fallen Angel, his blood pressure rose with his eyebrows. He sat bolt upright, with eyes wide as tea cup saucers: "What? You want that loan?"